"Mesa's debut mixes ... cal realism, and tons ... ... page-turning urban fantasy that takes the glitter of *Boardwalk Empire* and combines it with a story of found family, mob violence, and romance."

—LIBRARY JOURNAL (starred review)

"*Bindle Punk Bruja* is a book you will dive into, gorgeously addictive and impossible to put down. It will transport you through time to a 1920s world soaked in gin, glittering in gold, and edged in danger. Luna is a hero with an indomitable will, navigating blood-soaked city streets with dark humor and cutting intelligence. Sharp, smart, and utterly enchanting, Mesa's debut is a triumph that stayed with me long after I turned the final page."

—GRETA KELLY, author of *The Frozen Crown*

"Desideria Mesa puts the reader in a Kansas City Prohibition scene filled with gangsters, bigotry, and magic to give a thrilling read to historical fantasy fans. Her writing is strong and confident in a story that simply bursts with action fueled by a likable young woman bent on shattering the stereotypes of her time period. No stranger to a fine turn of phrase, Mesa balances raw action with lyrical prose and knows just when to pull her punches. Fans of emotionally strong characters and historical fantasy will find a lot to love in *Bindle Punk Bruja*. I know I did. Overall, the story goes down like good bootleg hooch: smooth and easy with a real strong kick."

—T. FROHOCK, author of the Los Nefilim series

"The friends and family surrounding Luna are a joy to meet. . . . Good flapper fun."   —KIRKUS REVIEWS

"*Bindle Punk Bruja* is the 'bee's knees' and the 'cat's meow.'"

—SEATTLE BOOK REVIEW

BINDLE PUNK JEFE

ALSO BY DESIDERIA MESA

Bindle Punk Bruja

BINDLE PUNK
JEFE

A NOVEL

DESIDERIA MESA

HARPER Voyager
An Imprint of HarperCollins *Publishers*

BINDLE PUNK JEFE. Copyright © 2024 by Desideria Mesa. All rights reserved. Printed in the United States of America. No part of this book may be used or reproduced in any manner whatsoever without written permission except in the case of brief quotations embodied in critical articles and reviews. For information, address HarperCollins Publishers, 195 Broadway, New York, NY 10007.

HarperCollins books may be purchased for educational, business, or sales promotional use. For information, please email the Special Markets Department at SPsales@harpercollins.com.

Harper Voyager and design are trademarks of HarperCollins Publishers LLC.

FIRST EDITION

Map by Jeffrey L. Ward
Title page illustration © tartila/stock.adobe.com
Chapter opener illustration © bewalrus/stock.adobe.com

Library of Congress Cataloging-in-Publication Data has been applied for.

ISBN 978-0-06-305612-1

24 25 26 27 28 LBC 5 4 3 2 1

*This book is dedicated to embracing who we are,
living a life of purpose, peace, and love.
The greatest of these is love.*

BINDLE PUNK: BIN-DƏL PUNK, <u>NOUN</u>
An early-twentieth-century term to describe one who carries his clothing or bedding in a bundle, usually derogatory in nature. Also used to classify a hobo, wanderer, migrant worker, tramp, or one who has no home.

JEFE: HEF-AY, <u>NOUN</u>
A person who is in charge of a worker, crew, or organization; a boss.

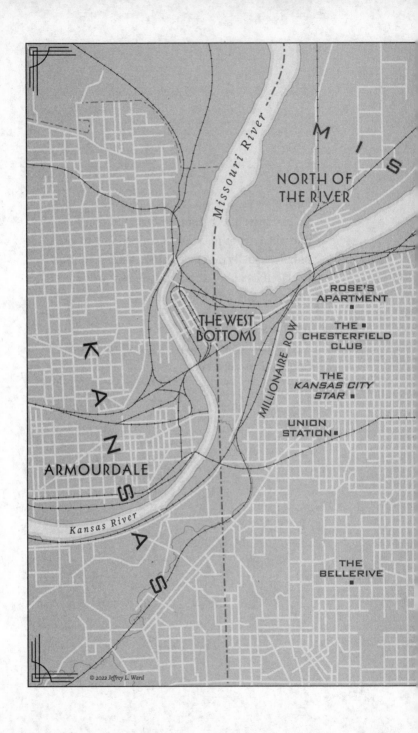

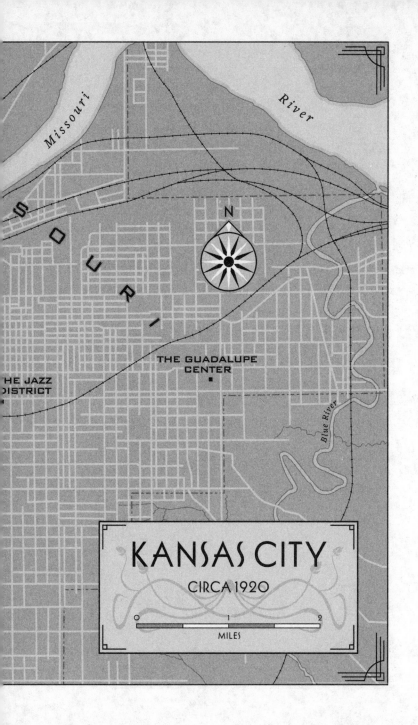

Missouri

River

MISSOURI

N

THE GUADALUPE
CENTER
■

THE JAZZ
DISTRICT

Blue River

KANSAS CITY

CIRCA 1920

0   1   2

MILES

BINDLE PUNK JEFE

1

BRUJA FALSA.

I got everything I thought I wanted these past six months—managing high-end juke joints, embracing my heritage, navigating true romance even though *that* now has to stay hidden from the public eye for a whole new set of reasons. Having a boyfriend and a husband doesn't exactly shine in the society papers, even if the faux marriage has set me up in ways I couldn't have done on my own up until this point. I should be filled to the brim with confidence. My life should be easier. *So why isn't it, then?*

A sigh makes its way out of my shuddering mouth in a puff of smoke that rivals the outward blow of any cigarette. I'd have one now, except my fingers are far too stiff from the dropping temperatures in the West Bottoms, where the river flows slowly beneath the icy film that lies over top of it. Even with the risk of muddying up my gloves to perform this spell, I'd still almost chance putting them on just to give my knuckles a barrier from the air. Earth magic, however, is particular about its need for my bare hands against the ground. *That* I'm confident about. With a word, I can render my enemies speechless, my will pressing into their minds. My palms can lay wet earth over a gaping wound and bring the tissues back together—save for a bit of scarring because I'm still learning. The parts of me I can't reconcile, though, are the recurring images in my head of screaming Klansmen as they reach for the sky with horror in their eyes while ghastly oaks become their tomb.

They were buried alive. And they deserved it. And yet, the sight of the riverbanks with these giant grave markers makes my guts twist into a ball of morbid dread.

Six months ago, I was a dangerous flirt at best. My legs were more potent than my magic. *But now* . . . It more than haunts me at night that I'm a witch powerful enough to bring someone back to life.

Let alone take it.

Shivering, I trudge down a sloping hill toward the rocky bank, dead grass crunching beneath my boots that I borrowed from my boyfriend because I've ruined enough pairs of shoes in these parts. Gio won't mind once I tell him. He hardly wears these industrialized foot trappings, anyway. Even with the extra stockings that I have layered under my slacks, though, my toes are still feeling the cut of the breeze. Just as my heart still feels the cut of the empty railyard that stands as a specter, which once held warm boxcars full of family and safety. *Home.* Or . . . it had been. The city wasted no time taking it all away, including this place that was once so magical. Only sadness and stillness remain. The emptiness feels like my fault. It's a feeling I've been able to ignore quite well up until I pulled my Model T into the frozen field.

The wind bites at me again. It stings almost as badly as my guilt. I'm barely aware of the ice breaking beneath my boots as I reach the shoreline. For the first time since saving my brother, I've come to bless a portion of dirt that will be used in all kinds of enchantments that my abuela plans to show me. I've come to do what I was born to do—not because I'm a dedicated student, but because my abuela isn't able to cast another spell again . . . and because we're running out of dirt. She's a witch, bound to the earth without her magic. And that doesn't just *feel* like my fault.

It *is* my fault.

The old railyard whispers with the wind, frigid in its accusations as I squat down with a metal bucket and a spade; I need to hurry this along. My hands haven't quite numbed yet, so the aching in my fingers is edging on unbearable. I tilt the bucket into the river, evermore thankful for women's slacks. My hair, as I pull the wool sides of my cloche down over my ears, acts as a flimsy layer that barely shields my chin. I don't know if it's because I'm in such a melancholy mood or if the fates are as upset with me as I am, but as I begin scooping and pouring clumps of dry dirt over my open palm, the wind refuses to sing. I expected the gray sky to give way like any other time I've blessed a handful of dirt. The stars should be greeting me, weaving my consciousness in and out of space and time. But the brown granules continue to sprinkle in silence past my fingers into the bucket of river water. My teeth grind on their own.

God, it's cold.

"Las ventanas del cielo abren sus portones," I say through

the chattering. "Lavan las montañas—ugh, you can do this, Luna."

My nerves take advantage of the temperature, giving my body a violent shiver. I don't recall this spell being so difficult. But then again, I usually have my matriarchal guide with me. The day was far too cold to bring my abuela this time. In fact, I haven't faced the fates alone since . . .

A tremble roars through my body once again as the images of screaming men dressed as ghosts steal what breath from me the cold hasn't. Their twisted faces in my memory are more present right now than the river in front of me. As bark climbs down their creased foreheads like brown, scaly snakes, they turn their bulging eyes to me, choking out the words that won't leave me alone. *Bruja falsa.*

Swearing, I shove the pointed end of my gardening tool back into the hard earth along with the memories. Saving the lives of my family that night shouldn't be tormenting me like this. I did what I needed to do last summer. The fates know that. They helped me do it.

They helped me kill all of those wicked men. But there's that word again:

Kill.

"Acuesta tus cargas sobre el viento," I gasp into the clouds my breath is making around me. "¡Mientras canta el río bendito!"

A clap like thunder, and there it is—the wind stilling itself as it should. Though the clouds are turning a shade darker, I can hear the stars behind them, giggling and welcoming me home. *Finally.* I quickly fill the bucket to the waterline. I even join the gentle melody that sweeps past my numbing cheeks. While I'm not much of a singer, I swear I'm more off-key than usual. My nerves are definitely not helping the performance. At least my ill-tuned vocals are coercing a smile to my drying lips. While my spade stirs the mixture, I stop my humming just long enough to shift on my feet. That's when I hear it— an odd sound on the wind. The relief on my face falls quickly. I tilt my ear, scanning the river to my left and then to my right. The unknown song is as lovely as all the others at first, but soon begins to shift on the returning breeze that also changes its course. It whips my hair one direction and then another. The goosebumps rising on my skin aren't just from the winter air.

What is this?

The mixture I came to create will be used for healing spells and protection, not for curses—to my disappointment, my abuela has yet to train me to perform a curse. But this gusty hymn sounds like one.

It *feels* like one.

I glance up at the clouds, which are bubbling into a brooding shade of slate. The playful laughter beyond them grows harsh. Cruel. Like the stars are laughing *at* me this time. But I've never heard of them doing that. The fates are a part of us, and we are a part of them . . . or something like that. Yet that doesn't stop the cackling from turning guttural. A bitter smell like dead moths and mischief invades my raw nose, permeating everything around me. My stomach mimics the angst of the sky. It's time to end the spell.

As I drop the spade into the mixture, a roar jerks my head back toward what was a tranquil river only a moment ago. Now, just inches away from my knee, a raging torrent threatens the shoreline. The rush of the water harmonizes with the foreboding music in the air. Such a dreadful song.

Frigid gusts bite at my stinging eyes. I want to cry. I want it to stop.

"H-hey!" I stutter, pushing my shaking body up from the ground. A screaming burst of wind shoves me back down, the bucket slopping everywhere. I realize I've been shielding my eyes with my arms once the freezing mud starts seeping past the cuffs of my overcoat and down my wrists. The pinch of the metal handle inside my elbow signals me next. I chance a peek over my arm at the riverbank that acts like nothing just happened. *Yeah, I'm outta here.* I got what I came for.

I think.

I hope.

The wind might be dying down, but my nerves are going to take a while.

Regaining some of my bearings, I find my way back to my feet, looking around like a sleepwalker who's been startled awake. My panting breath is the only sound in the desolate river valley—that and my beating heart. The cold air burns my lungs. With the river back to its rhythmic flow, I take that cue and sail past the trees, which clap their dead hands together in the light breeze. I'm not parking so far away next time.

The drive home barely registers, even along the back roads that I have to go down to keep from being seen. I thought I'd be past this by now—hiding in shadows. I also thought I'd found my way with my *gift*.

Mierda. What the hell do I know?

If I didn't have a business meeting in the morning, I'd head straight to my mother's house right now. Or Javier's. My brother almost always knows what to say. But at least I've got my dirt. He'd probably tell me to be grateful or something and to look on the bright side of blabbity blah. It's best that I just go home and down a few glasses of cordial with my—I almost can't think it—husband. It's usually funny. Right now, it's not.

I dig beneath the cloth seat for my emergency stash of Camels. Since I refuse to let any air in for ventilation, the cabin soon fills with a white haze, my heated breath fogging up the front window. My tire only hits a curb a few times. Everything I'm involved in might be illegal and dangerous up to my ears, but creeping along the boulevards at night in a smoked-up Model T with a bucket of magical dirt seems the least of them.

ALL I WANT IS A TALL GLASS OF SPIRITS AND AN ENTIRE PACK of smokes to shake off the unease brought on by my trip to the River Bottoms. My dream is quite thoroughly dashed as I inch down the tree-lined street where Heck lives. The house we share has presence with its pillars in front of pillars, all white and pretentious—just like everything else in this part of town. The only parts of me reflected here are the vines that climb up each column and down again, blanketing the home with protection spells that took me months to get just right. But it's not the house that's got my mood sinking; it's the lack of parking space in the driveway. One of Heck's dinner parties strikes again.

I'd try to sneak around to the back door, but our hired valets for the evening have spotted me. My stomach pivots at the sight of the Duesys and Royales lining the brick pavement. The convertibles have their covers on for winter, yet their bodies are still inlaid with shining trim and extra tires like encrusted jewels. Each automobile seems to stretch longer than the next, the newer models clearly in competition with each other. It's a wonder their drivers can turn a corner.

The uniformed young man sailing down the front steps soon rounds my Model T, opening my door and offering me an arm before I can protest . . . or hide my muddy bucket. His polite smile struggles to cover his curious frown. This isn't the first time Timothy has greeted me in such a manner.

"Shall I have a bath drawn, Mrs. Kessler?" he asks, guiding me up to the covered porch, then past the grand pillars with a hurriedness I didn't expect. "The hors d'oeuvres are nearly served."

I'm far too tired to argue with the boy about calling me by Heck's name. I've got enough names to keep straight tonight—bigger stakes, a bigger ruse. And I'm just not in the mood to be Rose Lane or Kessler or whoever the hell I'm supposed to be.

"I'll get the bath myself, and please tell Heck that I'm not well enough for dinner parties tonight."

Letting Timothy open the front door—since mahogany is obviously too heavy for a woman to handle—I slip into the entryway, making a beeline for the staircase. The warmth of the house hits my numbed cheeks in a way that almost burns.

"Gentlemen," a voice as smooth as bourbon and laughter calls out from somewhere beyond the foyer, "if you'll excuse me a moment, I'm going to see about my wife—I believe she's just come in. Kitten, let me help you get settled!"

"Oh, thank you," I call back. "But I can manage."

Thankfully, the entryway and the sitting room are divided by large arched doorways with equally ritzy doors. I'm nearly to the second landing as the brass handle turns below.

Knowing the stern look I'm about to endure, not to mention the lecture, I pause my ascent to tilt my head down toward what's sure to be a scowling man with a Rolex wristwatch standing in the foyer doorway.

I am, of course, right.

He shoots the room full of aristocrats a wide grin and a chuckling apology before turning back to me. The door clips shut with a curt tug. It's funny, the amount of silent words I'm able to make out on Heck's lips, although it's mostly profanity with grandiose gestures that look even more grandiose in the three-piece suit he's wearing. His side-slicked hair is absolute perfection, the color growing lighter as his face reddens.

"I'm *sorry*," I mouth back, holding up my bucket, which does nothing to temper him. His eyes light up like two cerulean hailstorms. Heck is suave and handsome, but he's damn annoying about things like propriety and punctuality.

Which is pretty ironic, considering our sham of a marriage.

He points upward before he scales the stairs on his tiptoes behind me, impressively keeping his wineglass steady. The wallpapered hallways get to watch as we both angrily make our way to the master quarters on the third floor, neither of us excusing the other while fighting to be the first into the room.

Another set of ridiculously large doors clicks shut. "Rose, just where in the hell have you been? We have until the Christmas Gala to nail down these acquisitions, and here you come waltzing in like you don't give a damn. Do you have *any* idea—you look as though you've been accosted. Thank heavens no one saw you!"

"I didn't think a trip to the river would take me that long,"

I snap back, shedding my coat and boots near the fireplace that still flickers with a few embers. Although this room has a radiator, the private balcony makes it too drafty to keep up with heating the place. Heck could have the doors sealed for the winter, but I think he likes strolling about these decadent quarters in vintage style—a roaring fire with a drink in one hand. Makes him feel like the old money that he is. And what do I care? I barely live here.

I toss my hat to the standing rack by a chifforobe that's more art than it is furniture, but my aim is off, and the hat falls to the floor. Heck complains the farther I venture into the room—something about dirt on the rug and how long it's going to take to untangle my hair. I drop into one of the largest wingback chairs I've ever seen, setting the bucket next to me with a sigh. "I just had a rough day, and I'm not in the mood for your nagging."

"I am not nagging." His fingers pinch every item I've dropped, setting it all by the door for the maid to deal with. "Okay—yes, I'm nagging. But I'm allowed to be angry when you've left me naked with embarrassment tonight."

"I want to be me for the night, Heck. In fact, I was planning to stay at Gio's."

"Oh, is he back in town?" He's genuinely happy for me, I can tell. Except then he says, "You two can gallivant after dinner."

"Three dinner parties in one week is unreasonable."

"This one is important, Rose."

"You said that last time," I say, shimmying my trousers up so that I can stretch my legs, "and I spent that evening watching your golf club beaus get drunk and handsy!"

"Keep your voice down," he hisses, planting himself between me and the fire I'm trying to use to warm my stockings. "They are not my *beaus*." His hardened jaw relaxes as he flicks a golden eyebrow. "As if I would date a golfer."

"*You're* a golfer."

"Swinging my club to get in on the gossip before Sunday brunch doesn't make me a golfer. Plus, I'm spoken for." His eyes go wistful, his teeth clenching over his bottom lip. It would be an adorably sexy look if I didn't know he was fantasizing about my brother. As happy as I am for them, it's still odd to think of my best friend (not to mention husband) making whoopee to Javier.

Heck quickly regains his steely posture. "In any case, we do not have golfers downstairs, my dear. We have lumber barons and a certain Kansas City politician who is, thankfully, running later than you are. Otherwise, I'd be downright panicked. At least we have time to gain our composure before he gets here."

Some realizations are slow, while others hit like six shots of moonshine. This one is the latter.

"P . . . politician?" I ask, my eyes widening.

"Should I start your bath?"

"You said being married was gonna be a piece of cake."

"I have *never* used that euphemism."

I shake my head with a whining groan. "I'll be down in ten."

"Take twenty. He hasn't arrived yet, and you smell like"— Heck waves his hand at the air around him—"outside."

The rest of my clothes are tossed about the room as Heck checks his side-slicked hair in a mirror before heading back downstairs. My nerves dance inside my bones, fully rejuvenated. And now with no time to recover. But I have at least *some* reprieve and within minutes I'm closing my eyes to take in the lavender-scented steam that fills my claw-foot tub. The water brings me back to a feeling of normalcy—back to a time when I was an unknown spinster who didn't have to schmooze the upper class with a faux marriage. I could kiss whoever I wanted, con whoever I wanted, and I sure didn't have to have dinner around a crowded table of jewelry-adorned suckers three times a week.

But the payoff *was* what I wanted. Heck and I are building a small underground dynasty in the booze business. And our lovers aren't exactly complaining. Hell, they're our partners in crime. The truth is, we all kind of like the danger.

Danger is sexy.

I'm all confident smiles by the time I'm pinning the side of my hair with a sparkling adornment the size of my hand. Heck says the color is the perfect complement to the contrast between my skin and the darkness of my hair. I think that's just a fancy way to say he likes green. Lip stain and rouge finish the work. And even though the crooked politician downstairs used to employ one of the men who tried to kidnap me and steal my magic last summer, I don't let that bother me. Too much. I want to play in the big leagues and hold favor in this city. Can't really do that without the man who runs it all.

I lift up my manicured nails with a sly smile, opting out of wearing dinner gloves. The former city councilman deserves a good, hearty handshake once he arrives. My magic is sure to glean something useful from him. He's got to be swimming in secrets.

Straightening the beaded fringe of my sleeves, I stare into the bathroom mirror like it's destiny itself. *Tell me everything, Mr. Pendergast.*

AS I ENTER THE ARCHED DOORWAY OF THE DINING ROOM with a slender cigarette holder between my fingers, I stop to admire the way the chandelier casts droplets of light across the pale wallpaper. Heck's muted color choices really are quite something, even if our tastes are different. A pine tree drenched with ornaments fills the expanse of the bay window, and I'm tempted to adjust a few pine cones and berries just to annoy him. My lingering also gives the room a chance to zero in on my legs.

Bruja magic isn't the only way to disarm a man.

Eventually, my eyes turn to a dining table big enough to seat a king and his retinue. I glance at every seat except the one in the middle, where the former city councilman's chair stands empty. *Good.* I'm too flustered to see the big guy just yet. The last time I saw Tom Pendergast was when I made a fool of myself at the train station back when I worked for the newspaper. Writer by day, vamp by night—my lies were easier to keep track of back then. *Simpler times.*

The host of the evening ejects himself from the head of the table with casual flair, doting on my dress and continuing a story he was telling when I came in. The room erupts into periodic light laughter, which helps me force my shoulders to relax. At least Heck being the entertainer saves me from having to actually say anything. *For now.* He pulls me to his side to guide me to our spot as he introduces me to what seems like thirty people. They all compliment the home's modernized-yet-traditional Christmas decor like I had anything to do with it. Heck's holiday parties are ones for the books. Holly garland wraps around lit candles as centerpieces. Utensils as golden as the long table runner await in neat rows on either side of the matching plates. I could buy a lot of gin for the cost of one of these forks. Speaking of which, Heck hasn't skimped on booze either. While several crystal decanters sparkle amid the flickering centerpieces, there's only one calling my name.

I cast smiling nods to the jeweled wives around me, taking my seat as my eyes scan the table for the cherry cordial. Sinking onto a cushioned chair beside me, Heck swiftly takes my cigarette holder before tapping his lips to my cheek.

His soft hand squeezes mine, a signal that he wants me to tap into my magic so I can know his thoughts about how this evening should go. "Darling, our guests are curious to hear all about your afternoon."

I shoot him a flat expression, refusing to read his mind or mood. I've got my own thoughts to keep together, thank you very much. Besides, I'm hardly nervous about impromptu excuses—I lie for a living, and I'm sure I can do the same tonight.

Maybe when I get some liquor in me.

I let out a long exhale as Heck pours a rich maroon liquid into my glass. I pinch the pencil-thin stem with gratefulness and let the cardamom and ginger mixture warm the back of my throat in a smooth burn. I want to wash it all down and ask for another but I take tiny sips instead. I've got to stay focused for Pendergast. The former city councilman might be a part of the same mob syndicate that I'm in, but his tenure furnishes him with a power that took him decades to build and that I'm no closer to obtaining—he owns Kansas City in ways that go beyond title deeds.

Pulling my hand away from Heck's, I straighten the long string of pearls around my neck, ignoring his subtle frown.

I love him—I truly do in our strange, beautiful way—and I understand why tonight is important. But my time by the river has me a little shaken, and I don't want to play his marionette tonight.

A brawny fellow dressed like an old-fashioned gentleman all the way down to the golden T-bar on his waistcoat nods to the young man between us to refill his drink.

"Oh, let your woman settle herself with a drink, Mr. Kessler," he says with a Southern air. His fingers run along the pointy end of his mustache as my eyebrows raise. "As much as I delight in the daily courses of such a pretty little thing, of course."

Your woman? Some gentleman. Even for this retrograde time, that language chafes. The streaks of gray in his brick-colored hair are a mocked wisdom to the snide look on his face. The younger man fills the glass with enough whiskey to take the old man down. Apparently lumber barons sure can drink.

So why are we giving it to them for free when they could be spilling money for it at my club?

"Father," the young man says, "I'm sure not everyone delights in telling stories such as you do."

The older man takes a sip. "Of course, you know stories are my predilection. But if I am *boring* you, feed on that new circular that's been making its way to our hotel doorsteps." He touches a cloth napkin to his sun-bleached lips.

"An anonymous woman scribbling theories about working housewives, filling our girls' heads with suggestive views such as seizing positions in society that belong to men—"

"Oh, Father, not this again."

"That have *always* belonged to men." His five-fingered glass soon becomes two- as he draws light praise from others at the table at his reminding us all of our places in the world—ladies belong in dresses and men in suits. *And my eyes belong in a looking-ahead position, rather than rolling back into my skull.* "And those damn belles certainly have no business mixing about without their husbands or fathers present."

The cordial burns as it threatens to come back up.

Heck pastes an expression on his face likened to a mannequin at Harzfeld's while the lumber baron's son stares down at his callused hands. I hide my own disdain behind my napkin but find myself also pressing an occasional smirk into the fabric. *Damn belles . . . such baloney.* My dearest friend, Margaret, nearly got herself fired over her antics and views at the job we used to share at the *Star*. Although her writing is excellent, her skills weren't enough to gain favor with the chief editor, even if he is her uncle. Starting an underground circular was the most brilliant and dangerous thing a spinster like her could do. And hearing how her efforts have ruffled this man's patriarchal feathers makes me think she might just be on to something.

I'll have to tell her when I see her next.

"No man would want to read that rubbish," the old man finishes with a fist rustling the utensils on the table.

I'm sure 250 miles southeast of here, his hometown in the

Ozark Mountains is praising the man's monologue with an identical accent and feigned charm. I immediately vow never to go there. If not for the money and lumber the barons bring to our city's development, I'd tell the man to go back to the apple-knocking hills where he came from. But then, I'd have to hear Heck's lecture later about how I snubbed Missouri royalty. *We're always surrounded by villains,* he would say. *We must never let them steal our focus.*

We also shouldn't let them steal our will, I would argue back. For now, though, I'll let this blustering buffoon have his piece.

The younger man, who could be his father's twin if not for the obvious age difference, catches my blank stare. His smirk is barely noticeable as he leans in while his father's rant segues to Negros working in white nightclubs.

"Oh, don't pay him any mind, darlin'," the younger baron whispers. "I surely don't. I'm Hiram, by the way. Hiram Wilmington"—he pauses with an overly smug purse of his freckled lips—"the *Third.*"

His eye roll makes me smile. I hate the handlebar caterpillar on his father's face, but it doesn't look so bad on Hiram. It seems softer somehow, due to his rounded chin, which is suitable for a well-fed heir, although there's no hiding the strength contained in the broadness of his shoulders. I don't usually find red hair attractive, but it's kind of stylish on him, along with his taupe suit, looking like he snagged it from Heck's closet. And clearly, they share the same love for pomade, although Hiram's smells of leathery musk and pine needles. A dastardly combination.

It almost makes me laugh, thinking about my love life now. Before I fell for Gio, this young baron was just the kind of pretty face and big money I'd go for—him, thinking he was playing my heart while I'd play right back. That's when magic was fun. Except when it came to the lovesick fools.

It's ironic that I've become one myself.

"So," I whisper back, although the other guests have moved on to idly beating their gums, "not all lumber barons share your father's sentiments on women and non-whites?"

Hiram shakes his head. "I can't remember the last time I was in the same room as my father," he says. "We're only here at my mother's request to keep our family in good standing with Pendergast. And Nichols. And Kessler . . . and whoever else dominates development in this city. We've got contracts to fill."

"Well, surely you've got the green to stay away." I glance down at the golden band on his left hand. "You telling me that ring hasn't set you free?"

Just like title restrictions, inheritance contracts have always been a dreadful tool of coercion. Heck and I had to marry just to gain his fortune. I can't imagine he's the only one whose reputation is tied to his money.

"Depends on how you define freedom," Hiram says, his accent slipping into a more casual flair, like that of the country folk who pass by at the farmers' market. It seems I'm not the only one who wears multiple hats. "We want the titles. Respect. And by God, even the power." He nods in his father's direction. "I stick around because I want the old man to know that I don't need to grovel at his feet with gratefulness like my brother. I've got my own investments. My own damn life. And I strive to never be his favorite son."

"I see." It doesn't take a bruja to feel the darkness shadowing his countenance. "So, big money in logs, eh?"

Hiram's eyelids lower in a way that could make the pope blush. "You know . . . they write songs about love. And lust. And drinking on the bayou." His fingers tease the boutonniere hole in his lapel. "But I'd rather they play us a tune about eighty-eight million dollars in real estate transactions in this city and let the melody show us what ferocity and passion feel like."

As a variety of vegetables and greens that could pass for artistic sculptures swirl around us on the platters of our caterers, I let the warm buzz of the cordial flow across my bare shoulders. Soon, on either side of me, Heck and the devilish baron's son with the devilish ideals spark a debate on men's watches. Hiram is no half-witted potato; I'll give him that. I used to share his views on romance and money. I still do in a lot of ways. I'm an ambitious woman who just happened to fall in love. And maybe he will too one day—as long as his wife is okay with it.

"Mrs. Kessler, come now," says a woman whose headpiece could easily be an entire peacock. "As soon as you and your husband are done *flirting* with the lumber barons, we're simply all *dying* to know how your afternoon went."

Heck's nervous laugh intercepts my raised brow as he reaches for my wrist. "Kitten, why don't you show everyone the bracelet I've given you as an early Christmas present? Aren't the diamonds just lovely, ladies?"

While light gasps and tittering fill the room, Heck's urgency filters into my skin, rippling up to my elbow. I might be refusing to read his thoughts, but he knows my magic will surely soak up his feelings—a very annoying tactic on a night that's got me so nervous. Especially when I was just beginning to get comfortable.

I swiftly take my arm out of his reach—he'll have to save his etiquette lessons for some other time—making a show of dangling my fingers in front of the starry-eyed wives as I take another swig of my fruity, spiced drink.

"Then tell us this, Rose, if you *must* keep us in suspense," the peacock says. "What made you decide on this Colonial Revival rather than a Tudor or Craftsman house in the newer neighborhoods? I've been *dying* with curiosity about it."

She pauses to take a drink and, I assume, to watch me squirm. Her smugness would have been a real victory for her if I cared at all.

I sip at the rim of my own glass. "Doesn't take much to kill you, does it?"

"I beg your pardon?"

"You know, darling," Heck interjects with a laugh as hard as the hold he's got on my elbow, "you were just telling me how obvious a Craftsman would be for a couple with our taste."

"Mmm, that sounds precisely like something I would say."

"Indeed, in fact . . ."

Matching his tightened smile, I nod in agreement to everything he says. We've decided to irritate each other, it seems. But it's the people Heck has surrounded me with that irk me, and he knows it. I want to tell the peacock woman that I would have chosen a condominium in the Country Club Plaza, where all the up-and-coming players play, but that Heck is from old money and chose for us to live in the part of town that said as much. But I guess we can't say truthful things like that in such affluent company.

"Begging everyone's pardon for the interruption." The director of the catering staff stands at the head of the dining hall, smoothing his tuxedo until he has all of our attention. "The former city councilman's car has just pulled up, but I've been informed that he has, sadly, again, been detoured by urgent business and must go. However, he has asked for a brief conversation with Mr. Kessler if it's not too much trouble."

My eyes level at the realization. *Pendergast is here?* And leaving. And he wants to talk to Heck. My husband can schmooze the upper class, but he doesn't know onions about the bootlegging business. What's he gonna do—dazzle the man with a smile?

The table around me looks as glum and startled as the deflating host beside me, who begins clearing his throat. "Well, thank you, Harold, and we will continue the evening with your fine menu and services." Heck dons his professional grin, straightening his shoulders once again as he turns back to our guests. "In light of this unfortunate news, I suppose we will have to eat more, drink more, and be all the merrier."

"Hear! Hear!" Glasses clink together around the room.

"If you'll all excuse me momentarily, I shall thank our brief guest for coming all the way out to Hyde Park on such a cold evening."

As he begins to stand, I lean forward, pressing my lips and a light flow of magic to Heck's smooth cheek with enough force to leave some rouge behind.

Rose should see Pendergast.

I know it's wrong—sending a thought into a man's brain that isn't his own. But I can't let Heck out there without me, and he can't leave me in here with these people. The impartation is the tiniest spell, anyway. And it's not like he's forced to accept an introduced thought.

His wide eyes turn to me as two cerulean jewels some-where between shocked and indignant. He lifts his nose to the faint scent of hibiscus coming from my lips. He knows. An inward cringe finds its way to my face as he lays a delicate hand over mine on the chair rail between us, my magic now letting in the floodgates of his thoughts—*How* dare *you?*

Really, the rest of what I'm reading through his palm aren't thoughts so much as feelings of betrayal. *What's he so sore about?* He's been trying to use my magic all night. I should set my elbows on the table and start another one of our adorable arguments in front of our fake friends, and I will . . . as soon as I talk to Pendergast.

"Stay here, darling. I'll give the former councilman our regards," I say, taking my hand away and tossing my napkin from my lap with what I hope is a fair amount of grace.

Heck's subtle hand clamps around the hem of my dress, sliding it backward to find my knee. This would be exciting in so many other circumstances but he's just desperately trying to find any connection with my skin. I give him a half-second audience and a look that tells him to hurry the hell up as another silent message filters through just above my stockings. *Rose, we'll argue later. But even you know it's uncouth for you to go.*

I push my chair from the table. "Really, dear, I'm needing some air."

The table murmurs with an array of kind agreements and "that's understandable"s with a few "of course, you poor things" thrown in as I stand.

"I shall walk you to the door," Heck insists, gliding across the expansive room beside me. His slight panic invades my elbow as we reach the entryway doors. He glances back at the dining room before pulling me closer. "They think you went to the doctor."

Huh? I scrunch my face. Whatever he's trying to say has nothing to do with me losing my audience with Pendergast, and the man is waiting.

"Okay," I say with a shrug, "tell them all about it."

With a blast of cold air from the open door, his fingers slide from my arm as I give him an apologetic frown before shutting his sullen frame in the house. I'm not losing this chance. Let Heck tell them I've got the dropsy for all I care.

HURTING MY BEST FRIEND IN THE ENTIRE WORLD STINGS almost as much as the Missouri wind on my arms that sends my skin rippling with tiny bumps. Heck and I can bicker like brother and sister, but we understand each other. And I have every intention of making up with him later. We always do. We're partners, and that means sometimes he needs to play my game as much as I play his.

Pendergast. Booze. Felonies . . . those are my games.

As crystal flakes swirl around me like tiny feathers, our hired man, Timothy, helps me in the careful ascent down the front patio stairs, leading me to the cream Cadillac with side curtains that protect the shadowed figure within. The headlamps stare straight ahead as twin beams, lighting the darkness in front of them—a stage for the dancing snow. And that's what this meeting is. Just another dance. I've played this role before. I'm smart and capable. I'm a bootlegger. And a damn good one.

Letting my breath out in a shivering misty cloud, I nod to Timothy to open the passenger door. I slide onto the cream upholstery and avoid making small talk about how chilly the night is. That's not what we're here for.

"Mrs. Kessler," the man whose presence and broad shoulders fill up the back seat says, "I'm not complaining here, but most guys don't send their wives out to see me unless they want them outta their hair."

I swallow a growl because everything on this man is big—his nose, his teeth—even the cleft in his chin that's much more prominent than mine. The darkness doesn't hide the amused curl of his lip either.

"Yes, well, my husband was never known to tear himself away from an adoring crowd," I quip with another shiver, "and I'm not exactly the life of the party."

While the crooked councilman and I have done most of our business through telegrams up to this point, he knows my ownership of the clubs that Heck and I run together. There's no question as to whether I'm the boss of my operations, but Pendergast's sarcasm precedes him. And he likes to poke at women in more ways than one.

I glance up at his gloved hands that he rubs together, blowing into them with a coughing laugh at my deadpan expression. There are a lot more things I'd say to a jerk statement like that one, but my snarkiness *might* not serve me well here.

"Ah, where are my manners? You must be freezin' your heels off in this weather." He points to his top hat. "And here I thought I was overdressed."

Before I can protest, he sheds his tuxedo jacket that nearly swallows me whole once it's wrapped around my trembling shoulders. Having a sit-down in thirty-degree weather is certainly one way to keep a meeting short.

"Mr. Pendergast—"

"Hey, Charlie, hand me that paper, will ya?"

The silent driver in front of us suddenly comes to life, passing a folded-up page of the *Kansas City Star* over his shoulder.

"Just listen to this." Pendergast nods to the page, pushing a pair of spectacles over his nose. "'If you want to see some sin, forget Paris, and head to Kansas City.'" His gloves tap against the crinkled edge. "What do you make of that, sweetheart?"

If I cringed every time a guy called me something ridiculous, I'd walk around with a permanently scrunched face. Instead, like most other times, I settle into whatever game he's playing.

"I can't say that I disagree."

He coughs and laughs again, handing the paper back to his driver. "Smart girl. I've always thought so. And now you're a part of the machine—my machine. And I've just gotta make sure we understand each other." His lowered brow gets lower. "Before you get any taller, if you get my drift."

"I do," I say, meeting his eye, and glad for the darkness. "I guess you just wanna hear that I won't get in your way."

"In my way?" He removes his spectacles, and I resist the urge to recoil as he pulls the lapel from my shoulder before slipping the tiny eyewear into the breast pocket. His hand nearly brushes my chin. "I like you right here where I can see you." Releasing the jacket to me, he settles back with a big sigh, the frigid air clouding around his mouth with each word. "This is a simple business. I get what I want and you get what you want."

My chin hardens, my eyes landing on the gleaming door handle. "Okay, so what do you want exactly?"

"No, no. You first."

"Okay," I say again. *Steady, Rose.* "I just want to keep making money without any trouble."

"Don't we all?" His chuckle fills the cabin with more white mist. He sure thinks something is funny. "Listen, I'm not out to hurt you, sweetheart. You're good for my bottom line. And I protect those who are good for my bottom line. That's what it means to be in the syndicate."

Well, that's good news. *I guess.* Al Capone's network runs from Canada to New Orleans and back again, with Kansas City as a favored stopping point. There's plenty of business to be had for everyone out here. So why don't I feel comfortable?

Probably because he's a powerful man.

A man who's done favors for me in the past.

A man who has yet to tell me what he wants in return.

Pendergast lifts a chubby finger. "I only respond to what affects me, you understand?"

"I do, sir."

"Good. Check your pockets there."

Reaching down into the silk-lined fabric, my stiffening fingers find an envelope. He also hands me a monogrammed card with gold detailing as fancy as the car we're sitting in.

"You know where my office is down on Main. Come by there on Monday after you've dropped that off. The information is in the envelope."

I nearly jump in my seat as the driver jerks open his door, leaving me looking around like a lost kid at the train station while he circles the car to my side. Pendergast's outer garment is barely a shield to the wind when my door opens for me.

"Wait. Hang on. What—"

"I've been short a man since your old boss met the river," the powerhouse next to me says. "Moretti got too cocky, but he was good at bribing cops. I'm giving you a front seat to how this machine really works."

¿Qué? I wanted Moretti gone, but I certainly didn't want his job. Besides, I'm already up to my ears in felonies.

"You . . . you want me to pay the police to keep them from arresting us for bootlegging?"

"You're the one who jumped in my car when I originally called for your husband." He lifts his eyebrow with a smirk. "Don't take this the wrong way, but you aren't exactly charming, Mrs. Kessler."

I sputter to cover my expletives. What a jerk. Charm is exactly what I do. I'm all charm.

"You're gonna hafta be more persuasive than that." Pendergast beckons for his jacket, all humor gone from his face. "Show a little more skin and a little less attitude, sweetheart."

Half a second later, I'm watching the wooden artillery wheels spin down the driveway as the vehicle makes its way back into the city. I'm sure there's a body that needs burying. I don't want any part of this—not if it comes with slimeball cops who will think they're getting a shot at me. Sure, I've got my magic to give me an upper hand. But dios, I miss using it for fun . . . and this does not sound like fun.

With a shuddering groan, I hop back up the front steps and ask Timothy to bring my car around. I'm more done with this night than I was before. I'm going to go lie in the arms of my boyfriend and let him thaw me back to life.

While I'm bouncing on the balls of my feet and rubbing my arms, the doors open behind me. Heck's nervous laughter carries from the dining room through the foyer beyond like he's being paid to do it. I'm just glad the figure joining me on the patio isn't him coming to demand answers that I'm in no shape to give right now.

The figure shuts the doors with a swift pull, and in seconds, another dinner jacket is thrown around my shoulders as the garment's owner stares down at me with a smirk on his freckled face. "I shoulda known you'd try to escape. Why didn't you send for me?"

"Every man for himself these days."

"Ah yes, troublin' times what with havin' to bear such gourmet meals with only the use of uncut gin and golden flatware to ease our trials."

"Look, if you're not gonna butt me, then you're useless."

"As long as you're partial to Lucky Strikes."

"I know someone who likes those."

"Well, they *are* the doctors' choice."

Hiram and I share a shuddering laugh against the cold as he produces a cigarette and a lighter almost as fast as my hired man produces my Model T. "Looks like your ride is here, darlin'. Let me know if I can be of further assistance."

That sultry look from earlier is back, and I respond with a brilliant cloud of smoke in his face before sticking out a shivering hand in salutation. A married man this flirtatious is always hiding something interesting. With eyes shining, he obliges. His hand is at least ten degrees warmer than mine . . . and his thoughts about ten degrees darker as he bends to meet my knuckles with his lips. The small smile I press to the filter of my cigarette drops into a stunned frown. My magic is picking up anything but the sexual tension he's fronting. Instead, a wild cyclone of grim emotion soaks into my skin from his mouth. It's only a flash, but the still frames of twisted faces and explosions in his memory make me nearly drop my smoke. The farewell ends quickly.

As Timothy leads me to my car, the lumber baron's anguish still shakes me as much as the cold, and I wonder how the most traumatized people seem so collected. Heck, smiling and laughing inside, was nearly killed last year while trying to save my brother, who, incidentally, was also left for dead—twice. *Dios.* He *did* die.

"Di-mi," I whisper in the cabin of my rumbling car as I head to a part of town not meant for wives of famous land developers. I can't wait to strip myself of this whole day with its volatile magic and volatile houseguests and this damn dress that presses a thousand beads into my rear. The poking fabric is as uncomfortable as my thoughts that keep trying to solve every problem that's been thrown at me since I set foot on the River Bottoms this afternoon.

I really do need to figure out what's going on with all of it. Just . . . not tonight.

2

"'EY."

I spin around in the empty alleyway, clutching my handbag.

Hidden from the streetlight, a lone figure waves me down.

"'Ey! You got any green on ya?"

"No," I lie, picking up my pace across the frozen gravel.

"Come on, baby. You ain't got two pennies? I gotta catch the bus."

"Buses don't run this late," I call over my shoulder, readying an impartation spell on my lips. My heavy exhale is a gloomy mixture of hibiscus within a great white cloud. The stranger tries to harass me further, but then he starts arguing with a man named Gerald from Tonganoxie. The most curious part of this display is that Gerald isn't in the alleyway. No one is in the alleyway except me and this nutjob. He bats at the air, holding his arms in front of his face in self-defense. Gerald seems like an angry guy.

Mumbled curses escape my lips on my way up a set of icy steps that lead to a long brick building with tiny windows. All I wanted when I started this day was to make some magic dirt and come home and have a smoke and a drink with my husband before going to see my boyfriend.

Now *that's* a mouthful.

Pulling Hiram's boxy suit jacket around my trembling body, I find my way beneath the cloud-covered moon to the door. The back entrance of the rooming house always squeals like a dying bird no matter how carefully I try to pry it open. My whole body cringes as the wind outside picks up and slams the door shut with my hand still on the knob. *Oh well.* No one here is likely to tell on me. The anonymity of living among other working-class folks is one of the reasons Gio picked this place since earning his stack of green glorious as my managing rum-runner. I remember his excitement when he showed me his two-room palace short of a single bathroom.

The people here are great, and it's worth the conditions, he told me. *I gotta stay close to the unda'ground, anyway.*

That much is true. The jazz district is where he works and plays, and his new place really does make our relationship work a little easier; I don't have to hide anything because nobody asks me anything. Most people in these makeshift apartments divided by the thinnest walls imaginable don't want to spill our secrets—because they don't want us spilling theirs.

The single bulb in the narrow hallway gives off just enough light to let me know I'm *in* a hallway. Beyond that, I have to squint and use a cigarette lighter to find Gio's door. I light up, letting the flickering aura guide me. The golden glow in my hands eventually reveals a door with a 27, the number dangling upside down. Pinching a Camel with my lips, I dig through my handbag for the key. The back door to the building squeals again—more like shorter squeaks this time. No slamming.

My increasingly panicked hand gropes and feels the inside of the bag, tossing a tin case of smokes and a few lip rouges to the corner. The squeaks draw closer. I tell myself it's just the door. *Find the key, Rose.*

Rapid movement as tiny as the squeaking patters along the carpet just behind me. I've got my hand shoved so far into the handbag that my frozen fingers can barely make out the smaller items. I'm not even sure what has me so uneasy. My abuela has used rats in her spells for as long as I can remember. It's not like I'm afraid of them. I just don't want them to see me or touch me or come anywhere near—*where the hell is that key?*

I've always imagined the fur of such a varmint to be as rough and nausea-invoking as it looks. And as the scritching creature's nose searches the toes poking through my open straps, I kick it away with a gasping squeal of my own. "¡Voy a hacer un caldo con tu cuerpo!"

Somewhere down the dim hallway, a baby's cry is followed by a swearing couple whose quarrel is barely muffled by their closed door. Seeing as how I've awakened the neighbors already, I turn to give Gio's door a solid series of raps with my knuckles when I'm suddenly staring straight into a myriad of beady eyes belonging to a creature far viler than my earlier hallway assailant.

Hell no.

See, wolf spiders are where I draw the line. I lurch backward like I've been hit by lightning before the door opens to my scream, sending the hellish creature scurrying toward room 28.

"You tryin' to get me kicked outta here or what?"

I rush past Gio's groggy face, completely shedding my composure in a high-pitched, full-body shudder that has him chuckling as he stomps out my dropped cigarette in the doorway. He takes in a big yawn, sliding a few locks into place on the door. "Who's jacket are you wearin'?"

"Oh," I say, still quivering in disgust, "some sap at the party felt sorry for me when I was having a smoke."

"Yeah, well, take it off, will ya? He smells betta' than me."

My eyes roll at the smirk in his voice and how he starts making a fuss about how cold my hands are. Three steps and we're in his bedroom, the wool garment falling to the floor. His deft fingers tease my shoulder blades as they make their way to my zipper. "Think I could get ten greens for that sausage casing?"

"No." I laugh, unleashing my garters from their straps. "I'm giving the jacket back. And I like the way you smell."

"I like the way *you* smell." I can't see Gio's nose in the blackness of the room but the softness of his breath traces my jawline, sending shivers down my neck. His hands slide to my hips before clamping around the backs of my thighs. "C'mere and get warm."

In a flurry, he has me on my back beneath a mountain of quilts even though the stove in the other room is letting off a fair amount of heat. I'm glad he was able to snag a room with such an accommodation in this building. I can't stand the thought of him being here, much less the thought of him being cold at night.

The rest of my undergarments are thrown here and there, Gio's mouth evoking swears and panting from me in the darkness—still, save for the argument that's still happening across the hall. My lips fill with blood and a good measure of magic as he works his own kind of incantation between my thighs. I grip his hair with both hands, letting the pressure build. The taste of lavender dances on my lips. I've trained myself to contain the allure spell that draws lovers in with a single kiss. I won't use it on Gio unless he asks me for it. But in this moment, with desperation seizing my body, I want to give him all I have. I want to pour myself out and have him drink of me.

My hips grind on their own, lifting from the bed.

The tension is enough to make me moan for mercy and forget my own name.

"Please," I manage to say in a choking groan. "Please!"

As my knees lock around his ears, he moans, his tongue coaxing me into a gasping frenzy. My eyes devour the darkness above me. The release is long and draining, but it's not enough. As his body finally joins mine, his arms slide behind my shoulders, my head cradled in his hands.

"I want all of you," he whispers just above my panting lips. I whimper with each strike of his hips against me—a choice, painful rhythm. "Will you let me have it?"

"Please," I beg again, pulling my knees up high beside his ribs in surrender. In a flashing series of acrobatics, Gio has my legs over his shoulders, his mouth claiming mine as he siphons my breath and allure from me. The spell unfastens itself from its holding place, freeing my burden and draining into his willing soul. His body trembles in a thousand curse words mixed with promises of devotion, struggling to hold out while I reach another climax before he finally collapses on top of me like a man on his deathbed.

My boyfriend tries to mumble some form of thanksgiving into my heaving chest. "Hrrmm, Rose . . . you killed me dead . . . some kinda drug . . . taste so damn good."

I can't help but laugh, reaching for the crate he uses as a nightstand where I know he keeps his Lucky Strikes. His matchbook contains plenty enough to light a smoke and a few candles. In the flitting light of the tiny fires, I trace the scar on the corner of his eyebrow, wishing I could heal it all the way. But scars are old wounds, as my abuela would say. Harder to manipulate.

My nails glide along his tattooed arms, all the way up to the shaved sides of his head and behind his ears. His lips pinch to hold in a grin. He always tries to pretend he's not ticklish, but I know better.

Gio rolls himself over with a grunt, reaching for my cigarette. "I think you're a sex witch."

"Well, aren't you lucky, then?"

As I lay back on the lumpy double bed with a pillow too luxurious for the place, the argument across the hall reaches a crescendo, and I'm not sure if the ladies are fighting or having some really aggressive nookie. At least the baby has stopped crying. Gio and I share some more of the cigarette as another neighbor yells down the hall for the heated duo to shut up and go to sleep while the couple's groans and crashing furniture only get louder.

"Oh yeah," my boyfriend says, "welcome to my winta' château. Can I get you a beverage?"

"I'm not drinking anything from a kitchen you share with ten other people."

"Ten otha'—what, you think they got a kitchen on every floor?"

My eyes widen as I blow out a slender line of smoke with a lift of my chin.

"Baby, the whole buildin' uses that refrigerata'," he says with a laugh that makes me punch him in the arm. "I know you grew up in that boxca', but you ain't neva' been poor since, have you?"

I want to argue it, but I can't. Between my abuela's money and what I earned on my own, I was able to set up a decent middle-class life for myself. I entered the world as Rose Lane for the low, low price of nearly losing the name I grew up with—Luna Alvarado. Truthfully, I almost lost more than the name. I'm just thankful I've found myself again. *Mostly.*

"It has been a while," I admit. "But I did sleep on the floor of the River Rose with Javi once when we had a big shipment coming in."

And I was too drunk to drive home.

Gio snags the dincher I've got left of our cigarette and drags it down to the quick. "I've slept on floors, in movie theatas, you name it."

"Not enough beds between the circus and the jailhouse?"

"Oh, it's the in-between where you're scrappin' for beds."

I try to imagine my clever boyfriend lying on concrete floors just after being clocked in the head with the butt of a gun—the first time. He might not be living the safest life right now, but at least he's got the shelter of my magic. The tall fern in the next room calls out a silent agreement. The protection spells I placed on their roots are more than enough to keep prying eyes off his place. Unless those eyes are somehow invited, of course.

"Well, you don't have to scrap for anything now," I say. "You make plenty enough to buy a house."

I couldn't convince Heck to buy a home for Gio any more than I could convince Gio to take it. Besides, Kessler money is constantly under scrutiny, and we don't want a dime traced back to our infamous rum-runner. I'm still a little miffed that he moved out of the colonnaded building I used to live in, what with the free rent because he's sleeping with the owner. But I get it—he wants to make his own way.

He turns on his side, his slender build stretching across the bed as he tucks a pillow under his cheek. "With all the Victorians around here bein' turned into apa'tments? I gotta move a little futha' out to buy a house, which takes me futha' away from the whiskey-peddlin' scene."

"I knoooow," I say with my best whiny face. "I do like that you're near Javi's new place. He seems . . . lonely."

"I don't know how you get lonely in the jazz district."

"Uh, probably because his lover lives in Hyde Park."

"So does mine." Gio flashes me a wry smile and shrugs his shoulder. "But when I decide I wanna settle, I'll get a house."

It shouldn't, but the statement sinks like lead from my chest to my stomach. I feel terrible when he and I can't see each other. And sure, the distance is unconventional, but . . . I thought we were solid. Until now, it felt solid.

"You . . . you don't know if you're ready to settle here?"

"Geez, Rose, it's not like I'm lookin' to leave."

"Doesn't sound like you're looking to stay."

I try to hide my watering eyes in the flickering shadows. His arm crosses my waist before pulling me closer. "Hey, don't do that." Gio brushes my hair away from my face, tucking it behind my ear. "Lotta new's been happenin' to me—more than eva' has before—and I'm just tryin' to move with it."

The embarrassment of needing to sniffle warms my cheeks. Thank God it's dark in here. I've never cried about a man. Ever. What a doozy this one did on me.

"You sound like you've got a lot of doubts."

"Of course I have doubts, baby. Who *wouldn't* have doubts?" I attempt to shroud my display of emotion in his chest, but he moves back so that I have to look at him. He lowers his chin like he's about to lecture me about the moonshine budget. "I got a hot sheba who loves the hell outta me, sure. I'll give us that. We're crazy about each otha'. But my girl is married—to a gay swell who could buy me a thousand times ova'. Oh, not to mention, she's also my boss in an illegal operation, she's betta' than me in every way, and she's got a magic mouth."

I must look like I'm not buying it because he lays his hand on my damp cheek and says, "Go on and read me."

The barrier between him and me comes down, and Gio's palm exposes his innermost self to me. If I were to open a window on a spring evening, I'd hear the chattering of birds and a symphony of cicadas joining the sound of bullfrogs, all announcing the coming of night. In Gio's mind, there are also songs. But they are often as sad as the swooning cry of the blues. His lip trembles, his eyes reddening as I push past the iris surrounded by a sable cloud. He worries that I'll find someone else—someone with more class and less of a rap sheet. He wonders if it's fair to force me into exclusivity with him since we won't be able to be an open couple for the foreseeable future.

The sad songs introduce a lighter saxophone as his thoughts turn to Javier. Gio loves how much I love my brother. And Javi and Heck will never in this life be able to have a public relationship either.

But they ain't gonna stop loving each otha'. Gio's thoughts echo through the chamber of blues and jazz music, drawing me back to the bed, where he smiles down at me. He wipes a tear from his cheek with his shoulder. *I ain't goin' nowhere . . . I just unda'stand if you do someday, that's all.*

"Gio."

"Hey." He lifts his hand up. "It just needed to be said."

"Ugh . . . okay," I say, letting him pull me to his chest as he lays back. His fingers along my goosebumpy arm fill the long silence with warmth until his breathing steadies with the rhythm of his heart. It must be hard to let someone else into his head—for him or for anyone. I lift my chin, nudging him awake. "Does my magic scare you?"

"The fact that you could scramble my brains by touchin' my face? Hell yeah, it scares me. But it also kinda revs my mota'."

"Well, that's romantic."

He groans as I pull away, reaching back for his pack of smokes, but it's so dark that I knock it off the crate. *Fantastic.* I am not feeling my way across the floor for that thing.

"Look," Gio says, pushing himself up on his hands with a sigh like a man who's trying to sleep, "we been beatin' all the odds for, what, six months? I think we're in a pretty damn good place."

"I like how you say how you feel now."

"Yeah, well, it ain't like I got a choice with you."

My gasp nearly makes him burst out laughing. "I wouldn't read you without your permission, now that you know!"

"Well, like I said, you're betta' than me," Gio says, cocking his head to one side. "If I could get inside your head, I'd be in it all day—in all the dirty memories." I don't have long enough hair to cover my face, but I try anyway. The bed sinks toward him as he draws closer, his hands sliding up my legs. "Rose, I wanna know what you think. Hear what you have to say. I like watchin' you sleep. Hell, I wanna watch you shave these gams—watch you brush ya' teeth if you'd let me."

"Okay, Mr. Cattaneo, that's enough allure for you tonight."

"Fine wit' me. Guess it's ova'."

"Oh, so should I take my magic back?"

It's his turn to gasp as he claps his hand over his mouth, shoving his arm between us to block my fingers stretching toward his face. His gritty laughter really is the best sound.

"Don't you dare—if I smell licorice, so help me, Rose, I won't kiss ya the rest of the night."

I've already got the charm spell that counters my allure ready at my lips—a new bewitchment that I've recently acquired, thanks to my abuela's weekly lessons. The taste of anise runs across my tongue, and as I blow my breath in Gio's direction, he doubles down with pleading laughter. We don't always get to be this silly. The joy in this tiny room is a spell I can't conjure. As we wrestle and giggle beneath the covers, I wonder if the allure helps us both lower our guard with one another—if this is how we'd always be without the pressures around us.

"Gio," I purr, straightening my body upright with my knees digging into the mattress. My arms dangle lazily over my head. "I just want one kiss."

His eyes stare up at me before trailing down the length of my frame. "Fine. But I get to pick where."

Telling me to stay right where I am, he positions himself below me. *Bossy little bootlegger.* I gave him enough allure earlier to make him desperate to give me what *I* want. He used to ask. Maybe Gio knowing that I'm charming him makes the spell less potent somehow. Or maybe he really is crazy about me. This is my first long-term relationship, and with my thighs beginning to tense around his head once more, I realize that he already knows what I want.

Danger might be sexy, but intimacy is even more so.

"OH, HECK, IT WAS HARDLY ENOUGH TO DO ANYTHING."

"There! See? She *admits* it."

I let my head fall back, closing my eyes to the ridiculousness. I knew I'd have to make amends with him for last night, but I didn't know he'd bring it up during our meeting with the whiskey team. Across the living room full of hand-carved furniture, my brother stares at the bustling street from the window seat of his new apartment. His place in Armourdale was a much farther drive, so it made sense when he announced his move to the apartment above the new River Rose. He can walk to work without so much as breaking a sweat. It should be an easy enough life he's built for himself. So why does he look anything but relaxed?

My brother barely looks up as Heck continues his fuming and Gio breezes through the door with an apology for being late and slightly disheveled. His rumpled hair is poking out beneath his taxicab hat, and his suspenders are pinching his dress shirt in all the wrong ways. He lives three blocks away. But I can only guess what the line was like to the washroom at the rooming house.

"Oh good," Heck huffs. "Maybe your boyfriend can get you to confess your misdeeds toward me last night."

I spin around, aiming my flared nose back at the fuming blond covered in pin-striped perfection. "It's not like I was trying to hide my impartation, you goon. I've never tried to trick you. I knew you would know!"

Kind of.

"You put a thought in my head that wasn't mine!" The floor planks creak under Heck's stomping as he crosses the room trying to get Javier's attention. "What if her allure leaked through?" His hands feel around his torso, aimlessly checking his pockets as though he's lost something. I scrunch my eye at a smirking Gio when Heck's accusing finger points at me. "Did it? I feel that you're very beautiful right now. Did you allure me, Rose?"

"You always think I'm beautiful."

A sigh escapes from the window seat. "Kessie, do you want to kiss her?"

Heck eyes my ensemble, silently judging my slacks and blouse to be an unfashionable shade of gray for winter, I'm sure. "If pouring a cold bucket of water on her head is kissing her, then yes."

"Then let it go, Kess. Dios, you're like her other brother, so take it as a compliment." A tiny smile peeks across his unshaven face, stopping just before his empty eyes that continue staring out the window. "You don't know the tricks she played on me when we were little."

When we were little. The time when my brother and I were carefree miscreants in the eyes of a white world, but we didn't know it. Children of immigrants have to learn about their station in life earlier than others. Our mother filled us to the brim with both pride and caution as a family who barely made it to Kansas City from Mexico when Javier was a baby. But as youngsters, we frolicked along the train tracks of our boxcar community, unaware that we were hated before we were even born. We played games of cops and robbers, jacks and dominos, and occasionally, I'd plant a kiss on my brother's cheek, using my impartation to make him think that I was a ghost and no one else could see me. Our mother hated that game.

Truthfully, I was just jealous because he could get away with having an accent and I couldn't.

Looking at my brother now, no one would ever think that he was ever a schoolboy with britches that showed his ankles when he'd grow three inches overnight. His smile isn't even enough to deepen the dimple in his chin—*our* dimple and the only physical feature I seem to share with the Alvarado family. Javier is tall and dark. And I'm not. He'll give me a good tongue-lashing if I complain about my light skin and blue eyes, though, so I don't bring it up. We used to joke about it. Now, he's grown distant and so serious—even more so since his death. That would sober just about anyone, sure, but I miss the Javi I'd always known.

"Heck," I say, breaking the silence, "I swear I wasn't meaning to cause any harm. I was trying to help us."

"I know. But that's not even the most pressing issue." He plants his hands on his hips, seating himself beside my brother. "I'm certain that you love me and I'm sure that you're sorry."

"I do, Heck, and I am. I just . . . panicked."

He leaps back to his feet like he's heard a shotgun blast. "*You* panicked?"

Gio snorts with a shake of his head as he pulls out his favorite hope chest, leaning against the damask wallpaper that Heck said would really light up the place. I want a smoke, too, but Heck looks like he's about to explode with anxiousness.

"I panicked," he continues. "You were late. Pendergast was coming. And they all expected me to know where you were, so I said 'doctor's appointment.'"

"Okaaay."

He takes me by the shoulders with a frustrated groan. "They immediately assumed that you were with child and I couldn't say no."

"You . . . *what*?"

Gio pushes away from the wall, choking on his drag. Even Javier looks up from his trance.

While I'm sputtering to find words, Heck talks over me, his hands performative as always. "Christmas Gala. New Year's. If I had told them you weren't expecting, they would have assumed we'd lost a baby, and you know we can't go into mourning. The lumber barons come to town once a year, for God's sake. We have contracts to sign, and those social events are where everything happens, Rose." His fingers pinch in front of my seething face. "Everything."

"Luna, I think you should focus on your deal with Pendergast," Javier says, settling back into his new home in the window. "Find your way out of this lie later."

I've never wanted to punch such a pretty face more than I do right now as Heck flashes a satisfied smile. *Voy a hacer un caldo con tu cuerpo.*

I would normally push back against my brother's bossiness, but I've learned it usually comes from a place of protectiveness toward our family. *Usually.* This morning, however, he doesn't even seem to be here.

"I'm getting a drink," Heck announces. "Would anyone care for a drink?"

All hands raise around the room, including mine, before Gio leads me to the printed couch. "Should you be drinking in your condition?" he asks with a grin and I shove him away just as I also shove a few stacks of newspapers and a wrinkled jacket to the third cushion to force Heck onto the love seat. Typically, my brother is so tidy, but even the ashtray on the coffee table is stuffed full of butts, their stale scent catching my nose.

Heck hands out tumblers before drizzling a Highland scotch into each one, leaving my glass for last just so he can ignore my icy stare. "I need the influence of the other land developers," he announces to everyone except me, "unless we plan to put this city together piecemeal like some kind of incongruous cheese plate."

"What's so wrong with that?" my boyfriend says, raising the rim of his glass to his lips. "I ain't puttin' on the ritz, even if I do have the cash."

"Same." Javier's eyes study his drink. "I don't wanna take my brown ass to a white neighborhood. I like blending in, not standing out."

Heck sips at the amber liquid with a frustrated eye roll. "But that's my point. If we can lift these title restrictions, then non-whites can live anywhere. We can—"

"Kess, give it a rest. No one wants to go where they're not wanted!"

Heck isn't the only one taken back by my brother's sharp tone. I shoot Gio a look, hoping he gets the message. Maybe it's time to change the subject and let these guys talk it out later.

My boyfriend takes a loud sip from his tumbler before filling the room with a satisfied exhale. "Yeah, well, what's this gotta do with rum-runnin'?"

Neither of the sullen men takes the bait, leaving Gio and me to drink in silence. I really should take up Heck's charge on this—if I wasn't so irritated with him. If someone found out that I'm a half-blooded tramp from the River Bottoms, then we'd be sued by any number of our socially elite rivals for violating title restrictions. Heck would endanger his claim to any of the whites-only deeds he holds in this town as long as he's married to me—his only beneficiary. Our nightclubs could fold and everything else we've worked for—and all that was the most boring outcome.

I don't want to think about the alternatives, yet images of oaks on the riverbank stir in my mind.

I shift against the back cushions. The discomfort of the silence is really getting to me . . . and the forlorn look on Heck's face.

"Well," I say, clapping my hands together, "I think it's such a heartfelt venture. There's no harm in trying."

"Javi . . . how can you be against this?"

My brother empties his glass, his lover's words finally coaxing him from his perch at the window. "White neighborhoods. Mixed neighborhoods. It doesn't change a thing for us."

"But—

"How much do you lose in valuation if you do this?"

"What? Ugh, Javi."

"Answer the question."

BINDLE PUNK JEFE · 47

Heck's manicured nail picks at a chip in his glass as he refuses to look up at my brother's approach. "Lifting the title restrictions could cut the land value in half . . . maybe more. And I don't know why you're being like this."

Javier's hanging suspenders tap against the love seat as he slides onto the arm next to Heck. My brother bumps his shoulder with his hip, but the frowning socialite still won't look up.

"All I'm saying is you can't buy their loyalty," Javier says. "Lemme give you an example. A few of these barons—they come into my bar, they take me out, and we just listen to each other. And they like that because I don't have an agenda."

Gio snorts. "Except they give a lotta money to your juke joint. Speakin' a' which"—he snaps his fingers—"why can't Rose just do a big charm spell? Bam. The city's ours."

"I've got a spell for you," I say, messing with the unshaven hair on his chin while he bats me away.

Our jokes do nothing to lighten the mood. Javier talks over our laughter that quickly dies down. "Sure, I have something to gain. Maybe they like my drinks. Maybe I wanna know more about the lumber business because I've got my own money to invest. It's a one-on-one thing, though." If I didn't know him any better, I'd swear my brother was angry with Gio—or maybe everybody. I can't tell. "It's not like I'm trying to change up their whole society."

Heck throws his arm down like a gauntlet. "And what do you think *I'm* doing?"

"You just said you need signed contracts, Kess. And support—from all of them. That's a *lot*. I'm just making friends with a few guys."

Gio grabs my hand, letting me feel the dam of patience

that's about to break inside him. He's not liking my brother's tone and how he's been dominating this meeting. I squeeze Gio's hand in return, pursing my lips at him. My Don't Do It look curbs his irritation for about two seconds before he leans forward to aim his nose at my brother.

"So what Heck's doing is silly, but your game is different, Jav?"

"Gio, let's go," I say. "I can't be late for Abuela."

But Gio will not be stopped. "Those guys who come to your club—their one Mexican friend is gonna make them change their political views and how they handle their money?"

"¿De verdad?" My brother's thick brows shoot upward. "Didn't hear you say that to Heck."

I emit a grumbling sigh that no one pays attention to, straightening my hat as I check my wristwatch. This pecking contest is ridiculously unproductive, and I've got places to be.

"He's got that alabasta' skin. Everyone knows those uppity jerks think the lighta' the shade, the smarta' the businessman."

Javier's hands tap his chest. "They're getting to know me, Gio. I'm making them know me. Hell, I think one of them is a jocker."

With an impressive amount of composure, Heck slides his tumbler across the coffee table, zeroing his cerulean gaze onto his clenching hands like they just challenged him to a duel. "You don't say?"

Oof. Gio and I definitely should go.

"C'mon, Kessie, I didn't mean it like that." Javi reaches around Heck's broad shoulder, sliding his hand around the back of his lover's reddening neck. "It's nothing to worry about."

"Okay, but don't expose him."

"I . . . I wasn't saying I was *going* to." Now Javier's neck reddens, their matching scars at the base of their throats staying a few shades lighter, although Heck keeps his mostly covered by fancy collars.

I stand up, pulling Gio with me toward the door, but not before my boyfriend turns around and says, "He's just sayin' it's different if your new snotty friends find out one of their own class is wearin' a mask. It's dangerous for you to even know it."

Javier surges to his feet, tensing his neck and leaning forward. I've never seen my brother so confrontational.

"I think I know what my own boyfriend is saying, Gio. I don't need you fuckin' explaining what it means to be fuckin' gay in our world, okay? I don't—"

"*Javi.*"

I say it just loud enough, just sternly enough to break his censure. His irises grow large and then narrow again. His long lashes fan in a series of blinks. *Oh, Javi.* I wish I knew what was wrong.

"Hey, look. I'm just tryna help," Gio says, his face softening. "And it don't help for you to believe that you're more than a bartenda' to them."

"I *am* more than that."

"You ain't gotta tell me, Jav. I'm sorry I got sideways and in your business. You're one'a my best friends." Gio gives my brother's shoulder a playful thump, his hopeful attempt to break the tension crumbling as the gentlest man I've known since I was a baby jolts at my boyfriend's touch. With a gasp, Javier pushes away Gio's hand like it's made of nails. "Jav . . . you okay?"

Javier's breath picks up speed, a strange stutter dancing on his quivering lips. "No," he utters as tears fill his eyes. Heck steps toward him, but he shakes his head again, fixing his turbulent gaze on the wall behind us. Alarm builds on all of our faces as his hands tug on the cuffs of his sleeves, rolling them up to his elbow. He's clearly expecting a fight.

Now there's no denying it. My brother's not just grumpy or tired. He's lost somewhere no one can reach him. *Unless . . .*

"Javi?" I take a chance, reaching for his wrist.

"No! ¡Sé lo que estás haciendo!"

"Javi, it's okay," I plead, tears springing to my eyes.

"You're doing this, aren't you! Can you see them?"

"I didn't do anything, honey. Please—"

"Cuddle up a liiiiitle closer, loooovey mine." A soothing voice breaks into the intensity of the atmosphere, sending my brother's hands to his knees as he tries to catch his breath. I've heard that voice a few hundred times before, and have always felt Heck's singing voice had presence. But I've never known him to be a siren. All eyes turn to the shockingly calm blond, who clears his throat, beginning again.

> *Cuddle up a little closer, lovey mine*
> *Cuddle up and be my little clinging vine*

Javier falls into Heck's steady gaze, his fingers curled around his elbows. Heck stretches a beckoning hand between them, and my brother moves forward, closing the gap.

Gio and I stand as statues, afraid to break the siren's song. I've never seen allure without magic—until I met Heck Kessler.

> *Like to feel your cheek so rosy*
> *Like to make you comfy, cozy*
> *'Cause I love you from head to toesie, lovey mine*

Soon, two of my favorite fellas are holding each other, my brother burying his face into Heck's shoulder. "Kessie, I don't know why I—"

"Sh, sh, sh, shhhh," Heck says into Javier's hair. "None of that. Let's rest, hm?" He pulls my brother's head back with a gentle tug so they're eye to eye. "We both work tonight. I say let's get under the covers and stay there until then."

"I don't think I have much of a choice." Javier nods at Gio and me as we stand stunned and speechless. "I'm sorry, I . . . I really need to lay down."

He leaves the room like a vagrant on the railroad tracks who's searching the iron bars for a stray nickel. A huge sigh empties the tension my body has been holding. Hell, the entire room takes a collective breath as soon as his bedroom door clicks shut.

"Heck Kessler," I whisper, wiping the wetness from my cheeks so it doesn't soak the Camel I stick between my lips, "what the hell was that?"

"It's the song that was playing when we first . . . you know."

"You know very well I'm not asking about the song."

Gio lights up a tobacco stick of his own. "I seen some soldjas in the circus have fits like that—sometimes right in the middle'a the damn show. Had to be careful what music we played or who was around fire, things like that."

"Okay," I say, "but Javi's not a circus performer. He's . . . he's sick or something. He needs a *doctor*."

"Doctors won't help him," Heck insists, signaling me to lower my voice. "They do terrible things to men with head sickness . . . terrible things." His eyes grow bitter and all the more beautiful. He really does love my brother. "After I was caught with my schoolmate in secondary, my father sent me for shock therapy."

"Oh, Heck."

The smoke blanketing my lungs is barely a comfort. My fingers tremble from the buzz that fuses with my anxiousness. I just want the pain to end for my family.

"I shared an isolation room with two other men who were there for nervousness. And I watched how they dealt with each other when the eyes of the doctors were gone for the day." Heck crosses his arms so tightly I'd think he was naked. "One would have a fit—screaming, crying, saying odd things. And the other, he would just start telling him silly stories and singing songs from happier times, and somehow, it got his friend's attention. It seemed to work, anyhow."

"Aw, man," Gio says with his eyes focused on the floor as he takes a big drag. "I'm real sorry to hear that. Sorry you went through it."

"I'm fine." Heck peers back at the bedroom door, his face melancholy. "He started sleepwalking a month ago."

My head snaps up. "A *month*? Why didn't you tell me?"

"He didn't want me to, and please, keep your voice down."

I almost snap at that—Javi is *my* brother—but take a breath instead. "Then we'll take him to Abuela."

"He won't go. I've asked him three times already."

My head falls all the way back, a cloud of smoke shooting to the ceiling. This doesn't make any sense. Javier isn't a soldier. He hasn't been through war . . . *But hasn't he?* Even *I* have trouble pushing away the memories of his marred body the day he died on our front steps last summer. I can only imagine what haunts him at night. Our enemies tried to burn him, beat him, drown him, and finally got it done with a noose tied to the bumper of a car.

Querido Dios.

I never should have let him go to the North witches to get that cursed dirt. Then he never would have been caught on the road alone for those mobsters to find him. Javier saved us all that day. But at what cost?

I shake my head to knock the memories back where they belong, and out of the front of my mind. Taking Gio's hand, I lead him out of the apartment that has returned to its cozy atmosphere. Heck hugs me, even kissing me on the cheek before turning to my boyfriend, who's less comfortable with embraces. He obliges anyway.

Heck and I nod to each other as the door begins to close.

"We'll figure this out," I say, swallowing a wave of emotion. "Take care of him."

"I will, kitten."

3

THE WHIRRING OF MY MOTHER'S VACUUM IS THE ONLY SOUND on the quiet street after I shut off my engine outside her bungalow. My heels sink into the dirty slush along the walkway up to the front porch that will have more hanging plants than Babylon once spring arrives. Until then, my mother keeps them safely inside the little house that's as warm inside as the sage-green exterior. Sleeping ivy hibernates along the rock foundation, the window in the attic room peeking at everyone who comes by. I can't wait until summer, when many of the other boxcar families who have relocated here will make tamales together and share Sunday dinner after Mass like they used to. I'll definitely swing by for a home-cooked meal. White culture has such ... white food.

God, I miss home.

I used to get curt waves and subtle nods when I'd visit my family at the River Bottoms. Now, when a neighbor passes, they either pull their children in the other direction with a frosty glare or ignore my greeting altogether. I know why they're angry. I'm angry too. But my abuela won't allow such musings. *What had to be done to save Javier had to be done,* she always says. Her encouragement only makes me feel guiltier.

From years of habit, I duck for cover any time a car that's fancier than my Model T drives by. Now that I've become Mrs. Kessler, the habit has turned into a ritual. Cars like mine aren't suspect in a poor Mexican neighborhood; that's why I keep the damn thing. There's no reason for an elegant automobile like a Duesy to travel to a part of town where no one can afford even half the payment. So when a black one with red trim meanders down the road, I dive into a corner by a pillar that's wider than I am. The half-wall around the front porch makes for a great hiding place.

As the Duesy passes, I glare up at the window above me for not giving me a heads-up. The door opens as I brush a few dead leaves from my slacks.

"¡Qué orgullo tengo!" My mother's hands capture my face in a not-so-tender grip. "¡Mi hija está casada!"

"Yes, Mother, I've been married for three months. Can we just—"

"¡Bendiciones! Para ella y nuestra familia!"

Do we have to do this every time? There's only one thing that will stop her gushing at this point.

"Mamá," I say over her continuing prayers. "I haven't eaten all day."

The affection lifts from her prim face, a sense of duty replacing her exhortations. We have a running agreement that I may read her anytime I please—because Gloria Alvarado has nothing to hide. Her maddening pride is also comforting;

my earlier edginess lifts at the sight of her hanging gardens in the oak entryway. Maneuvering past the potted cactus, and ivy that brushes the floor, she bustles me into a home as warm and inviting as the earth songs she hums under her breath. Javier's carpentry also adorns this house, the mahogany chairs and cabinets inlaid with dancing flute players and men with hats so wide they could catch a bucket of rain.

Tying an apron around her impeccably pressed dress, my mother sets herself to work in the kitchen. Parallel to the dining area, this part of the house is like walking into a mosaic painting with colorful tiles covering the tabletops and counter, where she lays a stack of flattened dough from the cooler. I'm still amazed at how many bowls of premade meals she has ready. She straightens her glorious bun of raven and silver strands and soon begins mincing pork while a cast-iron skillet warms on her cookstove. She's never had a gas range before, but has taken to it like she was born for such an appliance.

The air is soon rich and spicy.

"Tell your brother he is to come for dinner."

"He works tonight, Mamá," I say, hanging my hat and handbag on the back of a chair.

"Too much to see his mother?"

What is there to say? Honestly, there's too much to say. Our mother worries enough as it is. She would beat his door down with the spatula she's carrying if she knew how he lost it this morning. She'd want to know. But she'll become too upset, which will upset Javier even worse. Guilt seeps to the surface of my heart the more she cooks and sings. I really should tell her. *In time.* I just need to figure out what's going on with him first so she doesn't have to worry.

Additions are made to the spread on the counter—dark red sauce and sautéed potatoes.

"Aye, aye, aye, Mamá. I don't need a banquet."

"Still with the Spanish? What if you slip up at one of your fiestas, eh?" I start to answer but that spatula is really moving. "You should stop leaving your coat in the car—you'll catch a fever. And when will you give me los nietos? I should be an abuela by now."

Ugh.

"The fur collar is bulky," I interject over the start of her mumbled prayers of thanksgiving for the food and an appeal to God for my womb. "And the society papers already think I'm expecting. It's such a racket."

Gloria's commanding fingers pinch my chin from across the counter. "Just one night and a little magic, niña. That's all it takes, yes?"

"Mamá!"

The spatula flips with indifference. "Have Gio do it, then."

"¡Dios mío, Mamá!"

"That better be a prayer, and enough with the Spanish!" A freshly warmed tortilla smothered with a layer of pasty beans lands on a plate in front of me. Gloria's skillful fingers drizzle the pork and the other ingredients over the top. The food smells like childhood. My mouth is watering already.

The plate is big enough to feed two of me, and I'd usually complain, but this is my opportunity to go find my abuela. Scooping up the meal I hoped my mother would cook, I kiss her cheek and sail out to the back patio that's filled with a similar array of hanging plants as the entryway. And maybe it's because the patio is enclosed, or maybe it's leftover magic from when my abuela used to have her powers, but the greenery out here doesn't seem to know it's winter.

Mamá Sunday sits on a stool, her long skirt spread over her knees as she rocks side to side with a fennel plant on her lap. At the crown of her head rests a bun of nestled gray hair with little wispy pieces floating around her ears like tiny feathers. Her crackled voice shares an enchanting melody that tells a soulful story about ancient brujas and bravery. Two porcelain mugs sit on a bench between us, steam rising from the hand-painted rims.

"Ah, niña. Bebe tu horchata." My abuela's typical youthfulness plays at her hickory eyes before fading again. She loves heated rice milk as much as I do. It does me good to see her slurping at her glass, and I hope that it warms her as much as mine is warming my hands against the chilliness of the porch. The late-morning sun shining through the surrounding windows keeps it tolerable, though.

No matter how tightly I fold my tortilla, the contents spill to the plate on my lap, horchata dropping all the same as I wash it all down. My dignity is lost to spicy pork soaked in adobo that drips from my knuckles. I have to roll my sleeves up halfway through the meal to keep it from soaking my blouse. Yet I don't mind Mamá Sunday seeing me this way. Somehow, while the chickadees and blue jays sing their songs on the barren oaks outside, we are two little girls, drinking their milk and whispering secrets to plants. The patio room is so serene, in fact, that I nearly forget why I've come to visit today . . . until my abuela's hands begin trembling around her glass.

"Abuela, let me take that."

"Okay, niña."

Her knuckles tremble as she holds out her arms, the veins popping beneath her papery skin. I try to grab the mug in time, but the painted ceramic meets the stones beneath our feet in a delicate crash. At least she finished her horchata.

Her gums shine at me in a sly smile. "Don't tell Gloria."

"Never, Abuela," I say, jumping up to grab the broom my mother keeps in the corner. "It's not your fault."

Turning my face to hide the stinging tears in my eyes, I slide the jagged pieces into a metal dustpan. It's *not* her fault. *It's mine.* It's only been six months, but the spell we cast the day we saved my brother's life took more than just her powers from her. Most spells beyond an easy charm or read cost us something—the vigor of a night's sleep, or for a larger incantation, our health can suffer. But the suffering is supposed to be temporary. Even in her old age, she was always able to bounce back, the ashen coloring of her face returning to its usual dark glow.

But now . . .

Lo siento, Abuela.

Her spotted hand flutters to my chin, lifting my tear-soaked face. It's no question where my mother gets her proud look as the Alvarado matriarch beams down at me with both resilience and tenderness.

"Tears for sad times," Mamá Sunday says. "My niño is alive. It is honor to give myself for love." She pats the empty spot on the bench next to her. "I do same for you."

She produces a handkerchief in the same pattern as her skirt, and I give my nose a long blow. "I would do the same for you, Abuela." An idea hits me like Gloria's wooden spoon across a swearing mouth. "Abuela! The magic—can I give it back somehow?"

"No, no, no, niña. The stars have spoken." With that, she reaches down beneath her stool, pulling a large tome from behind her sandaled feet. My skin prickles with little bumps every time I see it—the twisted tree on the front cover, the gnarled bark that covers three limbs. Our spell book has been in our family for generations, and now, it's being placed over my knees like the passing of a birthright. I wasn't ready to become the only full bruja left in our family. I wasn't ready to become a full bruja period. The fates could have left me to frolic within the one branch of magic I knew how to use—it's not like I was causing havoc, save for a few broken hearts I'd left in the wake of my allure. I'm twenty-five—I *should* be leaving some broken hearts. While most girls my age have three and a half kids, abandoning their dreams to responsibility, I set out to really live my life. That didn't include being *the* bruja of Kansas City.

The weight on me now, however, is heavier than the idea of marriage itself.

Ay, ay, ay.

A withered finger points to the first branch on the book cover. "Abre."

I turn to the first section of three—the charm category. The corner of each page is marked by an oval stone wrapped in vines with tiny thorns. The cream coloring is speckled with blush streaks like the eggs our ducks used to lay, but the old paper of the spell book doesn't have the shimmer to show off the stone's brilliant granite. My childhood rushes back to me as I recall my tiny hands holding an even tinier rock egg. It was heavier than it looked then, and still is now. My now-grown fingers touch the crinkling page. The sketching is crude but lovely somehow.

My abuela waves me on, my hands flipping through passages that read like recipes written as poetry. They are songs with unwritten melodies. Once I reach the second section of the book, she holds up her hand. *Oh wow.* I wonder if I've said it out loud, because her toothless smile widens. Cradled in her bony fingers is a small egg—similar in size and shape to the sapphire oval that marks the corner pages of the healing poems. But this one is a real egg, white and filled with promise and yolk.

She reaches, tapping the page. "Para mi niño."

I tilt my head, silently scolding myself for letting my eyes mist again as I read the melodic recipe. *Rest for the Weary.*

"Abuela," I say, "you want *me* to create a healing stone? What if he won't let me use it? He's . . . Javi's not himself these days."

"You heal him, then."

Air fills my mouth, puffing my face with exasperation. Healing the mind is a far cry from healing the body. It takes more than walking through thoughts and memories. My forearms ripple with goosebumps once again. Dreams are where healing happens. And dreams are where the monsters live. Diving into a sleeping mind takes more precision than mending flesh—and a hell of a lot of guts. I don't like facing my own nightmares, much less someone else's. More, I've never wanted to even try. My drooping head is met with a light smack on the hand.

"Start with stone." The firm tone and burn on my knuckles get my attention enough so that I scoot down the bench so she can organize jars and decanters that appear from beneath her skirt, which is clearly hiding more than just her ankles. *What else has she got down there?*

The faded labels on the row of ingredients do give me a noticeable thrill, like being electrocuted, although I never have been. A tinge of sadness dampens the excitement as I recall Heck's admission from this morning. Those I love have been through too much for me not to at least try. I could bring a level of healing to all of them that they've never experienced before. My abuela's sentiment comes full circle. It's an honor to give myself for love . . . or at least make an attempt.

Glancing down at the page, I tuck my hair behind my ears and get down to business. Dried blackberries. Cigar ash. Rose petals mixed with rattlesnake skins. It all goes in a wooden bowl, and the old witch hands me a matching pestle that soon grinds the ingredients together. Reaching into a satchel of blessed dirt that's probably the same age as I am, knowing Abuela, I pinch a good amount before adding it to my mixture. A deep breath and a few drops of river water later, I look down at the handwritten words on the page in front of me and open my mouth to sing.

I'm always shocked when the air begins to change at the sound of my voice. The moment time slows down, the atmosphere becomes fluid, like jumping into lake water in the summer. Above me, the stars begin their tinkling beyond the plastered ceiling. The more I sing, the more they laugh. Abuela's voice joins the melody, although her eyes remain the same, faded yet tinged with hope and affection. The color of her irises used to twist and sway like limbs in the breeze during these spells as mine must be now, but of course, she is no longer able to call on the fates. She can't feel the heaviness of the air around us nor hear the harmonies between the sun and the North Star.

Or can she?

I hope so. I truly hope so.

"La piedra, niña!" Her wrinkled hand presses the cool oval into my palm.

The song grows louder and more insistent.

My hands hover over the mortar before lowering the egg into the mixture. "El descanso para los cansados."

My abuela's laughter and clapping hands are almost as lively as the ivy and potted bushes that shiver against an invisible wind. This is all so wild and freeing, and it's not as though I've never seen this spell before, but now *I'm* doing it. *I'm doing it!* Even my giggling sounds shocked. I don't mean to be so astonished. I am a bruja, after all. But as the earthy confection around the egg begins to recede, I gasp like a schoolgirl as the bowl dries up completely, leaving the tiny oval a dark shade of sapphire. The stars bid us farewell in a fading lullaby, the panels on the ceiling shielding us from the sky once again. The deep blue speckles in the stone shimmer under the sun's rays that are spread across the patio room.

In the returned quiet, the greenery lies back down to rest, its slow settling making me jealous for my own respite. The larger the spell, the bigger the drain on my energy. And enchanting an egg feels like I climbed a small mountain with lead shoes on.

"Abuela," I say through a giant yawn, "did you see all that? Could you hear it?"

Her hand slides around my cheek, her expression as tender as ever. "I see a river, powerful and strong."

I'm not sure why, but my nose begins to burn, the tears from earlier threatening to return. She's talking about my eyes. The twisting irises should calm soon and fade back to one shade of blue. As tired as I am now, my sweet abuela looks even more tired. I wish to lie across this sturdy bench that my brother built and hold Mamá Sunday's frail hand while I fall asleep—just like I did when I was little. Instead, I'm holding a granite stone and wondering how the hell I'm ever going to take her place one day in this family. Or in the world of brujas, for that matter. I don't want to think about it anymore—not now, at least. I just want to rest and listen to her sing.

"Abuela," I say after a long while, my hands folded as a pillow beneath my ear. "Something odd happened to me at the river yesterday." As she continues her whispering song to the fennel plant, I curl my legs up tighter on the bench. "The stars and the wind, it was almost . . . hostile."

I push myself up on my arms, looking up at the witch, who has ceased her singing. The wrinkles in her brow are deeper than usual. Dry, dead pieces of the plant in her hands are being picked by her pruney fingers as her song begins again.

"Abuela?"

"Many spirits at the river," she says in the tone she uses for spells and divination. My neck prickles at the cadence. "In the earth. Sky. Love and hate sometimes meet, sometimes dance. Mirth holds hands with sorrow."

She pauses to tell the fennel that it's good, leaving me with a dumbfounded look, although, I know better than to sigh. Her cane is always somewhere nearby.

"Abuela, are you saying not all earth spirits are friendly?"

Her finger shakes in the air. "Spirit of vengeance walks and talks the same as defense, but they not identical brothers."

Huh? I thought the earth spirits were made up of laughter

and love—stars and all that. Now there's hate, and sorrow, and vengeance, which is all enough to make me sit back up with my fingernails between my teeth. "So did I interact with those spirits? How will I know the difference? Is the dirt I made any good?"

Mamá Sunday waves my words away with her hand before producing her cane. "You powerful bruja. Dirt is powerful too."

"Okay, but how—"

"And tell Heck to come see me. I miss him." With a heavy exhale full of finality, my abuela pushes a shaking hand down onto the hook of her cane, and I jump up to help her stand. She's ready to go lie down.

"He misses you too, Abuela. You know how busy things are right now."

Leaning on my arm as I guide her across the patio, she smiles. "He smells like a baby."

"He acts like one too," I say with a laugh.

She shakes another finger up at my nose, her playful eyes glinting. "You and Gio—take time. Music players have skilled hands."

"Abuela!" A full blush blooms across my cheeks that are tight with spitting giggles.

"No rush love. No rush babies. No rush magic."

Soon, I'm tucking her beneath a thick set of quilts in a quaint bedroom that could second as a plant menagerie. I love it. I love her, and that innocent look on her face when she snuggles her pillow and closes her eyes. If she's not worried, then I shouldn't be. Tiptoeing around the bed, I touch the leaves of different vines—some fuzzy, some smooth. Maybe I'll make Javier a plant to calm his nerves.

I look back at my abuela as she begins to snore like she hasn't got a care in the world.

Hell, maybe I need a nap too.

I HATE WINTER FOR A HUNDRED REASONS, BUT THE WORST part of this frigid weather is the bulky coat I have to wear. Sure, raccoon fur is trendy and keeps me warm against the Missouri temperatures, but the bulkiness that reaches all the way to the hem around my calves makes it hard to drive. The snowy season also has shorter days, which means the sun sets before dinner, so a gal has to guess how her lip rouge is holding up in a rearview mirror when heading to a local juice joint.

My cumbersome outerwear better not wrinkle my dress either. I rarely get to don a flapper getup these days, what with my life being gentrified and all. Those dinner party aristocrats would get in a serious lather if they saw my stockings rolled down to my knees tonight.

It's possible that I might be the only Scrooge on Eighteenth and Vine because as I turn onto the busy street, Christmas shoppers bustle in and out of stores in the twilight. The mothers fluff their wool caps, tugging their little ones by the hand to snag that one last gift before the shops close and the clubs open. Most folks around here don't have much money, although no one would ever know it. The black businesses in this part of town more than rival the shops in the Country Club Plaza, in terms of their owners' skills and manners and otherwise, but whites rarely spend their money in the jazz district—unless they're buying booze and sex, of course. I know a few women in Heck's circle who would rather wear white chinchilla than Negro mink.

Shaking my head at the thought, I slow my car as I reach my destination. A couple of ladies in fox wraps up to their ears walk out of a hats and hosiery shop, which sits below Javier's apartment and above his juice joint. Nostalgia hits me immediately, both warm and bothersome. The old River Rose used to be mine before an attack consumed the whole building in fire. My brother not only made it out alive but he's turned our little venture into several thriving businesses for himself. As my car tootles down the side alleyway that opens to the back parking lot, I'm all smiles at the lot full of automobiles and patrons coming out for a quiet smoke. My heart swells with pride and affection. Javier didn't just purchase one of the basements to rebuild the River Rose. He bought the whole damn lot that the building sat on—the conjoining basement that used to be a brothel, and the gambling parlor on the other side. He even gets a nice cut from the legitimate businesses above the nightclub. As a landlord, he treats them well, and the families always return the favor. He should be over the moon about his accomplishments instead of lying in bed all day in despair. So when Javier runs across the gravel parking lot to greet me with a big hug, I'm honestly bewildered.

His freshly shaven chin presses against my forehead. *I'm okay, Luna*, he sends to me before pulling away.

"You smell expensive," I say with a light smile. "You're dressed nifty too."

With a blush, he runs his hands across his slick hair that was in no danger of moving, even in this breeze. "Aww, it's just a look I'm trying. I never thought I'd wear tweed. Or patterns. Or a jacket, for that matter. But I'm a business owner now, I guess."

"You're turning into a real swell."

"Baloney!" He wraps his arm around my shoulders to shield me from the wind as we make our way to the basement door that thumps from the music within. We duck inside, the door closing with a heavy bang that's barely heard above the raging toms and screaming saxophones. The only sound louder than the house band is the friendly jeering from a few familiar faces that are glad at my arrival. A man with a tiny mouth shoves past the patrons at his poker table before his loafers start sliding across the floor and up next to me.

"May I take ya coat, m'lady?" He smooths his hair, the middle part as greasy as his smile. I don't know if he tries to fit the stereotypes about gambling-parlor owners and their underhanded ways or if the stereotypes were written about him, but Giuseppe seems proud of the pigeonhole.

I shoot him a flat stare, hanging my things on one of the loaded coatracks. "Well, if it isn't the king of the under-ground."

"I've waited years to hear ya say that," he shouts with his grin growing wider. "Hey, whaddya think'a the place, anyway? It's almost as fancy as you."

"Mr. Alvarado is full of surprises."

"Yeah, he's all right for a bean eata'."

Most guys I encounter are potatoes to me—root vegeta-bles as dense as they are dull. My former business partner is no exception. But he's proven himself faithful to my crew, even if he is despicable in every other way. The underground rises and falls on such principles. It's the main reason I don't do something to him for disparaging my brother—and by extension me and my family—with his slurs.

Giuseppe grabs his dark lapel, standing tall to make use of our one-inch height difference. "Lemme be a good host and getcha a drink!"

"Make it a drink and a smoke, and I might tell people I know you."

"You got it, baby!"

He laughs at my narrowing eyes as he slips into the sweaty crowd, and I shake my head, turning back to the room my brother built. I'd been here a hundred times while it was being reconstructed, but the place still stuns me. Javier fixed up my old club in ways I hadn't thought of before. No longer do the patrons have to move tables and chairs to create a dance floor now that the wall between the bar and the basement brothel has come down. He still has plenty of storage and even made a deal with Giuseppe to turn a few rooms from the gambling parlor into private quarters for our flappers to make that late-night dough. Still, he was able to restore some of the previous charms. He even kept a few blackened floorboards throughout to remind us all of what we fought to get here. This smoke-filled, raucous room is as homey as it's ever been.

"Di-mi, woman!" Giuseppe's nasally voice edges its way into my musing. "You're lookin' tight, Rose. Real tight."

It doesn't take long for me to thaw around the heat of lively bodies and laughter. I'm soon thankful I chose a dress with such daring cuts. Mostly grateful. While the peekaboo neckline and the slits in the back are allowing enough ventilation to keep my own perspiration at bay, they're also giving this greaseball something to gape at. I grab the clouded drink and the cigarette he's holding out, and let him light it as I stick it between my lips. "I didn't think you were a Chesterfield man."

"I'm not. But that smoke is courtesy of one'a Javi's new pet barons."

As tall as the heels on my T-straps are, I still push up to my tiptoes, Giuseppe doing the same beside me. It doesn't take long to spot the company of patrons with back-slicked hair and Southern accents. Nearest the bar, the rowdiest group in the club shout vulgar jokes at each other with a variety of cigars poking out of their mouths. They tap their ashes onto the floor, pinching the backside of every waitress that walks by. And even though a few occasionally reach over the bar to help themselves to the nearest bottle of whiskey, my brother is all smiles, lighting a cigarette and telling his head bartender to keep the drinks coming.

"So you don't like them either," I shout between puffs, catching Giuseppe's disapproving frown from the corner of my eye.

"What's there ta like? John D's like that are always up to somethin'."

My laugh reflects the irony. "And guys like you aren't?"

"Aw, c'mon, Rosie." He takes me by the elbow, his gross thoughts leaking through my skin before I shoot him a look that makes him remove his hand. "When are ya gonna put the past behind us? I'm a swindla'. I swindle." He bites his nonexistent bottom lip with his grin returning. "But I'd leave this glorious life behind to get at that mouth again."

"Ugh, try to find anyone else to talk to tonight," I say, leaving him swiping at the cloud of smoke I leave in my wake.

"Always a pleasa', baby!"

A new song featuring quick raps on the hi-hat begins to play from the stage, my legs locking on to the beat as I saunter around the crowd and right into the den of lions surrounding my brother. If Giuseppe doesn't care for Javier's new friends, then they're either really great or really terrible. My money's on the latter.

"Hey, Rose!" my brother calls out. He's always got a twinkle in his eyes when he uses my white name, even after all these years of hiding our family tie. It's great seeing him happy in his element. Tonight, his smile is bigger than I've seen it in ages. "What's Gus got you drinkin' there? Lemme get you the good stuff!"

Several loud voices chime in their salutations, one of them shouting at Javier to fill up his drink as well. As a shot glass is tossed into the air, my brother reaches to catch it with a wince. He tugs his jacket sleeve, but not before I spot the bandage wrapped around his palm. *Curious.* His hand was fine this morning. Donning extreme nonchalance, I slide onto a barstool next to a dashing gentleman with glassy eyes that wander around my neckline like two hazel explorers. In a flourish, my brother slides a glass of amber liquid in front of me and this ogling stranger.

"So," I say, sipping the burning liquid with ease. It's already got my chest warming. "What have you all done to that bartender's hand?"

The stranger rolls his head toward Javier, who has moved on to directing a few waitresses and aiding his bartender with more drink orders. Turning back to me, the man leans forward, his sandy hair falling slightly out of place above his ear. "I daresay, as soon as I'm convinced I've had everything I've ever wanted, someone like you makes an appearance. I haven't seen you around here before."

"I was going to say the same about you."

"Ah, are we that obvious?" His glass makes its way to his smirking lips. "How do you know that we're not just another group of working-class men with fine taste in spirits and itches to scratch?"

Good grief. Men of privilege waste no time giving themselves away.

I straighten my back, crossing my arms and legs as a barrier to his roving eyes. "I just look for men with the best posture and the worst manners who have the nerve to talk to a married lady about how itchy they are."

"Hm, and your devilishly lucky man is, what, in a business meeting this evening?"

"I beg your pardon?"

"That rock on your finger is the only indication you're giving tonight that you are taken. My manners might be terrible, but my instincts are not. Married women who frequent juke joints unchaperoned are rarely happy women."

I hate to have to do it. But what's the point of carrying Heck's name if I can't sling it around every once in a while?

"I am Rose Kessler," I say, unfolding myself and lifting my chin. "And I am quite happy."

The stranger's swimming eyes round before he lets out a provocative chuckle. "Oh, *the* Rose? The formerly Rose Lane of this very establishment? Hell, that's right. Well, you may know my association, then. I am Dorian Luxberg." His tumbler empties into his mouth. "How is that old sport, Heck, anyhow? I haven't seen him in ages."

The long drag I take on my cigarette is my only response.

"Mrs. Kessler, surely you can extend some grace to an inebriated gentleman so far from his home. What can I do to make up for my offensive remarks?"

"Tell me what happened to my former bartender's hand."

"Goodness, that? Javi has been learning the ropes of the lumber business. All in good fun, I assure you." Dorian pushes his hair back to where it belongs, the deep slit in the top of his ear making me do a double take that I try not to let show. It's obviously an old wound, sealed over with scar tissue, but the damage looks like a drunken barber sliced into the cartilage.

A smooth stream of smoke billows from the corner of my mouth. "Same fun that chipped your ear there?"

"Now who's being rude?" His glassy eyes shine with a challenge, his gaze breaking when my brother appears at Dorian's side to offer us both a refill. The lumber baron claps Javier between the shoulders. "We are in constant search of men who work hard, like Mr. Alvarado. They're going places. Javi, will you be joining us at my suite this evening?"

My brother sends a tipsy laugh over his shoulder at a few fellas who are stuffing dollar bills into one of their friend's dress socks. "Aww, I would, but I've gotta rest tonight. You guys got five years on me, at least."

"Well, rest up, old man. We'll catch you at the next one!"

My eyes roll above my tumbler as he claps Javier on the back once more, sending him into the crowd behind us. Nothing about this exchange is making me feel better about the company my brother is keeping, other than the wide grin on his face. And it is nice to see him socializing for once.

But there's something about the way they talk him up, and each other, and everyone else. Who *wouldn't* like them? They're almost *too* nice.

I glance over at the roar of laughter as an ossified baron leads the other heirs in an impromptu rendition of "If You Knew Susie (Like I Know Susie)." The house band happily joins in. *Geez Louise.* Don't the sons of barons do anything other than merrymaking?

"Not during the holidays, we don't," Dorian slurs, offering a nearby ashtray for my dincher.

Huh? I hadn't realized I'd said that out loud—or left my smoke out to dry. Holding my tongue has never been a gift of mine, though. My criticisms have me sounding like a prude tonight. Of course I want my brother to be happy. And maybe these guys are jerks, but Javier's a big boy. It's high time for me to relax and stop shouldering everyone else's burdens for a while.

"Speaking of holidays," the baron continues, "I do apologize for my absence at your small soiree, but I will be in attendance for Old Man Wilmington's seventieth-birthday celebration at your husband's club—the Casbah Lounge, is it?"

I nearly choke on my drink.

"What do you mean?" I ask before recovering a cooler posture. "Also, you're clearly too sozzled to realize, but it's *my* club."

"If it's *your* club, how do you not know what I mean?"

I'd argue, but this guy's mouth is going at his glass again and missing the mark. Amber liquid dribbles from his chin, yet he doesn't seem to mind. Or notice. *Well, that's just dandy.* Heck is renting out the Casbah Lounge to that old beet from

BINDLE PUNK JEFE · 75

our pre-Christmas dinner, and I had to hear about it from the prince of the drunken hillbillies. Now I've gotta endure another night of Old Man Wilmington *and* this guy to boot? I'd hoped never to see that whiskey-soaked handlebar mustache again. Just wait until he gets a load of my Barlow girls. My club's dancers were trained by the best—Penny taught them to handle anything.

I better warn her, though.

My head flapper knows all about racist men shedding their disapproval in the presence of fine bosoms and legs—no matter their color.

As the music shifts to a moody blues tune, Dorian's eyes close to the acoustic strumming from the stage.

"Your town's been'a fine host, indeed, what with our country ways," he says, setting his empty tumbler down. I've never heard anyone try so hard to keep from slurring— slowing down his cadence to overenunciate. Propping his elbow against the counter and his cheek against his hand, he studies my dress with a lazy stare. "You know . . . we don't have beadwork and satin quite this s'phisticated in the Ozarks. I hope you don't mind my staring. What do they call that color these days—rose, like your name?"

I feel the shade of my dress rising up to my cheeks. I could learn a lot about this man were I able to follow my previous inclinations to scandalize myself in a washroom with such a *gentleman*. The secrets I could learn. But no, I have to find new ways to make a physical connection, what with being in a committed relationship these days. Sure, I need to keep up appearances for my marriage—Heck doesn't deserve any more scandal than I already bring him as a club owner with zero inheritance. But I won't risk breaking Gio's heart just to read a man's thoughts, no matter how pertinent the information could be to us. Not unless I absolutely *had* to.

"Something like that," I say, swiveling my head around in search of my brother. Time to call a night on this one. I can tell when a guy is zeroing in for conquest. Even if Dorian does follow me, I'll just end up filling his head with putrid thoughts. One thing about being less forward than I used to be—guys still try to back me into corners or catch me in an alleyway. My status, my hemline—none of it matters. The real creeps always give themselves permission, and they always regret trying to put their hands on me.

Dorian begins tapping his thumb against his slacks to the beat of the music. "Oh, I can tell you're not interested. A man can still dream. I used to have such flair with th' ladies before I went and married one."

"I'm sure you did."

"Please ac'ept my 'pologies, madam," he says, stumbling to his feet as his forehead begins to glisten. "But we cannot pursue our passions tonight. I . . . I must make haste to the lav'ratory."

Passions?

Dorian sheds his jacket, moisture soaking through his button-down like he'd spent an hour in a sweat lodge. Wobbling forward, he steps on his fallen garment, swearing about how slippery the wool is while reaching for my outstretched arm. I'm out of my seat and careening beneath his weight to try to keep us both steady before several other barons come to our rescue. The touch is brief but just enough. His palm gushes with determined feelings and a jumbled mess of thoughts that jump around from how hot it is in here to how my brother's lips would look on his—

Dios mío. This guy's got it bad for Javi.

"We've got you, silly boy," one baron says, coaxing Dorian's fingers from my arm. Donning a playful grin, his thoughts and eyes turn sharply toward the bar, where my brother is staring with amusement. My stomach lurches in an echo to Dorian's own nausea as his thoughts play out one line that is anything but affectionate in nature—*I've got you, silly boy.*

It sounds sweet—even cute. But . . . he means to only pretend to initiate my brother. Humiliation. Treat him like the bindle punk lowlife that he is. And he's easy pickings because he's a nobody immigrant with a gorgeous face.

¡Asqueroso! I could vomit from his thoughts alone.

Dorian's last finger is pried from my forearm, and the connection breaks, leaving me as unsteady as he looks. My brother's laughter, which I've missed so much, is suddenly at my ear, his familiar arm around my shoulders. "You need a cab too, Mrs. Kessler?"

I study his dimpled chin and shining hair, the trumpets louder than my stammering response as the group of barons carry their fallen comrade through a sea of people. My stomach squeezes again. I want to tell Javier what I heard in Dorian's brutish mind. I want to warn him, but as my brother's playful kiss meets my forehead, I read his vulnerability without his permission. He won't hear a thing right now. Inside, he's fragile as glass. Anything could break him, especially learning that his new friends intend to cause him harm. Or at least pressure him into some extreme form of hazing. And while none of that is truly my business, I know how much he loves Heck. He would never choose to ruin their relationship over the chance to impress some rich white jerks from the Ozarks.

Would he?

His loud laughter sounds above my head again as he calls an insult to a patron near the poker tables. This side of him should be a relief to see these days. But it all feels off-center. Javier's liveliness, his lifted chin, even his jokes—it's like he's reading from a script. The quick reads I glean from his occasional hand on my shoulder are all the more eerie; his insides are playing along as well. If I didn't know him so well, I wouldn't have noticed how his concerns are buried behind something I don't recognize. I can't feel them, and neither can he.

Javier glances down at me, his deep brown eyes flickering with annoyance before removing his arm from my shoulders with another fake smile. I try to act like I was doing anything other than intruding into his thoughts, plastering my own innocent smile on my face.

"Lemme get you some water, Rose."

Circling back around the counter, he soon slides a glass of clear liquid toward me, then busies himself with more drink orders. *Great.* This night is sinking faster than the *Titanic.* Six more greedy eyes roam in my direction. Swallowing about half of my drink and a ton of dark secrets, I push the putrid feeling down with the fluid, vowing to at least come up with a plan with Heck and Gio.

Gio. I wish he were here now. I wish we could link arms and bicker in public. I wish Heck and my brother could love without punishment. I wish a lot of things. My mood hits the bottom of the ocean. Finishing my water, I head back to the coatrack, giving anyone who tries to approach me the cold shoulder. Upper class. Lower class. Villains sprout up anywhere there are good men like Javier who just want to exist without wickedness trying to take advantage of them. And I've never been one to sit back and just watch it happen.

· · ·

THICK GLOVES AND WOOL STOCKINGS ARE HARDLY A MATCH for the drop in temperature since I first arrived at my brother's club. While he already spread what was left of my last batch of autumn dirt around the building, I still feel like I should walk the perimeter like my abuela taught me years ago when the speakeasy was mine. My hand hovers over the barren ground beneath the gravel as I whisper, "Bendiciones y prosperidad."

The typical pull from the roots below the surface is as absent as Javier's feelings when I read him inside the club. With most plants hibernating for winter, their lack of magical warmth seems normal. Although, this is my first winter as a full bruja. What the hell do I know?

Not enough. The new batch of blessed dirt I procured from the river yesterday could provide a powerful protection spell, but I'm hesitant to use it until I understand what happened with that mixture. Maybe something. Maybe nothing at all. Feels like I'm always one or ten steps behind my problems.

Across the parking lot, the basement door opens and a group of guffawing patrons staggers into the darkness. The moon hides behind the clouds, hiding me as well. In between the vehicles, a tall figure darts in and out of the glow of several headlamps, engines sputtering to life as he waves goodbye to the group that's so loud the lot becomes uncomfortably still when their cars finally head up the alleyway.

The figure draws closer to me, the flick of a match lighting up his face and the space between us. "You don't gotta do that anymore, hermanita. I got neighborhood kids to spread dirt around for a coupla pennies."

"Yes, well," I say, turning back to my earlier task with my hand stretched out to my side, "I like to tie it up in a bow, as they say—let the dirt meet the roots and bind them together."

The quote from our abuela softens his tense shoulders.

"I appreciate that, Luna. I really do." My brother falls into step beside me, and we stroll together in the frigid darkness with only the occasional glow on the end of his cigarette to light our way. His long exhales soon give way to chattering teeth. My concerned frown deepens as my eyes adjust to the darkness.

"Javi . . . where is your overcoat?"

Smoke sputters out from behind his shivering teeth. "Inside. It makes me feel trapped, I don't know."

"You'd prefer frostbite?"

"If I wanted a lecture, I'd go see Gloria."

"Did you just compare me to Mamá?"

My brother chuckles into the butt of his smoke.

"You know what? Don't answer that."

His laugh is subdued by the big drag he takes, the resulting cloud filling the air behind us. "Oh, *now* you don't wanna know what I think. Spent all night reading me and the big-time ganders every chance you got."

"Dammit, Javi, I am so sorry. I just—"

"Hang on. Just listen for a second." He pauses as we reach the far end of the lot, his gaze locked onto the entrance to the club behind me. "You can be a wet blanket all you want about my lifestyle and how much you think I've changed—"

"I never said that."

"Can you just *listen*?"

My shoulders are tense, gearing up for an argument, but the pleading tone of his voice and the etched lines on his forehead lower my defenses. A reluctant sigh coats the air around my face with a white cloud of my own. "Yeah, okay. I'm listening."

"You're over the line, hermanita, and you know it. What you did to Heck last night at that party, what you did to me in there just now"—he holds up a hand to my impending protest that threatens to burst from my face. I do my best to clamp my lips shut—"I don't need bruja blood to see why. I know you're worried. I know this is all so different from what we're used to. But I invited you tonight so you could be a part of something that *I'm* doing for a change."

Awww, hermano. My own lips tremble, but not from the cold. When he puts it like that, I feel like a huge jerk. I had my reasons for using magic on my loved ones lately, but those are my reasons. And they may not even be good ones now that they're being cross-examined by the kindest brother anyone could ever hope to have.

"Look," he says, tapping his ashes to the ground. "I know we've got distance between us, and it's not your fault, but . . . don't go making it worse. Okay?"

I nod with another big sigh, and turn to lead us back toward the door. A healing spell for hypothermia isn't something I want to learn tonight.

"Fine. But just so you know, your new friends are a little more upstage than I expected from country-born heirs."

"Oh, here we go."

"They're hiding something."

"*Everyone* is hiding something."

"I don't have to trust them just because you do."

"We're bootleggers, Luna," my brother declares with an incredulous laugh. "Those barons are about as on-the-level as we are—no better, no worse. Certainly not what Gio thinks they are, at least."

Most of that is true enough. I never aimed to police morality.

His loafers crunch into the gravel as he spins to face me with raised eyebrows and a lowered chin—his famous lecture-face. "Whatever you read in Dorian is Dorian's business. And before you say anything else about it, you gotta understand something: everyone has thoughts they don't want other people knowin' about. Everyone."

His dincher drops to the ground before he shoves his hands into his pockets. "Luna, can you let me handle this one? Just stay outta this one thing for me, please? I got enough going on. I've got this club, been a little tense with Heck, and I've got roaches all over my apartment."

"I really do under—what?"

"Yeah, didn't Kessie tell you? It's why I don't want anyone there right now."

Roaches? I didn't see a single bug when we were there, and surely Heck would have fled the scene months ago when my brother moved in. *Strange.* Between his odd claim and the way that his eyes begin a series of rapid blinks, my head starts cocking. Another chill fills the inside of my bones. Javier's attention turns upward to the third floor of the building, where his apartment sits in the dark—another window of warning, yet I'm not sure what it's saying. As he stares into the stillness, I'm overcome with the urge to wrap my arms around him. But he would just think I'm trying to read him again. *That was stupid, Luna.*

"I can give you plants for pests," I say, hoping my calm smile captures the corner of his eye. "Gio has a few of them.

They work wonders. Oh! And Mamá Sunday and I were working on a spell to help you sleep."

Ignoring his clouded expression that has finally turned back in my direction, I plunge my hand into the deep pockets of my overcoat. My fingertips loop around a small stone, the smooth surface shining as I hold the offering out to Javier. The moon sends a few silver beams to the parking lot, spotlighting his widening eyes. *Oh no.* I can't have him going into another one of those trances from yesterday—or even flying off the handle. Both would be awful and I don't have Heck here to sing him back down to earth.

I shove the granite egg back into my pocket. "Well, you know where to find it if you need it."

"Just . . ." Javier shakes his head, avoiding my fake smile. "Keep that magic away from me for a little while, okay?"

"I . . . okay."

I'm striking out left and right with my brother lately. Mamá Sunday's magic won't be much help if he won't take it. If I go back to her now, Gloria will certainly catch on that's something's up with Javi. If only I knew of some other witches nearby I could confide in—witches that provided cursed dirt in a pinch when we really needed it. Javier gave his life for it, after all.

No, Luna. Scratch that option. Desperate ideas are bad ideas. At least that's what my mother tells me. She's also the one who warned me never to seek out the witches in the North. They *only* deal in curses. That's the opposite of what my brother needs right now.

I feel like I'm quickly running out of options, though . . .

As he slouches his way to the speakeasy entrance, I finish my walk around the perimeter with determination. Telling me not to have magic is like telling me not to be Mexican. But I'll definitely keep it under wraps around Javier . . . until I figure out how to use it to help him.

My hands spread over the ground one last time while I make my way to my car as I declare to the darkened parking lot, "Bendiciones y prosperidad . . . y protección."

4

"YOU GOT HOME LATE LAST NIGHT."

Heck's crossed knee shakes with his foot, the agitation reverberating into the newspaper he's holding. He gives it a swift crack in front of his face. He might be nose-deep in his favored society section, but I swear he's frowning. From the far end of the table where he sits when he's peeved at me, he reaches around the black-and-white pages for his coffee mug. His cuff links glint in the sunlight that spills past the drawn curtains in the dining room. The sight of the jewelry on his suit sleeves makes my shoulders relax a little. He wouldn't be wearing them if he was *that* mad. I got him those golden trinkets of vines and leaves to celebrate our marriage a few months ago—a promise to always remain the best of friends through this sham. *For better or worse.*

"I told you I was visiting Javi at the club," I say, biting into a cookie that's shaped like a spear. The deafening crunch is almost as off-putting as the dry texture.

Heck normally would lecture me about speaking with my mouth full, but he remains unfazed, his coffee mug settling back into its matching saucer on the tablecloth. "Yes, but you did *not* tell me you'd made such an impression with those barons."

I force the bite I'm working on down my throat before I choke on it. "I *what*?"

A blond eyebrow rises above the top of the newspaper. "Are you saying Margaret's sources are unvetted?"

"It does not say that," I declare, storming across the rug. My cookie and I are soon settling into the seat directly in front of Heck, the paper lowering just enough to show his classic glare.

"No, only that an anonymous tip came in from someone spotting you at a club in the jazz district, unchaperoned, and drinking with a Dorian Luxberg."

Oooh, scandalous. My smile can't help itself. "Jealous?"

Heck's eyebrows pinch together. "Only that you got to spend time with Javi. Or at least, that's what you were *supposed* to be doing."

"Yes, I'm a terrible wife. I get it."

"Do you?" The paper snaps again, folding down to reveal a perfect set of pursed lips. "Do you truly understand how our every move is being examined—that the connections we make and break right now have every bearing on our ability to get those contracts signed?"

"Oh, please. This isn't just about the contracts."

"Exactly!" His eyebrows pinch further. "It's about what these contracts represent."

I hold his glare, but I hate that he's right. Land development contracts will be plentiful from now until long after we're both in the ground, but the deals Heck is trying to make with these barons may not be something he can just buy into later—not with the way land developers around here hold on to property for generations. And Heck is the only one with an actual heart. Which means he'll lift the title restrictions that keep people like my brother (and me, for that matter) out of the affluent parts of town. Yes, there's money involved—big money—but there's also change, and he's the best chance this city has to affect that. So yes, I know what he's trying to do, and I love him for it.

I think I'm mad that I can't stay mad.

Letting the newspaper fall to the table, he runs his thumb along the lace tablecloth. "You must understand what it would look like to those on the outside if I were drinking and conversing alone with a single woman in a low-class speakeasy until one A.M."

I guess I can be a *little* mad. It's unfair that I can't be treated as equal in our venture for equality.

"But you go to Javier's all the time!"

"I'm an investor."

"So am I!"

"But I am a man visiting a man." Heck's eyes fill with apology and I understand what he's saying. He doesn't make the rules society lays to trap outliers within a barricade of coattails, deceit, and dresses—starving us of our will to fight back while we eventually die with frozen smiles on our faces. Perhaps the real rush is how we break as many rules as we pretend to follow in the face of our captors (if only for the sake of agency). I know, to Heck, every subtle look of desire from my brother is an unspoken victory, just like Gio's hand when it slides across the small of my back in the dark juke joint. But it's still a sore spot, having to bow to ordinances and expectations as though the rules themselves are lords over our own kingdom—especially knowing that I, out of the three of us, have to do more bowing and scraping than the others.

With a heavy exhale, I let the tension in my shoulders relax, matching the softening expression on my best friend's face as he reaches for my hand. "Rose, it is different, and you know it. No one is going to think twice about how much time I spend at a club . . . or with Javi."

A rush of tears burns my nose and nearly makes it to my eyes. "How fair is that?"

"I didn't say it was fair, kitten. I am simply saying what it is."

His affection toward me warms my knuckles, his thoughts all the same. He loves me. Dearly. And I love him. What we have is something better than romance, and that's how I know it will be lasting. There's nothing malicious or manipulative in his concern. I *do* need to be more careful.

I take to biting down on the hardened pastry with my back teeth, crumbly pieces falling to my blouse and skirt.

Heck straightens once again, his eyes back to glittering orneriness. "I didn't import biscotti all the way from Tuscany to have you gnaw at them like a beaver at the breakfast table."

"Maybe you should import cookies that haven't gone stale."

"You're supposed to dip them into your coffee to soften them."

"Then why not just make them soft in the first place?"

"Oh, I don't know," he huffs as he waves his biscotti in the air like a conductor at a symphony, "history, culture, tradition." The cookie takes a delicate dip into his glass before meeting an equally delicate end between his teeth—a crisp and clean concerto. Even the man's chewing is as though he weren't chewing at all.

Melancholy touches the small smile on my lips. Unlike mine, Heck's poshness isn't forced. Truthfully, he seems to enjoy the velvety world around him, and I imagine he finds me as frustrating as I find him. I rarely stop to think I may not be the only one losing myself in our merger. That doesn't mean I'm going to keep my nose from wrinkling next time he has the kitchen staff serve up a late-morning brunch of codfish and grapefruit (I prefer cooked oats or nothing at all), but I can at least try to stop making him feel bad for just being who he is.

Our dissension against societal norms is how we found each other in the first place.

"Darling," I say, mimicking Heck's cosmopolitan dialect as I brush crumbs from my skirt, "if we're planning to bicker about breakfast, then have the chef bring around a good stiff glass."

His eyes glance down at the wristwatch he wears everywhere just short of bed. "Of course. All the classy girls get half-seas over before noon." He lifts his finger as if to signal an attendant before pausing. "Oh, wait. We should probably consult the doctor on which liquor is best for this trimester."

He cuts me off at the gasp. "And do stop that squinting glare. It's unbecoming of a woman of any station."

"Dios mío, I thought Dorian was a cacafuego!"

"Swearing and speaking Spanish?" Heck's flashing grin

lights up the breakfast table as he excuses himself with a nod. "If Gloria could hear you now."

"Well, we can't all be her favorite . . . and where are you going?"

"Javi is clearly your mother's favorite," Heck replies into my hair with a quick kiss, "and I am headed to deal with the ongoing shenanigans of the upper class. Nothing to unsort yourself ab—"

"Old Man Wilmington's birthday celebration at our club. I'm aware."

Heck's snow-white collar freezes above me, his nervous laugh mixing with his musky scent of patchouli and shoe polish. He takes to brushing invisible dust from my blouse with a guilty bite of his lip. "That happened before I could stop it."

"All the worst things do, really."

He makes a comment about how funny I can be when no one's listening and asks the doorman to ready his vehicle. Then, the first man I ever trusted outside of my own brother lowers himself in front of me further, squatting, so we're eye to eye. I can't believe he's allowing the creases in his slacks to flatten like this.

"We'll make it, Rose," he says, pressing his thumb to the dimple in my chin. "We'll get through this part."

This part. And all its new rules—for both of us. But I'm the one who has to change how I dress, where I go, what I talk about, and even how to eat my damn breakfast. Despite myself, my nose burns again, but I hold it in just like everything else. "I don't like codfish and grapefruit."

"And you shall never have it served at our table again."

My hand juts out to rustle his pristine hair, but he's onto

me these days, dodging away with a chuckle as he straightens himself once again. From his jacket pocket, he produces my favorite brand of cigarettes, bending ever so slightly to light one for me. A peace offering.

I'll take it.

"We'll answer the press that you went to the new River Rose on my behalf," he says, waving away the cloud around my face. "And say I was under the weather."

"You having a baby too?"

Heck's deadpan stare is usually my favorite, but I find little satisfaction in annoying him right now, even with a Camel between my lips.

My smoky exhale is long. "I'll never forgive you."

"Yes, you will. And you cannot, under any circumstances, be caught with Mr. Giovanni Cattaneo outside of work."

"I'll be the epitome of virtue from now on."

"That's my girl."

Why, you little . . .

Heck's laughter trails behind him as I shoot up from my chair and begin chasing him to the front door while the staff stare at us like we're a couple of lunatics. And we really are off our nuts. At least we're not like everybody else.

HECK'S PRIZED CHRYSLER IS A DISTINCT FUSION OF LUXURY and classic mobility. It vibrates less violently than my Model T and riding in the back seat makes me feel like a celebrity. *Maybe I am.* The thought is as jarring as it is intriguing.

There are some real perks to being married to the heir to a not-so-small fortune. How Heck's grandfather built that money by displacing non-whites to build city boulevards seems inconsequential now that that same inheritance is funding much more improved investments—such as the apartment above the new River Rose, which provides Heck and his boyfriend a private place to spoon. It also bankrolls our clubs that service at least three human vices explicitly forbidden by Missouri law. The Kessler money *used* to capitalize on the disadvantages of the darker-skinned, but recently has secured a raise for our mixed jazz band and flapper girls. The irony is excellent.

I smile down at the cream cushions, stretching my arms across the seat like a bigwig gangster. My fur overcoat and riding boots were made for this car. I'm dying for a smoke, but Heck would choke on his own gasp if I lit up in here. Plus, my tall, dark, and handsome driver would freeze to death if he had to roll the front window down.

"Lookin' sharp back there, boss," he says, turning into an empty alleyway. "But don't get too comfortable. Those rented cops'll be here any minute."

Dios, dios, dios. Cops. Bribery. I'm oddly clammy and warm at the same time.

Heck's warning from this morning is nearly drowned by the thumping in my chest. Surely, he didn't expect me to attend my first Pendergast mission alone. And I can't exactly bring just anybody with me to graft city cops in the middle of the day. My boyfriend is perfect for this sort of thing, and I never agreed to stop seeing Gio.

I agreed not to get *caught* with Gio.

"Tell ya what. Wood-rimmed steerin' wheel, leatha' interior"—he twists in his seat, his arm snaking behind him until his hand finds its way to my knees—"I could go to work on you in a car like this."

A twinge of excitement joins the nervous rhythm in my chest as he lifts his head just enough so I can see his eyes darkening beneath the shadow of his cap. The cold from his palm bleeds through my stockings, but my thighs don't seem to mind. I can't believe this is revving my motor. I should be a wreck by now.

Gio's fingers make their way like they've been there before.

"No bloomas," he says with a pleased grunt as I shift to give him room to creep further.

I meet his gaze, unflinching. "Someone could see you."

"Baby, I'll have you done in two minutes, the way you're lookin' at me."

My breath hitches. So does his, but those sable eyes break away as he yanks his arm back and then smashes his hat down over his ears. "They're pullin' in. I'm keepin' the engine runnin'." Letting me adjust the sprig in his cap, he tucks his hair beneath the rim. The green feather pinned to the ribbon might not look like a scrap of fennel doused in a newly cast protection spell, but I'm also hoping folks don't examine it too closely. "You really think this flowa' will work?"

"It's magic, not a miracle."

"Great. That's real comfortin', Rose."

By the time Gio opens the passenger door for me, sleet is falling fast and hard, the stinging crystals racing each other to the ground. The patrol cruiser behind us is still running, just like our car. This meeting isn't meant to last long.

The two henchmen in official Kansas City Police Department uniforms both blow into their hands before rubbing them together. Uncovering a shining head, one tucks his Stetson into his underarm, extending a hand to me. *Oh, perfecto.*

The thoughts I immediately pick up on when our palms meet are not quite so dandy. This protector of the law is already thrilled with his assignment for the day. By the time he starts picturing what undergarments I'm wearing, I'm already yanking my hand back, abandoning any hope for a gleaned notion that might be helpful. I wanted a motive, a weakness—anything. But sometimes, it shakes out like this.

Boys will be boys. Ugh.

I turn with a nod at Gio like he didn't just have his hand up my skirt. "Mr. Cattaneo."

The simple command springs him into action, the policemen frowning at the envelope in my driver's hand.

My eyes dart between them. "Is there a problem?"

"You ever been handcuffed, Mrs. Kessler?"

"I . . . huh?"

While baldy's question throws me, it seems to fully entertain his partner, who makes no attempt to hide his gargled laughter. Gio lowers the envelope and his chin. The guffawing men laugh even harder as his expression turns to stone.

"Great," I mumble under my breath. *This part.*

I don't exactly *not* miss this part of the game; using my allure to gain an advantage with potential enemies is downright fun in the right context. But it also gives them the wrong impression, which used to be fine. Having a boyfriend can be rather inconvenient when flirting for information, however.

I glance over at Gio, who has produced a cigarette out of nowhere. He refuses to break eye contact with these goons. I can't signal him if he won't look at me. Not a single guy in this parking lot is being helpful.

Gio knows what I've had to do at times to read a man in a hurry. He's always telling me it's no problem. *I trust you.*

And even if you gotta go fartha' than I'd like, I still trust you. My heart sinks into my twisting stomach every time he says it. He just doesn't want to know about it. He certainly doesn't want to *watch* it.

"C'mon, sweetheart," the snorting cop with the hat says as he raps the wooden door to their vehicle. "I've got a Kingston heater installed in this baby. We'll warm you up in no time."

"Hey, you ain't gonna talk to her like that."

The henchmen's shining eyes turn menacing as they land on my driver.

Come on, take it easy, Gio.

Baldy takes a wide step between us, cutting me off from seeing my boyfriend's expression, although it isn't hard to guess. He makes a certain face right before he's about to let his mouth run off the pages. If his jaw is cocking, we're all in trouble.

The jerk between us straightens his back. "That's a real gutsy thing to say to a couple of cops who know exactly who you are."

Oh boy. They can't be onto us already. Pendergast must know a lot more about our operation than illegal booze and bad reputations. Does he know about my relationship with Gio? About Heck? A much larger fear dries the roof of my mouth. How much does the former city councilman know about me?

"All right, officers," I say, doing my best to flash what I'm hoping is a smile, "let's just get back to busi—"

My boyfriend's snorting laugh is unmistakable. His chin has to be twisting like it's loading one in the chamber. "Yeah, I got nothin' to hide from two knuckleheads who parade around as civil servants while tryna put the squeeze on some otha' schmuck's wife in an alleyway."

The officer between us tenses his own jaw, his head reddening. "Her husband pays you to drive, bimbo. And if you don't dry up, we'll make sure your employer knows all about that rap sheet of yours."

"We're well aware of Mr. Cattaneo's prior arrests." I attempt to circle around the miffed policeman, who's returning the hat to his head, but his partner cuts off my path. *Damn*. That fennel is really letting me down, or maybe that dirt from the river really wasn't a good batch. But I needed something in a pinch. Just like I do now. "Gio, give them the envelope, and let's go."

My tone says it all. This is no time for his ego. He knows how important this is.

The cop in my way sneers his greasy nose down at me and then over his shoulder. "Tell you what, Mr. Cattaneo, do what you're told, and then get back in that Chrysler."

"Like I'm gonna leave her with a couple of drugstore cowboys pretendin' to be the law."

Damn rum-runners! I curse myself silently for not bringing Nickels, the Casbah's bouncer. Or even Timothy, our doorman. Anyone other than my boyfriend, who has the temper of a bearcat with a bellyache. Wringing my stiff fingers, I attempt another interjection, but baldy is dead set on stoking Gio's fire.

"What did you call me, you lackey?"

"A piece'a shit with a badge. Now, fuck off!"

Two eye blinks later, my boyfriend is swinging and lands a few good ones before they've got him face down on the pavement. Snow smears dirt and granules across his chin as he struggles against the boot on his head. While the tangle of men jeer at each other, I wrap my overcoat around my legs and squat down to scoop up Gio's fallen cigarette. No sense in letting it go to waste.

The one with the greasy nose stares at my mouth while I take a long drag and stand to observe the brick walls around us. They chose this location because no one can see us or hear us. No one can see or hear them either. They clearly didn't think this all the way through, or they really don't know my witchy little secret. My lips tighten in a smile around the filter as I whisper through my teeth, "Deja que el tiempo se congele como el aire."

As tobacco smoke fills my lungs and strengthens the spell, my observer's eyes squint. Then, his head tilts. The taste of dried, dead things floods my tongue, and the bitterness is a bit more shocking than usual. It's only a small spell to buy us time, but that's all I need—they literally won't know what hit them.

Like crashing into still waters, the air becomes fluid but still cold enough to turn my slowing breath into puffs of white vapor. Tiny ice drops cease their downward race and begin floating in the stillness around us. The car engines cease their sputtering. Since my recent visit to the River Bottoms, I've found the silence of magic a little eerie. It's always spooked Gio, who doesn't waste any time, sliding himself from beneath a muddy boot that rests over him in midair. "Good thinkin', Rose. Now let's drop this money and get movin'."

I square my shoulders with a satisfied grin, poking at the slow-moving smoke from my exhale. The fringes of Gio's suit float around him while he moves to push himself up from the ground. The two goons stand stiff as mannequins. It's a comical scene. But my boyfriend is anything but entertaining.

At first, I think he's still mad or embarrassed by the situation, but the way he's fixating on his assailant's boot chills me from fingertip to bone marrow.

"Rose?"

I step closer as tiny crystals cover the thick soles. My wonderment and panic have my chest heaving as they climb higher, forming an icy crust over the laces, then the socks. It only takes a quick scan of the situation to see that both officers are in serious trouble—trouble that I'm causing.

"Rose, you gotta stop whateva' this is. We can't kill these jokas, baby."

"I . . . this wasn't the right spell." The cigarette drops from my fingers.

"Make it stop, Rose!"

"I don't know how!"

Gio's arms spin me around, his hands braced against my cheeks like a vise. "Look at me. Don't look at them."

No, no, no. I choke on cold air and terror. I didn't know I could cough this hard. I didn't know I could cry this hard. I'm not a killer. This isn't what I wanted. The fates got it wrong.

"Look at me, Rose!" Gio gives my head a moderate shake, his thumbs pressed against my cheekbones. The desperation in his face and palms matches mine. "You were gonna unfreeze time after we left. Just do it now."

"What if it doesn't work?"

"Then they die . . . but you gotta try. I know you can do this, okay?"

My eyes blink hard to shed the wet crystals clinging to my lashes. Gio pulls me close, hiding my face in his chest that rumbles as he begins to hum an old river song he learned from my mother. His throaty voice and tightening arms soothe my breathing just enough so that I'm able to utter a tear-filled incantation into the wool of his overcoat. "Deja que las estrellas duerman."

The maddening rush of time returning to its normal state startles us both with the weight of the air and the roar of car engines around us. Behind me, a series of confused swears and the scuffle of shoes on wet pavement has Gio and me clinging to each other in relief. "Go weak in the knees," he mumbles by my ear.

I let my body go limp. I can't believe it hasn't already.

"What the hell's goin'—how'd you get over there? What's wrong with her?"

"Look, officers," Gio says, half dragging me toward the Chrysler, "girl passed out, and I just got her to come to. Got a baby on the way, this one."

He's not even wrong about some of it. Exhaustion usually does hit me after a spell. It should be threatening to steal my consciousness by now. My palms dampen when one of the cops begins swearing again. "Can you believe this shit? My boot's stuck to the goddamn ground."

"What in God's name—" I lift my head to the sound of a thud followed by a grunt. Baldy has one shoe in the air while the other is stuck to the ground like it's been cemented there. "The bottom of my boot is frozen! I . . . I hardly got the strength to stand. Can you believe this, Ralph?"

Ralph mumbles a sludgy reply.

Gio is already opening the car door to the Chrysler, dumping me into the back seat before trotting out to the fallen policeman. "Eh, don't get up, offica'." He leans down, plastering a wary smile on his face, and tucks the envelope into the cop's front pocket before backing away with a series of nervous chuckles and waving hands. "You just take ya time gettin' your bearin's. Can't go rushin' around on icy streets."

The two cops stare after him in bewilderment as he dives into the seat in front of me. Wheels screeching and engine roaring, our car bails out of that alley faster than a heist gone wrong.

Because it did. My magic, the money drop—it all went wrong.

And yet, my bones feel strong enough to fight again.

And I have no idea why.

MY BOYFRIEND AND I DO NOTHING BUT BREATHE AFTER I awaken on chilled leather seats. I haven't performed a cursing spell since summer. I haven't cast a spell that *potent* since summer. From the driver's seat, Gio stares into nothingness as the car slushes around city block after city block, although the sleet has let up for now. *How long have we been driving?* His hand reaches back and squeezes mine as he parks in another alleyway, this time behind a closed bakery.

"What are we doing here?" I whisper into the frigid cabin.

Gio takes his hand back, grabbing the door handle on his side. "You couldn't read me?"

"My magic's got me worn out." More like freaked out. And exhausted. I could sleep until next Tuesday. "You stopping for a smoke or what?"

Ejecting himself back into the cold, Gio jogs around the car, letting himself into the passenger seat beside me. A gush of crisp air rushes into the cabin before he closes us both inside. He looks as shaken as I feel.

"C'mon, you're tremblin'," he says, pulling me onto his lap and tugging my overcoat down. "Take this off. There's plenty'a room inside mine for both of us." As he stretches his coat around us, I cling to his shivering body, tucking my nose into his neck. I start stammering about how wild and scary it was to nearly turn cops into an ice pop, but Gio shushes me, his arms locked around me until my body relaxes along with his. "You're a powerful woman, Rose. And I know it's scary. Hell, I almost pissed myself back there. But this one's on me and my big mouth. I'm so damn sorry I got you all shook up. I ain't gonna let anything like this happen again. You can count on me. I swear to God."

I never see this guy tear up. I either really scared him or he feels really bad. Likely both.

Aw, hell. What's with guys making me want to cry today? My nose sniffs back the burn in my eyes.

"Naw, none'a that." My boyfriend presses his mouth to my forehead, sending me thoughts and feelings of devotion and tenderness. "Mamá Sunday'll have some answers. We'll work out the kinks."

"I just . . . don't want anyone to get hurt. Especially you." More sniffling.

Gio pulls me away from him so our foreheads can touch. "I've seen what you can do, and I'm still here."

"You shouldn't be."

"You can't boss my heart around."

We sigh against each other's lips before a long, slow kiss takes us over. The softness of Gio's mouth feels like a long saxophone solo in a dimly lit club—smooth and soulful while sending warmth down my neck and shoulders. I want to hang on to him and not let go. My hands cling to the back of his shirt in agreement. Any other guy would be running in the other direction. By all accounts, he should be terrified. I certainly am. But the way his hands are moving down my spine tapers my fear for the time being.

I break away after becoming breathless. I'd almost forgotten where we are. While the abandoned stores surrounding our car aren't really drawing shoppers, I still feel on display. "We can't stay here necking in the middle of the city."

"Baby, neckin' ain't what's on my mind."

While I'd love to hear those sultry thoughts he reserves just for me, the thought of tapping into my magic right now has me on edge. Hell, my allure isn't even attempting to climb while my nerves are bedding everything down. However, Gio's eyes are saying quite enough—pleading and demanding at the same time. I don't need to read this man.

"Yeah, well," I say, running my fingers along the stubble of his chin, "sometimes, it's fun guessing."

"I'm hearin' ya, boss." His lips travel down below my ear, sending another heated ripple through me. Snaking his arm around my waist, he fastens his hand to my hip. "No allure. No reading. Lemme finish this job."

My head falls back with a moan as his mouth travels down my neck. "You sure?"

"I just want you."

Neither one of us lacks experience in automobile debauchery; our clothes unbutton and shift expertly within seconds to allow the overcoat to conceal our grinding bodies. And since the privacy of the cabin and the alleyway conceals our moans, we let them out louder than in a back room at a brothel.

5

"AND SO IT HAS COME TIME TO RAISE OUR GLASSES TO THE patriarch of the hour—my own dear father, Hiram Wilmington the Second!" As the cheers die down, an austere man caked in pomade and freckles lifts his rounded chin with a hand on his hip to square his shoulders. The command in his presence is more than enough to silence the rowdy room. "The patriarch who somehow survived an entire world war!"

More cheers.

"The Spanish flu!"

The room sounds again.

"And the invention of aspirin, which any man would need to survive my mother," the younger Wilmington says, grinning at the reciprocating laughter. "And let us acknowledge his harrowing escape from the sinking of the *Titanic* by selling his ticket to a German soldier. Yes, from the first Kentucky Derby to the grand opening of Woolworth, my father has experienced an entire lifetime of both misfortune and innovation. And so, before he passes on like a good old chap"—forty-plus pairs of hands begin drumming against wooden tables around the club, the band throwing in a few notes from the stage—"I shall lead us in a song we used to sing in Barbados before it became famous here in the States. Y'all might be familiar with it now."

Hiram the Third beckons toward the stage, lifting his arms to lead the room in a silly tune I've heard a few of my musicians sing a time or two.

> *Some time ago, I'd a cold in the chest*
> *And the doctor advised me to go for a rest*
> *So I went to the coast for a couple o' weeks*
> *The weather was fine, and it colored my cheeks*
> *I went for a sail ev'ry day I was there*
> *I didn't care, weather rainy or fair*
> *The last sail I had was a bumping success*
> *I got acquainted with Nelly McNess.*

As the band joins the patrons in the chorus daydreaming of a summertime wedding, I note the small drop in Hiram's smile as he jumps down from the chair that served as his podium. He throws back his drink and then makes his way through the merry crowd to the bar in the back of the room before the band can hit the second verse.

My eyebrows pinch together. That was some send-off. The disdain he has for his father rivals mine. The only reason I'm tolerating the old man myself is because he offered Heck nearly double our normal rental price.

And, more, because Heck finally asked me.

The Casbah Lounge used to be my fortress in enemy territory and still is in some ways. Only my closest staff members there know about my unconventional marriage, but the high-fluting patrons laughing and sweating around my club can never be trusted. Their pockets are too deep, and their motives too shallow. If only one could capture them below a glittering nightclub accessed only by a hidden staircase that led to a hidden juke joint adorned with crimson curtains and gold trim. Such a place would offer Missouri royalty the perfect amount of discretion to aid in their mastery of debauchery without consequences—a place where sophisticated sin is served in a variety of glasses. And a variety of colors.

A striking woman as tall and dark as my brother saunters through the crowd of men, who sling their dinner jackets over their shoulders with one hand and jingle their glasses at her with the other. She flutters her lashes as they beg for a kiss and then offers them her exposed knee in reply. By the time she reaches my side, her rolled-down stocking has been stuffed with several dollar bills. My head flapper sure knows how to sell the services of her Barlow girls. Our brothel rooms might be hidden in this underbelly club beneath a grand ballroom, but there's no hiding the exchange of goods tonight. It's Old Man Wilmington's seventieth birthday and the presents abound.

"Plum looks tight on you," our head flapper says, patting the arrangement of jewels that are woven into the stack of fuchsia curls on her head. She leans down as the hi-hat starts tapping from the stage. "You almost wear that dress like you mean it."

Penny has a way of making me smile, especially when

we're surrounded by drooling root vegetables in three-piece suits. At least I've got the sequins of my handbag to fidget with if I get too antsy.

"Well, I've always wanted to wear a getup that costs more than the rent on my old apartment." I flick the fringes that hang down to my elbows. "Don't get me started on how heavy this beading is."

Wrapped in lace gloves, her hand reaches to lift the dangling teardrop from my neck. "And this adornment? Is it difficult to wear as well?"

"That and the earrings—they belonged to Heck's grand-mother," I say. "I know. It's terrible."

The woman would have hated me and anyone else who wasn't a full-blooded Anglo. It almost makes me love the ensemble even more than I already do. I fit just as much into silk skirts and ruby-encrusted jewelry as I do river boots and my abuela's cotton dresses I used to dance around in at bedtime. I've been working my whole life for a dress like this. To own a club like this. The revenue from tonight alone is something I used to dream about.

My dreams forgot to mention fraud in broad daylight.

It was different when it was just me and my brother scamming a dumb gambling-club owner to run a sleazy gin joint in the jazz district. Money flowed and so no one asked questions. My identity and magic were safe enough. How-ever, with my marriage (and now the supposed child within my womb) becoming a public spectacle, the weight of deceit is heavier than the sparkling gemstone around my neck.

Penny snorts with a delicate smirk. "Nothing terrible about it, honey. It's not like Grandma Kessler's old bones have a use for them."

"Penny!"

Our laughter is drowned out by the final chords of a temperate foot-tapper, the microphone squealing from the stage as it comes to life in front of another dazzler of a woman whose white dress and long gloves shine as bright as her smile. Doris can win a crowd over with her voice alone. If she'd stick to the script Heck wrote for her, she'd have this place in the palm of her hands. But our lounge singer doesn't often bother herself with things like following directions or chewing gum with her mouth closed.

"Ain't it been a great decade so fah?" Doris tosses her blond waves and sweeps her arm at the round of jeers and applause. "Movie stahs. Men finally discova'd the clitaris—"

Several mouths throughout the room spray moonshine into the air, the crowd roaring even louder as I succeed at not choking on my own drink. I cannot *believe* she said that. But then again, yes, I can. It's Doris. I'd sink into the ground if she did that in front of a more uptown crowd, even though we are down in the basement bar room. The underbelly of my high-end club might be a gambling parlor with a harem, but the uppercrustmen still expect a *certain* amount of finesse to their entertainment.

"But don't worry, fellas," she continues, "I'm sure they'll outlaw that too."

My expression must register a good measure of shock because Penny whispers to me to relax. "Doris knows her crowd, Miss Rose."

I'm glad *she* does. Personally, in all my years running a gin joint, I've never seen a group of whiskey-soaked men so amped up and crass. Their ringleader sits in the center of the room with his belly hitting the table with every squawking laugh. Old Man Wilmington is having the time of his life, snapping his suspenders at the dancers onstage and grabbing himself between the legs. It's a mystery how his heart isn't giving out with the way he's coughing between puffs on his cigar. He and his entourage flick their tongues like vipers at the passing Barlow girls, stealing their trays and pulling them onto their laps until our bar security has to pry the ladies away. Some of them want to preen, but Nickels's face and bulging arms mean business. The country boys back down quickly.

I don't know why I expected better behavior from the South. They don't smell any more sophisticated than city men; the Aqua Velva isn't enough to cover the perspiration in the room anyway. They're supposed to be famous for their good manners, but all I've seen so far is a slew of hateful speeches against women and anyone with skin darker than mine while those same men grab at the skirts of Penny's array of colored girls, stuffing obligatory dollars into their stockings. Clearly, their lust doesn't seem to be so preferential.

If only their mamas could see them now.

The barons' bad behavior reaches a crescendo as one of them offends Doris in the middle of a song, to which she hoists her heel onto a step stool, hurling a series of comebacks so discourteous the offender plops down in his chair in silence. I'm surrounded by bearcats these days.

I squeeze Penny's shoulder. "I'm gonna check on Javi."

I mostly mean it. While Heck's constant assurances that he's able to handle my brother's mood shifts have provided some solace, Javier still has me wound up tighter than my wristwatch. But what I'm really after this evening is to eavesdrop on Heck, who has been entertaining Hiram the Third at the bar. The old man's protégé seems to be the more subdued Wilmington, albeit the red handlebar above his lip is just as brassy as his father's.

Through the smoky haze, Heck is in his own world, gabbing and laughing on a barstool beside Hiram, whose eyes glint at my approach. *Damn*. He *does* know how to wear it, though— the mustache, the wry smile, the three-piece suit—everything. The other barons might be fancy potatoes in fancy ties, but Hiram has already proven to be keen in the short time I've spent with him. His lip curls upward at my attention. *Settle down, boy*. I don't want what he thinks I want. It's simply my business to know who's in my club drinking my drinks with my faux husband, whom he's obviously taken an interest in. Given what I've discovered about the other barons, I decide on a subtler technique, landing at the end of the bar where my brother is training one of my new bartenders in the art of tray placement.

"Thanks for helping tonight," I say to Javi as he sends the nervous young man to fetch more cases of rum.

He pours me a two-fingered glass, then pinches the dimple in my chin with a wink. Javier is in such a good mood; I wouldn't dare read him. It's not like he'd know, but I feel like he'd know.

And after what we discussed last night, *I'd* know.

"That's a long face, Miss Rose," he says. "We've got plenty of nights to be troubled, so why choose this one? Besides, Kessie wouldn't want you chewing your lip like that."

He winks again, evoking a snorting laugh through my nose.

"You can't possibly be having a good time surrounded

by men who hate us." I nod my head toward the center of the room. "I mean, look at that old bigot and his cohort. It's gonna smell like underarms and aftershave for a week."

"Yeah, I get what it feels like. But this is your den. Don't forget that."

My brother leans his arms on the counter, staring past me into the sea of barons. I know Heck said he's been working on Javier to go see my abuela, but he's been refusing under the guise of "feeling better." The forlorn look in his eyes tells me something different.

"Javi—"

"I know they're not my friends, okay?"

"Then why do you go with them?"

My brother's gaze lands on me so pointedly, I almost feel it. "They think I'm with them. But they're actually with *me*. I hear their secrets when they've had a few too many. I see their balance ledgers and roaming fingers. It's no different than the games you play."

I blink back at Javier. *Games?* My face tightens at the allegation. Everything I've done as a bruja has been for a purpose. *Nearly.* Before I met Gio and Heck, I used my charm to protect my family and gain favor—and gain a few chiseled bedmates. And maybe a discount or two. And sometimes, when I just felt like it.

Dios. It really isn't much different.

My brother leans closer, his eyes locked on the crowd in front of us. "Manipulation is magic in its purest form."

I let out a small grunt, tipping my glass to my lips. The dark liquid is rich going down—bitter and sweet on the back end. For the first time in days, my brother's musings are making some sense. Heck's got the magic of charm that needs no conjuring. Penny's touches are as methodical as my abuela's potions. Hell, even Doris can enchant a man with her curves in a way that makes them thank her for slapping them across the face. Who am I to say how Javier should use his own gifts?

The part that's hard to swallow is the kind of gifts I didn't know he had. Deception has always been my arena while he remained an observer—a man of few words, unless he's arguing with me, of course.

I take another burning swig. "Who's the mateo at Gus's table?"

"Spanish, mija," my brother teases in a whisper, following my gaze to the roulette wheel in the corner. A tall man in a pair of spectacles watches the dice roll, stoic as he wins another round. "Oh, that guy who looks like he could use a few minutes with a flapper?"

"Doesn't seem to notice them."

"I've seen him prowling—some Wall Street–type reporter from Chicago doing a story on the barons' investments."

A reporter? *Great.* That's just what my life needs—more busybodies looking for a news break. Scrutiny keeps upping the ante around here.

"Well, he's sure cleaning our gambling manager out of his green."

"Sí, but Gus'll swindle it back before the night's over."

"Good," I say. "I'd rather a gumshoe like that stay distracted." And far away from me. I've got enough people lining up to ask me questions at luncheons and cocktail parties. I don't need it here too.

Javier steals my glass for the final sip. "I'm more interested in the guy dropping pins in front of your husband all night."

"I wouldn't worry, Javi. Hiram is a big flirt but all gas, just like his dad."

"Oh, Kessie is just being Kessie. I just . . . know the barons." The glass in my brother's hand clinks against the countertop. "Speaking of which, I gotta run. Take care of our boy for me?"

"You sure you don't wanna stay?"

He pushes away from the counter. "I'm meeting the guys at my joint. Great seeing this place again, though—and you, hermana. I'll see you and Mamá soon." Giving me a salute, he throws a subtle nod to Heck, whose face struggles between a pouting lip at Javier's exit and a laugh at something Hiram just said. My heart sinks for them. We're all playing roles here.

Refocusing back on fancy veggies in fancy fedoras, I tug at the sequined strap dangling from my shoulder. There's enough smoke in the air to share, but I want my own. As much as the ferns around this club have flourished in their ability to blanket the atmosphere with congeniality as they were blessed to do, they're hardly touching the ruckus inside me. My handbag holds at least one remedy to my restlessness tonight. As I stroll to Heck's side, he has a match waiting for me. The flick of the fire lights our faces in the dim room, Hiram watching with a droll smile.

"You don't look so country in that getup," I say before pulling a fresh drag into my lungs. The toasted flavor warms me immediately.

"You city folk are so lacking in the complimentary," he

fires back in his smooth twang, "that I'll dare to take that as a commendation . . . especially from a creature as alluring as yourself. Mr. Kessler, how do you keep your hands to yourself with this prized possession?"

Disgust crinkles the side of my face. It doesn't take much moonshine to bring the man out of a man. Yet, the challenging spark that flashes in his eyes tells me he's looking for a fight. Like my mother always said, *A man that teases your sensibilities wants to tease your skirts later.* But with Heck standing here?

Hiram is either daring or half-seas over with moonshine to flirt with another man's wife right in front of him—and in his own fortress. Another proverb of my mother's comes to mind as I suck on the slender end of my cigarette holder: *There's always something you haven't thought of yet.*

A spitting chuckle bursts from Heck's lips. He's somehow the only guy I know who becomes more adorable when he's had a few. "Well, for starters," he slurs, "by not calling her a possession. She'd smother me in my sleep otherwise."

Hiram's forehead wrinkles, his gaze holding mine. "My apologies, Mrs. Kessler. You'll forgive my old-fashioned conventions?"

"Not a chance," I say before blowing a small stream of smoke above his slicked curls.

Heck's laughter is drowned by the booming voice of the birthday boy in the center of the crowd. "Hear! Hear! for this Negro jazz band! Come now and play somethin' sultry so that I may find a pair of rouged lips to carouse!"

Hiram's face turns as red as his hair. But this isn't the first time our club's band leader has had to abide a drunken patron. No matter the insults, no matter the crowd, Charlie "Clip Lip" Williams always says he'll play until they rip the saxophone from his calloused fingers.

The younger Wilmington lays his hand on Heck's forearm. "You won't have to rent to my father again. I can absolutely assure you."

"Not to worry," Penny says from over his shoulder. The flush in Hiram's cheek deepens as he jolts in his seat. "If we denied clientele for their views on our blackness, we'd have hardly any clients."

From the stage, Clip exchanges a knowing grin with her while she thumbs her nose toward the old man. The tension fades from Hiram's face.

"Of course," she continues, "it's hard to take seriously a man who parades like a stallion while his hairline is in full retreat and taking cover inside of his ears."

Heck is back to giggling and claps Hiram on the back, who casts a smug grin back at her. "His eyebrows have their hands up in full surrender."

"Look like they tryna leap off his damn face."

"His mustache seems to be making an escape too, I'd say."

"Probably from his breath, if I had to guess." She bolsters up her cleavage. "Hell, I'm takin' every dime he has."

Seconds later, Penny plants herself in the middle of the lions, the old man's hand ricocheting off her backside. The lower she bends, the more dollar bills her stockings collect. After a signal to her Barlow girls, another monstrous glass of amber liquid appears in front of him. It'll take seven stout men to carry him out of here later.

"I'd rather he slap *my* ass than sing that sailor's song again," Hiram drawls against his own tumbler.

"That's right," I say with a raised eyebrow, "Barbados, wasn't it? You're well traveled."

His lower eyelid pushes up in a squint, half covering an iris the color of wet sand, his nose lifting with the tilt of his head. Like bringing up a man's wife in bed, I've touched something he doesn't want touched. He takes to studying his glass as he thumbs the rim. "They're putting radios in cars now."

The tension in his shoulders is clear enough. He'll walk if I pry any further. I do my best to look interested.

"My father sent his man all the way to Philadelphia to get me one." Hiram reaches for an ashtray, then holds it between us. Could be an offering of thanks—or a barrier. "Your Model T is rather known in our circle. How is he forcing you to drive such a relic?"

"I choose to drive it," I quip, tapping my ashes. "I earned it myself."

"Why not upgrade?"

"It reminds me of what really matters."

"Not even tantalized by the radio?"

"If I wanted to listen to men yap about themselves, I'd stay at this counter."

Leaning against the bar, it's clear Heck has reached the point where he'll laugh at anything.

"Rosie!"

A man with a middle part so slick it could survive a hurricane pushes through a pack of shouting roulette players, finally reaching for my arm with a sweaty palm. Sending my magic to work, I pick up on his nervousness—and his enjoyment of how my neckline reaches his chin in these heels. *Mierda*. Can't Giuseppe think about anything else?

"I beg your pardon, sir." Heck's drink splashes as he points the glass down at our gambling manager. As Gus removes his hand from my elbow, Heck's eyes widen like two cerulean, crocked marbles as he realizes I was trying to get a read. "Oh, uh . . . I mean—"

"Yeah, sure, whateva'," Gus says, standing on his toes to see his table over the rowdy heads behind him. "Listen, bosses, that guy ova' there ain't no regula' reporta'. He's askin' way too many questions."

Dammit. I knew it. Never trust a guy in a gin joint who doesn't want gin.

I shake Gus's shoulder, relaxing my face as much as I can with the way Hiram is staring. "What kind of questions?"

My gambling manager's tiny mouth pinches tighter. "*Questions.* About your business, my business."

Reaching for Heck's sleeve, I pinch a golden trinket, un-pinning it from its place as I pull him from his stool. Even with the cuff link now pressing into his palm between our hands, he doesn't understand the signal; his mind is a jumble mixed with worry. We've got seconds to communicate while these two other guys are exchanging curious stares.

I chance a read, Heck's message to me rushing in. *What's wrong, kitten?*

That sounds like permission. With the aroma of hibiscus filling my nose, I ready a thought to send through our clasped hands. It'll sound like his own in his head, but he'll know it's from me.

It's time to go home. Let Rose handle the stranger.

There's hardly an argument here. Heck is way too sauced to engage an investigative reporter. And if he comes at me, at least I can get a read to find out what he's up to.

Heck's eyes close with a quick nod, pulling our hands to his mouth to kiss my knuckles before gripping the cuff link in his fist. He turns to the puzzled baron. "Mr. Wilmington, it's been a pleasure, but I hate to keep my driver out all night."

"Ah," Hiram says, his glass clinking against the counter. "I also hate the press, my friends. In fact, I'll go alert both of our drivers, Mr. Kessler. I've had enough of my father's shenanigans."

"That would be divine."

As Hiram disappears up the stairwell, Gus spins around with his hands behind him like a schoolboy with a confession to make. "I, uh . . . mighta told that reporta' that you was my sista'."

Heck and I drop our chins collectively. "You what?"

"Yeah, well, at first, I wanted the clout—thought he was some poindexter lookin' to spend some serious green glorious." My gambling manager shakes his head, the guilt on his face turning to fret. "But he kept just bettin' with pennies, so I said, 'Lemme get you a drink.'"

Gus pulls a decanter from behind his back, holding it up to us in the dim light. *What in the . . .*

"They're all like this. Every bottle in the new boxes."

I lean in closer, my cigarette dropping to the floor with my stomach. Floating in the amber liquid is a tiny ball of fur, its tail like a long dancing thread in the pool of rum. The crystal jar glitters as much as the sweat of Gus's palm. *Dios mío.*

My fingers reach out and touch the glass, the mouse's lifeless eyes staring right through me. Its body rolls gently from one side to the other in the crystal tomb.

"'Ey, Rosie . . . it . . . it's like it's lookin' at you."

Heck's hand claps over his mouth. "I can't . . . I'm gonna be sick."

Upside down now, the grotesque creature twists its head around, its beady gaze on me once again. The sound of Heck's retching fades beside me. I should see to him—get us both out of here. But I can't take my eyes off those bulging black dots . . . and the flicker of the spidery claw.

"Not possible," I whisper.

Gus's nervous breath turns into panting. "This shit ain't happenin'. That thing ain't movin', right?"

A bitter flavor floods my mouth, nausea draining the blood from my face as the mouse leaps at my fingertips, ramming its body against the glass. Gus and I rip our hands away from the decanter, stumbling backward as it crashes on the floor. As I back into a sea of loutish barons, my heels mash gin and vomit into the carpet. *Where is it? Is it still coming for me?*

"¡Criatura asquerosa! ¡Soy tu muerte!" Bile burns my throat. Gruff voices swear and jeer around me in the throng of crude gentlemen. I've lost sight of that . . . *thing*. Several hands grab at my wrists. What minds they have—sickening appetites for the snake charmer with the pretty dimples. Vile breath and wild laughter threaten to drown me before a strong grip spins me around.

His thoughts are not so carnal. I've made him drop his dice . . . and his life savings.

A pair of glassy eyes stare down at me through a fringe of greasy locks. "Watch it, you damn skirt!"

The man's fuming emotions rise like a volcano threatening to erupt. He doesn't care for my dimples—doesn't care that I'm a woman. And he sure isn't afraid to deck one.

"I apologize," I say, attempting to appeal to his ego. He doesn't like forward ladies or lipstick or anything that I am. But like my friends, I'm a chameleon in this world. We are who we say we are. "I'm sure my husband will allow it—let me cover your drinks for the night, sir."

"You gonna cover the bet you made me lose too? Runnin' around here like you're something!"

Dammit, dammit, dammit to hell. He's too drunk. Too angry. I might have to tap into his mind. As with impartation, I can access his mind, but I don't know how potent that spell would be with my nerves on six cylinders. A shiver thickens the uproar in my stomach. I haven't walked through a man's mind since . . . Moretti. Salvatore. And they're both dead now.

I don't want to be responsible for that ever again. And I sure don't want to drop a guy in such a public place. Not in front of such a wild crowd—and that damn reporter taking notes somewhere in the fray.

"Hey!"

That nasal voice has never been more comforting. From somewhere around my captor's elbow, Giuseppe's chest puffs, his finger poking the man in his double-breasted suit. "Yeah, keep it up, tough guy. Nobody hits my sista' unless he's married to her!"

The boulder of a man that's holding me lets me go. Gus pales. Yanking a drink from a passing tray, Gus takes a swig hearty as a frat boy on graduation day. As the smiling boulder rears back a tightened fist, Gus sprays the entire contents of his mouth in his assailant's face. Gus ducks away and bolts for the stairwell before the startled patron can wipe the moonshine from his eyes. I'm not far behind, pressing through sweaty arms that seep agitation and folly. I check over my shoulder at the shouts rising behind me. The boulder is shoving his way to the center of the throng. He seems to have forgotten his goal—and doesn't seem to care. The first swing he takes lands on a swearing baron whose pack of brothers answers with a few blows of their own. Soon, lions are pummeling lions, Old Man Wilmington's laughter following him as his entourage whisks him away.

I yell for Heck, spotting him near the stage where another group is flicking coins at Clip as he attempts to finish a solo. The saxophone halts; the drummer points a stick down into the crowd. Heck grabs the mic to calm the commotion, but nobody can hear him. I've never seen the band pack up so quickly.

¡Mierda! How is this happening? I've got damn ferns all over the place. They're what kept the River Rose from this brand of chaos. But now, my castle has become a battlefield.

Clip sends his last guy toward the stairs, clutching the instrument case in his hands as he helps Heck put the microphone back into its holder. Finding a clearing near the bar, I climb onto a stool, waving at him to come down. Heck finally catches sight of me, frantically pointing toward the door.

Yeah, okay. It's sweet of him, truly. But there's no way I'm abandoning my keep. Or him. Or any of my crew.

Clip pulls on Heck's arm with desperation on his face.

Before any of us can make a break for it, a large bottle hurls through the air. It shatters against Clip's temple. Heck's face wilts—as does my heart and all time and space. Our beloved band leader crumples to the ground. His saxophone case slides across the stage.

"Clip!" I scream, my voice choking at the loud blast that

silences the entire room, save for gasping breath and a few whispered curses. Standing on a poker table, a slender blonde holds a pistol in the air like Texas Guinan, with the same provocative and deadly look in her jade eyes.

Doris. The Casbah Lounge's very own lead singer has once again commanded the club's attention. In a dress. With a gun.

Her straightened arms sweep the barrel over the ducking crowd. "Now, I ain't gonna ask you nicely. Walk the hell outta here, and don't cause no more trouble. And if you see the cops, pay 'em off."

Rubbing their heads and grabbing their hats, the Southern gentlemen stumble single file up the stairwell, the door slamming shut after the last of them.

"BEARCAT, DON'T YOU EVA' DO SOMETHIN' LIKE THAT AGAIN!" Nickels wails, scooping up Doris in his burly arms. "You coulda been killed or killed somebody. Then, what am I gonna do without you?"

"Aww, nerts," she says, as he smothers her face with kisses, "would ya calm down, Nicky? It's not a real gun. They was blanks from the props room."

While it's always lovely and nauseating watching those two suck face, I can't be bothered too long with whatever the hell just happened. I've never been more grateful for Doris's wild spontaneity. Every member of this team has come through for me more than a time or two—including Clip.

"We've got to get him to the hospital," I say through chattering teeth, hugging myself near Clip's feet as Heck holds the saxophone player's head in his lap. Heck's slacks are soaked crimson, the blood still oozing from the large gash on Clip's temple. I lower myself to the stage, hugging myself tighter. I'm unable to maintain any semblance of stoicism, the sobs around the room choking me with my own. While these people are my infantry, they're still not my inner circle. They don't know about my abilities, and while I can trust them, I'm not sure I can trust them with this. They already carry so much.

"No hospital is gonna help him, Miss Rose," Penny says, her voice grating with anguish. "And we'll wait hours at Wheatley Medical."

She's right. Dammit, she's right. The hospital for the poor and darker-skinned is not a quick drive nor a quick wait. Clip doesn't deserve to die in a cramped holding room. Nobody does. Hot tears spill down my cheeks as I look over at Heck, whose face is streaked as well. He presses his lips together, the pleading in his eyes asking me to do what I cannot.

"Rose."

"Heck, I can't—"

Squatting down in front of me, Penny lays her hands over my shivering knees. "I know, Miss Rose." I start to stammer a response, but she shakes her head. "I know you can heal him."

Once again: not possible. I've been so careful. *Haven't I?*

A moderate amount of panic rises to my chest. I've come out into society too far. I'm too visible. This is too out of hand. It was scary enough trusting Heck and then Gio. More people knowing about my magic means more danger for my family. Any more layers to this fortress, and it won't hold.

Penny grabs my hands, pulling them to her chest. "I know

you're scared. But this was my daddy when I had none. You've got to heal him."

"What's she talkin' about?" Nickels whispers to Doris, who shushes him.

"Mr. Ibina, Miss Fenton," Heck says, sniffing the pool around his nose, "thank you for your services tonight, but we would like a private moment with Penny."

Doris lifts her head, dabbing the tears from her defiant chin with a handkerchief. "We ain't goin' nowhere. This is our family. And betcha we know a lot more than you think."

A small groan seeps from Clip's mouth, his jaw growing slack.

"We're running out of time, Miss Rose," Penny pleads. "Please."

Dios ayúdame. I suppose if I can trust them with this, I can trust them with anything. This crew already knows enough about Javier's preferences (and my fake nuptials with Heck) to get us all killed. Why not add divination to the list? The truth is, if they wanted to offer my secrets to the highest bidder, they would have done so already.

I straighten my back, throwing caution to the tempest as I meet Heck's hopeful stare. "It's gonna take a lot of dirt."

With wide eyes, he orders Nickels to fetch a large bucket of dirt from under the counter. "Fill it with enough water to make a paste!" Heck turns back to me, his nose running across his suit sleeve. "Javi still has the batch you made."

"It hasn't been tested with healing spells—*I've* barely been tested with healing spells," I argue, scooting to Heck's side, where Clip's breathing is becoming shallower. "My abuela was supposed to look at it. I just haven't had time!"

But that's just what we're out of—time.

Nickels's sturdy hands set the bucket beside me before he gives Doris a shrug.

"Nicky," she says, "don't you see what's goin' on? The secret Miss Rose been keepin'?"

"Aw, I already know she's barnymuggin' Gio and not Mr. Kessler."

"Not that, you dimwit."

"Goddamn, is Heck barnymuggin' Gio too? Cuz him and Javi ain't no secret—"

"Just watch." Doris pulls Nickels down between her and Penny, whose hands now caress the wrinkled fingers of the man who practically raised her.

Clip's head lies cushioned within Heck's lap, his brow relaxed and free from the worry around him. His groans have dissipated into light breathing. *Where are you, Charlie?* He could be too far gone for me to reach him by myself. Maybe we really did wait too long. I'd never forgive myself.

Swallowing the lump in my throat, I lay a hand over his forehead. The clotting blood sticks to my palms, but I push the sensation away, searching beyond the outer wounds. A soft song plays in his mind. It's an old tune from childhood that his mother used to tinker with on the keys. The piano is so faint I can barely make out the melody. He's fading.

But I can still hear the music.

Plunging my hand into the bucket near my thigh, I lift out the cold paste, covering Clip's wound with a generous handful. Determination warms my fingers, and the paste melts to mud beneath the heat. We're not losing anyone today. My head tilts back, seeking the taste of ashes, blackberries, and cloves. My mouth whispers a secret to the sky.

Este día te reirás.
Este día vivirás.
Este día cantarás las canciones
que cantaba tu madre.

The room hushes like a taciturn watchtower, unsure of what lies on the horizon. My thoughts turn to the moonrise, reticent then bold in its stillness as all the world sits in awe for those few glorious seconds when the glowing sphere takes the sky over at dusk. With the same reverent splendor, this bloodied jazz stage plunges into the stillness of floating within what I can only describe as fluid air. Magical air. Time exists somewhere else. I could live in this realm, but then, the company around me would be forever frozen as the edges of their hair and clothing waft in the invisible waves, the rest of their bodies stranded within the moment. My companions can't see the ceiling giving way to a splendid black sky radiating with stars that sing their river melody. But maybe, just maybe, my friends can hear the laughter of the moon as the song of the celestial bodies runs through me. Soon, the hymns dissolve, the ceiling covering up the sky like singing children running off to play while waving goodbye.

With the final note, the room releases gravity back into the atmosphere, and my body is heavy with weightiness and the need to lie down. I could stretch out on this floor and sleep for hours.

But Nickels has his ovaled eyes planted on me. "Yeah, I think I'm gettin' it, Bearcat." He gives me another once-over. "Miss Rose is a damn Mexican."

Another groan rumbles from Clip as he pushes my hands away, attempting to sit up. His lips pale, and he thinks better of it, allowing Penny to lower him back down as she offers her lap to take Heck's place. "Don't you get up too fast, now, Charlie."

"What the hell is everyone goin' on about? Penny, one'a those damn fools got me in the head, I think."

"Oh, they got you, all right. Now, Charlie, I said don't you stand up too fast, and I meant it. I'll have Nickels carry you outta here if you keep tryin' to act tough—"

"Girl, if you don't let me be . . ."

The room is full of grateful smiles and relieved chuckles as Penny fusses over Clip, who fusses right back. Feeling like I fought the boulder man myself, I decide to go ahead and lay myself out on this wooden stage in case I pass out. But as Heck swings my arm over his shoulders, I realize I'm not as spent as I thought I'd be. "Let's get you home, kitten. We can regroup tomorrow."

If Clip had gone any further, I'm sure I'd have to be carried out of here. My yawn is still wide but bearable. "You're in no shape to drive."

"That, my darling, is why we have a driver."

I lean into his side while he shuffles me to the basement door. "Well, it's a good thing Hiram went to . . ." My heel stops midair as Heck squeezes panic into my hand, finishing my sentence in his own thoughts. *Fetch the car.* Heck's panic spikes again. *Hiram went to fetch the car.* The realization surges through us both, our arms tangled together at the bottom of the stairwell like two frightened children. My eyes land on the tiny gap between the frame and the latch. Heck's body tenses around me. In all the ruckus, no one thought to lock the door—or close it all the way.

Sucking in a small breath, Heck nudges the bottom plate with the tip of his loafer. His silent prayer turns to silent swears. Mr. Handlebar Sailor himself is standing on the landing, gripping the back of his neck while his eyes search the enclosed walls. Hiram's attempt to appear lost and confused dies when he finally smiles, letting his hand fall with a shrug. "Well, kiss me till I'm grinnin'. I seem to have lost my way to the lavatory."

Shock tightens my chest.

"Give me your hand," I blurt out, his eyebrows arching at my outstretched fingers.

Heck squeezes my elbow. "In salutation, of course."

Through my skin, he asks me to remain calm, echoing my own thought that the baron's son may not have witnessed a damn thing. Maybe he didn't see anything. Maybe he just heard us talking nonsense, completely unaware that he was caught in a magic bubble of suspension. To him, nothing happened. Time froze, but he wouldn't have known it.

Fidgeting with a button on his waistcoat, Hiram lays one of his palms over mine. "In salutation, I do bid you good night. My father had the birthday of his dreams, so I thank you."

As he brings my knuckles to his lips, I pick up on his unending curiosity. And he is genuinely thankful for our hospitality. He wonders where we get such elegant brandy. He finds Heck charming. And he can't decide if I'm like the same bruja that gave luck to Luciano or if our power differs from each other's.

Nerts.

. . .

MY BODY IS FULL OF LIGHTNING—OR SO IT FEELS. THE SHOCK must be keeping the exhaustion at bay. Clip let Nicky take him home, but the rest of the gang stuck around to clean up . . . and to keep an eye on the young baron who shares a cushion next to me in one of our private rooms. Beyond the coffee table, Heck's body is sprawled across an overstuffed chaise. He props his neck up with his hand to try and stay awake, but he's losing the battle. Five or so brandys will do that to a fellow.

"How long are you going to be holding my hand?" Hiram drawls, stuffing a cigarette between his lips.

"Until I know you're safe."

"I have nothing to hide from someone who's got something to hide." He takes a long drag, then holds the Lucky Strike between us. "Smoke?"

Now there's *a peace offering*. This baron's good manners put him at a disadvantage—he couldn't know the power he's handing over to me. Men never do. They just want to stare at my neckline and light my cigarette, among other things. As my abuela loves to say—*never give a witch something from the earth*.

I want to climb inside Hiram's mind—make him forget. I could do that and more if I wasn't so exhausted . . . and unpracticed. My mind flashes to Gio and the men I nearly froze to death. It's too risky to try something so delicate without Mamá Sunday's guidance. *So frustrating.*

What's the point of having power I can't use?

At least I don't need help using charm. Pressing my mind through Hiram's damp palm, I am able to read his loyalty. His allegiance is mainly to secrecy, but he has no marks of betrayal. He doesn't ever spill secrets—not because he is particularly devoted to any one person but because he believes secrets to be personal and sacred. He certainly has his own.

Turning his hand over, I tap my ashes into his palm. Mind-reading spells love tobacco. It strengthens the read and keeps me from having to tap so much into my own energy, although reading has always been as simple as breathing.

"You knew a bruja before me," I say with smoke billowing around my mouth.

Guilt streaks across Hiram's face. "Celeste."

Without a hint of resistance, Hiram invites me past his current thoughts, and before I can back out, I'm face-to-face with a beautiful lady in a floral dress. She picks daisies with a laugh so catching I hear myself giggle. I didn't mean to go in this far, but I feel steady enough.

Looking past me, the woman's eyes turn glassy, her smile melting. Several men with fitted gloves rush to pull her from the flower bed, thanking Hiram as they drag the wailing woman into a covered limousine.

"That's the bruja that helped Lucky," I whisper. "Di-mi."

Hiram's fingers clamped over mine bring me back into the crimson speakeasy, both of our hearts pounding. My breath struggles against my chest; a full-speed foot chase from the cops would be a milder pursuit.

"I'm the one who helped her escape him and the rest of the mobsters, but . . . I'm also the one who gave her up to them in the first place." Tears gather in his sandy eyes, making them even sandier. "I didn't mean to."

Stormy contrition soaks into my palm.

"Listen, Hiram—"

"I didn't mean to."

The whites in the young baron's eyes grow like glowing spheres, his pupils shrinking as his upper lip twitches. His wild gaze is locked on mine.

"Hiram?"

Heading past his sandy irises with the tiny black dots, my power rushes back into his memory with the screaming woman. I watch them drag her away, and then it starts again. The volley from the room to this eerie garden strains at any magic the tobacco is providing. I doubt I'll be able to stand when this is over.

"Hiram, you don't have to show me this."

"No, I . . . I need you to show it to *me*."

¿Qué?

I spin at the shriek behind me, where a slightly younger Hiram throws his arms around a long metal pole to keep from slipping to the deck beneath his feet. His dark blue service coat and trousers hang heavy on his frame, soaked by the deluge falling from the sky. Igniting and roaring, the clouds pour out onto the cargo boxes around him. The ship groans and pitches, followed by several more screams as the earth itself seems to split in half. The deep cracking sound is louder than the thunder, drowning out the barking orders of men in uniform running past Hiram while others jump from the swaying sea vessel into foaming black water.

"Come on, Three!" A gasping man grabs the edges of Hiram's collar, but the young baron clings to the pole that struggles to hold several cranes in place. The pleading sailor has the same red hair, even the same damn freckles. Hell, if he had a mustache, he'd pass for Hiram. "The manganese blew the engine room. We gotta get off this boat!"

Hiram sobs wildly, his face contorted as he tightens his grip on the pole. "This is God's judgment! I deserve to die!"

"I never should have said that to you. And I won't tell Dad I saw anything. I swear it. Just"—the man's arms fasten around Hiram's neck and chest—"let go!"

"Leave me here, Julius! And think better of me!"

"Stop this nonsense!"

The two Wilmingtons struggle, each ordering the other to save themselves. Hiram swipes at his brother's arm, ripping the lustrous black braid from the gold bands on his sleeve. Plenty of military photos passed my desk when I used to work at the *Star*. Hiram's twin isn't the average seaman.

"Chaplain," I whisper.

The squealing of the swinging cranes echoes through my mind. Or are those Hiram's cries from the couch? *¡Ay, no!* He doesn't want me here anymore. Dammit, I don't want to be here either. Yet I can't seem to leave. Maybe I've run out of magic for the voyage back. It doesn't make any sense, but none of this makes any sense. Getting out should be like walking backward.

"I . . . I'm trying. I can't seem to . . ." The strain on my energy is like climbing with sore muscles. The sudden fatigue is unbearable.

With a guttural groan, the vessel lurches, its beams splitting under the weight of the cranes. Hiram and his brother finally let go of each other, clutching the pole as the ship's bow tips toward the angry sky. A hundred feet below them, the sea swirls and crashes, swallowing up the stern like a ravenous water demon. Its teeth are made of snapped poles and wires jutting out as crude javelins.

"Don't you let go, Three!" Julius clamps his hand over

Hiram's, their legs dangling. "When she sinks, swim outta here—soon as our feet touch the water!"

"I'm so sorry. I didn't mean to—"

Hiram's brother kicks at his boots. "Hey, you didn't do this, and neither did God." Julius gives him another kick with a know-it-all grin. "He doesn't work that way."

In the most life-harrowing event of his life up to this point, Hiram laughs.

Thunder cracks. Lightning flashes. The ocean roars beneath the lurching boat.

The pole between his fingers rattles and shakes, and Julius stops smiling. There's no time to grab him as his hand slides from Hiram's knuckles. There's hardly time to gasp. Beyond his shock and flailing feet, Hiram dares to look, his screams lost in the storm. The demon below has speared his brother's abdomen with its teeth and soon pulls him into a deep blue darkness where he will never be found.

Let go!

Is that Hiram? I've never heard thoughts of memories before. Not like this. Did he want to let go and die as well? He clearly feels responsible for his brother losing his grip.

Please, let go.

You've got to let go.

Look at her eyes.

No, those voices aren't Hiram's. They are familiar, however. They're arguing over something in my handbag and whether they should knock me out or not. They're worried about the baron's son. They're afraid I might kill him. So am I.

Put it in water!

What's that supposed to do?

Just do it! Crack it first, you ninny.

Like air being sucked out of a room, or rather into one, I find myself back on the couch, falling to the cushions as Hiram pushes away from me. It takes me a full minute to gather my bearings. My skin still feels wet from the storm at sea.

"I . . . I'm so sorry, Hiram," I stammer, reaching for his hand. His body jilts me, so I fold my arms instead, and we both sit shivering for a moment before I turn to my friends, who all sit wide-eyed on the carpet next to a large bowl of water. Even Heck crouches on the floor, his hands gripping some kind of broken stone. The pieces are pretty, sort of rounded, with tiny sapphire flecks.

But I don't know what Heck would be doing wrinkling his trousers on a brothel room floor next to a bowl of water, holding broken shards of granite stones. My eyes drift to the floating yolk in the water.

Actually, yes, I do.

I lower my chin. "Heck, is that—"

"The magic egg you made for Javi?" he replies, glancing to his left. "Yes, but I told Penny you could make another."

"You . . . how did you know how to use it?"

Heck sits back on his forearms, a stunned expression settling on his face. "Penny told me."

Penny? Am I the only one who didn't know that everyone knew something more about me? And what's more, she knows the spells.

My head flapper pushes herself from the floor with the bowl in hand. "That's a story for another day, Miss Rose. But look. Somethin' bad was definitely here."

Shaking away my curiosity about Penny, I focus on the

concoction in her hands. The muculent egg whites have spread like slimy tendrils as the water separates them from the yolky center. The more they spread, the darker they turn, as though the bowl is filling up with slimy hair made of ash. The incantation continues to pull whatever seedy things are in the air tonight. *Finally*. While my plants should have kept the club from pandemonium, at least that dirt is good for something.

The dark strings float and swirl—just like the rat's tail. Before this party turned to hell.

My bones tremble beneath my skin. "Where's the floating mouse!"

"It's okay, kitten," Heck says, rushing to my side. "Nickels disposed of it before taking Charlie home."

"It was dead?"

"Likely stomped on in the fray. Foul thing."

As my breathing returns, Hiram pulls a flask from his jacket pocket, downing at least half the contents. A crude burp escapes his lips. "Now I recall."

"Recall what, exactly?" I ask.

"Why I didn't want to recall." Letting the last few drops drip from the flask onto his tongue, he then throws it to the carpet before folding his legs up to his chest. "I helped Celeste escape. In return, she took my memory of . . . of the night I lost my brother. I came back from the Great War as a ghost—the only survivor on a ship that sunk, and no one knows how."

"We're all deeply sorry to hear it," Heck says. "Was it the Germans?"

"We don't know what blew the manganese in the engine

room. I was . . . preoccupied just before the explosion. We capsized, and I lost Julius . . . I lost a lot of things that night."

As Hiram's face grows even emptier, my crew helps us both to our feet, and we agree to reconvene about this when we've had some rest.

"You need to be more careful, Miss Rose," Penny says, holding my hip to keep me steady while Doris grabs my hand-bag and coat. "It's a good thing you can trust this man, but you're not exactly blending in like you used to."

I scoff, leaning my head on her shoulder. "I can't fit another diamond or sequin on this getup."

"I can't believe I'm sayin' this, but more diamonds are not the solution."

"What's that supposed to mean?" I shoot a warning glance ahead of me at Heck, who's thankfully busy escorting our newest member to the stairwell. I don't need him chiming in. I'm outnumbered, and my legs are gelatinous.

"You bring too much negative attention to yourself by hating your station." Penny shakes her head as I protest. "No, you actively rebel against having an uptown image."

Doris pops a cigarette between her lips. "Yeah, you need class."

It doesn't even make sense to argue against their points. They're absolutely right. I love ritzy clothes but hate the kind of people who wear them.

But Heck wears them. And Hiram. And my friend Margaret. They even seem to enjoy their places in the world.

"All right, all right," I grumble on our way up the stairwell. "But I'm not having this baby."

6

IT'S ANOTHER BRISK MORNING AS I CLIMB THE STEPS OF MY mother's front porch. The metal bucket in my hand bangs against the door as I search for my key; it's too cold to wait for Gloria to decide to come to the door. Plus, this metal handle is pinching my fingers even through the gloves.

"Oh, good! You've brought it," my mother's voice sings from somewhere in the house. "It's too cold for porch sessions today, yes?"

Mamá Sunday is already smiling at me, patting the floral cushion beside her as I hang up my coat in the entryway. My abuela's housedress is buried beneath a crocheted blanket that she no doubt made herself. A fireplace full of burning applewood warms my aching fingers and lifts the dread I've been carrying for days.

"Abuela," I say, sneaking my legs beneath her blanket like

I'm five years old again, "I don't know what's wrong with this dirt. And I don't know what's wrong with me."

With storming in my eyes, I tell the matriarchs all about the fight that broke out in my club. The rats in the rum. Everything. I snot through several kerchiefs as I recount how I almost iced a couple of cops and got stuck in Hiram's mind. I admit how much my power scares me.

I blow my nose into a pattern of orange sunflowers. "I'm just trying to learn to defend myself with more than magic kisses. I know I can do so much more."

If I didn't keep messing it up.

"I have old plants you take for now," the old bruja says. "One helps with sleep. Now, let me see dirt." As she gums her bottom lip, I place the bucket on her lap, and her wrinkled palms turn the dark granules over and over again. "Extraña."

I lean over, hoping to capture her gaze. "Abuela, do you think you could let me, uh, take the book home?"

"You very powerful, but not ready for all, niña."

"But—"

"No magic today. I must examine dirt."

My heart sinks more than just a little. I would never press my sweet abuela. She's an expert in her field—a legend in our community. I doubt they'll ever regard me the same way. I can't say I blame them. They know what I'm capable of— and what I'm *not* capable of. They know who I am now. They just don't quite know who I'm not. But I'm certain I'm not a villain. *Right?* Can't tell that to the village of my past, though.

My dejected stare idles on the red and green tinsel that adorns the sitting room tree. The dreaded holiday will be here in a few days. The cruelest December our family can recount since the day my mother found out she was expecting me was on a Christmas Eve. My abuela held my screaming brother in her arms while his daddy took his last breath. The town of investors and mariachi players Javier's father came from told big stories of life in America. They left out the plague that would end his life.

La gripe. Spanish flu.

Whites blamed the Mexicans. And the Mexicans blamed the brujas.

One of my mother's savory meals slides onto the end table beside me. "The earth always answers, mija."

Yeah. Just always in the nick of time, though. I was hoping to be a few more steps ahead and far more advanced by now. And now abuela is telling me I need to wait. *Well, this is the bee's knees.* I can't even be trusted with the spell book.

"Thanks, Mamá, but I'm not hungry. I think I'll head to work."

Planting a kiss on my abuela's papery cheek, I leave her to dip her tongue into her hand, grinding the granules around her mouth. Gloria stares in bewilderment before following me to the door with a knitted shawl around her shoulders.

"Listen, Mamá," I say as she shoves a small fern into my hands, closing the door behind her. The chill of the front porch is like jumping into ice water compared to the warmth of the cozy fire inside. "Can't you talk to her about the book? I can practice from home and—how often does that Duesy show up on your street?"

Gloria tilts her head as we watch the red-trimmed wheels saunter down the road. "Ay, ay, ay, those ladies have been doubling their efforts from the Guadalupe Center. It must be one of them. They actually knocked on *my* door last week to offer assistance cooking what they call 'proper American meals.'" She pulls her shawl as tightly as her lips. "They can sooner take the brown from my skin. ¡Absurdo! There's nothing wrong with who we are."

Her knitted fabric reaches out, lifting my chin so that I can meet my mother's proud eyes. "Mija, perhaps there's nothing wrong with your blessed dirt. Perhaps it's precisely what you meant for it to be."

The cold and confusion furrow my brow.

She pinches her eyebrows back at me, almost sorrowful. "Bruja de maldiciones."

¿Qué? ¿Cómo? Did she just say—

"Curses, Mamá?" My hand pushes her shawl away. "You think that is my only gift—like the witches of the North?"

"Hardly! Wickedness is in *how* we use our gifts. You are nothing like those sorcerers."

My cheeks flush with hot shame. Those brujas may have provided the dirt I used to take down Moretti, but it was their dirt, not mine. Growing up, our house barely permitted talking about the sisters of destruction, much less seeking out their secluded shack on the outskirts of a small town only known for one nice hotel. I imagine Javier's journey there and back wasn't an easy one. He still doesn't speak much of it.

"Last summer," my mother continues, rolling her eyes as though my entire identity and destiny aren't being brought into question, "Abuela still had her powers to heal Javi and also Gio."

"Sí. So?"

"And you joined her in these spells, surrounded by blessed plants that Abuela made, no less."

"And you think she, what, borrowed my power like extra fuel to bring Javi back?"

How can my own mother be saying this? Surely, my abuela would have discerned if I wasn't a full bruja—or even worse, if all I was good for was destruction and divination.

The sad look is back on my mother's face. "Luna . . . who have you healed since Mamá Sunday lost her gifts?"

"I healed Javi of many headaches over the fall . . ." The ground threatens to tilt beneath me like Hiram's sinking ship. "Oh, Mamá. Is that what's wrong with him? Is that why Abuela lost her power? Was it all me?"

"I'm not saying you did anything at all. I just want you to be cautious."

My throat squeezes out an angry sob. "But Mamá, I can also charm!"

"All brujas can charm, niña." Gloria's brow pinches further. "You must now find a way through your perils without using magic until Abuela can properly train you. I fear someone could truly get hurt."

Could? Like Clip? What if something terrible happens to *him* now? Like those cops? Like the hoard of hooded men who tried to murder my brother? I want to throw myself into my mother's arms. But we're in public. I choose, instead, to straighten my face, squaring my shoulders back. There'll be time to cry later.

"Yes, Mamá."

I LEFT MY MOTHER'S HOUSE FEELING ALL BUT CONFIDENT IN who I am. Pendergast's cramped office on Main doesn't do anything to help the matter. Pulling my sweaty hand from one of my gloves, I give his meaty paw a firm shake. The quick exchange gives me very little to go on, but he doesn't seem upset about his paid law enforcement being strong-armed into silence. In fact, he doesn't seem to even be aware that it happened.

I know my mother said no magic. But I've never had issues with reading.

The former city councilman is punctual and quick about our meeting, commenting on my fur coat before handing me a small piece of card stock with some very concerning instructions.

"Hold the phone," I say. "You want Mr. Cattaneo to lead these drop-offs?"

"Whatever he did last time, keep that goin'." Pendergast leans back in his chair, folding his fingers over his belly like he doesn't know why I'm still here. "I know you didn't give the cops what they were hoping for, yet they backed down on their price even more. So yes, take your muscle with you, and don't ever tell me what happens. Fair and square?"

Mierda. There's nothing fair about it. Bribe a few cops—sure. Charm their socks off—that's just my game. But intimidation is way more than I signed on for. Again.

I don't even have to say it out loud. My face does it for me.

"Give me a break, Mrs. Kessler. You're in a squirrelly business," Pendergast says. "You know what affects my bottom line? Snitches." His smile lines deepen around his mouth. "And sinking land values. And guilty cops. I keep their salaries low so they'll take the money. They just like dinner and a show so they don't feel like criminals, most of them."

"So you thought I'd just trade their loyalty for a necking session in the back of their car?"

"Nah, I'm surprised you didn't slap 'em. They'd've gotten a kick out of it."

I'm glad I didn't sit down when I got here. I'd be leaping from my chair. "I'm surprised you gave such an assignment to an upper-class woman."

"You're a snake charmer," Pendergast says, his laugh mingling with a few coughs. "Since when was a lady bootlegger considered upper-class?"

"Since I married Heck Kessler."

"You shoulda sent him out to my car like I asked, then."

I shut my fuming mouth, flaring my nostrils at the glaring city councilman in the three-piece suit. I loathe that he's sort of right. I'm in the big leagues and I've got to pay my big-league dues. I'm also married to one of the richest heirs in our district, with one of the shadiest reputations. I have responsibilities to both identities. And I have to stop acting like such a rookie in all of my roles.

Pendergast and I bid each other a curt goodbye as I sail from the unassuming office of the most powerful man in Kansas City. I've never looked forward to frigid air more. Once the icy breeze hits my burning face, however, my nerves rev higher as a lanky man in rounded spectacles approaches. He shuts the red-trimmed door of his vehicle, then extends his gloved hand in a greeting. Since I can't read him, I see no reason for courtesy. This man has been on my case for days.

"Why have you been following me?"

His breath billows like fog around his mouth. "It's all fairly simple, Mrs. Kessler. That new name you carry is visiting questionable places with questionable people—a crooked councilman's office, speakeasies in the jazz district . . . wonder what I'll dig up next? Or you can just tell me what I'm searching for."

"So, you're an investigator."

"Investigative *journalist*," he snips, arching a condescending eyebrow. "Now answer me. Why do you spend so much time in that greaser neighborhood? Selling hooch to the immigrants? Or are you cozying up to that former bartender of yours? Rumor has it you were extremely close."

Damn. Penny and Doris were right. I have been way too obvious with my attitude and lifestyle.

"Oh, you mean my charity work at the Guadalupe Center?" I shoot back. "I've been sponsoring that family for a few years now." Straightening my posture in a way that would make Gloria beam, I saunter past the frowning journalist toward the parking lot. "A big-shot investigator like you should know that."

"Ah, then perhaps we can run a spotlight piece," he says, straightening his spectacles. "A recitation of the charitable works of House Kessler."

I give him a shrug, digging through my handbag for matches like I haven't brought the entire town to my front door. "Indeed, but don't take too long to schedule. It is the holidays, after all." Before he can say anything else, I have a smoke lit, bolting away to my Model T with a quick glance over my shoulder. "You know where to find me."

Ugh, what a rat. The guy wants to make his living looking for dirt on me. *Not gonna happen.* My driver already has the car running, holding the back passenger door open so I can slide in quickly. I'm thankful I didn't have Gio take me to this meeting. The sleuth's prying eyes are prying too closely—a bulldog with no bone to chew. I'll have to give him something to write about.

"I'M SO GLAD THE KESSLERS COULD PAY MY ROOM THE COURTESY of a visit in one way or another. The accommodations are more than sufficient."

Dorian's accent is just as twangy as Hiram's, but not in an apple-knocker kind of way. His baritone vibration is a mix of sticks and well-bred stock. That alone is enough to make me hate him. His curved smile and manicured hands finish the job.

Crossing one knee over the other, he slides his finger across the scar tissue in his ear. "So tell me what business brings you here. Or have I convinced you to run away with me after all?"

He chuckles at my deadpan stare. "Women like you are why men drink, you know."

His rudeness doesn't shock me, but I need to act like it does. "I beg your pardon?"

"Oh, come now, have a sherry with me. I've always wanted to share a drink with a snake charmer."

In front of the slow-burning hearth, the suited lumberman tips a golden liquid into the tiniest flute glasses I've ever seen. The fire crackle, glints of the flames lighting the smugness on his face. This isn't my den; it's his. And he knows it.

I made sure the investigator was on my tail as I checked my lip rouge before heading to Midtown. The keen lobby of the Hyde Park Hotel has me quite jealous, although the Casbah Lounge is just as glittery. Heck was fairly insulted when we learned the visiting barons chose the newer hotel for their holiday stay, but their presence in the city has brought us enough hassle without inviting the whole lot beyond our doorstep. So here I am visiting them. Dignified wives would normally have nothing to do with them at all—which is why I had my driver accompany me to shake suspicion.

I let him out on the second floor. Anyone posh enough to care saw him escort me in. The fact that I'm here is message enough to the man who's beginning to watch my every move. If that investigator wants to sniff around for something foul, he can set his sights on Dorian Luxberg.

My sights are certainly set on him.

"What do you want with my former bartender?"

"Again, with the immigrant?" Dorian's laugh is incredulous, sending my face burning. "Do you fancy him or something? Don't worry, gorgeous, I am neither judge nor jury. But I have to admit, it's rather disappointing."

"Have you ever worked a day in your life?"

"Cute." He sets my drink on the sofa table, eyeing my crossed legs before settling into the chair across from me.

"What's disappointing is your view on a professional woman," I say as he tilts the glass to his lips. "As you were quick to point out—I am a lady bootlegger. And the immigrant, as you call him, protected me on my way up."

"So you feel the need to reciprocate."

"I am responsible for his well-being."

Dorian's smirk darkens, his hair falling over his forehead as he props an elbow on his knee. I can only imagine how much he despises not having my brother to himself. "Does he know that?" The threat in his tone chills my neck. "Does he *want* that?"

Well, no. But that's none of Dorian's business. It doesn't take an investigative journalist to decipher the bad shape my brother is in. He's no match for these manipulators in his condition. He needs help—whether he wants it or not. At least, that's what I tell my guilt for even being here. I don't need Dorian spilling his yap about it either.

Letting the annoyance fall from my face, I decide to restructure my approach. Once again, I'm giving too much away. It's hard trying to get a read on a man without distracting him with a little allure. The spell has become one of Gio's favorite bedroom games, making him ravenous and desperate for me. My boyfriend made it clear as mud that I should use my abilities should I ever find myself in trouble.

I think that clause counts toward family as well.

Scooping the tiny glass from the table, I uncross my legs, watching Dorian's trailing gaze as I shimmy my dress in order to stand. "I'm sorry for my poor mood, Mr. Luxberg. I've become quite flushed."

"Oh, goodness," he says, rushing to help me to my feet. "Let's get you over to the window."

Perfecto. The window won't have a sofa table between us. And the window is close to the bed.

Again, guilt reverberates through my chest, but I shove it back down. This villain means to harm Javier. And this might be the only opportunity I have to get a solid read on Dorian. Gio said he would understand if I ever had to do something like this, but even if he doesn't, it's my brother I'm looking after. *Mi familia es todo.* Period.

Dorian is taller when he's not hunched and slurring over my dress. As predicted, he takes my hand, placing it over the frosted glass. "You were too close to the fire, it seems."

He's unsure of me. I have to stay vulnerable. Studying his fingers over mine, I relax my jaw so my lips can part. "That is something I'm known for."

"Is your drink too warm as well?"

"I'm not thirsty."

As he leans his face down along with his guard, his fruity breath hits my mouth. "You aren't the slightest bit curious what it tastes like?"

I've got to be careful about this. I promised my mother I wouldn't use magic. Surely she knows I meant the kind I haven't spent my whole life perfecting. My very bones are made of charm.

Mi familia es todo.

Dorian's forehead wrinkles. "Come again?"

I didn't mean to say it aloud, but as the icy pane stiffens my palm and Dorian's hand heats my knuckles, it doesn't matter. His tongue is now my prisoner, and so are his emotions. I don't want to enter his mind; that's too risky. I just want to feel him, hear his intentions. And he's full of them. The lumber heir is all want without giving thought to my feelings—or Javier's. Dorian sees him as a stray animal like the turtles the village boys used to torment down by the river when I was a girl. They would coax a turtle out of its shell with the skin of an orange, only to scare it back in again by tapping on its belly like a drum.

The same ridicule happened to Dorian. The woods are apparently a merciless place.

He wants to play a ruthless rhythm on Javier. His twisted fantasies bleed into pain. He'll start with hazing games—have the other guys make him crawl through the snow and call them princes. These barons' games are not underground politics. These men are miscreants in tailored suits. I feel no mercy toward the gasping heir as I impart instructions to fall to his knees.

Grabbing a fistful of his hair, I jerk his head back, and he gapes up at me, his chest rising and falling. Making him care for Javier would only last as long as my presence in this room, and I've already gone farther with my magic than I wanted to. If I took it all the way, I could make chorizo out of Dorian's brains. But I'm not a monster. I'm not like him.

The baron will become suspicious again if I leave him like this, however.

I press my fingertips to his scalp to finish what I started. Dorian's breath picks up speed, my mouth filling with the taste of rose and lavender before I bend down, pouring a spell of passion and desire past his lips. He drinks in my kiss, groaning, and his thoughts become savage until he finally slumps over. His light gasps land on the carpet next to a spilled flute that once held sherry.

Vanquishment and a regenerating disdain swell inside me. *Sieso.*

"That was . . . Rose, that was just—"

"That was just nothing," I say, crossing the room to the coatrack. "Just another man fantasizing about something he can't have."

"You are so very cruel to me."

"Do not harm my bartender."

A wicked grin crosses Dorian's face as he leans back on his hands. "Will you come to see me again? At the Christmas Gala, perhaps?"

"You won't want me to if anything happens to him." The heat in my chest climbs to my ears. I'll make this imp of a baron into a mute if he messes with my brother. I'll drain him of both tears and joy and turn him into an empty husk, but the only threat I can come up with to say out loud is, "I'll tell everyone you're responsible for this baby."

Dorian drops his head back with an eye-rolling sigh. "There's hardly a need for such derision. No harm will come to your beloved Javier."

I don't believe him. He's all hopped up on charm spells, but hopefully, I loaded him with enough harmony to buy some time for my brother to realize what kind of predator he's dealing with.

"You wouldn't really pin your condition on me, would you?" Dorian's lazy drawl calls after me. "I figured a girl with one on the way would be the most discreet among scandal-mates."

I flatten the curved brim of my hat over my ears as I crack open the door to the hotel hallway. "Do I seem like someone who cares about her reputation?"

The closing door cuts off the view of his slumped body, and I vow to wash my mouth out with moonshine and a pack of Camels.

7

HECK HAS NEVER LIVED IN A HOUSE WITHOUT A DRAWING room. I've never lived in a house with one. And now that I do, I rarely breach the threshold of Heck Kessler's leather-adorned whiskey sanctuary and all that is man. Today, however, I have debutante lessons to attend to.

The two boys in the Winston chairs clink their glasses together in front of an empty fireplace. The temperature outside has finally risen to a balmy forty-seven, so there's no need to roast our faces during such a crucial meeting.

"You realize this space is just another one of your studies without the desk," I interject into their joviality.

Heck swings his pin-striped leg over his knee. "Kitten, you might not like having more rooms than you need, but you *must* convince your peers that you like them."

"I daresay," Hiram says with a raise of his glass, "act as though you deserve them."

I dread to ask, but I do. "And why is that?"

"Because we are rich."

He and Heck have another good laugh at my scowl, exchanging golf game numbers and the best place to acquire heel ointment. I glance at my wristwatch, wishing Heck would let me smoke in the house. He should if he's going to make me sit through his dissertation on the importance of posture.

"Oh, we're boring her," Hiram says. "I almost thought to bring my wife this time."

My eyebrow raises at the idea of Mrs. Mustache regaling us with stories of the Bootheel of Missouri. I hope Hiram's not the type of husband to leave his doting wife in a quiet house far from real civilization while he gallivants to the big city once a year. I've had a lifetime of dealings with traveling businessmen with itches to scratch. I thought he was a better spud than that, and I'm surprised at how disappointed I am to find out he might not be.

"Bring her?" I snort, spinning the ring on my finger. "You rarely mention her."

"That is not by happenstance." The young baron smooths the closely shaved sides of his head, darting his eyes around like he's got a secret. "Much like you two, she is my best friend. Unlike you two, she is also my lover. We give each other the space we need for our inclinations—marriage is a lifelong commitment, after all. I only wish I could provide her and our son with a better provider."

The confession is anticlimactic, given the information I gleaned from my walk through his memory. And the way he's been openly flirting with Heck for the past hour.

"But you are rich," I tease, my smile falling at his melancholy.

"Only at my father's bidding."

Even his mustache is sad. *Damn.* I always looked at wealth as the path to my freedom. Hiram speaks as though it were a vice.

"Which is why," he says, perking back up again, "you must heed my guidance. Your husband can teach you to discourse, rave over the art hanging from these walls and where to find peaty scotch. But I can teach you how to feign interest."

Heck gasps, holding his tumbler to his chest. "You said you liked peaty scotch."

"I do. But she doesn't."

I'm going to need my own drink if I have to ever know what "peaty" means. Maybe if they keep their glasses full, I can avoid being talked to altogether.

True to its name, and with the help of a little more liquor, the drawing room shelves our itinerary for the day and, instead, evokes pre- and postwar stories from Hiram that make me wonder how he's ever able to smile at all.

"Of course, my father sent me to Virginia boarding schools since I was a boy," he confesses, Heck nodding in understanding. "He wanted to instill me with Southern pride. All I saw there was Southern shame."

I may not understand the way Heck does, but I get the idea that their childhoods were not as rich as mine and Javier's in regard to tolerance and identity. My mother accepted my brother's attraction to other boys, although she taught him well how to be true to himself within a society that was not so accepting. The wealthy gentlemen in front of me, however, lacked the basic protection every child needs—love.

I do my best to follow along as they swap horrifying memories of torment shrouded in delighted tones of irony.

Heck beats the suede arm of his chair. "Oh, oh, oh! Did they ever try the electric heat baths on you? They are *harrowing* this time of year."

"I'd take another dip in a claw-foot tub with a lamp any time of year over one of those sickening milk diets."

"How about hypnotism?"

"Clamps and machines were more my father's savvy."

Seeing my falling face, Heck beckons me from a sofa apparently made for fainting and then to his lap. This safe place in his arms is just that—a safe place. A respite we can run to when we're feeling grummy without the nagging expectation of sex or catching feelings. I do find him handsome. But it's his soul that I love.

The way he lays my cheek on his shoulder and gives my head a motherly pat makes me giggle. "Now, now, kitten. All of that is behind us."

Maybe so. But my stomach twists anyway. I nuzzle my nose just beneath his jaw, refusing to tap into his feelings. Whatever he's recalling, I don't want to see it. I wish he never had to.

"Oh," I say, tucking my toes between the arm of the chair and his thigh, "I'm just sad because I'm the only one in the room without hysterical nerves disorder."

His lips press to my forehead, his nose laughing into my hair. "You're still young, my darling. We've always time for a traumatic finish."

"I shall drink to that," Hiram says, refilling their glasses as I drift off to their bubbly conversations about insomnia and paralysis and other ways the world tried to kill them yet did not succeed.

. . .

AS HIRAM'S ROLLS-ROYCE MEANDERS DOWN OUR DRIVEWAY past an incoming taxicab, Heck and I wave and smile from our front porch like Scott and Zelda Fitzgerald. The king and queen of flappers keep their modernness sophisticated. And I intend to do the same.

Brief domestic tranquility is shattered when a car door slams, and a familiar voice gabs about the storm that's coming. It feels hard to believe, given the dripping icicles along the portico. Fur coats aren't needed today. Instead, I've chosen a long jacket in the same pattern as my skirt to honor my acquiescence to my title. The wide pillars and the cover over our heads provide the perfect hideout to meet an ornery rum-runner playing the part of my driver.

A pair of eyes, my favorite shade of sable, approach from the side parking corral. The way he blows his smoke always makes my heart skip a bit.

"One would think you've plans to devour him, the way you're biting your lip," Heck muses while picking lint from his tie. "We can always send him to . . . repair the fireplace in the master suite if you need some warming up."

"The staff won't buy it. Gio's no good at masonry."

"We'll *make* him good at masonry."

My boyfriend jogs to Heck's side with a handshake and a "Hey there, boss!" and then bows toward me with his cap pressed to his T-shirt. "Lady boss."

Charcoal fringe falls over the twinkle in his eye. We hold each other's gaze for about two seconds before he breaks.

"C'mere!"

The potted evergreens muffle my light shriek as he spins me around, shielding our kiss beneath the wool beret I've got on today.

"Look at this swanky getup," he says to my hat, my laughter sputtering from my chest as he messes with the decorative flower pinned there. It's been a while since I've donned a genuine smile. "You could run for president in these threads. Own the whole damn town."

"Yeah, president of bridge club, maybe."

His thumb pinches my dimple. "Hey, I'd vote for ya—if that's what you wanted. But somethin' tells me you're made for bigger things." Taking my hands, he curls my fingers over his suspenders, his nose leaning just under the giant flower. "But tell me my flapper girl's still unda' there somewhere."

¡Ay, guapo! I'll show this piano player exactly what I've got under this frock.

"How do you feel about masonry?"

"*Ahem.*"

Gio and I turn to the tight-lipped investor with the ruby cuff links. Heck looks as bored as I felt during his and Hiram's earlier conversation on croquet strategies. "I hate to interrupt your caller's hat-whispering, but we have urgent matters to discuss, and also, I am still standing here."

"Oh, gimme a break," Gio says as he pulls me closer. "How many times did we have to watch Javi pry your hands from his buttons when you've had a few too many?"

Heck's face turns as red as a cardinal in the snow, although his eyes drift off in what is certainly a shining memory. The man isn't known for shyness in acts of affection . . . or anything else. His lashes flutter, blinking back a mistiness that steals at my joy, but I'm content to let it go. I'm worried about Javier too.

"You couldn't get him to go, huh?" Gio asks, pulling my back to him so he can rest his head on my shoulder. Only Heck's forlorn headshake answers back. "Yeah, well, I got guys digging up the flower beds around the parking lot to replace that dirt he spread around, but the almanac's callin' for a six-foota'. I also had the inside plants removed, 'cept the ones Mamá Sunday gave him."

Heck dots his nose with a handkerchief. "Did you see him? Did he talk to you?"

"Sorry, bank's closed on that. He acts like I stole his pomade or somethin'."

"I've been trying to get him to stay with us for *weeks* now," Heck says, setting a course for the next closest pillar. His pacing is usually comical, sometimes downright annoying, but all I want to do is wrap my arms around him so we can both cry. "I told him the dirt might be contaminated, but then he says he's not even been home much lately. To that, I can't say I'm not concerned."

The barons. Heck's loafers tap against the pavement as they journey. He's right to be unsettled. Dorian and his lions are lying in wait at this point; they can't wait to play with their new mouse.

"Come on, Kess," Gio calls out to the third pillar. "Javi is nuts for you. You know that. He prolly just don't want people he cares about seein' this side of him. These new guys—he can put it away for a while cuz no one's there to make him face it." Heck pauses, his fists unclenching by his hips. Gio continues, his tone steady. "He loves you. That's why he don't wanna see you."

That sounds like typical Javier. He's as proud as our mother and just as stubborn. He might not want anyone seeing him in such a condition, but he might not have a choice.

Another pillar becomes Heck's destination as he recovers his straightened back. His business face signals the end of his quest around the porch. "I trust him completely. And we *will* find a way to bring him home to heal."

His exit is quiet. The entryway door closes just as solemnly.

I tug my boyfriend's arms around me with a sigh. "It's them I don't trust—the barons."

"Hear! Hear!" His breath comforts my ear. "Did you tell hubs about that jerkface's thoughts about Javi?"

My sigh turns into a groan. "I couldn't do it. He'd go through the rafters and then go after Dorian, which could send my brother right to them. Javi is . . . fragile. Like something in him is close to breaking in a bad way. Thing is, now that I know Dorian's plans, I don't know what to do with them."

"You know, I, uh, won't ask how you got them."

Unhinging myself from his embrace, I spin my burning cheeks around to face my wincing boyfriend. "You said you didn't want to know!"

"That's cuz I believe everything you do, you try to do for the right reason. And ain't that the point of it?" His gaze studies the braided trim of my jacket. Chanel isn't that fascinating. Gio finally shakes his head with a short laugh that sounds more like a sob he's trying to swallow. "I ain't lettin' go of someone like you. Not eva'."

"Gio—"

"Hey, *I'd* sleep with Dorian to save Javi."

"I didn't sleep with him. I—"

Gio's hands fly up in surrender, his eyes squeezed shut. "Good enough. Let's, uh—" Spotting something around the patio furniture, my boyfriend scoops it up from the chair.

"Look at this, huh? I been collectin' these circulars cuz they remind me of you, what with how you helped her write her first article. They got real news too."

Good grief, this man. As the piano player reads me an article on book recommendations for newlywed couples, the corners of my lips rise in a teary-eyed smile. He was always too good for jails and circuses.

"Speakin' of real issues," he says, tapping the rolled-up newsletter to my nose, "I mighta already did the drop."

My mouth does just that. *From the instructions I was given?* He did *what*? Pendergast wanted us both to go. Even though I can handle myself.

"You . . . you're afraid I'm gonna freeze people's legs off."

"Hey, I know you got plans with Penny this afternoon," he says, trying to shake the tension from my shoulders. "Also, that dick's been tailin' us. Plus, I thought you might be busy today gettin' classy and all." He gives my flower a playful tug. "I was right."

He's sweet, but I'm still mad. The man who runs the city is testing me with that list. I want the opportunity to find the best way to come out strong without giving anything away. I can't *have* that opportunity if my boyfriend swoops in and takes it from me, even if he is going for chivalry.

"You should have at least called. Those assignments were given to *me*."

Gio's thumbs clamp down on my shoulders. The circular crunches against my sleeve. It doesn't hurt, but I pull my head back at the hardness of his jaw. "Pendergast don't know what he's askin'—sendin' me to do the muscle while you do the skirtin'. No way in hell, Rose."

"That's not how this works. How did you plan on doing this without me?"

"I'm a fighta'. I don't want you worryin' about it, baby."

Don't worry? Baby? Since when did Gio become Rudolph Valentino? Piano players may be dramatic, but I've never seen him so worked up before.

"Listen," he says, his face softening as he sets my arms free to fiddle with that damn paper. "Pendergast also made me an offer. A day job kinda thing. Insteada' just cops, I visit businesses to give 'em quotes on new concrete. Quick drops without the law thinkin' they can feel up my girlfriend."

My evening with Dorian weighs with the return of guilt in my stomach. The breeze picks up, but my hat is safely molded to my head. *Wool was a good pick.* Heck's array of evergreens sway around the porch's edge, and I suddenly find our shoes interesting. All I can think to say without crying out in frustration is, "Is that what this is about?"

"No, look." When Gio pinches the bridge of his nose, he's gotta be counting to ten. "It's somethin' I can do to legitimize my image, all right?"

"Since when do we care about image?"

Gio's exasperation has his hands gesturing to the pillars like they're in agreement. "I mean, who knows? One day, you and Heck might lose the handcuffs and, I don't know, divorce. And I wouldn't mind bein' the guy who scoops you up while you're out on parole, but I ain't neva' gonna be accepted into the crystal-glass class as a tattooed, rum-runnin' jerk."

Again, sweet. Again, still mad. I just wish he would have talked to me. The wind slips under my jacket, and I pull it tight to keep myself from floating away.

"I'm still your boss, Mr. Cattaneo."

"Then go, Mrs. Kessler." My boyfriend cranes his head around before giving me a quick peck on the forehead. "Quick, before someone sees you."

He darts toward the car corral with his hands shoved in his pockets like the guys at Giuseppe's table who wagered a bet they couldn't cash. The touch from Gio's lips was so fast; he didn't think I could read his arrangements for this evening. *I'm still your boss, Mr. Cattaneo.* I might want to pin him to his mattress, but I'm still his boss.

"I BELIEVE THESE TREES HAVE MAGIC OF THEIR OWN," PENNY says while pinching her corners of the quilt we're wrestling to the ground. It's warmer today, but the occasional gusts tell me something is coming. The long willow branches surrounding us lift their tendrils to the east, and then they fall again.

The Blue River is singsongy in the afternoon shadows. Penny has a great instinct for hideaways and ducking for cover. Unlike me, there are parts of town she's not allowed to frequent. Javier, Clip, Penny—hiding in plain sight isn't an option for them like it is for me. She said I need to learn to shake reporters and cops, even admirers, off my tail. Her plan to switch cars in a few back alleys after exiting Columbia Phonograph Company's basement and a few other record stores was brilliant. We had to head to Midtown to send off a package anyway—or so the investigator thought. He'll be parked outside Western Union for a while.

Putting twenty miles between us and Midtown, Penny and I headed to a secluded riverbank with a row of weeping willows to shade us from prying eyes. Being so close to the running water, I can feel the plant roots beneath the ground. They want me to call to them so they may tell me earth secrets. If I hadn't endangered so many people lately, I would. As much as I hate getting my hands dirty, I begin to miss the scent of herbs lingering on my fingernails after I've gathered a bundle in the greenhouse.

Using our handbaskets to weigh our quilt down, Penny and I soon settle in to take advantage of temperatures we likely won't be seeing for a while. Once Missouri turns cold, it stays cold. Tamales and a small variety of fruit and nuts make up our spread. Penny was even able to find a pomegranate.

"Merry Christmas," she says, slicing it down the middle with a grin. She hands me half, exchanging it for one of my masa-wrapped delicacies. They're still warm from Mamá's kitchen.

My nails dig for the tiny seeds, popping them into my mouth once I set them free. The juicy crunch has me smiling as well. Penny bites into her offering, the corn husk falling to her lap, and she swears about wearing a satin jacket to a picnic. With the breeze and the willow floating around her, I think it makes her look divine—like a fashioned flapper goddess with knowing eyes.

"Why do we have to work twice as hard?" I ask the dead grass in front of my toes.

Penny lets out a grunt, shaking her head. "Sex and booze, Miss Rose. Businesses run by men are full of peacocks who don't know what to make of strong women. They don't like their feathers plucked."

"Well, I wish they'd find something else to peacock about."

Gio's earlier outburst almost spoils the sweetness of the pomegranate. We removed all plants from his apartment, leaving behind a single fern from my abuela. The truth is, he's got me more worried than angry. Gio is a spirited man full of music and adventure, with more potential than most guys put together. He's making a way for himself and not because I'm sleeping with him. He doesn't see what I see. He doesn't understand. I'm already proud to be with him, just as he is.

Because of who he is.

Penny and I rest in the quiet of our chewing and the trickling of the river down the ravine. There's so much I want to tell her, confide in her, but I've never been the best at having girlfriends. Or any friends. This year has held a lot of firsts for me.

"I, um, think I plucked a few of Gio's feathers."

"Nah," Penny says, "just ruffled them a bit. Don't pay any mind to musicians. They're spittin' mad one day and writing love songs the next."

"I guess, I guess."

It feels good to giggle over guys. The custom I'd long criticized isn't so bad after all. But they've also taken up enough real estate today. There's something more pressing than Gio's ego that I've been dying to ask Penny about.

"So . . . are you a bruja, too?"

It makes sense. She knew what to do with my charmed egg.

"Goodness, no." The satin goddess picks at her masa with a laugh. "I've just seen some things—things folks shouldn't naturally be able to do. This world is full of the unexplainable. In every culture."

Instead of expounding on that, my head flapper stares

at the swaying branches of the tree with the dancing hair. She won't break the trust of whoever she's talking about. She won't break mine either.

"I'm thinking of going to the witches in the North," I blurt out before I can rein myself back in. She's the only soul I've told. Even with the covering of willows and miles of countryside, I feel as though I've told the whole world.

Penny pats the pleated cap around her head; the turban style is modern yet modest, even with the glittering brooch in the front. "You want me to go with you? How far north are we talkin'?"

On the other side of the Missouri River, a grove of hedge trees soaks its roots into the soggy ground where my family and I sat stupefied on the flooded banks . . . after the screams of the hooded men subsided. Heck used to flinch in his sleep after that night. When I'd wake him, he'd say he felt like he was drowning. It took a long time for him to sleep in his own quarters after that. *Or maybe that was me.*

"Too far north," I say, holding a half-eaten fruit in my lap. "Javi went there for me once."

"Protecting you like always."

"Yeah." A long sigh empties my lungs. The fresh air feels nice. "I wanted to protect *him* this time. Now, I don't know if I even can."

Penny's long legs push out in front of her as she grunts with a hearty stretch. Taking me by the hand, she tugs my back to the quilt, so we're facing the lazy sky. "It's okay to be scared of what you've got. I used to be the same way. I'm black. I'm smart. I fill out my dresses. And I enjoy exploiting the weaknesses of bad men. But my worst crime—I have a special place in my heart for women. You know this."

A fair amount of pride and determination runs into my palm from hers. She could serve jail time or worse for her bedroom activities alone, and with skin as dark as hers, they'd maim her—if she was lucky. But she's not afraid to die.

She's afraid of dying under someone's heel.

"They tell me my gifts are wicked," she says, just above a whisper. "But then again, they don't know what wickedness is."

My stupid lip begins to tremble. "But how do *we* know what's wicked?"

"My former suitor tryin' to burn my hair to the scalp for kissing a waitress—that's wicked. Knocking him in the head with a trumpet—that's not."

I shudder at the thought and the dropping temperature in the air. It's a well-known story in our club of misfits. Penny's survival of a sixteen-year pursuit by a man who wouldn't take no for an answer ended her employment as a nurse—and nearly her life. Fraught with pride and injury, the man reported her at the hospital as a whore who tried to bribe him for sex. Of course, she wasn't believed—if she hadn't been black, she was still a woman, and neither of those helped give her any credibility. Instead of collapsing, though, she rose beyond it—she calls it her phoenix-rising origin story. She left that dank hospital run by white men with drifting hands and made a life for herself. And a damn good one at that.

But I don't feel like a phoenix full of fire and determination. I'm more like the sun wishing to play with Icarus. My head shakes with the same deflated notion—I'm in way over my head. "That seems too simple. You were defending yourself."

"Intention, Miss Rose, *is* simple. It's so damn simple." Penny's teeth shine as she grins, a grin so wide she shuts her eyes. I've never heard my head flapper sing, but as the melody floats through her thoughts, then out of her mouth, I wonder why she doesn't more often.

> *Make my enemies my footstool*
> *Pull them deep into the ground*
> *Muffle the words over their tongues*
> *So they'll never make a sound*

As haunting as my mother's songs, the melody runs through my bones, my magic creeping to my skin. The roots beneath this weeping tree appeal the hiatus of my power. Brujería is a part of the earth as much as it's a part of me. *Simbiótica.*

With our fingers interlaced, Penny and I are one in a rising hope that she shares with me. The wind carries her song away as an unearthed treasure, delighted in the richness as it dances over the rocky bank. It's a blessing to have friends who will sing for me. And fight for me. And who don't want to sell me to the circus.

"We're not wicked," she says after a while. "We're powerful. Evil is a heart issue."

She's not wrong. I have hurt—even killed—to save my loved ones. And I would do it again if I had to. I just don't want destruction to be all I'm good for.

"You just don't know what you got yet. That's all. But your friends do. I do. And I'm certain the earth does as well.

"Intention is everything."

Exhaling fresh air from my lungs for once, I take in Penny's words and let the cardinals on the branches chirp their troubles for a while.

· · ·

TOOTLING PAST THE ROWS OF GLITTERING BUSINESSES WITH miniature evergreens decorating the outside of the storefronts, I all but ignore the strings of lights along the Plaza. The shopping district boasts Spanish architecture and brick-inlaid walkways, but my car is gunning for one retailer—Suydam Decorating Company. Heck ordered enough "statement mirrors" to keep the place running for a year. And he's not their only lofty patron. High-end furniture clearly has as much say in this city as political advertisements.

And Pendergast wants their pledge of loyalty. Well, he wants the entire shopping district, but he's having me start here.

Pulling my Model T up to a curbside thick with Christmas cheer, I stroll past a holly-covered pole passing as a streetlamp and head into the den of an inconspicuous adversary with a skip in my step. I want to get this over with to show Pendergast I can play in the big leagues. And I want to do it before Gio gets here.

He's gonna get an earful for planning to do this without me. But I've got to focus on the task at hand.

Sure, they may not be quintessentially "bad" people, but I have to give myself a good reason to bribe or threaten them to comply with the bootlegging climate our former city councilman has lied so hard to achieve. Those of us in the underworld understand this arrangement. We weren't all born with the privilege given to the store owner, who is now staring down at me with a wrinkled nose.

I laid out this skirt and jacket just for this occasion. But my ensemble smells like nature and pomegranates. I thought I was sneaky. I thought I was ready. I was going to waltz in here like the big name I am and start making my way in this town—with or without the magic.

My waltz turns into an unsure sashay as I realize I'll need to tap into the charm Heck was trying to teach me in his leather enclave. I can't use my impartation or anything else here. I doubt this store owner would be as grateful as Dorian for my . . . gifts.

Arranging a set of fabrics, the squinting store owner adjusts his spectacles at my approach. "Mrs. Kessler, delighted as always. However, your husband's order hasn't yet shipped, as I already told your employee earlier today."

"Oh, that's okay. I'm not—did you say 'my employee'?"

Giovanni, you son of a . . .

"Yes," the store owner continues, scribbling some notes next to the suede samples on the counter. "That inked ruffian you call a driver was here already, and I told him I would be contacting his employer about his unseemly proposal."

"Mr. Ballard, I am so sorry—"

"Hm, yes, he apologized as well. This is not how we do business here, Mrs. Kessler. My family and I will not be coerced, threatened, or otherwise. As if Pendergast thought he could bribe a hallmark family of this city."

Ruined. Gio ruined our first assignment on that list. These are delicate matters. The police were one thing, but stuffy upper-class men are a whole different world with different rules. They've even got rules for what forks to use at the dinner table and what kind of glasses they drink their booze out of. These business owners aren't so easily bought. I'm just relieved he didn't take to roughing them up; then, we'd have to bribe them, *and* the cops, who would surely be called.

I straighten my overcoat, keeping my tone as light as my expression. "Mr. Ballard, we would never send our driver to discuss our politics on our behalf. That financial offering was meant to be a pledge of support that we'd hoped to present over coffee and brunch. Rest assured, the employee was supposed to drop off an order."

Behind me, the doorbell chimes, and an older couple shuffle in, rubbing their hands together and chuckling about their windblown hair. Mr. Ballard greets them and sends them off to meander through the selection of rolltop desks before leaning across the counter with a pointed look in his eyes. "Is there anything else I can do for you today, Mrs. Kessler, or shall I call your husband about your behavior as well?"

Heat climbs to my ears. I've been working with Heck on what he calls my "judgment problem" with wealthy people. It's not my fault every single darb I meet falls right into my expectations. As the door dings again, I give a nod to another set of shoppers, the frost on the edge of the display window catching my eye. *Dammit.* It's time to calm down and re-strategize before I freeze the spectacles to this guy's face.

"Oh, don't look so panicked, Mrs. Kessler," the store owner says. "My wife and I understand you're still learning the ways of civilized city life. God knows the environment you were used to at that old hole in the ground they called a club—the jazz district, no less."

I could give his entire body frostbite, starting with his tongue. I bite mine instead.

"How about we call this one a fold and pretend today never happened?"

"I, uh, of course," I say, gripping the strap to my handbag in a hurried turn for the door.

"Tell your husband thank you for the fennel."

"I will, I—" My heels glue themselves to the carpet. "The fennel?"

Mr. Ballard points his pen to his left. "Yes, the one your driver left. We'll have it with trout once the season comes."

The store owner frowns as I rush back toward the cash register. Next to it sits a wiry herb in a rounded pot. *Gio, you didn't.* My thumbs brush the tiny sprigs, my power searching down into its roots. A subtle yet familiar spell answers back. It was cast for good luck—one of many around the Kessler mansion. While my new home is adorned with plenty of my abuela's blessed plants from my old apartment, I had Gio dispose of any new cuttings I made. That's what he was supposed to be doing today. Not this.

I can't let this stay here. It could do the opposite of what it was intended to do. Bad luck could sink this business. A sunken business could make a store owner desperate. It's a smart plan . . . for a villain. I won't use my magic this way.

"I'm sorry, Mr. Ballard, but this gift was given by mistake."

"Mrs. Kessler, I was attempting formality and kindness—"

"You cannot have this plant!"

Several heads turn in our direction, their whispers giving the kind of attention the store owner clearly does not enjoy. He promptly whisks the potted plant away, then tucks it beneath the counter. His spectacles resurface with a renewed scowl. "Will that be *all*, Mrs. Kessler?"

"I mean, I . . ." Shifting on my feet, I scan the stares around the room as well as the crystals forming across the window. "Yes, I . . . I think so."

"I should think so."

The doorbell signals my exit and growing frustration.

The wind slaps my face like I'm the one who did something wrong. My jacket is no longer warm enough. My relationships, my career, my magic—they're no longer safe enough. Not from me. I have so many questions about who I really am.

It's time to find the brujas who can answer them for me.

8

"GIO, WHAT THE HELL DID YOU DO TO THOSE STORE OWNERS?" The door to the drawing room shakes, although it took me both hands to shove it with enough force.

My boyfriend flinches at the rattling door panels. "My job. Jesus, why don't you break the door down?"

"That's *not* how we do things."

"I'm a criminal. I break the damn law. Now you wanna tell me how to break it?"

Heck sighs, lighting a candle on the sofa table as the chandelier flickers. The howling wind beats against the grand window, threatening to throw us all in the dark if it doesn't let up.

"I'm delighted to interrupt whatever this is," he says, "because the fourth party to our bootlegging quartet has yet to show on the eve prior to the most important acquisition gala of the year."

That does simmer down the glares Gio and I are sharing. Javier is rarely late to a team meeting, especially one so important. All four of us have fronted enough money to cover the liquor orders that were damaged in shipment by those deranged rats. We found boxes of them at all of our clubs. Not that my brother was involved in the inventory counts. Acquiring contracts with the barons will not only cover those shipments but will secure enough orders to get us through the year—under the guise of Kessler land developments, of course.

Gio makes for his jacket pocket with a shrug; it's even cold enough for him to have his sleeves rolled down. "I guess we keep track'a the orders without him. Divide and disperse and settle up later."

"He'll be here," I say, cocking my jaw. "We're waiting."

"Oh, that's right, cuz you're the boss."

"You bet I am."

What is this ego *on him lately?* He hasn't disrespected me like this since we first met, and even then, it was just to get my attention. He's not going to like the attention I'm getting ready to give him now.

Heck's sigh sounds more like a whine as he plops onto the arm of an overstuffed chair. "I miss arguing." The mist forming on his lower eyelids cools my ears a bit. As much as I miss Javier, I can only imagine how Heck must long for him. I'm upset with Gio—enraged even. But at least I can look him in the eye and say so.

"I'm jealous of the barons," Heck says softly. He dashes away a falling tear with his eyes on the crackling fireplace. "I'm not stupid. I know their allure and their prestige and how he's always wanted to make a way for himself."

"Heck . . ." I don't know what else to say. Javier was the most faithful, gentlest man I knew before Heck came dancing into our lives. The two met like a flame met a candle, and they've burned together ever since. My brother's not the kind of man to throw something like that away.

Heck lifts a dismissive hand as if lowering my unspoken words to the ground. "I like to think I hold up fairly well—I've spent a lifetime performing. But the truth is, I'm devastated." Another tear makes its way down his splotchy cheek before he dabs his eyes with a handkerchief. "Anyway, we'll have them tied up for the next week for business, and they'll be gone by the new year."

Gio leans against the wall with his arms crossed. "It's okay to be angry, Kess."

Sliding his hands to brace against his knees, Heck looks up from the fire, his eyes streaked with redness and pain. "I can forgive almost anything."

Muffled voices beyond the drawing room give way to a startled shout as the door is swung open by the man who swept Heck off his feet six months ago.

"Sir, he would not allow us to announce him, and he's—"

"That's all right, Timothy," Heck says, rushing to his feet. "Please close the door behind you." His wing-tips click across the hardwood. "Javi, I thought your automobile had been tipped over by this ghastly weather, or perhaps you were laid out hungover in your nightclub. Lord knows I don't have time to drive to Eighteenth and Vine to sober you up when you *know* we're packing for Excelsior—"

Heck's shoes and expression soften as he reaches the carpet, which stains from sage to red with each drip from Javier's fingers. Suspenders hang from his hips. Erratic breathing sputters from his mouth. The dawning hits us all at once.

"Gio," I spurt out, "grab the auto kit."

"No need!" Heck calls to him. "There's one in the humidor."

Gio returns from the cigar cabinet with a tin box in his hand, the Band-Aid label without a scratch on it. It's never had to be used, so hopefully, there's plenty of gauze and antiseptic to patch the gash on Javier's arm. My brother's shocked frame is led to the fainting couch, where Heck and Gio work quickly to cut away his sleeve. The crimson-soaked fabric falls to their ankles, and the piano player is chosen to suture on account of his deft hands. The velvet cushions are smeared by the tossed cotton balls almost as much as Heck as he slides down behind my brother, holding Javier's face to his chest.

As Javier weeps into his boyfriend's tie, Heck shushes and sings their calming song, his fingers combing through raven hair.

The medical kit snaps shut. "Okay, I know you don't wanna say nothin', Jav, but if you're too juiced to talk, Rose can read ya if you want."

My brother moans bitterly as he clings to Heck's shirt-sleeve. Touching the tip of my finger to his pinkie, I jump in behind his eyes, scanning his thoughts for anything he'll allow me to see without pushing. The first sign of resistance, I'm out of here. I can't get stuck here as I did with Hiram.

Beyond the blackness of a blindfold, Dorian's distant laughter becomes the sound of several henchmen from a long time ago. Moretti's teeth gleam like the trim of his car. Water splashes around my calves. The hooded men pray.

"Enough, Luna."

At the echo of my brother's voice, I pull back, but a flash of scarlet follows me like a rising red sun. Almost. I want to know what it is that has Javier's heart thumping. But I have to make a break for it. In the shrinking horizon, and wearing the sunrise itself, a woman with stringy hair hunches over, her skin thick and coarse as oak wood. As she begins to stand, her ragged appearance turns soft—save for her hardened gaze when she notices my escape. The horizon lunges after me with gaping teeth, and Javier's eyes close me out, leaving us both gasping in the candlelit room.

None of it connects to the blood all over him. I shake my head at Gio. *I tried.*

"All right . . . Jav," my boyfriend says more gently than I've ever heard him. "You gotta tell us what happened tonight."

I lower myself to the coffee table as Javier takes several deep breaths, keeping his eyes squeezed shut. "They . . . they wanted to use my business to funnel money. I was gonna make a lot on the back end. I was—I was . . . training for liaison positions in their network—kinda like what Leone Salvatore did for . . . for Pendergast."

Did they? Sounds like Missouri's Bootheel has a bigger moonshine game than they're letting on.

"Take your time, darling," Heck whispers against my brother's damp forehead.

"Like, finally, someone sees my success," Javier continues more slowly. "Sees what I'm capable of, and he's promising the whole damn world. I should've known I wasn't anybody. Then he starts getting hopped up on this powder." My brother flinches at whatever's behind his eyelids. "I knew what it was. He wanted me to do it too. Called it initiation into the big times. It wasn't a request, you know?"

Gio's eyes widen at me while Heck's face remains set as stone toward the hearth. Even as a distributor in the illegal market myself, I'm still jolted. My house never had a need for an opium powder prescription. We had a healer in our home. I'm not judging the use of such a potent painkiller. I'm not loving it either. There's a reason its use is more regulated than it used to be.

"After that," Javier says, "he brings out this blindfold. Starts slapping me around. Calling me a greaser and tells me if I catch him, I get to stay and become one of them. That's when he tried to tie my hands . . . and you know I can't . . . Luna, I . . ." He grits his teeth, wet drops spilling from his eyes that pop open wide as two full moons. "I always keep a blade on my thigh."

"Javi," I cry through the hand I have clapped over my mouth.

Gio grabs the edge of the couch like the earth is rocking. "What does that mean, Jav?"

Burying his sobs into Heck's jacket, he pulls his legs up to his elbows, repeating the muffled confession, "I always keep a blade on my thigh."

The blood drains from every face in the room, my lips tingling with anxiousness I haven't felt since the last time I saw my brother with binds around his wrists. Anybody would lose it if their last memory of rope and mocking laughter included Moretti or the Klan. Javier vowed never to let anyone do that to him again. And he didn't.

But now we've got a body to find.

The way the other two men in my life are looking at each other, they're thinking the same thing.

Heck's eyes flash with the flames he's staring at. "You're certain you were alone?"

"Yes."

"Was he breathing when you left him?"

"Yes? Maybe ... I ... I don't know."

Dios mío. Nerves shake my bones worse than the limbs outside the window as Gio leaps from his seat. "Whoa, Dorian mighta survived? We gotta get there—or to the hospital."

"And do what?" I ask, my teeth chattering. "Finish the job? ¡Maldita!"

"Hey, I don't know. I'm tryin' here. We shoulda done somethin' when you read Dorian—"

Not now, Gio! Can't this man do anything I ask him to do the way I ask him to do it? I should have kept my encounter with Dorian to myself.

From the end of the couch, Heck's stony face turns to cement, his eyes burrowing into mine. "You *knew*?"

"Not all the details. Mostly the intentions."

"She actually worked her magic to hold him off awhile, Kess."

The more we flounder, the more agitated Javier becomes, twisting in Heck's arms. He begins humming while shooting us an exasperated glance. It's best to remain steady if we're going to keep Javier calm.

"Here's what we're going to do," Heck says with an icy calm. "We find out what Dorian knows." His hand swipes dried flecks from his cheekbone, only smearing the blood further. "Then, we make him forget it."

It's an easy plan for someone who's not brimming with the power of death and doom. It's also not a request. I don't blame him. I'm angry with me too. But mostly at Dorian. If my magic is going to melt a brain, it may as well be his.

"We're gonna need another egg."

As a gust howls against the far window like a ghost trying to beat its way in, Heck lowers his chin in a gaze that challenges me to dispute him. "Then make one."

TOWERING FIVE FLOORS, GENERAL HOSPITAL LOOKS MORE like a grand English estate house than a place of healing with its grim brick and terra-cotta trimming. The hardwood floors and marble windowsills are features Heck would typically be going on about were we not headed to the second floor to burn away a man's memory. The deed is so malicious it feels like anything but two days before Christmas.

Not long after sending Gio to make sure Javier stays safely hidden away in Heck's bedroom, our house received the call asking about our bartender's whereabouts, and to let us know that Dorian Luxberg nearly bled to death in Longview stables. He was alone, but they wanted to question anyone who had an interaction with Dorian earlier in the day. The second bit of shocking news: he hasn't woken up yet.

Heck pulls me by the elbow past rows of white curtains, his emotions all bluster and vengeance as the cursed egg bangs against my hip from within my handbag. While I don't appreciate being dragged around like a scolded toddler, honestly, I would be the same way toward him if he kept something so important about Javi from me.

We slow ourselves to nod at a few passing nurses on our way to the baron's private corner of the ward. Pinching a piece of the makeshift wall, Heck pulls back the curtain just enough for us to slip through with minor detection. No one's going to ask a couple of our caliber what our business is here—now that we've washed the blood off anyway—but it doesn't hurt to be discreet.

"He looks . . . salvageable," Heck mumbles at the patient in the roller bed. Pale and swollen in the jaw, Dorian groans in his sleep, the morphine injection doing its job otherwise. Heck and I link hands, unable to take our eyes off his shoulder, which is wrapped in bandages as thick as the dressing around his head. If the stab wound to an artery hadn't nearly killed him, the blow to the head certainly could have. But miraculously, he survived.

Some miracle.

As tough as Heck talked back at the house, we both are running hot and cold on what to do about Dorian. We're all still reeling from the last men I sentenced to death. Did they deserve it? Sure. But what did I do to deserve being the executioner? I don't want to take another life.

Divination by itself is a punishable offense. One would think Missouri could stand to modernize its law code, considering magic is make-believe in most people's eyes these days.

At least my intention here is to *save* a life—Javier's. And in turn, Dorian will have nothing but a blank spot in his memory, which will hopefully be rumored as a bad night on hop.

If I can pull it off.

"We don't even know if this will work," I say, my eyes darting to the curtain.

"If it doesn't, you know what to do."

My insides curl around themselves. Spinning to face my best friend, who has donned a feigned nonchalance, I rip the granite egg from my bag. "Hardly, but for my brother's sake, I will try."

Guilt, and not Heck's persistence, is what drives me toward Dorian's seemingly lifeless fingers. I hook my pinkie around his. That seems safe enough.

Easing into Dorian's dreams is effortless, like entering a storybook written just for me. It's about a prince in a castle with every brand of delicacy surrounding his lavish table. I'm led into the great hall, and he spots my arrival, ordering my clothes to be only silk and lace. The ensemble I traveled in falls from my shoulders, and his eyes gleam as his concubines drape my body with soft fabric from the waist down.

Come on, Rose. We can't be much longer.

Heck's reminder echoes from the stone walls but is cut off by a harpist as Dorian leads me to the table with his hand on the small of my back. The air cools my breasts. But it's the way his fingers slide down my arm that sends my skin erupting with goosebumps. This would be an enjoyable dream . . . if it didn't involve Dorian.

"Look at the feast I've prepared for you," he says, his voice sweeter than his eyes. "We'll dine on pain and vengeance."

Following the point of his hand, the "meal" comes into full view, and my stomach threatens to empty itself. Surrounded by delicacies of every variety, my struggling brother chokes on the grapes in his mouth. His feet crush mulberries as he twists in his binding of tomato vines. I've never seen skin made of orange peels and other types of fruit before. I'd never thought to imagine such a putrid vision. The sharp scent of overripeness hits my nose. My stomach flips again.

Dorian wants to devour my brother—and not in a suggestive way. The baron lost control of his newest turtle. Javier must be brought back in line. From crushing my brother's business to crushing his legs, Dorian's thoughts permeate the entire hall.

Rose, get a damn move on.

"Get a move on, baby," Dorian growls. Like many in a restless sleep, he can detect the outside world—the clacking shoes of nurses outside the curtain, the coughing patients in the ward. He won't recall most of it, but he's not that far from consciousness. I've got to figure out what to do here.

Rose . . . they're coming.

A tiny crack and Heck's apology for breaking the spell hurl me back into the room, where he waves his frantic hands. Grappling the air with his fingers, he mouths something I'm supposed to be able to understand.

"What?"

He always looks like a teakettle when he's about to explode, but this performance has him just shy of whistling. His thumbs pinch his nose before he tents his hands below his chin, whispering, "Put your magic away."

"It *is* put away."

"The eye thing!" he hisses. "Stop doing the creepy eye thing. Someone's coming."

The creepy eye—is he lecturing me about my swimming irises? Of all the things!

"It's not like I can control it!" I hiss back.

"Fine, whatever. But did it work? Did the magic work?" His sorrowful eyes fall to my scarf at my silence. "Well then, we just need more time. Maybe if we—"

The curtain makes a crisp snap, and I yelp as Heck tugs my arms to burrow my face in his collar. My cap is promptly pulled over my eyes. "There, there, darling. Let's get you out of here before you have to see any blood."

I attempt to peek from under the brim (and to get a breath), but our wrestling just makes us look like a poor sap trying to calm his hysterical wife. *If he says "hush now" one more time . . .*

Ignoring our plight, a nurse wheels in a tray full of hypodermic needles and a fresh change of gauze as the two of us shuffle away through the makeshift wall.

Nearly there, Heck sends to me, lifting my legs from the ground as though I am faint when a few businessmen stop for a chat. Hearing of my condition, they give him a hearty congratulations and wish us well. No one wants to risk being rude, after all.

Except for me. I want to be rude—if he doesn't get us out of here.

Once the chill of the parking lot hits my stockings, I wriggle from Heck's arms, releasing my hair from its cap, which nearly flies away in the wind. My breath turns to wispy fog in the night air. "Di-mi. Where did you find a bowl of water for the egg?"

"That jacket isn't nearly warm enough." Heck slides his overcoat over my shoulders. "You should have worn your fur."

"You can be so damn frustrating."

"As can you, my dear flower. And I used the bedpan for the egg, if you insist on knowing."

"Ugh, Heck Kessler."

"It brought you back, didn't it?" A gust whips his blond fringe from its perfect perch atop his head, giving him the look of a lost traveler as his woeful eyes finally lose their sternness. If they keep watering like that, we're both going to have icicles on our eyelids before the car gets here. "I acquired a few vials of that morphine to keep Javi calm until . . . until we . . ."

Until we get another chance to fix this.

An ivory Chrysler rumbles to the curb. I raise my face to the stars, which poke through a veil of racing clouds, with a vow on my lips. I hope the sky can feel my intention. I hope heaven and earth know I haven't lost faith in them.

"We will," I say to the crescent moon. "Lo haremos."

"IF WE'RE GOING TO BE SNOWED IN AT A HOTEL ON CHRISTMAS Eve, at least the Acquisitions Ball Committee had the forethought to include accommodations with a spa." Heck straightens his bow tie with the finesse of a movie star. "Being the chairman of said committee doesn't hurt either."

As our vehicle skids up the long drive of the Elms, the hotel and health resort for rich whites only, a familiar discomfort bites at my heart; as long as I'm a Kessler, I'll be expected to spend my favorite holiday dancing and schmoozing with southern Missouri royalty as Heck nails down purchase acquisitions for the new year. Makes me miss my abuela already. I bet my mother is making buñuelos or tamales or anything more delicious than the saltless spread this "health" resort is bound to have inside.

How is a lack of flavor healthy?

The stretchy band around my middle finger pulls taut as I tug my gloves up past my elbows. The hand wear I've chosen for this ensemble is a smart statement in more ways than one—my exposed fingers will give me a leg up with every handshake offered by the barons. From the way the nude underlay of this dress hugs my curves, I should be getting plenty of them.

"We might not stay the entire week," Heck says, tucking a rogue wavy lock of hair into my bandeau. The silky head wrap brushes my cheek as it dangles down one side, and I wonder if it's going to annoy me as the night wears on. I keep my hair short for a reason. Heck seems just as irked with his headwear, adjusting and readjusting the grand thing around his forehead. "This all truly depends on how long it takes to nail down the lumber. However, Giuseppe can take you where you want to go during the day."

Our driver swivels his head around, his middle part as greasy as ever. "I'll keep my hands where I can see 'em, baby, don't you worry."

The cabin is too dark for him to see my eye roll, but I hope he can hear my grunting sigh. With Gio watching my brother, we needed someone trustworthy enough to keep their nose out of our business . . . or at least a guy easy to bribe. Gus was less happy to volunteer once I told him he's not to speak to any darbs whatsoever. We're not here to swindle this time.

"I don't know why you wouldn't make full use of the amenities here," Heck continues. "I highly recommend the bathhouse. Tie your coat, my dear, we're nearly there."

As he goes on about how mineral springs would fix the dry skin on my elbows, our driver opens the door in front of a hotel as grand as I've ever seen. The limestone exterior gives the look of a bastion in conquered lands, proudly displaying its trimmed evergreens and arched verandas. Gasping as the wind slips down my throat like frozen fingers aiming to choke me, I tug the heavy fur around my body. Heck's paisley oxfords have us sailing inside and to the coat check almost before he can complain about the amount of snow accumulating on his topper, but he finds a way. While I brush a few flakes from the brim, he curls his thumbs around my palms, lowering them to his chin. Fondness reflects through his skin, reaching the warmth in his eyes.

"For what it's worth," I say, "I started to tell Javi about Dorian's intentions—or what little I knew about them, anyway. He didn't want to hear it."

Heck touches his lips to my knuckles. "That lover boy of mine is as stubborn as you. He wouldn't have listened to me either." Tucking my arm around his, he leads us to a set of mahogany doors. "We have to remember—they're the bad guys, not us."

Two doormen pull on carved handles in front of us with a slight grunt. The heavy wood gives way to colorful tapestries adorning walls lit by chandeliers of varying heights, their crystals glittering as much as the tree in the center of the dance floor of a ballroom fit for the top hats and sequined dresses that fill it. Spinning couples shimmer and laugh, the ladies drawing smoke through long stems as their fellas coax them into a subdued Charleston. Tonight's band must be hitting on all sixes to get these stiffs moving. Either that or Pendergast really knows how to throw a party.

Heck and I make our way around the edges of the room, and I adopt a posh accent, commenting on the assortment of meat and cheeses that pass by on golden trays.

"I absolutely *adore* burrata," I muse with a flick of my bandeau. "Isn't it just *everything*?"

My smile hits the grave wall that is Heck's pinched eyebrows, his nose in the air as though catching the scent of something burning.

"Geez, I never thought I'd have to tell you to lighten up at a party."

"Something's off." His eyes survey the ballroom as he draws me close, so our backs face the wall. He slips a tall flute into my hand from a passing tray. "Drink this. Stay calm."

"I am calm. Heck, what are you—"

The man who lives to love and be loved takes my hand and tells me everything he can't say out loud. Formerly betrothed couples are seated separately, dining and drinking with their fathers. A pair of brothers who were on the outs are now laughing at their family's table. The lake households shake hands with each other on one side of the room while those from the Ozark forests are circled up nearest the buffet. Even the Bootheel families—the smallest yet richest of Missouri royalty—have staked their claim on the tables closest to the main exit. No one is dancing who they should be dancing with tonight. No one is drinking what they should be drinking tonight. The barons are dividing into factions.

Dorian.

Heck's thoughts widen the scope on politics I hadn't cared enough to pay attention to until now. The court of public opinion has ruled—the families suspect each other of the baron's deadly attack. It makes sense. His family is the wealthiest in the room; their monopolization of contracts from Kansas City to St. Louis has always been a bitter spot for the rest of the barons. But the bitterness has never been enough to stop business . . . until now.

"So let's just make the rounds and choose a side," I whisper into my champagne.

Heck leans into my ear, laughing as though I'd said something funny. "A normally strong strategy, my dear, but we would need contracts from both the lake and forest regions. If we sign even one contract with a single family, the other factions will abandon us, which only leaves us with one option."

Standing on my toes, I swivel my head back toward the mahogany doors, the lace-lined tables filled with scowling faces.

Don't look at them! Heck's thoughts are a foghorn, pulling my heels back to the ground. Understanding squeezes into my fingers. The Luxbergs haven't come to greet us. In fact, no one has. The suspicions surrounding Dorian's attack must include our bartender, who hasn't been seen since that night. While our house has tried to head off that suspicion by sending cards and well-wishes, our ruse doesn't seem to be taking hold. They think we're protecting Javier.

And we are. But they simply cannot know it.

"What if," Heck mumbles, his palms beginning to sweat," what if they find out we have him here? And what if Gio falls asleep and Javi sleepwalks out of there? We should have taken him far away and restrategized."

As his breathing picks up speed, I set my flute on a passing tray before reaching up to straighten Heck's topper. "Don't you look dashing?" I stand on the tips of my toes once more, planting a quick kiss on his mouth. The distraction flusters him just enough that he lets out a small chuckle. It's a rare thing to see him blush. "Dance with me?"

"I . . ." The bleakness returns to his face. "I just don't think I can."

"Heck Kessler, don't lie to me," I chide with false poutiness. My fingertips slide down the side of his jaw, lifting his chin where it belongs. "If anyone can dance through this moment, it's you."

Although reluctance seeps through his fingers, he lets me guide him to the sparkling tree in the center of the room as the band shifts to a lazy jazz tune with a piano solo. I follow Heck's lead almost without needing his cues through his thoughts, which works well enough given the worry dominating his mind. While I'm confident Gio can keep my brother calm, especially with the morphine at his disposal, Heck is less sure. He wants his Javi back. We all do. My heart bleeds for my brother as much as Heck's does. And I have a plan to fix all of this. Heck just doesn't know it yet.

We just need to survive right now.

He squeezes my hand, as if hearing that last bit.

"May I cut in?" a familiar voice drawls from behind me. A handlebar mustache and a wide smile greet me as I turn around, and Heck uses the interruption to excuse himself for a "light refreshment" that's sure to be at least three brandies.

"Well, he's fairly blue," Hiram says, leading me in a three-step. Clearly, he soaked his neck in that woodsy charm these fellas call cologne. "Seems an unconventional strategy if he is, in fact, hiding your brother."

I have to swallow my gasp.

The baron heir pulls me close enough to be inappropriate. "If I wanted to give you away, I would have by now." His palm presses into mine, and I pick up on an odd, urgent sincerity. "The Luxbergs have dominated timber for nearly a hundred years. The lake families couldn't be more thrilled to be rid of that deviant of a man. I could get every one of them to sign a Kessler contract and provide Javier a ride to the Ozarks in *minutes*. Your businesses will be safe. Your brother will be safe. Just say the word."

What?

Then . . .

No me gusta.

No one is that kind to a stranger. I'd ask him if he's serious, but I can read that he is. I trust that of him, but I still don't understand his motive. He knows I could scramble his brains, yet he's not afraid of me doing so. Fear doesn't seem to be driving him at all. It's something else, but he sets my hand on his shoulder before I can read him any further. Along the far wall, Heck is preoccupied with tiny shrimp and the rest of the land developers seeking to drink away their concerns. As the band signals the final song before intermission, Hiram offers his arm for a waltz. I hadn't realized it was getting so late. But then again, we're never on time. All of which is to say I can't spend all night cavorting with Hiram. I have much bigger deals to make tonight.

"I need to find the lavatory to powder my nose," I say, giving my dance partner a quick curtsy. "Then I'll need to consult with Heck. We should have an answer for you by morning."

"And here I thought you were the boss."

"I am, but I don't think that's how relationships work."

Not anymore.

Whether or not that's a good thing, I'm still trying to figure out.

"Well, do give it proper consideration." Hiram bows his head in farewell. "We'll speak then, Mrs. Kessler."

9

DAMN LUMBERJACKS AND MOONSHINERS.

Because that's all they are. They might have fancy suits and money from here to the Arkansas border, but it doesn't change what they are deep down.

Which is something I should know a hell of a lot about.

What I also know is that they're ruining my marriage and my brother, and now they're wreaking havoc on Christmas Eve. Noche Buena used to light up the night sky in the River Bottoms with fireworks, each family hosting a savory treat on the evenings leading up to it. I bet these clans of the lakes and woods can't even pronounce *piñata*, much less take a swing at one with any sort of accuracy—not with the amount of liquor they keep in their fuel tanks.

Yet none of that matters either—Christmas is on hold until I find a way to save my brother. And for that, I'm definitely *not* going to go powder my nose.

Scanning the room, I catch sight of a woman whose orange hair stands a foot above most of the men around her. Her protruding belly doesn't seem to keep a single one of them at bay. Why should it? She's a poor widow with a truckload of money her late husband left behind. Margaret's looks are as plain as the food here, but she's got a classic style, like her husband is running for governor . . . if she had a husband. My stomach squeezes just a little. She still doesn't know I set his body in a tree by the riverbanks. She doesn't know that I *can*. And I'm not sure if she'd hate me or thank me, and I don't want to risk it.

Before she can catch my eye, I duck behind a large nut-cracker by the punch bowls. As much as I love Margaret, I have no time for my old friend's gabbing. She'll take hold of my arm and never let me go. The guilt I feel right now is real—I need to see her more.

Not now, though. The exit I'm aiming for is just beyond the throng of tuxedos surrounding her. It's possible to slip by her unnoticed and make for the patio, but it's dicey. The main entrance isn't an option with the way Heck keeps staring at it. I could try the servers' hallway, which leads to the kitchens. They might give me a few questionable looks, but they won't venture beyond that.

I take my chances, following a line of empty platters as they head into a side hallway. If the fates are trying to stop me, they're doing a decent job, because the investigator who cuts off my path is now sneering down at me.

"Mrs. Kessler," he says. "How do you do?"

"I didn't know they made tuxes with a waist size that small."

His flat mouth sinks lower. "I'm finished with your games,

Mrs. Kessler. We can either do this here or in a private room for a proper interview. Your call."

"Or not at all, you flunky," I say with urgency rising in my chest. I only have a couple of hours to get out of here and back undetected. And I don't owe this guy anything. "Get out of my way. Now."

"Then we'll do it here." He pulls a small notebook from his pocket, his spectacles falling down the ridge of his nose. "You did not disclose to your current landlords that you are of Mexican descent. Why was that?"

Heat rushes to my neck as the trays weave around us.

"How dare you?" I hiss, using the blush in my cheeks to look indignant at such an accusation.

"Is your husband even aware that he's been lied to so you can use his white pedigree to run these illegal businesses for you?"

If it's one thing Gio taught me about his run-ins with the law, it's "deny, deny, deny." Then let the money do the defending. Heck and I will bury this guy in a lawsuit if he says one more word.

As cool threats fight their way out of my mouth, a pile of orange waves appears above the investigator's shoulder. "There you are!" Margaret's singsongy voice says with a laugh. She's already talking by the time I turn to greet her. "I was hoping you were well enough to come tonight. I thought I was the only expectant mother at the ball, and now, look at us! I cannot *believe* you didn't tell me yourself, you secretive thing."

She grabs me by the hands, and I pull her into a hug, to her confusion and delight, as I'm not known for my affectionate side.

"Speaking of secrets," she rambles on, "I have one for the books, I tell you, but that's for another day . . ."

I know I'm limiting my magic; however, I press the thought into her palms without hesitation. *Help Rose.* Of course, I hate to make my own friends think thoughts that aren't theirs, especially the ones who don't know about my magic, but I'm not sure she's picking up on my angst.

"Mrs. Kessler," the investigator says, "shall we?"

Margaret's eyes dart to mine, finally understanding the situation. She knows all about secrets—and many of mine. Her late husband, Archibald, was the definition of cruelty. They lost their first baby due to his violent temper, and he disappeared not long after. She explored romance with a few men (and women) before settling on the single life once she realized she was pregnant again. Her previous doctor was paid off to stay silent about the miscarriage, and the second "Archibald heir" gained her even more sympathy from high society—as long as no one pays too close attention to counting the months. Suitors send flowers weekly. She sets them in vases and vows to never again be beholden to a man.

I really like being held by some men, but I get where she's coming from.

"Rose, you look just ravishing," she gushes, her belly bumping against the investigator's elbow. He clears his throat as she hooks her arm around his sleeve. "Sir, could you be a dear and grab us both a table? You can't expect women in our condition to be chasing down waiters."

The man pushes his spectacles back up, eyeing the clamp on his arm. "I . . . well, I . . . suppose I could."

"That's *wonderful*," Margaret says, pushing his body forward. "And what is it you do for a living? My, aren't you stronger than you look."

"I'm a reporter of sorts—"

My friend's gasp parts a sea of partygoers. "Isn't that the bee's knees? I'm an author myself! You *have* to tell me what you've written . . ."

As the investigator drowns in unending small talk and a tide of people, I bolt for the kitchen to find the back door. A few service staff on a smoke break get the privilege of watching me pretend like I'm not running around the back of a grand hotel in a dress in the middle of a snowstorm. *Drink it in, boys.* Adrenaline drives me through spinning flakes and down a walking path covered by what has to be three inches. I'm glad I listened to the almanac and came prepared. This is no light snowfall. My heels crunch along the path, halting beside a row of bushes; my mouth mumbles a few swears. My waves won't hold if my hair gets damp.

But I came prepared for that too.

Giuseppe isn't the classiest criminal, but he knows how to hide a suitcase of clothes in the hedges.

My God, it's cold! Ripping open the clasps, I take off my heels and shove my feet into a pair of hunting boots I won off a guy during a card game just because I could. I throw on heavy fur with matching mittens and cram a wool cloche over my head. The warmth burns my frozen ears.

Following the directions my brother gave me, I throw a satchel over my shoulder and begin the hike—only one mile north. The Elms is the only thing in the small town of Excelsior; the journey would normally be a brisk walk up a few dirt roads with a sharp cut into the woods for the final trek. Unfortunately, my venture through the countryside is as serene as a blizzard. The lack of moonlight makes it hard to see. The swirling snow makes visibility impossible. Coming to a crossroad, I pull a flashlight from my pack and fumble with the button. I'm not about to enter the woods without seeing what's in front of me.

My shins slam against limbs, as I nearly trip over exposed roots like I've lost all grace, but at least the tree cover has slowed down the snowfall. In the silence, a deep hoot sounds in front of me, then behind. A flap of wings follows a shriek of something that scuttles around my ankles. My palms dampen inside my gloves as my breath comes out in small, white puffs. I'm more spooked than I should be. I should have spent less time learning silverware placement and more time learning how to walk in the forest.

The instructions Javier gave me were simple as a childhood song. In fact, the directions *are* a childhood song. Our mother taught it to us when we were little. I thought it was fun to sing such a chilling melody. Singing it to the dark woods now has my body shivering from more than the temperature.

> *Camina por el camino, niña*
> *Norte, norte*
> *Corre por el bosque, niña*
> *Oeste*

A twist of thorns catches the fur of my coat, and I have to tuck the flashlight under my arm to tug free of the vines. The shadows around me dance in the struggle, but I'm able to shake loose, although Heck will surely notice the snag later.

Whether or not that matters more than him noticing my absence will remain to be seen.

Another long hoot greets me as I start down the path of dead leaves and snow. To my left, another owl answers back with short bursts. I leave them to their argument, only to be found in the middle of another skirmish, different hoots bombarding the forest floor. Behind me, in front of me, all around me, they lament, and I can no longer hear my little eerie song in the mayhem. Their flapping wings have me picking up the pace, crunching and crashing my way through the branches.

Nearly there.

By the time I reach the clearing, the air has scraped out my gasping lungs with a frigid burn. I stop to catch my breath, clicking off the flashlight. Of all the moments, the thought occurs to me now that this is absolutely crazy. And dangerous. I can always just turn back. I probably should.

But the house has already seen me.

Hiding beneath the peeling sycamores around it, a silhouette lit only by the glowing moonlight behind the clouds begins to take form at my approach. The flickering candlelight within the shack ahead makes my old boxcar seem uptown; I'm sure the darkness makes it worse than it is.

Probably not.

The scraping of fur over the bumps on my arms provides more stinging than relief. *What are you doing, Luna?* I should come back during the day like a normal person. But I've already ripped up my best hosiery.

In for a peso . . .

The sick will to know what devilry goes on behind that thorn-covered door plants my weighted boots on the first creaking step. My confidence plummets as the second stair gives way, rough wood digging into my hand that grips the railing. *Damn these man-boots.* Wrenching my wrist to disentangle it from a vine wrapped around what's left of the splintering handrail, I glance up with a gasp through my nose. Small puffs of white join mine in the quiet, a shadow studying me. I'm no longer standing out here alone.

And the owls have stopped their hailing.

My thumb hits the flashlight once again, and the yellow beam shines on the curious silhouette. A girl with a mousy expression stares at me from the open doorway.

A girl? These are the brujas everybody is so frightened of?

These are the witches who are supposed to give me insight into deadly magic that could help me save my brother?

Glowing firelight behind her hugs her tiny frame. Not from the eeriness of the owls that called around me like a cacophony of warning, nor the disdain settling in the stranger's eyes, but from the clinking within the netted bag gripped in her hand, I swallow hard. I want it to be filled with stones. Hell, the rumored sack of rotted hide these witches carry could've provided some small comfort compared to what she holds in front of her.

Dios ayúdame. Dread keeps my gaze locked onto the ivory skull that lies atop the clinking bones inside the netting. Hollowed eyes. Gleaming teeth. The remains are human . . . or were.

My panic battles the ivy along the banister for my wrist. *Luna, what are you doing?*

"Excuse me, I . . . I . . . I think I've gotten turned around."

"They don't want you here." The girl's voice is as spectral as the look in her eyes—empty and lost.

"They . . . I'm sorry?" I tug at my arm again, the wiry vines nearly binding me as a disgusted frown pinches her petite features. There's no time to figure out why she's so offended. I don't want to know. I just want to get the hell out of here and back to boring parties and mindless conversation—away from this vine that's starting to cut off my circulation. Scrunching my face, I pause in the struggle. *What the . . .*

I thought my nerves were causing this raucousness, making me clumsy. But as the ivy coils on its own, a cold realization flashes across my sodden skin. My heart answers the frozen feeling with a rapid drumming. *It's moving.* The damn vine is moving. What's more—it's tightening. Plants have always been my friends. And now, for the first time, one is hurting me.

As blood thumps in the ends of my fingers, the glaring girl grunts like my civics tutor when I'd ask about women's rights. "They don't *want* you here!"

Okay, I get it now. She's crazy. They're crazy. I'm definitely crazy.

I turn my mouth down in a fast nod. "Well, I never argue with foliage. I'm happy to get outta here—unless they wanna keep the hand."

Dios mío, Luna. My nervous humor spills out of my dumb mouth at the worst possible times. It usually works as a minor distraction, but this Jane of the Woods isn't buying my attempt at natural charm. I should've let Heck get me tipsy.

I rear my head back as a slow smile struggles its way across her face, and she bounces on her bare toes with delight. "¡Vaya, mira quién ha venido!" She bends at the hip, sneering at the tugging vines. "¡Suelta!"

Like withering arms, the vines shrink away, releasing me

from their shackles, and I welcome the splinters from the handrail as I nearly slide back down the steps.

"Don't go, por favor! You've only just got here."

I don't want to find out why she's changed her mind even as my boot sinks into the broken stair at the bottom, startling whatever varmints were hiding beneath the rotting wood. The beam of my flashlight catches several rodents scurrying away, and I tug my heel from the wood fragments. The girl calls after me once more as I dash into the icy breeze, which rips into my heaving lungs in a metallic burn.

"WHAT IN GOD'S NAME—YOU MISSED THE ENTIRE BALL. AND your overcoat. You do realize that is *mink*."

"It was," I mutter.

"*Excuse* me?"

As Heck lectures about the state of my hair and my absence being the highlight of his embarrassment, I yank my legs from my boots and let the fur fall to the floor. My dress has shimmied nearly to my hips, but I don't care. I just want to plop in front of this fireplace and thaw the hell out.

The reclining sofa is everything I wanted it to be.

"I didn't think you would *abandon* me. Is this because I left you on the dance floor? Also, I didn't realize Margaret was so chatty, which proved to be useful with that investigator prowling about. Not to mention Hiram had to leave early because his father became ill . . ." Heck's sharp gaze falls to my knee, his face flattening. I follow his wide eyes to the top of my knee, where a soft creature clings to my garter with eight hairy legs.

With both of us shrieking, the thing falls to the floor, and

Heck recovers himself long enough to chase it down with one of the boots. A heavy heel slams against the baseboard, and I crumble back to the sofa with relief. A renewed energy steadies my breathing as I meditate on the chandelier above me. I can't believe it. I just met one of the witches of the North—and ran off like a frightened schoolgirl. What's the worst she could have done besides shake her eerie bag of bones at me? I guess she could have tried to choke me to death with ivy, but either way, I blew my first meeting with the infamous sisters.

Or at least one of them, anyway.

I shouldn't be so mad at myself. Being attacked by plants would send anyone running back into a blizzard.

"Ugh, I hope the hotel isn't crawling with these things." Heck drops the entire boot into a wastebasket.

"You don't see many spiders in the winter."

It's an oddity in the midst of so many oddities lately. Sure, insects could survive if they stayed indoors, but I never went inside that cabin. Maybe my escape and reentry through the kitchens were the culprits. Food waste can draw all kinds of unwanted pests. I brush my knee with a shudder. Makes me rethink eating breakfast in the morning.

A pair of silk sleeping shorts and a matching tank float to my lap as Heck finally sits, taking my hands. "You're ice cold, darling. Let's get you ready for bed. I need to relieve Gio of his shift."

Sadness reverberates from his warm hands, his tie loosened and hanging. He won't get a wink of sleep watching Javier, but he'll pace the floors if he stays in here. It might make him feel better to know I tried to get help for my brother tonight . . . even if it didn't go well. This is as good a time to tell Heck as any.

I push myself back up, hiding my knuckles inside his cupped palms. "I didn't want to worry you until I knew if they could help us."

The awareness of what I attempted tonight shoots through him and up my forearms.

"You went without me."

"You would have tried to come."

"Of *course* I would have!" Bursting out an annoyed growl, he sets to work unfastening his collar buttons. "Please tell me you didn't go alone."

"Of *course* I did," I shoot back. "I'm a bruja, Heck Kessler. There's no way I'd expose you to someone like me until I knew it was safe—which it *wasn't*. That witch has the power to command vines."

I fold down my fancy hand wear, exposing the scratches around my wrists.

He ceases his aggressive undressing with a gasp, pulling the gloves from my fingers. "Oh dear God, Rose! You're hurt!"

It stings worse than a slap on a sunburn, but the man who would search the earth to save my brother is stressed enough as it is, so I say, "It's okay. I got away from the one I met. And it goes without saying, but . . . I don't think they're the ones to help us."

Heck's face sinks further. "Well . . . what about the other sister?"

"The one I met was holding a human skeleton in a sack."

"Di-mi, I'm running out of expletives." He rubs his hands all over his face, his fingers stopping on the bridge of his nose. "Perhaps we should consider Hiram's terms . . . Don't look so annoyed. You left the party. Naturally he spoke with me."

I fumble around with my garters, releasing my stockings before slipping into my night shorts. "I just wish I knew what he wanted."

"An unknown favor, he tells me."

"A what?"

"I don't know."

"And that doesn't scare you?"

"Yes, it scares me! But what are we going to do?" Heck is flushed, staring at me, and then leaves me to finish dressing as he does the same on the other side of a large partition by the wardrobe. I hear his voice continue, calmer. "The lake contracts will cover more than half of what we need. At least it's something. And most importantly, Javi will be safe—"

A lump forms in my throat at the break in Heck's voice. And the thought of my brother struggling with nightmares and confusion while hiding among strangers on the outskirts of an unknown town. We'd have to absorb his business—or sell it. He would never be safe at home again.

Heck's jacket slings over the side of the partition before I hear him hit the floor. Rushing around the wooden divider, I throw my arms around his slumped shoulders, and we cling to each other, our tears running down each other's necks. His anguish pours into me and breaks what's already broken for my brother. Heck and I both feel like failures, letting down the man who saved us both in different ways. We're unable to save him.

And so, we cry on our knees, failing and rocking each other.

GIO'S LIGHT SNORES AND WARM ARMS GIVE ME NO SOLACE. Once Heck went to relieve him, my boyfriend and I exchanged a few tender kisses before he drifted off quickly. Javier spooked him a couple of times, mumbling disturbing things in his sleep, leaving Gio on edge from the moment we snuck my brother into his room. I should probably get some rest myself, but the fire died in the hearth ten minutes ago. The warmth was the only barrier between the bed and the drafty windows. But I've made a toasty nest within the tangle of my boyfriend's limbs beneath the feather comforter.

At least the storm has passed, serenity taking over the night. Even a few stars sparkle beyond the clouded panes. I squint at the window as another draft wisps across my bare arms, sending them prickling. The glass in my old boxcar used to get foggy like that when my mother would leave the door cracked open on autumn nights. I always thought it made the air way too crisp by morning—just like this hotel room is now.

As the fog fades and then fills the glass again, for a moment, the window looks as though it's breathing, the pane pushed up halfway like an open mouth.

A sharp spike of fear stills my own breath. Gio and I didn't open that window.

The tingle across my tongue tastes of dread as a tiny cloud puffs from a silhouette beside the frame, its slow exhale hitting the cold. Something is definitely breathing.

And it's in our room.

"Hey!" My body tenses with the frigid fire of panic as I lurch up to my knees, throwing back the blankets.

Gio fumbles for the chain on the bedside lamp. "Jesus, Rose, you okay? You got a cramp or somethin'?"

"Gio, don't move."

As the glowing bulb floods our corner of the room, an unsure smile stares back at us from the shadows by the window.

"Oh, fuck." My boyfriend's tone is rising like a scale on his piano. "What the—shit, it's that creepy girl with the bones, ain't it?"

The little bruja giggles, using her fingers to brush her tangled hair to the side. She looks older than I first thought—ten, maybe eleven years old, with hair and eyes as raven as my mother's. Her boots stand in a puddle of melted snow, her wool coat hanging open and threatening to swallow her tiny frame.

"Don't worry," she whispers, "I left my sister at home."

I blink to adjust my eyes to the light. *Your sister?*

Before I can ask, the girl dashes across the room, her bony arms and legs crawling up onto the foot of the bed.

"Holy shit, hang on," Gio pants, his arm crossing my body like a barrier. "We did not mean to offend you in any way. We just wanted—"

"You wanted our help." The girl's hand grips the bedpost, and she stretches her arm until she's hovering with her matted hair suspended over my wide-eyed boyfriend.

"That's right. But I had to get back to the party," I lie, attempting to push him behind me. But he's not having it and it doesn't take his thoughts to tell me so.

The girl's face pinches in an expression unbecoming to such delicate features. "I sent my criado to bring you back. But the man with the golden hair smashed it. Collecting even that much light is a terrible burden."

Gio's arm tenses. This time he does share his thoughts. *That damn spider,* he sends to me. *First vines, now bugs. Now creepy lil' girlies.* He's practically screaming an exit strategy into my thoughts. My unease must be frustrating her because she doesn't look pleased.

"I thought you would know it was a gift from me," she says, with her thin lips disappearing as she presses them together. "Don't you know anything about us?"

Gio clears his throat and runs his mouth before I can shush him. "About . . . about you and your sista' bein' a sack of bones or—"

"¡Bruja de maldiciones!" The sheets soak up the water from the girl's stomping boots, and my boyfriend and I press our backs to the velvet headboard. "Why do you kill my criados?"

Kill them? Have I? My mind retraces my steps from the last time I saw a beady-eyed insect staring at me—Gio's apartment, the rat in his hallway. Even my brother made mention of a peculiarity I brushed off as his mind breaking down until now. *I've got roaches all over my apartment . . .*

I squeeze Gio's hand, sending him a thought to stay calm. This bruja is a destruction witch who can do vile and unconventional things—like teaching me how to manipulate Dorian's memories. If she wanted to hurt us, she would have already. The distressing pout on her face is a clear enough signal, even in the low lighting—she wants to help me.

She also carries around her sister's remains half the time. *Tread carefully, Rose.*

"The mice in our shipments," I say, while echoing Gio's thought back to him. "Those are your servants too."

The little bruja squeals and claps her hands together.

"What were those for?"

"Energía. Neque."

My face asks the question, and so she answers. "*Healing,* silly Luna. Without draining your own life force like all healers do." Her secretive grin has my hair standing on end. "And now you don't have to!"

Gio sends me a silent suggestion at the same time I'm sending it to him: she doesn't know I'm not a healer. She doesn't need to know.

My boyfriend shifts against the headboard. "So, Rose won't get tired no more when she uses her power?"

His thoughts swarm with prayers of repentance as she snaps her head back in his direction.

"Exactly," she says, baring a set of crooked teeth. Biting down with a sickening crunch, they split like crushed ice before she hisses, "Because brujas like me take it from something else—or someone."

Gio's back can't press any farther into the velvet. "Aw, hell, tell me I'm asleep."

A skeletal hand slides from the armhole of her coat, where her arm used to be, and reaches for his heaving chest. "Would you like to sleep?"

As the air in the room thickens, the stars beyond the window begin to squeal like the brakes of a barreling train. There are no songs this time. Just the heavens covering its eyes and waiting for it to be over. Gio groans before her touch even reaches him.

This witch's fingers will never make it that far.

"¡Para ya!" My hand shoots out, clamping around the bony wrist, but it shrinks away like the vines at the shotgun house. The overcoat thrashes about, choking on the girl as she crashes to the floor. Disappearing beneath the thick fabric, her groans are lost in the coat's gurgling gulp.

As my boyfriend and I scramble to peer over the foot of the bed, a tiny lump pulsates from within the possessed garb, where the girl's giggle can be heard once more.

"We gotta get outta here," Gio says, but I resist the tug on my arm, to his consternation.

The stars have ceased their screaming and are back to twinkling their nightly dance near the moon. The bruja's spell is broken. Or at least she stopped. Either way, with the way the air is thinning out and freezing my nostrils, I think the worst part might be over for the time being and I touch my shoulder to Gio's to tell him so. *Somebody tell it to my lungs, though.*

"I hear that," he whispers, trying to control his own gasping.

If I didn't know any better, I'd say she was playing with him. Or testing me. Or both.

Unfolding herself from the wool flaps, the disheveled girl rights herself once again, her dark brows lowering. With her odd smile back and her teeth returning to their straight, pearly rows, my breath starts to head toward normal. The crushed teeth, the hand of bones—none of it was real.

I lean against the bedpost, leveling my eyes at her. "Show me how you did that."

Gio's got a thousand wisecracks on his tongue but he uses his head this time and keeps quiet.

With her irises swirling like worms in a bucket, the little bruja's fingers float to the spot just below my ear, and I do my best not to cringe. What a perfect opportunity. I could read another bruja. But then she'd read me, which has its own set of consequences I haven't weighed yet. Maybe a quick assessment. No thoughts. Just motive, and then I can get out of there before she realizes my intrusion.

No. She'll undoubtedly taste the magic working—or smell it, at the very least. *Speaking of which . . .*

The bitter flavor of cinnamon without the sugar still coats my tongue from when she reached for Gio, and I continue to think better of tapping into my charm as her fingertips tickle my jawline, stopping at the dent in my chin.

"You are used to wearing different faces, aren't you?" she asks, the humor stolen from her expression. "If anyone understands that, I do. My name is Idoya. My sister is Sol."

The tightness in my shoulders eases a bit. This feels like progress.

"That bitterness—what is that spell you're doing?"

"I'm just showing you what it should taste like . . . when you walk through that baron's dreams."

My shock perks Idoya up as she takes her hand back to fasten the giant buttons of her coat with a melody humming in her throat.

"Were you reading me just now?"

I didn't sense it.

"No," the little bruja says, "I've been watching you."

"Oh . . . right." *The criados.*

"You will need a properly blessed egg—one that will absorb a memory without taking one from you."

"Okay, but what does that—"

"Meet me at Union Station in five days' time. The third hour of the night," she says, her boots clonking over the rug. "I'll bring what you need. And I'll make sure my sister is rested."

Gio tightens his arms around his shivering torso. "So, uh, the dead need sleep?"

Idoya hoists her body over the windowsill, her eyes peeking into the room as her body disappears into the darkness on the other side. "The dead can do everything we can do."

As the little bruja vanishes, a slight breeze lifts the curtains, and Gio and I watch them flap around in paisley eeriness. Vowing to return to church, my boyfriend stalks across the room and slides the window shut before yanking the window dressing to block out the moon. "Bones, rats—what was with the teeth thing, huh? Now we gotta meet up with that crazy broad and her dead sista' in a place more isolated than this one? At least we got people in the other rooms who can hear us scream."

"First off—yes, I have to go. And second—no," I say, snatching my robe from its hook by the door.

"No?"

"You're not going with me. She seems to like messing with you."

"End of story there, Rose. You're not going to that place alone."

"You know, it's funny." Padding across the room to the hearth, I stop to grab an armful of kindling and shove it into what's left of the glowing embers. "Those were my exact words to you before you used my fennel to curse an entire furniture store."

"That ain't the same and you know it—hey, lemme get that, will ya?"

Pointing the nozzle of the bellow into the orange coals, I tug the wooden paddles open and closed like an accordion. "I've got this, Mr. Cattaneo. And it sounds like I've got the brujas too. What I *don't* have"—I let out a grunt, giving the paddles a few more pumps—"is your trust or respect. You certainly don't have mine."

Several flames jump around the kindling, lighting Gio's stony eye roll as he sets a few wooden bricks to keep the fire going. "Fine."

With the air between us heating, we storm to our sides of the bed with our backs to each other and nothing more to say. Of course, we're just angry. And traumatized. And missing simpler times when dodging the law to sell booze was our biggest contender. But we've been through worse or just as bad. My piano player has scars to prove it.

As does my soul.

I slowly let my fingers creep behind me and find his hand is already waiting there. He curls his pinkie around mine, sending me a silent apology. We're still too worked up to say our regrets out loud, so we settle on a silence more peaceful than anything our voices can give right now.

And fall asleep with the lamp on.

10

"WHEN WERE YOU GOING TO TELL ME YOU'RE EXPECTING?" Margaret's long legs dangle from the arm of her couch like those of a schoolgirl who's delighted to sit on the edge of the furniture when no one is watching. Her apartment is an identical replica of my old unit—a dainty living room that walks out to a balcony held by giant white pillars. Of course, she has it decorated with all imperial pieces. I never had a use for a luncheon table. When there's always a willing guy to spot my meals for me, why would I?

"Don't knot up your knickers," I say, strolling down the single hallway this apartment affords. I'm not sure if my excitement is more from seeing this old place or from escaping the lumber-bum convention after five days of drowning in tea and dinner parties. "I'm *not* expecting."

Her claw-foot tub is smaller than mine, but I miss having one in an apartment all to myself. And the modern rugs and fashionable wallpaper have my face lit up with nostalgia. Those were exciting days. My heart pricks with a small aching for the modesty of my former life—kissing fellas and breaking the law with far less responsibility and consequences.

Her poetic voice follows me. "But everyone thinks you are."

"Thanks to Heck, yes."

"And you need people to continue this charade for a while, I'm guessing?"

"One of many."

"All right, then. I'll help you."

I spin to face her squared-off neckline. "I didn't ask—"

"I will send in a nice fluff piece to my uncle to publish about affluent women in Kansas City," she says, adjusting the satin belt above her bulging belly. Her elegance is unmatched, even in a housedress made with checks and panels. "And you are hereby summoned, young lady, to the Guadalupe Center, where you will hobnob with women of like station as we all give back to those less fortunate—for the papers, of course."

My eyes drink in the hexagon tiles that signified my former independence. I hate the idea she's presenting . . . except for the fact it's actually a good one. Regardless of how I feel about being whitewashed by the practices of the affluent women at the Guadalupe Center as a child, they unknowingly implemented my mother's plan to smuggle me into society as a proper American-born girl. My ivory skin wasn't enough. Having my accent and name stolen was the price I paid to get to where I am. If only I could enjoy the benefits of such a trade.

Yes, I know I *have* all the benefits. I just don't enjoy them. Margaret's lips disappear into a sympathetic frown in response to the silent melancholy. "As senior editor of a secret circular promoting women's rights, I've learned infiltration is the best way to find weaknesses in a broken system. Don't you agree? Why am I asking you? You're married to a queer man while lying with your felonious rum-runner all while operating a speakeasy as a white-passing Chicana. Of course you agree."

Her words sink into me like lead truth. I'm an expert at pretending to be something I'm not. This new balancing act has higher stakes, and the benefits seem an uneven exchange. I've already got an investigator on my tail, and I haven't even begun to figure out how to shake him off. If he can see right through me, can't everyone else?

The brooding woman in the mirror stares back at me, her dark hair framed by the tiles surrounding the edges of the glass. "How am I supposed to do this, Margaret? I do my best acting when I'm saying nothing from the corner of a cocktail lounge."

"Liar. Look in there." Her painted fingernails wrap around my shoulders, her chin brushing my forehead. "That ravishing debutante next to you is pregnant with a bastard. No one suspects that she received the seed which created this child weeks after her husband's disappearance. Of course, I didn't think I could conceive that quickly after losing my first." The hair pointing to her jaw is crushed between her cheek and my temple. "Good riddance to that dreadful man. I heard he ran off with his secretary, but who leaves all this money behind?"

Who does, indeed? A moderate streak of guilt jolts my chest. I did what I had to do to save my family when I killed Archibald. And I know I did Margaret a favor, really. Her delicate emotions, which leak into my skin with one of her tears, tell me there's only so much reality she can handle, however. These are the burdens I am willing to carry.

"Well," I tell the mirror to avoid Margaret's eye. "All that money has to come in handy, right?"

"I didn't have a smidgen of guilt using it to pay off my old doctor to keep quiet about the miscarriage."

"Regardless of the curious timeline, I say it's uncouth for anyone to ask."

Her lips stretch into a pleased grin. "See? You're learning manners already. And with this newfound fortune, I could start a whole new life."

As she dabs beneath her eye and straightens her back, I lean to check the rouge on my lips. "Who is this man of mystery, anyway? A doctor? Another lawyer? I thought you and Penny had a kind of . . . arrangement."

"Penny and I continue to be close. She did, after all, teach me where certain things are, if you know what I mean." Margaret's side smile is a rare sight, the dreamy look on her face saying more than words ever could. But she's never been one to bridle her thoughts. "She encouraged me to explore the wanton side of myself. You wouldn't *believe* how many men and women, mind you, want to neck with a fashionable gal in the dark corners of a proper speakeasy."

If anyone would believe, it's me, but I let it slide. Instead I say, "Yes, but who's responsible for killing the rabbit?"

Margaret's cheeks turn the shade of her hair. "Well, he's . . . he's kind of a blue-collar."

I hate how squinting creases my face, but I can't help it. "Margaret, you're not refusing him because he's *poor*? I'm the last one who's going to judge, and it's not like you need anyone's money."

"It's not that. I'm not marrying him because I don't want to ever lose my freedom again. You, of all people, should understand that." The indignation that fuses her hands to her hips smooths my face into a grin. "Why is my circular anonymous? Why do *you* hide? Because, foremost, we're women. We hide because our opportunities will be stolen from us for things that aren't even wrong!"

Once again, I can't argue with that. I'd write it on the walls of city hall if I could. Women like us have so much to say but few places to say it. I'm beaming inside at my friend's liberty from the prison of her former life—jealous of it, even, in some ways, and only slightly concerned.

"But, Margaret, the father . . ."

My sentence withdraws itself. Given that my own father didn't want me, I can't imagine denying a man the opportunity if he wanted it.

Margaret's jaw lifts, her eyebrows flattening in defiance. "He didn't want it. I know, shocking. Archie used our baby to imprison me. This man uses it to leave. And so goes the lessons I've learned about darbs who love the smell of my hair."

Ahhhh. That explains a hell of a lot. Searching despite the lack of my own maternal instincts for comforting words, I struggle for something helpful to say but come up with nothing.

"I will raise the baby with Penny," my adamant friend says. Before I can object, she drags me back to the living room, where she sets me on the couch and then offers me tea from a set too elegant to drink from—which I guess is the whole point. As we sip the bergamot beverage, she hones in on my pouting mood.

"It's not a settled plan, darling," she says.

I manage a sigh in response. Penny never told me she planned to rear a child with Margaret. But she's good at keeping secrets. And certainly doesn't need my permission. I don't know what I would do at the clubs without her, though.

Margaret, as bold as I wish I could be, sets her cup down into a dainty dish. "We've spoken of moving to a home where we're away from scrutiny. Maybe somewhere on some acreage in upstate New York. I think I'd like to fight the good fight from somewhere a little less . . . conservative." Even Margaret's sigh is mannerly. "Rose, there's an entire culture of people who love freely in the bigger cities. It's still illegal, technically, but so is drinking. However, the law can't dictate hearts, I suppose."

"And it shouldn't," I reply with more than a bit of dolefulness.

"Oh goodness, Penny's not quite ready to leave the flapper life. I told her when the time comes, I've got a home and place for her—just like she gave to me."

The prim couch isn't made for leaning, but I settle back like a cowboy watching a sunset from his rocking chair. My friends deserve every good thing that comes to them in a world that won't offer them more than minimum wage and the obliteration of their dreams. I would gladly accept the sacrifice of losing them to happiness.

Margaret tilts her head, catching my lazy stare out the window. "You could come too. Anytime you're ready." The sweetness of such a gesture draws a smile to my face, which seems to satisfy her as she drops a tiny cube of sugar into her cup. "The city is getting more dangerous all the time, anyhow. Suydam Decorating Company, what a shame. And with all the new pieces they just acquired. I can't see how the Ballards will recover—"

Alarm sends my tea spilling onto my lap. My legs barely register the burn. "Re . . . recover from what, exactly? Are they all right?"

"My gosh, Rose, I didn't mean to give you such a start. They're fine. It's their business that got ransacked." A floral kerchief blots the front of my blouse while my mouth drops open. "Every stitch of furniture, even the till and the safe in the back room."

Dios mío. What has my magic done? Mr. Ballard might be a rude old man, but he didn't deserve this. Why couldn't he just give me back my damn plant?

"Gio," I mumble at the void growing between my boyfriend and me.

In my peripheral, two perfectly penciled eyebrows draw together. "Gio? Isn't that your beau? You don't think he—"

"Oh no!" I choke out a laugh, my smile full of lies Margaret can't detect. I set my tea glass on the sofa table to stop its quivering. "He would never. I only meant that Gio told me about it, but I'd nearly forgotten with all of the barons and their dramatics—wasn't there a secret you were wanting to tell me? I already know you've got a bun in the oven."

Her head ducks down like the purple drapes have ears. "Well . . . do you know that dirt that Javier spreads all over the place?"

"Y . . . yeah."

Where is this going? The alarming quiver settles back into my hands.

"Well," she continues, her voice squeaking with happy guilt. "I happened to maybe borrow a tiny, tiny bit when I went to see Penny at his club yesterday."

"You . . . you . . . you . . ."

I may faint. I wish I could. What is Margaret saying to me right now? What does she know? I swear I can feel my heart pumping blood all the way to my fingertips.

"Well, someone has to hold down the fort while he's off on holiday," she says like I've slapped the excitement off her face. "Being a working woman myself, I offered to wipe down the sink area and accidentally discovered it while we were looking for cleaning gloves."

"Margaret, are you serious!"

"Good gracious, Rose, it wasn't even a handful."

"Oh my God, Margaret. What did you do with it?"

If cold river water were to course through my chest and down my arms, it could freeze and tighten my entire body, and it would be less strain than I feel right now.

"Wait, is it bad? Is it bad dirt?" My friend's eyes widen like rounded emeralds, her fingers hitting her mouth. She even sets her tea down.

"Margaret, I . . . we should probably talk—"

"I remember Javi telling me it was for good luck. I thought it was a Mexican thing and kind of interesting. I thought about running a story on it—with your permission, of course. Mexican superstitions and what have you. It could be so catchy."

Oh, good grief! She doesn't know about my magic. She thinks the dirt and mentions of good luck are cultural conventions. The revelation relieves me for half a second.

I grab her shoulders, giving her a shake that widens her eyes further. "What did you do with it, you knucklehead?"

"Well," she says with a curious gulp, "you know how he spread it around gardens and in planters and—"

"Get to it, Margaret!"

"I put it in the ink for my circular and sent it to every darb in the city. I wanted some good luck with the equal rights campaign. That can't be a bad thing, right? Rose?"

She hoists herself from her seat as I rise to my feet, both of us steadying ourselves. For likely the first time in her life, Margaret is silent, eyeing me as I shuffle to the door. I smash my hat over my head, searching the room for an unknown answer. "Honestly, I . . . I really don't know."

"I'm awfully sorry I offended you, Rose. I never intended to."

"It's okay, Margaret. You always have the best intentions. Really."

She pulls me into a tight hug as I reach for the door handle, her relieved laugh above my ear. "Most folks throw my little paper away, anyhow. I think Gio might be my only dedicated reader. I wouldn't worry about—"

I'm not sure what else my friend is gabbing about. I'll catch up with her later when I'm not running out of colonnaded apartments like the building is on fire.

DONNING FLOPPY GLOVES I FOUND IN MY BOYFRIEND'S dresser, I take three wide steps toward the collection of circulars he has stacked in the corner of his bedroom. Even in the havoc of huffing swears through gritted teeth, I don't want my fingers stained with newspaper ink.

The room door creaks open, but that doesn't deter my mission, the heel of my shoe pressing down into a trash bin to make room for more paper. *How many copies does Gio have?*

"What the hell are ya doin'?"

"What the hell are you doing?" I call over my shoulder. "You're supposed to be watching Javi."

"Heck wanted to be with him. I came home to get some clothes, for God's sake!"

The last stack crashes into the bin before I whirl around, holding the bin to my chest with my face burning. "The ink was made with cursed dirt. I'm getting rid of them. No arguments."

My boyfriend's hand runs through the side of his hair, which falls back over his eye again. He starts a retort, then stops to study my determined expression. Settling against the wall, he crosses his arms as a barricade, holding in whatever he's fighting on the inside. "I . . . I don't know what to say, I guess."

My eyes fill with moisture before I can stop them. "Say you trust me."

"It ain't like you trust me."

"You ransacked the furniture store with my magic."

His gaze breaks away, his shoulder brushing against an imaginary itch on the scruff of his chin. "That wasn't my intention, but good and bad is relative." Gio glances at the bin in my arms, his face tightening. "I know you think that ink has somethin' to do with it, but maybe it doesn't."

"I know that it does."

He shakes his head, finally looking up at me with a glare he usually reserves for lowlifes, effectively making my stomach twist. "I'm a criminal, Rose. A goddamn criminal. You didn't change that. Nothin's gonna change that."

"I'm not trying to change that. I'm just trying to get you to remember that's not all you are." There's no keeping my voice from cracking. The sound makes him waver too.

"Not everyone's got a golden heart like you, doll. If I had that magic, I'd lay waste to anyone that got in the way of the people I love."

"Gio. Just stop."

"Why?" he snaps, his own voice gritty with emotion. "So you don't have to hear things you don't wanna hear? You wanna be with a bad boy but get angry when you find out bad boys aren't good men?"

He doesn't mean it. He can't. I've read him hundreds of times. I know his heart—at least, I think I do. Whatever he's saying now—it's not him. Curse magic brings out the worst in people. The part that bothers me is that this side was in him to begin with. But we all fight something. And one thing our crew excels in: we never let each other fight alone. My boyfriend may be a criminal—hell, so am I. But he's not a villain.

I'm not a villain either.

Which is why I'm going to end these curses and figure out how to stop hurting people I love . . . even if that means ending the use of my magic for good. We'll have fewer advantages and the occasional mundane romp. That's another trade I'm willing to make if happiness is the return. What good does it do to gain the whole world and lose my soul, anyway?

A parade of tears falls to the paper below my chin, blurring the ink in the politics section. "You'll feel differently when this wears off after a while."

Gio slides across the wall, leaning to grab the door handle

before holding it open with a sweep of his arm. I trudge across the warped hardwood, pausing as his eyes fall to the crumpled circulars. "Is there anything real about us?"

"How can you ask that?" I whisper.

But he doesn't say anything.

My face twists with a sob while his expression remains entranced by the Trojan horse in my arms. I understand, all too well, his sentiment. The fear of a fabricated romance was the reason I never entered into one until now. What Gio and I have is real. I know it is. He just needs time away from the wicked webs I've unknowingly spun. He needs time away from me.

"Do you care for Javi?" I ask, hardly bothering to sniff up the mucus from around my nose.

My boyfriend tears his eyes away from the bin with rapid blinks. "Like my own brotha'."

"That's real enough for now, isn't it? So take care of him. I'll take care of this." I nod to the vile papers, rushing from the room and down the dim hallway before he can say anything else.

What's great about curse magic is, it doesn't affect me. And I know what's real. And I'm really going to settle this nightmare. For me. For Gio. For all of us.

UNION STATION IS LIKE A SMALL CITY INSIDE A BUILDING. During the day, the neoclassical architecture and tall pillars give off the essence of Old Europe, welcoming the bustling passengers on their way to shops and to catch the train. At three in the morning, however, the dead silence is louder than an announcer declaring the next departure. The mural painted on the ceiling looks like a portal to Hades, the clouds set against a dark background without the charm of daylight behind it. The carved pillars stand as guards ready to send the hounds to drag me into the marble encasement. *No me gusta.*

I shake off the image of Margaret's husband screaming behind thickening bark and tuck myself away in the shadows at the bottom of a staircase. With my eyes long adjusted to the darkness, it's still difficult to make out the winding railing that wraps around half of the station. The staircase—the grandest I've ever seen up close—leads to the second floor, where visitors typically stand and gawk at the splendor of the place, stopping for coffee at the restaurant. It could make a good lookout for a girl who's waiting for a wicked witch in the dark.

Gripping the railing with a sweaty palm, I glance up at my destination, my whole body freezing. The figure at the top of the landing sends my skin flashing with dampness and trepidation. As dark as the room is, the crimson of the figure's dress is unmistakable, her black veil giving the illusion of a headless maiden. My hand aches against the iron railing as she makes her way down the steps with the grace of a floating bride. This is no flapper. And she's certainly not Idoya.

Sol.

It can't be. Her bones lie in a netted bag. I saw them myself.

But I'm also seeing this.

Her beaded hem brushes the ground as she reaches the landing. My nose draws in a sharp breath.

"Why is your face so defeated?" she asks, her voice far

away, yet close at the same time. Her veil tilts with her head in an odd direction. "Why does fear poison your lips?"

I lean away, praying my grip on the railing doesn't slip, and try to find a way to answer her question. "The sky has . . . become silent. I'm afraid the fates have turned against me."

Much like her sister, she laughs for no obvious reason, the outburst startling me so much I nearly fall backward—which only makes her laugh more. With both of my hands bracing my shaky body against the railing, I reel even farther back as she rushes to stand over me. I hate how tall people use their height as an intimidation tactic. I've learned not to let it bother me. But the way she arches her elbow above her head, her fingers tugging at the bottom of her veil—it bothers me. I don't have much experience with ghosts, but running seems like a futile option.

"When the stars stop speaking," she snickers, the veil revealing a set of sneering full lips, "know that the trees have an awful lot to say."

My forehead tightens. These brujas make absolutely no sense.

"¿No crees?"

"Uh . . . y . . . yeah," I choke out. "The trees have definitely gotten me out of a scrap or two."

She doesn't appear satisfied with my answer. "The earth groans for a bridle, dear sister. It wants to be controlled and wielded."

"That doesn't sound s . . . simbiosis."

As the veil climbs higher, my widening eyes fall into a squint at the ghastly creature who isn't so ghastly after all. Her eyes are thoughtful, albeit a bit wild, her skin a flawless sienna like the desert at dusk. I must be staring at her like

Gio was staring at those circulars because she tilts her head again, contorting her mouth back into its previous sneer.

"Simbiótica doesn't work for us," she says like an evening breeze. "Your relationships, your businesses, your life—you try to share, to lighten the loads that are meant for you. But we are brujas. Jefas of the earth as you are in life. And if you keep sharing your power, others will use it for what they want. They will make decisions for you every time."

"Listen, I . . ." I can't believe I'm arguing with a dead person. "My decisions affect people I care about."

Her upper lip rears away from a decent set of teeth. "You can rule—or you can share your will and lose it."

Time to move this along. This isn't a place anyone should linger, even a bruja from the River Bottoms.

"Thank you for the advice," I blurt out, "but I've come here for—"

Her shattering scream knocks me the rest of the way off my feet, my rear end hitting the cold granite, although my overcoat takes the brunt. The fur trim slides across the tiles, my heels shoving me away from the screeching woman as her face erupts with bubbling boils. Foaming pus spills from each lesion, her eyes filling with the color of her dress, and I swear I'm choking on my own terror that rams my heart down into my rib cage. Cinnamon and the fresh cut of dandelion rage on her breath before she vanishes, her screams echoing with the clink of a small stone as it hits the floor. My chest rises and falls like an accordion at a hoedown. I briefly wonder if a person's heart can just stop beating from such breathing. The sapphire egg waiting near my toes—the very reason I came to this cursed meeting— barely registers.

I don't know what I've gotten myself into. I don't want to know right now. I just want to get the hell out of here before I end up slinking around in a bag of netting.

A little girl's laugh from the center of the room has me scrambling to my feet, pocketing the egg on my way up. Dressed in the same rags from the other night, Idoya claps and bounces on her feet. "Oh, how fun that was! Isn't she preciosa?"

"Yeah, she's . . . demonstrative."

Idoya's tiny face puckers. "You should be grateful. She gifted you straight from her bones."

"Oh, well, give her my thanks," I say, sidestepping toward the entrance to keep my eyes on the younger of the insane duo. "I hate to give you the bum's rush, but I've gotta lot of witchery to do myself."

Ignoring her off-tempo song about weeping trees, I bolt through the doors, my breath raking across my throat in the cold as I sprint to the safety of the back seat of my car.

"Whoa there, baby," my driver says. "You rob the place or what?"

"Drive, Giuseppe!"

"Holy shit, okay, geeeez."

The tires squeal, and I lie in the back seat with my hands tucked in my pockets, but he doesn't question me any further. As a lifelong member of the underworld himself, the gambling-manager-turned-taxi-driver knows when to keep his mouth shut.

My fingers stretch around the haunted stone in my pocket, my skin almost too numb from the cold to grasp it. I wish anxiousness worked the same way. Maybe I *will* move to upstate New York when this is all over. I'll buy a farm and watch

Heck learn to feed a chicken. Gio can teach Margaret's child how to play the piano, and my mother and abuela can sing river songs while making tortillas and chile sauces. We just gotta get through this part.

I can do it.

I think I can do it.

I have to.

11

THE TREES HAVE AN AWFUL LOT TO SAY.

What did Sol mean?

I haven't seen the stone-stacked building with frost-printed windows that is the Guadalupe Center since I was a little girl, but the nostalgia is lost in a sea of worry and questions that have no answers. I only stop biting the tip of my thumbnail when I catch a group of mothers staring at me in a small waiting area. They bounce their toddlers on their hips, mumbling to each other in Spanish like I can't understand what they're saying. They think I'm just another brainless deb from the upper-class charity club, throwing my husband's money at their well-baby clinic.

"Rose, there you are, darling. You must have slept *horribly.*"

I tried to powder the circles under my eyes before leaving the hotel this morning, but nothing escapes Margaret's critical eye. At least Gio was asleep by the time I got to our room. I didn't have the energy for another fight.

I secure the strap of my handbag to my shoulder like I wasn't up all night hunting ghosts and divination, and do my best to prepare for my first encounter with the pregnant wives club—an annoying yet brilliant setup by Margaret for photo ops. Heck, of course, was thrilled with the idea, and I wanted to get as far away from Excelsior Springs as I could for the time being.

Leading me away from the snickering bystanders, my friend drags me into a meeting room filled with round tables adorned with lace cloths. The brunch being served has to cost more than was raised to put on the event, but these pearl-draped ladies don't seem concerned with things like bookkeeping.

Or the fact that giving the money to these mothers would have been a better use of resources than this make-me-feel-noble meal it's being wasted on.

"Ladies, I have a pressing matter to bring to the table if you'll hear me," one woman says while we take our seats. Her cloche, shimmering with a purple band that may as well be a crown, matches her frock. "That circular has gotten quite out of hand."

It's a good thing Margaret blushes a lot, or else she'd be giving herself away.

"Oh?" she replies, taking a dainty sip of her coffee and avoiding my eye. "How so?"

The woman next to me waves down a waiter, her fingers flashing with an impressive diamond. "It's true. We've had hired help walking out in the middle of prayer meeting—just as soon as it arrived on our doorstep."

"Well, there are *worse* things," Margaret muses into her mug.

"I told *my* help to dispose of it," a third debutante says, adjusting her long gloves with a curt nod. "My husband doesn't want me touching the morbid thing." She leans toward the center of the table, glancing over her shoulder. "One issue recommended a book on *sexual relations* . . . as in 'how to please a woman.'"

The diamond-studded hand grabs my wrist in stunned dismay. "That's so emasculating. My husband doesn't need such a book."

I don't know her or her man, but I'm almost positive he does. Of course, she can't say that here. Or anywhere in her world, for that matter. I almost feel sorry for her, the way she pushes her disappointment down with her toast and butter. Poor darling.

Her secret's safe with me.

While the waiter tops off a few beveled juice glasses, the crowned woman raises her fork in the air. "Which is why we cannot have those grotesque messages landing on our porches for our children and butlers to see. Do we really want immigrants and darkies tending to our kitchens and vehicles while thinking of our underthings?"

The waiter, as sable as the earth, shows no hint of anger at her language. He serves the table like Clip serves up jazz music—with a polite expression and a nod of thanks at the tip pressed into his hand. He's been born to it, inured from it. He probably hates it as much as I do but has learned to hide it so much better. Meanwhile, my ears are on fire, but this table wouldn't be aware of its bigotry if I burst into flames.

The lady with the gloves wrinkles her nose at the pulp floating in her juice. "As my William says, we must control the narrative, or else the devil will."

The surrounding brood nods and hums in agreement, although Margaret has become incredibly interested in the polka dots on her skirt.

The diamond-studded woman to my right finally relents, releasing my arm and shifting her upturned nose in my direction. "I hope you don't think us mean. Most of *our* help are immigrants, and they don't really know any better. But we can't have them thinking this is how we run society. That's why it's important to actually go into their homes—to help *them*."

Ahhh, yes—the heralded philanthropy of the center's many projects, helping indoctrinate other cultures into the American way of life in the name of charity. Through these efforts, immigrants receive free education and health clinics. They learn English. Learn bland ways to cook. And dress. And speak.

And unlearn who they are.

The coffee isn't nearly as bitter as the words on the edge of my tongue.

Margaret clears her throat, but the obvious leader of the group shakes her head in earnest, the purple band glinting along with her eyes as she swallows a bite to get her words out. "That's why we're going to keep them out of our schools until they can prove decent hygiene and home care. The grade school in Argentine is how Hank Nelson got Spanish flu."

"I thought that originated in Fort Riley, Kansas," I pipe up, unable to hold the disdain from my tone. It doesn't shake the brunch princess at all.

"Perhaps the Mexicans are more susceptible to carrying it, then," she quips without so much as looking in my direction. "They have all kinds of diseases, which is why we're so careful to teach them to clean properly. That boxcar community, for example—absolute *filth*. Good on the city for taking it down."

I break their nodding session with the scrape of my chair across the tiles. "How clean would your home be with seven people sharing five hundred square feet?"

Margaret bursts into a nervous giggle, joining my side with some excuse about pregnancy moodiness. "The Kesslers are such altruists, anyhow. We should be more polite. Why don't you ladies set up the Parcheesi board while I get her photo?"

"Really, Rose," she mutters into my ear as we reach the hallway. If she says one more word about my attitude or this stupid frumpy dress I had to wear . . .

"Don't you start with me, Margaret. Those ladies are—"

"Terrible? Dreadful? Deviant?" My friend smooths her cardigan, pulling me close as a man with a camera tells us to smile before I'm blinded by a *poof!*-ing flash. He runs off as fast as he showed up, Margaret's grin melting. "You don't know the half of it."

"God, do I want to know?"

Her head bows low, her hand cupping her mouth like we're being tailed by Russian spies. "That vile woman with the hat—her husband is some kind of imperial wizard."

"A . . . what?"

"A top Klansman," she hisses. "You know how the Mexican classrooms in Armourdale and Argentine are segregated from whites?"

"God, yes."

"Of course you do. What am I saying?"

"I'm not sure."

Margaret huffs, balling her hands into fists in front of her rounded belly. "They were behind it all. They roughed up the superintendent to get it done, and I think . . . I think Archie had something to do with it too. I found some strange things in his desk."

My eyes widen, and we both feign a light conversation as a few ladies stroll by before we turn to each other again with vehemence.

"Listen to me," I say, my words as soft as air. "You cannot chase this story."

"Why?" Margaret's eyes narrow. "Do you know something?"

"No! I just . . . it's dangerous, okay? Those people, they're dangerous." I tuck my handbag under my arm, laying a hand over her fist to shake it loose. "Those pearls and diamonds are the masks of monsters. Please, don't chase this one. You're free and clear to live your life."

My friend's forehead creases with burdens she should not have to carry. "But . . . what if Archie gets away with his wickedness? He's just out there getting away with it."

Squeezing her fingers, I read the fading of her determination as it turns to sadness so deep I almost hug her. But that would make her cry, and then I'd cry. And I'm damn tired of crying already.

"Wicked men never get away with anything," I say instead. "It eventually catches up to them."

Margaret stares down the hallway with a longer silence than she can usually tolerate. "I suppose you're right," she finally says, righting her posture once again. "Maybe . . . maybe he was a liability, and they buried him somewhere."

"God, what makes you say that?"

"Just . . . wishful thinking, I suppose." She shrugs at my fallen jaw. "Like I said, who leaves behind all that money? I sure don't want him coming back for it . . . or me."

My stomach swallows any indignation those ladies at the brunch table lit inside me. I never thought of how Margaret might lie awake at night wondering if her husband might show up someday and drag her out by her hair. Again.

What a terrible thought to fall asleep to. I want to tell her she'll never have to see that sorry excuse for a partner again. But I can only console her with another truth.

"Even if he does," I say, lifting my chin in a debonair fashion that coaxes a smirk from her, "you're too strong now to put up with it. And you're not without friends."

Margaret's belly presses into my chest as she tugs me into an embrace, her cheeks wetting mine. She sends me on my way before heading to the powder room to touch up her face, and I wipe her rouge from my shoulder. Of all the days to wear black. But this isn't the only event requiring such bleak attire today.

To add to the dismal morning, I find that damn investigator leaning his lanky body against the hood of my vehicle in the parking lot. Right on schedule. *Just great.*

"All right, so your story checks out," he says, popping a cigarette into his pruney mouth. "Sponsoring that immigrant family, as you said. The center here confirmed. I just thought . . . it seemed like the Alvarados were family. My instincts are usually spot-on with these things."

I tap my heels on the pavement but decide to open my own door to get away from this guy. Giuseppe is a better gambler than he is a chauffeur. "You're not a real reporter, are you?"

"No, ma'am. I am not," the investigator says. "I was hired by the Kessler family when Heck was barely a thought. And don't worry about firing me. I've been paid up. I protect the Kessler interests, if you will."

"Well, you've got nothing to worry about from me."

"Time will tell, won't it?"

I don't feel a thing about my door slamming in his face. He needs to get in line behind all the other slimeballs waiting to get at me.

"Shake him," I order my driver.

Giuseppe sticks his thumb in the air. "You got it, baby."

"HOT DAWG, THE OLD MAN FINALLY SHUT HIS MOUTH."

"Hiram!" A woman about my mother's age jabs the young baron with her elbow. Her accent is about as Ozarkian as her late husband's, but with fewer swear words. "You two may not have been congenial, but you will be respectful as long as I am present."

Hiram clicks his tongue as he scans a chandelier. "Fine. I am most thankful he decided to pass in his native city. I would be most put out to have to travel back home in a snowstorm."

"Have you no conscience?" she asks, her eyes darting

about nervously. "He *wanted* to be buried here. He looks forward to the holiday week all year."

"I'm sure he does," Hiram replies with a droll eye roll.

"Respect, Hiram!" Mrs. Wilmington's hiss is quickly covered by a fake smile as passersby send her well-wishes. She's got a point, even if the geezer lacked a single honorable attribute. It is his funeral after all.

Sipping at a wine too sweet for smooth drinking, I busy myself with eavesdropping and people watching while Heck makes the rounds during what feels like yet another luncheon for these Missouri royals. No one seems to be too broken up about Mr. Wilmington—even the dress code is a lot less gallant than at most of their gatherings. I suppose they're saving those getups for tonight.

Since the Christmas Eve Gala, Hiram Wilmington the Second's sudden illness took a turn for the worse. His passing effectively halted holiday festivities and all contract negotiations for at *least* a couple of days. They didn't even bother to host the memorial at a downtown location, citing the accommodations of the Elms Hotel as an appropriate respite for traveling family members of the infamous baron. Why waste his money on a funeral when the funds could be divided among his kinfolk at an exclusive spa resort?

A familiar gangster dressed as a politician sidles up next to me near the deviled eggs, a fat cigar between his big teeth. With all the money in the room, I'm shocked I haven't run into him this week already. The notion and the nearby stench of appetizers stuffed with mayonnaise and yolk have me taking a big swig of my sparkling wine.

"Mr. Pendergast," I say, grimacing at bubbles in my glass.

"Mrs. Kessler, your hair looks nice without a hat smashed over it. The waves and all."

"I . . . thanks."

I'd compliment his hair, but it's slicked like every other man's in here. We stand in silence for a few moments since I don't know how to beat the gums, until he lets out a smoky sigh. "That was some surprising work you did on that furniture store."

My eyes find an empty chair across the room, and I smile and wave like I've spotted an old friend. "That wasn't intentional."

"Hey, you don't hafta reason with me. You got their attention *and* their vote." He cuts off my protest with a light clap on my back. "Keep it up, kid."

After his broad shoulders disappear into the crowd, I fill my glass with more bubbly sweetness and head to find my overcoat. Thank the fates for fifty-degree temperatures. At least I'll be able to feel my fingers enough for a quick smoke. Or a long one. The south balcony is deserted enough to hide out for a while. The lone gentleman with a tall glass of champagne has the same idea, tipping his flute to me as I close the French doors to the buzzing room. I don't blame Hiram for getting as far away from this crowd as he can at a time like this. Not every showman wants to put on a show, no matter the occasion.

I light up a Camel, and we chuckle at a few birds fighting over seeds they've discovered under the melting snow.

"I know it's terribly rude to ask, but . . . how did he pass?"

Hiram's mustache lifts into a side smile, smoke streaming into the air. "Apparently, he choked to death on his own vomit after a night of Christmas Eve revelry. His escorts couldn't revive him."

"Oh," I say, glancing through the windows at the widow in the center of the ballroom. "Does your mother know? About the escorts, I mean."

A snort shoots from Hiram's nose. "They're the ones who called her that night." He raises his glass with a bitter smile. "It's how he wanted to go."

Something between a laugh and a groan pushes a plume of smoke out of my mouth, my own flute lifting in the air. "He deserved nothing less."

"Hear! Hear!" Hiram says flatly. He gives his glass an unbecoming slurp, followed by a belch that sends the birds flapping. "I'll forgive your rudeness if you forgive mine— I'm half under myself. I've just been meanin' to ask."

"Sure. Anything."

He raises an eyebrow at me.

"Almost anything."

"Well," he says, his smirk fading. "I was wonderin' . . . did you do this?"

¿Qué? I flick my ashes over the balcony. "Did I do *what*, Hiram?"

His glassy eyes level at the trees, water dripping from their bare branches. "You know what kind of man he is— what he's done to me. I wouldn't be angry in the slightest."

Old Man Wilmington was one of the most disgusting excuses for a gentleman I've encountered, even in the speakeasy scene. He was harsh and outspoken about his disdain for women, people with dark skin, and anyone who didn't tell him how right he was about his bigotry. He earned his terrible ferry ride out of this world. But . . . is Hiram really asking me if I *killed* his father? He doesn't know me well enough to know I'm not that kind of bruja. I mean, I am, but I'm not—even though I am.

But I'm not!

"Mr. Wilmington—"

"Lord, I despise that title."

"I don't even know *how* to perform a curse like that." However, my mind rushes to show me an endless reel of ghastly things that *could* be connected to that damn bucket of dirt. "But, um, just out of curiosity . . . did your father read the circular?"

"No," Hiram admits, rubbing the back of his neck. "He pissed on the first delivery and told his driver to burn that paper if it showed up again. Why? Did that kill him?"

"No," I insist. "Vomit and lust killed him. And . . . I'm sorry. I'm sorry he left you like this."

Even a bad father is still a father. It can't be easy knowing the man who raised you is never coming back.

Hiram flicks his Lucky Strike over the balcony, then braces his palms on the wood grain. I should let the man grieve for a while. The loss of the family patriarch, as well as his greatest critic, is a lot to take in.

"He left me with nothing, you know."

My heels stop just outside the door. *Oh, Hiram.* The old man was vile, but even in his death, he cut out his only living son. What kind of father plans such ruin in the afterlife?

"It's called 'the spite clause,'" Hiram continues, acidity seeping into his voice. "It states that the inheritance money shall only be released to the heirs upon the death of his son. I will never see a penny of his fortune as long as I breathe."

Whoa. That's scandalous. Unprincipled. Debased.

"Hiram, again, I'm so sorry."

However, the sinking in my guts is sorrier for my brother. Without Hiram's family money, there are no contracts to be had, save for possible contracts from the few other barons in the lake towns. It was a bleak option to begin with, but at least it was an option.

Not anymore.

"At least my children will benefit from his hatred of me." Pushing himself away from the bannister, the Baron Heir of Nothing attempts a grin. "Don't fret your pretty self about my predicament, darlin'. I've got a nest egg of my own—a much sounder investment than waiting on a ruthless rummy to kick off."

"Hey, at least that's good to hear," I say, eyeing his teetering stance. I might need to track down a family member of his to come collect him later. I also need to find Heck and give him the update. "I'm gonna head back in. My nose is getting cold."

"I'm much obliged to the lendin' of your ear, you phenomenal snake charma'."

"You're welcome," I say, leaving him tipping his glass upside down to catch the last few drops on his tongue. *Yeah, there's gotta be a cousin in here somewhere.*

Halfway across the ballroom, a familiar middle part with enough grease to lubricate all the engines in the parking lot catches my eye. With a look that deters anyone from stopping to chat with me, I make a beeline for the gambling manager in the awkward-fitting suit. He holds up an index finger at my flat stare as he chews the bulge in his cheek. I'm not sure how he's fitting all that food into such a tiny mouth.

"Why aren't you with Javi? It's your shift," I say, sending Giuseppe's jaw chomping faster.

His loud swallow is followed by a cringeworthy suck as his tongue fishes debris from his canine. "Heck rushed outta here to get him outta the hotel, seein' as how that baron is stayin' on the same floor."

Damn smoke break! I was gone for three minutes. I wish someone would have told me Dorian had arrived, but I wouldn't have bothered to go find Heck either if I heard the news before he did. We were prepared for this, however.

"Okay," I say, setting my flute on the serving table before I drop it. "So, we're going to Plan B."

"These darbs don't know nothin' about makin' meatballs."

"If you take one more bite while talking to me—"

"Jesus, baby," Giuseppe hisses before lowering his fork to his plate. "You're always gettin' in a latha'. It's taken care of. Gio's gettin' the car ready. I'm drivin' him to the *undisclosed* location and comin' right back so as not to arouse suspicion."

Okay, good. This is good, I think, although it feels like we're just short of jumping off a cliff into icy water. While I was away on my fluff mission at the Guadalupe Center, Hiram offered Heck to set my brother up at his vacation home in the city. No one would suspect another baron of giving refuge to the guy suspected of trying to kill one of their own.

Hiram felt it was the least he could do after all the trouble his father and the other barons dragged into our world. None of it was Hiram's fault, of course. But the gesture wasn't one we could afford to reject.

Remembering that Giuseppe is still here with a silent plea

to take another bite of his entrée, I give him a nod, my lips tucked between my teeth. "Listen, Gus—"

"Look, I don't know, and I don't wanna know," he says, shoving a forkful into his mouth. "Knowin' stuff gets people killed."

That it does—which is why I have to see this plan through to make sure Dorian doesn't know a damn thing.

THE WAY FLAMES DANCE IN A HEARTH OR ANY OTHER BED OF wood and coals mesmerizes the onlooker with a sense of both safety and danger. The orange glow promises warmth, even survival, but the fluid way it spins as though it is both air and water also beckons with a warning. The threat of the power to consume anything it touches pushes sweat to the surface of my skin. This couch in my hotel room has become the seat of my entrancement as I hollow out a place in my heart to do what I must do one night from now.

The door behind me squeals open, then clicks shut. Yet, my eyes stay locked onto that fire.

"We got him set up," says a voice with a familiar grit I typically find comforting. The shuffling of shoes and drawers accompanies my boyfriend around the room as he gives me the report of Javier's transfer to the younger Wilmington's holiday residence. "Heck is passed out from a few mint julep cocktails, and Gus is runnin' a game of poker in the basement. Keeps the barons busy, anyway."

"Good."

The silence is interrupted every so often with Gio's occasional sigh, his shoulder coming to rest on one of the big window frames. I chance a glance in his direction, his lost gaze half hidden by his frizzy fringe. It must have been misting outside. The dewy moisture on the window pane agrees.

With the moonlight swallowed up by the night, only the yellow flickering of the fireplace captures my boyfriend's pinched eyebrows. I've seen this expression before—the first time we kissed outside my car. He refused to sleep with me. And I refused to give him my heart. The part he didn't know yet was that he had it already.

Just as he does now.

My eyes mirror the misted glass in front of the man I never meant to hurt. Hell, that's why I wanted him far away from me and my magic. It's why I kept everyone away. The truth burns into my chest like the heat from the fire. I'm not angry with Gio. I'm angry with myself. And, quite frankly, the fates. Being blessed with only the power to curse isn't a blessing at all. My abuela called my powers a gift. But now, I just want to call it what it is.

"Gio . . . I'm honestly just . . . so sorry."

As my voice cracks and my hand hits my mouth, he crosses the room. I close my eyes, but I feel him kneeling in front of me, pulling at both my wrists. "Hey, you look at me. C'mon, look at me, Rose." From his touch, his heart tells me it's breaking—for Javi and for us. For everything that was said. "You know, believe it or not, I knew what I was gettin' into the night you saved us all down by the riva'."

"You *couldn't* have," I sob.

"Well, maybe not everything. But, my God, I watched you fry a guy's brain."

"Ughhh, Gio—"

"That jerk deserved it."

I hate how vulnerable I feel. At least the water in my eyes is blurring the way he's looking at me. I've never felt more like a monster. "Why would you want to even *be* with someone like me?"

"Why would I—" The cotton blend of Gio's sleeve mashes against my eyelids and finishes with the drip from my nose. "The more I learn about you, the more I want to be with you. And that's not the evil ink talkin'. The real question is, why would you wanna be with a joka' like *me*?"

Kneeling there in his undershirt, he hands me the wad that was once his button-down, letting me turn it into a giant handkerchief.

"You . . . you're not a joker."

"And you're not bad," he says, tilting his head to catch my gaze. "Maybe a little dangerous. But it ain't like we met at church."

I shake my head to hide the smile twitching on my lips. "Have you ever been to church?"

"Hey! A synagogue or two before they kicked me out."

A small laugh shoots through my nose, widening his ornery grin. "So, hey." Gio presses his lips to my knuckles before settling his chin on both of our hands. The fire backlights the earnestness in his eyes, which echoes through his skin. "If ten guys didn't tell you already how incredible you look tonight, I'd be a little sore."

Get out of town. My makeup is smudged. My hair's a mess. And he's definitely not going to want his shirt back until I've sent it out for cleaning.

"You're nuts. It's a simple black dress."

"Ain't nothin' simple when it's on you."

I still have no clue how he does it without charm magic, but I suddenly don't feel like crying anymore. I want him more now than I ever have. It occurs to me that what used to turn me on in former relationships no longer holds a candle to sincerity. And commitment.

And a little bit of danger.

My boyfriend's thoughts swirl methodically with the same sentiment as a storm building inside him, waiting for release. Sliding my fingers beneath his chin, I lift it higher, letting his silent apologies and urgent wantonness surge through me.

"What do you want?" I whisper.

His lurid gaze drops to my lips. "To forget this damn world for one night."

Pendergast. The barons. The witches with the dreadful bones. It all will fade to the background with one kiss—for the both of us.

Roses and lavender and everything sweet swell every taste bud on my tongue, the scent drawing his mouth up to mine, where we drink our fill of everything we've been holding back from each other.

12

"AIN'T IT BEEN A GREAT DECADE SO FAH?"

The crowd of New Year's partygoers erupt into applause, some of them clinking their glasses while others dance. The largest ballroom in the Elms Hotel has given my club's entertainers the great honor of providing our highly acclaimed jazz music and ragtime skits on the biggest night of the year.

I'm just crossing my fingers that Doris has enough sense to schmooze an audience on the brink of a baron territory war. She somehow always comes through. And I've got to start trusting my crew with the jobs I've given them.

But . . . they don't call her Bearcat for nothing.

"She can do it," Heck whispers in my ear, giving my hand an encouraging squeeze.

"I know she can."

"Movie stahs, kippy styles," she proclaims into the silver microphone with a smile so wide, I swear it's making the chandeliers sparkle. "Men finally discova'd the secret to makin' a woman happy." Her jade eyes shoot me a wink before she juts her hip out with a finger on her chin. "Oh, wait. No, they haven't." The crowd's laughter joins the crashing symbols. "That's why I'm ringin' out the new year without a rock on my finga'—so, single dolls and fellas, get ya hot feet on this dance floor and do what you please before somebody does something crazy—like fawl in love!"

With another round of cheers and whistles, a glittering dance troupe sashays across the stage, accompanying our lead singer's tune she's become locally famous for performing. Between her sultry vocals and the troupe's high kicks, the Missouri Rockettes have these upper-class gentlemen on their feet and swinging their ladies like the old friends they all used to be. Heck and I would join them if we weren't on the verge of our greatest con to date—erasing Dorian's memories.

I just don't want to accidentally erase Dorian.

My nerves spike again as Heck and I saunter about the edge of the room, feigning gratitude from the salutations of half-drunk patrons. They compliment the collection of kiss curls on the side of my temple. They can't know I'm wearing my hair up to keep strands out of my face during the incantation I'll perform later. While they prattle to us aloud, Heck's thoughts are an endless scroll of names and memories as cousins of barons twice removed gab to him about the catering and its Latin-inspired flair. Pity I'm too nauseated to enjoy it tonight.

Heck checks his wristwatch, giving me a subtle nod. It's time.

My stomach somersaults behind my rib cage. I finally

have his approval to leave a party, but this was not the reason I ever dreamed would be my escape. Still, I steer myself into the lavatory. Some cold water on my face should bed my angst back down.

The pedestal is as pale as my face, though the stark rouge on my lips contrasts well with the emerald sequins of my dress. I've chosen a close-fitting cap encrusted with jewels in lieu of feathers. I don't want anything falling off inside Dorian's room that could be traced back to me. The thought has queasiness crashing back over me, my mouth watering like I've got rabies. Other ladies rap at the door, but the toilet bowl and I are having it out. Five more minutes of splashing water and patting my face with a hand towel have my body feeling much better as I tell the mirror to get itself together.

This is for Javi. This is what I can do to save him and make this nightmare go away for all of us.

Knuckles rap at the door again, and after freshening up my cheeks and lips, I swing it open with the gusto of a bruja who's about to go scramble someone's brains.

"Geez, take it easy—!" I stop short, letting the door slam behind me with a heavy sigh at the pursed-lipped investigator with the ugly bow tie. "You keeping an eye on my bathroom habits now?"

His tight mouth squeezes into a sarcastic smile. "So, how far along are you? For the doctors to give you a positive test, you must be, what, three months?"

"This is really none of your business."

"The Kessler line is my business. Especially if one is being carried by a vamp."

"Mr. Investigator," I snap, searching my handbag for a

cigarette so I can blow the smoke in his face, "I have no intentions of giving the Kessler line a damn thing."

The newest bane of my existence blinks, taking a small step back. "So, you're going to . . . end the pregnancy? I will go tell him right now."

"There *is* no pregnancy."

More blinking. He really needs to accept I'm no debutante and get the hell out of my way. "You . . . lied to him. To everyone? For the society papers?"

"We did what we had to do." My thumb lights my Camel like I was born with a set of matches.

Dios. He looks like I stole his favorite pen.

"What kind of wife feels this way about bearing her husband a child? How will you protect his line?"

"How many times do I have to say it isn't your business?" Blowing a large plume at his spectacles, I push past him without apology. "You want a Kessler baby, go have one."

His hand fastens around my arm—a poor choice on his part. "You will give this line a baby, or else I will tell the world about your half-blood connection to a brood of filthy immigrants. I can't prove it, but it's a gut feeling, and I can't *believe* Heck would agree to such dirt in his bed."

His thoughts are full of the same drivel he's spewing. At least he's not hiding his bias. *What a saint.*

"And how does this protect Heck, exactly?"

"He will either have to come to your defense and lose his claim on the land he owns," the investigator says, covering a cough from my smoky onslaught, "or he'll have to say he was lied to. As the titles state: the land shall be bequeathed to a Kessler heir, pure of blood and clean of record. What do you think he'll choose? Losing his fortune for a loose skirt who clearly doesn't love him, or keeping what he is owed. I'll make sure the divorce is quick, and you will never be seen in society in this town again."

Why are all these patrons of intolerance so bent on running my family and me out of our homes? What did we ever do to them? The answer is: nothing. And that satisfies me, somehow. Heck taught me not to put any stock in what others will or will not accept.

"I am a Kessler whether you like it or not," I say, flicking my ashes onto his wing-tips. "You might work for the Kessler family, but you, sir, will *never* be a Kessler. Now, release my arm, you turnip."

As he turns three shades of red, a head of side-slicked, golden hair rounds the corner. "What do you mean, sir, by handling my wife?"

The investigator drops my elbow, backing away with his hands up. "Mr. Kessler, if I may—"

"You may not," Heck says with the same indignation in his voice that flashes in his eyes, both of which will make me love him forever. "I will have you removed from the premises with a court order—I know every judge in that ballroom. Or you may remove yourself." Heck steps closer, somehow towering over a man who is actually taller than he is. "Or . . . I will remove you myself."

Shifting on his feet, the investigator lowers his eyes to the floor, his chin lifting before he sails away without another word. *Good riddance.*

"Oh, darling," Heck says, examining the red mark on my arm. "Are you all right? I will lodge a formal complaint. I had no idea he was stalking you this way."

I flash him a guilty smile. "Well, he's been stalking us both. I guess he's some private investigator for your estate, and I know I should have told you. But I didn't want to worry you with everything else going on."

"Ugh, ugh, ugh, Rose."

"I know. I know."

"Something to talk about later, I suppose," he says with a sigh, his eyes shutting.

"Exactly. Let's focus on the task at hand, I . . ." Taking another drag, I try to suffocate the shivering in the pit of my stomach, but the tobacco isn't working this time. I have to face the likelihood that I could really harm Dorian. I feel like a government assassin who only knows how to shoot to kill.

Kill.

My stomach trembles again. The back of my neck flushes with heat and dampness. I can't just end someone's life pre-emptively, even if they *are* twisted. If he tried to kill Javi, in the moment, that would be different. I've had way too much time to think about this.

"I can't kill him, Heck. I can't."

My best friend's arms are tried and true, wrapping me up into a hug as safe as my own brother's. "I know, kitten." He pulls back, rubbing my temples with his thumbs resonating with reassurance. "That's how I know you won't."

I stand on my toes, touching my lips to his cheek before walking off to what will surely be my destiny . . . or my fate.

THE WALLPAPER ALONG THE HALLWAYS OF THE HOTEL IS A calculated pattern of cross-stitching that was made to feel uptown, but now adorns my long walk to a door that approaches me slowly, as if I'm in *Maciste*, a horror movie about a man who is taken by the devil into hell, to try to corrupt the man's morality. The silence of the film adds to the morbidity and eeriness of the story. Just as do this hallway and the baby fern gripped between my hands.

Using a key I acquired through Giuseppe, I turn the long knob after the click, letting myself into a room with a large fire and the devil himself. Dorian's hooded eyes slowly rise as I secure the door, and that hazel stare follows me to the fainting couch, where pillows prop him on every side. The bandage is still bound to his head, his hair scruffy in all directions, but he looks rather well . . . aside from the stupefied expression on his face.

"Come for me again, have you?" he drawls as he attempts to sit up. His teeth gleam as they grit together. "I wouldn't save your bartender if I had you bent over these cushions."

I withhold a gasp and force my jaw to relax. *He knows.* There is no going back at this juncture. I do this now or my brother dies because this man thinks himself a god. Invincible. So many men do.

"I'm here to apologize on behalf of my staff's actions, Mr. Luxberg," I say softly, setting the plant on the couch table before seating myself at his hip. I cross my legs, pushing my handbag behind me. "I brought you a peace offering."

"Ha," he laughs, grimacing as he settles back into his pillows. "You better have something to offer me other than a plant. We'll start with putting your mouth to good use, and maybe I won't have him beaten before handing him over to the authorities."

His fingers fall to my thigh, tickling my knee. He lets out another grimacing chuckle as the muscles in my body tense.

"Get out," he says, "or do what you do best."

What I do best.

"Oh, I certainly will."

Humming a haunting melody, I slide my hands up his thighs and over his hip bones, and he groans as my thumbs trail the patch of hair beneath his belly button. He arches his back, jutting his hips upward with a satisfied smile.

"I knew you were a good girl . . ." His mouth widens in a big yawn. I keep my gaze steady on his glassy stare as his eyelids lower. He fights to keep them open, mumbling about how tawdry I would look on my knees, before he finally succumbs to the bewitchment of the fern—an age-old recipe cut straight from one of my abuela's own plants.

Good night, Mr. Luxberg.

He won't feel a thing.

Hopefully.

Shaking off his icky hand, I rush to the bar and grab the ice bucket, then fill it with water from the private lavatory. The handbag at his hip gives me quite the fumble as adrenaline courses through me, but I manage to crack the gleaming stone, dropping the yolk and its slimy membrane into the bucket. I set it on the carpet and anchor my fingers around his ears and jaw.

Like stepping into another room only separated by a curtain, I descend into Dorian's consciousness. *No.* Not a room. A hall of stone, occupied by a prince who's waiting for me. His smile gleams as nude ladies drape my body with silk and lace as before. The song of a harpist accompanies

Dorian as he once again leads me to a long table, his hand teasing my shoulder blades.

"Look at the feast I've prepared for you. We'll dine on pain and vengeance."

My heart thumps with the rhythm of the harp, my nipples hardening at the chilly air and the coldness in his voice.

When he gestures to the banquet at the table, I'm no longer shocked, but still disgusted as my brother struggles within his bindings of tomato vines. Fat grapes bubble from his gurgling mouth. His heels slide across rotting berries to no avail. The pungency of the spoiled fruit stings my nostrils, and I have to hang on Dorian's arm to keep myself upright.

The baron's thoughts echo across the hall. *Eat.*

The message is clear: *Eat or be devoured.*

A knife slips into my hand, the edge sharp and ready. The gleaming tip shakes so badly, my wavy locks fall in front of my eyes, the strands trembling like the willow branches near the river. It takes both of my hands to keep the knife steady. My breath comes heavier now, the sound reverberating with Dorian's laughter as he reaches to push my hair back into place. The bitter flavor of cinnamon overpowers the stench of the decaying feast before me. That taste. It's so familiar.

Trailing his fingers down the side of my jawline, Dorian's hands stop to pinch the dimple in my chin. "Dine with me, Rose."

That taste!

Idoya said I would recognize it. The spell is activated. And now . . . I know what I must do.

I swallow the bile climbing to my throat and pray a desperate prayer, turning back to my writhing brother. "¡Es un desconocido para mí!"

Dorian gasps, backing away as I hunch over my brother, sinking the knife into Javi's temple. With his sickening screams ringing through the hall, I slide the edge down his jawline and around the other side, mind retching as I peel his face from his skull.

As the blade clinks against the stone floor, I pull my hands back from Javier's face, dry heaving until my head starts spinning. It takes several long gasps for me to realize it's no longer my brother's face I've pulled away from.

It's Dorian's.

The young baron's light snores harmonize with the crackling flames in the hearth while I swallow hard to keep my stomach from convulsing once more. The contents of the ice bucket at my feet have turned black with putrid sinews floating around the yolk.

"It worked," I whisper, forcing my quivering legs to stand. "I think it worked."

I waste no time emptying the bucket into the toilet before gathering any trace of my presence and leaving the wicked prince to his slumber. I pray a thousand prayers of thankfulness as I check the hallway, making sure no one is there, before I sprint to my hotel room, vowing to lock myself inside for the rest of the night. Tomorrow, we'll all be going home. *All of us*. And for the first time since this all began, I give myself a break. I free myself of my getup, don my coziest sleeping gown, and finally let myself rest.

THE WARMTH OF GIO'S BODY ON MY BACK MAKES ME GROAN from happiness as my eyes peel open to the darkness of the hotel room. The fire has gone to coals, and I have no intention of getting out from under these covers this early. Turning to bury myself in my boyfriend's sleep shirt, I smash my face into the bare skin of a rather brawny chest I've seen many times before.

"Heck Kessler, what are you doing in my bed?"

Gio's rumpled hair shoots up from the other side of me, his eyes swollen from a deep slumber. "Huh? What? What's happening?"

"Dios mío, Giovanni, what is wrong with you boys?"

Heck groans, turning onto his stomach and burying his head beneath a pillow.

"Funny thing," Gio says, shifting to lean on his elbow. "We both got spooked afta' we saw you passed out last night with that creepy eggshell in your handbag."

"You went through my handbag?"

"You wouldn't wake up! We thought you was, I don't know, passed out like usual when you do your voodoo shit."

Passed out? I knew a spell like that could take a lot out of me, but I was flying high on relief when I came to bed. My irritation fizzles at the sight of these two disheveled misfits tucking themselves back under the quilts.

"So, it musta' worked, right?"

"Honestly? I think it did."

Heck's muffled groan rumbles the mattress. "I'm not singing any victories until we hear the word about what Dorian knows—or rather doesn't."

He has a point. Of course we need to wait to gather Javier until we know for sure that Dorian won't identify him—which means we can't leave this hotel just yet.

"Ugh," I groan in return, flopping back down on my pillow. "I just want us all to go home."

"Me too, kitten, but we cannot just yet. So let's just try to rest." Scooching closer, Heck leans over me, shaking Gio's shoulder. "Would you be opposed to sleeping with the light on?"

"Um, I would," I say with an exasperated sigh.

Heck swears, settling back down with his arm still draped over my waist to clasp my boyfriend's forearm. Gio slides up against my other side, and with their chins at my ears, I lie there for a few seconds before I burst out laughing.

"Oh, sure, poke fun, Rose. But Heck ain't the one that had a creepy witch girl in his bedroom last week."

Heck gasps into my hair. "Oh, I nearly *forgot* about that."

"You know, none of us are going to sleep if you two keep talking."

"Well, I'm certainly not going back to my room *now*."

"Then, go to sleep."

"Hey, doll, we can't all drift off into blissful snores like you do."

My eyes shoot open. "I do not snore."

"You do."

"She does."

¡Dios mío!

13

MY BELLY BUTTON PROTRUDES FROM MY SWOLLEN BELLY. I giggle at the kick that stretches my skin, and I see a tiny footprint sliding across my navel. *It's nearly time.*

The white of my frock glows orange from the crimson sun ahead of me, which rises from a horizon so close, I can almost reach out and touch it. But I know it will burn me. It's too red. Too hot. And the cramping in my abdomen already has the cotton of my underarms soaked.

The sharp pain comes again, buckling my legs beneath me. The sun is rising higher, and getting closer—like it's preparing to chase me down. Fear twists the life within my womb as the crimson orb billows, flowing and floating into a woman's dress. Her body is curvy and stunning, but as her limbs take shape, her skin sags, hanging from the bones. The woman's stringy hair falls over her face, the hunch in her back growing larger.

"Who are you?" I ask, but as the pangs hit me again, I cry out, falling to my knees. The soft earth below me peels away at my touch, leaving only cracked ground for me to kneel on. I don't understand everything that's happening. But I can't let her have my baby.

The haggard woman tilts her neck, the bones jutting through her skin as she pauses. Her eyes study me with contemptuous curiosity before they narrow. She's coming for me.

In a panic, I take off into a dead run, the horizon lunging after me with a wide mouth full of sharpened teeth. The ground stretches on forever, and my body finally seizes me, throwing me to the ground with searing pain down my legs. I rock back and forth, my palms and knees digging into the dry earth, and my thighs begin to quiver.

"Someone help me!" I cry and rock, my body pushing as my belly pulsates to expel what's been growing inside me. With one final push, I fall to my back, both relieved and horrified by what I've given birth to. The trembling girl at my ankles wipes the blood from her skin—as thick and coarse as oak wood. She looks at her sister, who is wrapped in the sun, before turning her face back to me with a trembling chin.

"We store the light once we take it," she utters. "And send it into los criados . . . and into the bones."

"What? What does that mean?"

"Ask the trees. They have an awful lot to say."

The haggard woman screams behind us, her bony fingers driving into the ground as she claws her way across the earth. Terror has frozen me.

The little girl pulls at the wiry tree limbs in her hair. "¡Despiértate, Luna!"

. . .

"WAKE UP, ROSE!"

I gasp as my eyes shoot open, Gio's hands jiggling my sweaty shoulders. The tension in his face and that terrible dream would have me shaking if he weren't shaking me already.

"What's wrong? What's going on?"

The shouting in the hallway has my attention next, Heck running to lock the door to shut out the commotion. The sun's rays blanket the bedroom with a serenity that counters the apprehension on his face.

"Get dressed, Rose," he says. "Something has happened. And we need to go."

"What is it, dammit?" I fling back the covers and jump from the bed to fish my trousers from the suitcase Gio is packing like a man running from a heist gone wrong.

"Dorian talked," he says, the words rushing out with erratic breath. "Pinpointed the guy who tried to kill him."

O, no. Oh no. Oh no. It didn't work. I failed all of us. My fingers fumble with the buttons of my blouse.

"Javi?" I ask with tear-filled eyes.

Gio's hands gently push my palms down to my sides, and press my blouse buttons through their holes. "No, sweetheart . . . he says it was Giuseppe."

"*What?*" I cry, gripping his wrists.

My boyfriend looks back at Heck, who leans on the door with his face in his arms.

"I'm so sorry, Rose," Gio continues, his lips twisting. "They found him floatin' in the bathhouse this morning. Said it was a drunk drowning, but we all know who did it."

My boyfriend pulls my shocked frame to his chest. *No, that can't be right.* This makes no sense. Gus wasn't even around Dorian.

"But . . . but . . . but . . ."

"Just breathe, Rose." Gio sniffles against my temple, his skin emanating heavy guilt. "It's not your fault. We . . . it's not our fault."

But it is. Gus is dead because we made a choice to dabble in things we don't understand. My mother warned me not to use my magic, and we did it anyway. An innocent man was killed.

"We . . . were just trying to save Javi."

"I know."

But he can't. Because I don't. All I can say over and over is, "I don't understand. Gio, I don't understand."

"I know, baby. I know."

The cursed egg didn't make Dorian forget. It made him remember something completely different.

I am a killer.

14

"ABUELA!"

I can't scale the steps to the front door of her bungalow fast enough. Swinging it open, I run for the living room, but her cushion sits empty.

"Abuela!"

My mother's comforting face rushes from the kitchen. "Luna, what's wrong? It is Javi?"

"It's . . . it's everything," I wail, tearing the hat from my head. I let my coat fall to the floor, shaking off her arms as she tries to calm me. "I need Abuela."

"She's resting, mija. Come sit down."

"¡Mamá, por favor! ¿Dónde está Abuela?"

Gloria's eyes widen, but she stays the thousand questions she has on her lips, pulling me to my grandmother's bedroom. The old woman lies quietly, staring at the hanging plants around her, mumbling a song to herself.

"Abuela, I—"

"Niña," my mother says, her commanding tone snapping my head back in her direction. "She is sick with fever. Just last night."

"No, no, no." Rushing to Mamá Sunday's side, I grab her withered hand with both of mine, pulling it to my tear-soaked face. "Abuela, please, I'm so sorry."

The old bruja turns to me, the brown in her eyes more dismal than ever. "The dead often know what the living do not."

"What does that mean, Abuela?"

"I don't know," Gloria answers, circling around the bed. Her hand lies on my shoulder. "She keeps repeating it—over and over again."

I'm crying so hard, it seems like everything is crying— the colorful quilt around my grandmother's tiny body, the ivy hanging from the pots near the windows, the worn cane leaning on the footboard. Even worse, I can't heal her. I never could.

But I do know what made her sick.

"The dirt, Mamá," I gasp, leaping to my feet. "The dirt she was examining for me. We have to get rid of it."

My mother crosses her arms, standing straight in her matter-of-fact way. "I sealed it this morning in a case your grandmother made for such a time as this. It's safely stored and can cause no further harm."

"Oh . . . but what about the dirt Margaret spread all over the city?"

"She did *what*? How did that girl get her hands on our dirt?"

"It's a long story," I say. "I just need to know how to get rid of it."

Gloria breathes a deep breath, her forehead creasing. "You can't remove dirt once it's settled."

My abuela links her fingers through mine, her eyes shining with as much love as she soaks into my skin. "The dead often know what the living do not."

"Then what do I do, Mamá?" I press a kiss to my abuela's knuckles, making her smile. "Can I defeat a curse with a curse?"

"Luna, mija, you do not know how to perform these spells without knowing the consequences." Gloria paces to the window, checking the plants' leaves as she has done every day of my life. Keeping healthy plants means keeping good dirt. Earth magic takes a lot of loving care. I'm sure she's just distracting herself, but the last thing I need her to focus on is—

"Good dirt!" I cry out, leaping to my feet. "If I can't control the curses right now, I'll take them down with a blessing!"

With my mother on my heels, I run to the linen closet, tearing pillowcases from their folded pile. I rush through the bungalow, dumping every hanging plant in sight. Gloria catches on, shaking the granules from the roots of the hanging ivy.

"Maybe I can even heal Abuela," I say, spinning the top of a loaded pillowcase to keep anything from falling out.

"I will save some dirt here, Luna." Her busy hands place several plants into larger basins with leftover soil so we don't lose the plants entirely. "Once you figure out what's going on, we can have you try."

After giving Heck a quick call for an update, I finally hoist the pillowcase from the floor and cradle it in my arms as Gloria holds the front door open for me. "Mamá, I've done something terrible. I have to bring Giuseppe back."

"I don't know if you can undo what's been done," she says, the caked dirt on her fingers brushing my cheek. She lifts my chin to align with hers. "But there's always an answer in the earth."

The dead often know what the living do not.

If the stars are trying to speak to me, I only recognize two things: the earth and the dead.

And there's only one place I can think of that has both.

HEDGE TREES ARE ONE OF THE MOST HIDEOUS OF THEIR KIND. They shed barbed apples that taste like fruity bitterness, not unlike a grapefruit, but worse. To augment their unseemly appearance, they have several trunks, which twist around each other like snakes fighting their way out of the ground. The higher they reach, the more they twist, breaking off into separate arms that bow down again—a terrible resting place for those entombed within.

Cielo ayúdame. The grove around me is just as grisly in the daylight, the large nodules nearest the ground bulging as clumps of orange and gray bark around the base. This is where they keep the souls they have captured. I haven't visited this cemetery since the night I created it.

The woods are a merciless place.

With reluctance one could paint as dread, I pull my heels from the soggy ground, thick mud sticking to the soles of my shoes. The ice on the river keeps the flow from its happy trickle; a few vultures squawk above me as they search on the wind for something to die. They've come to the right orchard. Death soaks the very earth I'm standing on.

With my breath clouding around my face, I locate the

tree I'm aiming for, just on the edge of the water. The spot it grows from erects as a memorial to the wickedness that ended last summer. The last men who came for my family were never seen again. Nor will they be.

Sloshing closer to the bark-covered coffin, my shoes sink into the frigid water. My heels ache, sending a deep chill up my body. It hurts. But not as bad as what I've done to my loved ones. And I have to find answers to undo it. With a handful of my abuela's dirt, I dip my fist into the river, then place my muddy palm against an orange nodule on the side of the trunk.

"Dime la verdad," I say, a surge of wonder pulsating from my hand on contact. Giggles jingle from the sky like tiny bells, the river answering back with a soft melody. *Oh, that's it.* That's the sound I've been missing for so long. Joining the melody, I sing an enchantment about virtue and truth, drawing the bark away from the nodule like peeling an orange. My joy is short-lived as a familiar sneer between pointed ears takes a horrid gasp of cold air beneath the tree's skin. A name escapes my lips, interrupting my time with the stars. "Archibald."

The bark is still a part of his neck, holding him in place so that he can only drop his eyes to me with a menacing scowl.

"What . . . do you want of me?" he chokes out.

The wind slips through my overcoat, my feet turning numb in the water.

"I want answers."

He coughs in an attempt to chuckle. "What makes you think . . . I have them? And why . . . should I give them . . . to you?"

My teeth clench with cold anger as a determined growl

escapes me before I lay my caked hand right over his scoffing face. Archibald's memories give in quickly, his swearing fading as I enter a time when he was curious about earth magic. Too curious.

Archibald, as I used to know him, messes with his receding hairline before knocking on the door of a shack. His attempt is so soft it would be impossible for anyone to hear it. He may as well go home. No one can live this far away from the city in such depraved conditions, anyway. Why should anything work out for him? Nothing has ever gone his way.

As he retreats from the rickety steps, the cabin door swings open, and a tall woman covered in a shroud greets him with silence. Archibald sputters the best explanation he can put together. "I . . . wonder if you can tell me where the nearest filling station is."

The woman laughs, her silky hair cascading down to her full breasts, which she has pushed up beneath her frock. This does nothing for Archibald.

"I will read your fortune, Mr. Swinson," she says, gesturing him through the doorway. Her voice doesn't sound as raggedy as she appears. Rather, it has an intriguing timbre, as though she were a young woman with a very old soul.

"You will? That's exactly what I"—he clears his throat, squaring his pointy shoulders, which poke through his dress shirt—"I mean, sure. If it obliges you. As long as you tell me about that filling station."

He cringes at the layers of dust covering everything in this hovel—the herb jars, the books, the hanging plants that would knock him in the head if he was a taller man. The pot on the stove seems to have been boiling awhile, the peppery scent of burning stew coating the air. Archibald scoops the dust from a chair at the table as the shrouded woman lowers herself to the seat next to him. Taking his hand, she pries it open, chuckling something about his fear as she holds it with his palm facing upward. A scoop of tobacco is sprinkled into his palm, but he thinks better of complaining of the stale smell that will surely linger on his fingers later. This is the very reason he came here. And offending a witch would ruin his chance to glimpse into his future.

"Could you tell me, in particular, which stocks to buy? Or what woman to pursue? They don't really gravitate toward me—"

"Be silent," the bruja says, lighting a match. What she does next widens Archibald's eyes like two beady moons.

"Hey!"

His protest is too late. He was too late by the time he first reached the door. The matchstick drops to his palm, lighting the tobacco into a blaze of colorful fire. He tries to pull away but is too entranced, the purple and green flames holding him prisoner within the witch's spell. At least, that's how he recalls it.

The shrouded woman groans, singing a discordant melody he can't understand. Spanish wasn't worth learning because there was no one, in Archibald's mind, who spoke that unrefined language worth talking to.

"Unlucky Archie."

If he would dare to peek beneath her shroud, he would swear she was smiling.

"What does that mean?" he asks.

"You are going to be murdered."

The delight in her voice seeps into him, manifesting as a redness that climbs to his cheeks. *How dare she?*

He wrenches his hand back, the flames extinguishing. "Is that supposed to be funny?"

"Not at all, Mr. Archibald. You are destined to die by the hand of one who holds magic."

How dare *she?* Women were always mocking him—always taking him for a fool and leaving him for someone richer and taller and with a better sense of humor. He should never have come to this devil house. Nothing good was going to come of it.

"I'm leaving, you wench," he snaps, but her grip clamps around his wrist once more.

"Don't you want to know how it happens?" She lifts her head, revealing a set of enchanting lips that only serve to annoy Archibald.

"I want you to unhand me, miss." Standing and straightening his suspenders, he shakes off her hold, then brushes his hands together. The dust settles in her lap. "Now, go back to dying alone, or whatever it was you were doing before I arrived."

"You are disgusted with yourself. Not me."

No, it's not possible. Archibald's fingers curl into fists at his sides, his face flushing. She may as well have undressed him. The humiliation of her knowing even a single one of the wicked thoughts his mind often conjures has his breath struggling through his nose.

"You want to ask me to take away qualities you consider debased," she continues, ignoring his seething. "But it's self-loathing that is your ailment, not the way you fantasize about both men and women in silk dresses. Neither hate nor your desires are something I can take away."

"I will not have your demonic sorcery telling me who I am!"

"You will always be the kind of man you hate."

"I said, close your tarnished mouth."

Her sick laughter mocks him beneath the edge of the shroud, her neck stretching as she throws her head back. "It was foolish to think earth magic can change what you are."

"I *know* what I am," he says, revulsion scraping his tone like sandpaper. "I will show you *exactly* the kind of man I am!"

Lunging for her outstretched neck, he seizes her with both hands, her chair rattling against the warped wood. Her boots swing wildly as she tugs at his arms. But her struggle is no match for his contempt. He doesn't care if she dies. He hopes such a worthless creature *does*.

The gangly fingernails digging into his thumbs grow weaker, her upper lip retracting to show her bared teeth. Another gasping slew of Spanish nonsense escapes her constricted throat—hopefully, a prayer before he sends her to meet her judgment.

Her drooping arms pull back the shroud from her face, her cheeks red, eyes bulging. She halts her struggle. And so does he.

The searing pain between his legs forces him to do so.

With the blood draining from his face, he braces himself on the table as his knees give out from under him. Crimson soaks the front of his trousers . . . and the shroud she twists to hold the bloody contents within. He's afraid to ask—afraid to feel between his thighs. The rush of burning pain doubles him over as the teeth in her smile crack like cubes of ice in a crusher.

"Should I keep them?" she rasps, chewing on her own enamel. He cringes, drool pooling in his mouth as the little bag is shoved in his face. "Or should I rip the light from your body and cast your soul into a dog? I'm always adding to my collection."

"Please," he says between stuttering gags, "just kill me. I am no man without my manhood."

The bag jiggles against his nose. "That's where you're wrong. But I am not the bruja charged with your death. The fates have already decided—or perhaps, I told them."

The torture between Archibald's legs ceases as the bag drops to the floor, empty yet stained with a promise of what this abomination could do if she so pleased.

Falling to his chair once more, he buries his head into his knees, covering his head as he weeps for mercy. A delicate hand strokes the back of his hair, a delicate voice telling him not to be troubled.

Archibald lifts his face, his eyebrows snapping together at the little girl staring down at him with concern scrunching her petite features.

"You angered my sister," she says.

"I . . . I don't want to die by the likes of you. I wish I didn't know. I don't *want* a witch to kill me—that could . . . that could steal my soul."

The girl presses her lips to the side in a sympathetic frown. "Then find the magic before it finds you."

Archibald snaps his head up, pressing his elbows into his knees. "How?"

Her sideways frown twitches into a sideways smile. "Curanderos, brujas—they're all the same." Leaping toward him, she points her nose inches from his chin, his shoulders hitting the back of the chair as he rears but can't escape her bitter breath. "Look for vines that never cease their blooming. Businesses that do well when the odds are against them.

And watch for the gardeners, who spread their spells into the soil. You'll find them walking the perimeter of their stronghold."

"These . . . these gardeners," Archibald says. "Do they have magic too?"

"If one spreads magic, is there really a difference?"

Fascinating. Archibald's eyes grow until his eyelids disappear.

"Tell me more."

Settling into his seat, he listens intently as the girl cautions him to follow the trails of gossip and corruption. My stomach churns with vengeance. *Idoya and Sol—they're behind this.* This memory of Archibald's gives me clues into who my real enemy is—or has been this whole time. The Klu Klux Klan were just a set of pawns sent to wreak havoc on my domain. The answer I need now is: Why?

Idoya reveals nothing more during the hypnotic lesson between her and Margaret's ex-asshole. His eyes shine, the blood drying on his slacks, as he fills himself with determination to rid the world of wickedness in hopes that my kind—bootleggers, fast women, minorities, and witches take it all with us to hell. I shiver at the thought and the ice around my ankles that I can still feel outside this memory.

"Look for those who stand in the background," Idoya says, her eyes flashing with secrets. "Valets, waitresses . . ."

"Bartenders."

"ROSE! WHAT IS THAT YOU'RE HAULING IN HERE? IT LOOKS dreadfully heavy."

The pillowcase of blessed dirt hits the drawing room

carpet with a thud, a paper-thin layer of ice splitting and falling from the bottom of my trousers as I kick off my shoes near the door. The catchy wallpaper usually brings me some cheer; however, the warmth of the hearth is my only object of admiration. The heat burns the numbness from my toes.

Heck skips across the evergreen rug, pinching my wet stockings and lifting them from the floor where I've tossed them. "Darling, you must slow down just a little. You can't save anyone if you lose your feet to frostbite. And, quite frankly, you can't save everyone no matter what."

Folding my legs like a pretzel, I cup my palms around my aching heels. "Yeah, well, my abuela's dirt worked. It may just be enough to save Javi, and maybe even Gus."

Healing my brother will expend most of the energy I have—it'll take at least a day's recovery. Hopefully, Gus's soul will be retrievable at that point. If I can reach him, all I'll need is the equivalent of a life force to restore him to his body, according to the spell book. I don't exactly have one of those hanging around, so I'll have to trade my magic saving that rat, but it's worth a try.

"Rose, I . . . didn't want to tell you over the telephone. You were already so upset before you left your mother's, but . . ." Heck hangs my stockings over the mantel. "They burned Giuseppe's body. Something tells me that's a little too far—even for earth magic."

My body crumbles into the stuffed cushions, leaving my feet to dangle above the rug. *Whoa.* He's *gone*-gone. I killed an innocent man. He was a sleazy man, but in this case, innocent, drowned for a crime he didn't commit.

"I swear, we're all cursed."

I jolt in my seat, craning my neck toward the drawling voice coming from one of the wingback chairs in the lounging area nearest the bar. I had no idea Hiram was even here. Hell, the pattern of his suit practically blends into the wallpaper.

"Hello, darlin'," he says, raising a half-filled glass of amber liquid. "Now that we've returned your brother, I have lost all purpose other than consuming your husband's bourbon before he can get to it."

"Don't spout that nonsense." Heck shakes his head, his eyes rolling toward the ceiling. "You've plenty of purpose—with or without your father's money. What's more, you have your own investment."

"Ahhh, yes, that."

It doesn't take a bruja reading to discern the defeat on Hiram's face. Can this day *be* more dismal?

"Oh, friend," Heck says, beckoning him to come and sit with me. The lost baron accepts the invitation with reluctance, trudging to my side, then plopping down. "How much did you lose in that stock?"

Hiram's shoulders slump even lower. "All of it. And I owe every one of my investors." He downs the remaining contents of his glass. "With interest. All I do is wreck things. I am most deserving of my fate."

Ah, God's judgment. It's a ridiculous mantra that he tells himself, of course. But not only him—his father. His enemies. It's difficult to find ourselves when everyone around us tells us who we are. That's definitely something I can relate to.

"Well, we'll help you find a way once we navigate these contracts," Heck offers, ignoring my pinched eyebrows.

So much for not saving everyone. "Let's go through your books next week and—"

Hiram shakes his head, his curls bouncing. "I . . . you see it's . . . I love my wife."

"I'd hardly call that a curse. I love mine as well."

"Yes, however . . . I'm *in* love with her. We're lovers and best friends." Hiram sighs, the lower lids of his eyes watering. "She knows I'm . . . different. She's known since grade school. I know it's unconventional—even for 1926. But we allow each other our freedoms." His voice cracks, his face falling like that of a man who has lost all hope. "We've really built something together . . . and I've just ravaged our future."

Heck and I trade glances. I don't know why we're shocked. We've seen all kinds of lifestyles. Well, almost all of them.

"Come on," I say, "it can't be all that."

Heck lays a hand on my shoulder. "Rose is right. If it's any kind of love, your wife will stand by you, and you'll build again."

"You don't understand." Hiram's lips push to the side as he chews on the inside of his cheek. "We have children—two of them. And one of them is very ill. He has treatments. I tell you, I'm cursed."

"Come now, stop that, man."

"No! I . . ." The baron releases his lip, his eyebrows raising. "Curse . . . that's exactly it. I need a curse. I can't just hang myself; it's loathsome to put that burden on her, but I will if that's what I must do."

"You will do no such thing," Heck insists, his hands hitting his hips. "We don't deserve ropes around our necks for being who we are or any other reason."

My stomach turns as my mind flashes back to the summer when Archibald's men tried to take Heck from this world. We are also best friends. And I don't know what I'd do without him. Hiram's wife shouldn't be made to endure such a thing, especially for money's sake.

Heck shares my sentiment. "You can stay with us until we find a solution."

"Javi is back under your care now," Hiram argues. "Furthermore, I will be no one's burden."

"But—"

"All I'm asking for is a curse."

Is he serious? He must be. But I will not be a party to his despair.

I straighten my back, leaning forward like my mother before a grand lecture. "I will not end another innocent life. You will not ask this of me."

"The spite clause," Hiram says, the insistence in his voice matching his expression. "If I die, my heirs get my father's money. And my son—what decent father wouldn't sacrifice himself for his family?"

"This is not the answer, Hiram Wilmington." I point a finger to really drive my point. This man is talking madness.

His frustrated hand slaps the cushions between us. "It's not like it has to be painful or drawn out. I want to go quickly—like a sudden fever that will make me delirious before it takes me."

Heck lifts his hands, calling for the floor. "All right, let Rose and me discuss this—"

"You cannot be serious," I snap.

"Go ahead and take the other guest room. Javi is sleeping

well under the medication. The house is quiet. We will talk no more of this tonight."

Heck's fingers slip around the back of my neck, sending me his intentions. He just wants our defeated friend to pass out from his three glasses of bourbon, to give his mind some rest. He'll likely think differently in the morning.

Hiram thinks on this a moment, eventually slogging his way out of the room with the escort of our house manager, leaving Heck and me staring at each other in disbelief.

He rushes to the empty seat beside me. "Can you believe he *asked* for such a thing?"

I can only shake my head. Desperation leads men to lonely places.

"Well, the dirt from your mothers obviously worked. So what is the plan now? Do we have enough to help Javi—and undo any of the other curses?"

"We're going to fix it all," I say, pulling my legs back under me like a giddy girl at a sleepover. "We'll use a small amount to make gifts for the lumber barons to help them settle their disputes. That should take care of our contracts." Heck's nodding drives my fervor. "I've got a plan for the circular debacle too. If that goes well, we heal Javi and Mamá Sunday."

Heck clasps his hands together with a victorious grunt. "You've done it, Rose."

"Save that for when I actually do."

"You will. I know it."

Melancholy pulls the cheerfulness from my face. Even now, he believes in me. If only all men were rooted in the garden he grew from.

He places his hand over mine, stopping them from rubbing together. "I know it."

15

"ROSE, ARE YOU EVEN LISTENING TO ME? UGH, SAME EXASPER-ating Rose!"

With a rapid blink, I press the telephone receiver back to my ear, gripping the candlestick. "I'm sorry, I've got a lot on my mind."

"As always," she says, her voice squawking through the earpiece. "Now tell me your big plan. I feel like a sleuth. It's thrilling!"

I slide my rear onto Heck's desk since he's gone to bed and can't whine at me about smudging the mahogany. "I want you to tip off the *Kansas City Star* and tell them I've lost the baby." Her gasp gives me a smiling eye roll. "Then, I want you to plant more dirt in that circular of yours."

"Come again? You want me to what?"

I swear into the receiver as I look down at Heck's treasured map of the city I've accidentally creased with my thigh. "It's a Mexican thing. Just do it for me?"

"Of course, I will! I love superstitions." Her airy laugh ends in a satisfied sigh. "As far as your previous request, I'll just tell my uncle you didn't want people to know due to the holidays and the contract negotiations."

Smoothing the papers beneath me, I let Margaret go on with ten or so more ideas to change my image in the public eye. Just like Hiram, I made the choices I made. I'm in it now, and I couldn't ask to be in it with better people. But I'm not having a damn baby.

I'll hold Margaret's from time to time, then get back to my rum-runner and the crazy life we've built. And when I don't want to do this anymore, I won't. The public and the investigator are just going to have to accept that.

That's the beauty about life choices. They're mine to make. And they're mine to change.

THE INSIDE OF PENDERGAST'S OFFICE HAS BECOME MORE familiar than I care for. The minimalistic decor and tiny office give zero hints that the ground below an everyday building on Main is filled with tunnels for his bootlegging operation. That's where I come in.

"Come on in, Mrs. Kessler," he says, gesturing to a chair with no cushion. The wood pokes into my back immediately. He clearly doesn't like folks to stay awhile. "I'll get straight to it—I want you to align with Dorian Luxberg."

My chin lowers, my mouth dropping open. This is too

much reach. I won't be told which contracts to sign—by him or anyone else.

"Sir, our arrangement with him has nothing to do with rum-running."

"Oh, but *his* money does," the former city councilman says, his tone as patronizing as ever. "He's threatening to pull *all* of his investment from the city. I heard you two were chummy at one time. I need you to be chummy again."

I slap my hands down on the armrests, my back rigid. *What nerve!* And how did he *know* that? Heat climbs up my neck to my seething jaw. "I am *not* that kind of woman."

His giant eyebrows shoot upward with his wide smile. "I just figured, if you're going to mess around with your piano player, you may as well take on the baron's son too. Or can you not afford to hire a proper driver?"

"I can afford whatever I want. What I can't afford is to be told what to do with my body."

"And I'm saying you can't afford not to. Or, rather, find another way," he says, his face hardening. "Because this is not a request. You want my big fat help, but you don't want to reciprocate?"

"Of course I do. But—"

"Good. Report back to me when it's done."

What was that I was thinking about this glorious life I've built? The thought of Dorian's sneer fills my chest with good, old-fashioned disgust. I've got charm magic, sure. But that baron isn't going to have any more lavender sessions with me. A plant would be an easy option. And I *do* have access to dirt that won't harm him. Still, the request tastes like bile in the back of my throat.

"You want me to kiss you too?" I squint my eyes at the towering politician, and he squints back.

"I don't shit where I eat, Mrs. Kessler," he finally says. "Now, get these barons to play nice."

"What's the return on my time in this matter?"

His eyebrows shoot up again. "You're asking me for something else? Besides a free ride in my operation?"

"Nothing in this business is free," I say with a shrug.

Pendergast pushes his tongue into his cheek, shaking his head as though a woman has never spoken to him like this before. "Fine, then. Out with it."

"I need you to get an investigator off my tail."

"Mmmm," he says with a knowing nod. "That guy."

I hate how much he knows about me.

"So, is it a deal or not?"

"Depends." He takes up a shining pen, twirling it between his thick fingers. "You want him killed?"

"*No.*"

Dios, if someone else dies at my expense . . .

"Aw, fine." The pen clinks back to the desk. "But you make everything so much harder."

"I appreciate it," I say, digging through the satchel at my side. A sprig of ferns sticks through the opening. "Listen, Heck wants me to give our contacts a belated Christmas gift. He's so damn sentimental."

"Keep it," Pendergast says, standing and straightening his jacket. "They give me rashes."

His signal of the end of our conversation doesn't need explaining. I'd hoped to give him a plant to increase amiability—he's the one who's hard to work with.

I'll just have to sneak it to his secretary when he's not in the office.

"Have a good day, then, sir."

"Good luck out there."

THE SHOUTING FROM THE FOYER CAN BE HEARD BEFORE I reach the front door. Heck is really going at it with someone. Panic spikes through my arms. I hope Javier is okay. He was in a daze from the medication when I left this afternoon.

I pause outside the door, pressing my ear to the oak panel.

"I can't trace a background on a 'Rose Lane anywhere in or around this city. She and that musician are after your fortune!"

The voice is all too recognizable. That slimy trustee-turned-investigator had the nerve to find his way to my home. I'd storm in there and give him a piece of my mind. But Heck has beat me to it.

"She's *not*," he says, his muffled voice filled with insistence.

"She's hiding something. She's not who she says she is."

"Yes, I know."

The silence has my eyes widening. If only I had some popcorn. I can only imagine the flabbergasted expression on the investigator's face.

"Then . . . we can pay her off to leave," he says. "I only threatened to out her to the press to scare her. We have no intention of sullying the Kessler name. Your father would be so disappointed if he were alive."

The door swings open, the two of them glaring at each other with the lividity of men with large bank accounts. Heck looks at me, pulling my hip to his side before going back to his eye battle with the intruder upon our lives. "Then it'll be just another Sunday, won't it?"

The investigator tightens his mouth, studying me from head to toe like I imagine he would a homeless man asking him for a quarter, then stalks past us on his miffed trek down the driveway. Heck and I watch his taxi roll away.

"Thank you," I say, squeezing the arm he has around me.

"No bother." He plants his lips on my forehead. "As I said, we'll make it through this part. Soon, we'll be back to bickering over biscotti."

The hope from his touch gives me hope. We might just make it, after all.

16

AS IF MY MOUTH COULD STAND ANOTHER LAYER OF CARMINE, I press a Chanel stick to my Cupid's bow. In the hand mirror, my eyes have become wide ovals, the tension tight across my forehead. Heck curses the dark plaid of his suit jacket as he brushes dusty residue from the lapel, which only lasts as long as it takes to shift the large satchel in his arms.

"This is my best suit, *honestly*."

I spin away from the conference room door. "Oh, Heck, what if he remembers?"

"If you keep wrinkling your forehead like that, those lines will become permanent before your time."

"I'm serious."

My best friend sighs, grabbing the golden door handle, which leads to the meeting that could decide our financial future. "If he remembered, we would have surely heard.

Now, help me open this before I drop these plants and run for Paris."

Taking a deep breath and letting my shoulders drop, I toss my waves and push against the door. An unmarked conference room inside an unmarked office building welcomes us with fourteen sullen barons, all sectioned off into clusters like feuding princes who would rather be anywhere but in this room, much less seated by each other. Papers are lined up in front of each man, yet they haven't touched them. It's a room without windows or portraits. It's a room without mercy. *Well*, this *should be awful.*

The lake barons greet us warmly, each taking a baby fern with feigned commendation toward Heck for the courtesy of such a late holiday gift. Of course it's an odd gesture. But thankfully, these Southern boys are too polite to reject his offering.

Hiram's appearance is diminished from his typical swankiness, which is understandable considering what's weighing on his mind. I doubt he'll have much input at this meeting, given he has no funds to pledge this year.

Opposite the lake faction, the forest region thanks Heck kindly, holding the tiny pots in their laps. But the barons from the Bootheel only nod, allowing Heck to line the ferns on the tabletop in front of them. A pair of hazel eyes follow me to the table, where Heck scoots my chair in before taking his place at the head. The conference table gleams like the barons' pomade, its length stretching so far it feels ridiculous. I picture old kings negotiating at such a table or perhaps throwing a grand banquet.

Ugh, banquet. My insides quiver, recalling the spoiled fruit in Dorian's dream. The brooding baron tilts his head when I catch his eye, which then trails down to the neckline of my blouse. I'm certain he disdains women in suits; however, I don't want anyone to forget why I'm here. I'm not a flapper today. I'm not a vamp in a hotel room looking for favor in exchange for nookie, as one of these darbs believes me to be. I don't *intend* to piss Dorian off. We need him.

But I won't be his pet either.

As the prince at the farthest end of the table tilts his slick head to light a cigarette, Heck mirrors Dorian's gesture by pulling a golden case from my handbag. I cradle the side of my neck with my hand, cocking my head to allow my hair to hide my expression from the rest of the room. Heck ignores my questioning glare brilliantly. *What are you doing?* He doesn't smoke! Ever.

I try to save him by reaching for it. The barons may think him a gentleman if they think he's lighting it for me. But he arches away, pinching my chin to the chuckles in the room.

¡Atrevido! . . . he rarely acts like a common man. However, when he does, it burns me more than when others do it. Sure, he's got a reason. Politics is his game, and he wrote the book on posturing. I always try to trust he knows what he's doing in these scenarios. It's honestly more comical than annoying in this circumstance.

I force my irritation back down to save it for when it matters as he lifts the filter to his lips. I almost can't watch. Propping his arms on the table like he doesn't give a damn, he opens the ledger in front of him, letting the men sit in silence as he inhales what he always refers to as "poison fog." His eyes scan the numbers, the creases at his elbows almost more alarming than the Camel in his hand. The cough is subtle, but he swallows it quickly, blowing a stream of smoke to his right, so it doesn't cloud me.

Well done, Mr. Kessler.

Dorian's face smushes into the most unbecoming expression he's donned so far. "We didn't come here to watch you smoke and read, Mr. Kessler, so unless your wife plans to lead this colloquy for you . . ."

"Colloquy?" Heck glances up from his ledger, taking another drag. "I'm simply calculating the pledges I've received from every faction since the start of our negotiations and allowing you time to review your contracts." The smoke from his mouth points at the forest region. "You *do* intend to keep your word to me, gentlemen, do you not?"

Dorian snorts, throwing himself back in his seat. "I know a palooka isn't trying to tell us what to do with our money." The men around him snicker, clapping him on the back. His sparking gaze scans the other factions. "Especially one without a morsel of leverage."

Interesting tactic on Dorian's part, pointing out Heck as an outsider. What the baron hasn't counted on is that Heck has spent his entire life schmoozing a society that hates him. He can handle this Bootheel brat.

Heck lifts the corner of his ledger, unfazed. "I have pledges, sir."

"The only thing you have is an abundance of lawsuits comin' your way," Dorian says, his tone stripped of its polish and sounding like the hillbilly he is. "Your gamblin' manager—what was his name? Gus? That short, slimy weasel tried to kill me, and you're wantin' me to pay you for it?"

The barons in the room are finally in sync for once, murmuring in agreement. But we knew this was coming.

"Pay? Goodness, no," Heck says, flicking his ashes into a golden tray. His fingers nearly lose the cigarette, but no one is paying attention to his hands with the way they're whispering to each other. "We're talking about investments, gentlemen. Unless you truly believe we had anything to do with the attack on Dorian."

"Well, did you?" the man next to Hiram asks. "It's all *very* curious and quite disturbing."

"What would I gain from such an act?" Heck's hand flips to the side, the smoke from his cigarette trailing past his hair. "Losing the Bootheel means losing most, if not all, your investments. It's offensive to assert that *I'm* the reason Dorian ended up in a squabble on a farm in the middle of nowhere."

The prince on the opposite end of the royal table grits his teeth, gripping the edge of the tabletop. "Just what *are* you asserting?"

"Not a thing," Heck says, his face smooth against the stress in the room. "Only that we're not detectives. This crime has nothing to do with our contracts." His lips find the filter again, his inhale as grandiose as his posture as his eyes lock on to Dorian's. "I think the other barons are actually more resentful of *your* faction's accusations while you were in the hospital. However . . . no one but *you* knows what really happened that night."

Dorian's glare is a barreling train chugging just before the whistle. "What happened to Giuseppe is exactly as I said— he attacked me like the lowlife coward that he was—just like the crew he came from! Your entire operation isn't anything I would sink a *dollar* into."

My neck tightens. I want to defend our honor—give Dorian a piece of my mind. However, Heck and I assigned jobs to each other for this meeting. And mine is to wake up the magic in the hibernating ferns since they were cut from my abuela's pot. *Dios, this better work*. My abuela told me not to rush my magic. It'll come to me when it's time.

As long as we *have* enough time.

I relax the tension in my jaw and shoulders, folding my twisting hands in my lap, and try not to count the seconds.

"And your wife," Dorian continues, his upper lip curled. "You are aware, Mr. Kessler, that she came to my room."

The shocked murmur from the barons fills the room, my body rigid once more. A flash of sweat soaks the underarms of my blouse, my jacket hiding the stampede of panic running through me. *He remembers*. Our cards are on the table. I hope that rat can't see the color draining from my face; I should have listened to Heck when he told me to eat something this morning.

His ears rise, his eyebrows separating with nose-flaring fury as his dincher smashes into the ashtray. "My *pregnant* wife could be heard becoming ill in the ladies' room on New Year's Eve, *sir*. Several ladies can vouch for it. She spent the rest of the night sleeping in our room."

"Goodness, man," Dorian shoots back with a sly smile creeping along his mouth. He thinks he's winning. I bed down my angst and ready myself, praying to the fates that Heck can hold this man down long enough to allow me to focus. "Who said anything about New Year's? I meant when she threatened me regarding her *bartender*." The room casts curious stares in my direction, my face flushing. "Javi and I had ongoing negotiations—a job offer in my hometown—yet I haven't seen him but a few times since your wife's intrusion on business which did not concern her. The way I see it, you owe me damages for a failed negotiation."

The murmuring in the room turns to outright clamor as Heck attempts to maintain his position, but they speak over him.

"This is not the way to do business, Mr. Kessler."

"I'd be livid if my wife visited another man's room!"

"My wife is the most upstanding—"

"Let Pendergast find us another developer."

"Gentlemen, please. If you'll simply hear me—"

A pile of brick-red curls rises above the rest as Hiram stands to his feet, two fingers between his lips quieting the room with a low whistle. "Gentlemen." He lifts his chin at the forest region. "Brothers . . . let us *try* not to be as foolish as our fathers to think a woman cannot engage with us. We deal in lumber. Not gold, for God's sake."

The barons pass around glances, leaning in to hear what their fellow heir has to say. They don't seem to care he's penniless. Perhaps they aren't aware of his recent loss. Either way, I'm thankful for his intervention.

Hiram's eyebrow lifts sharply, his hand pushing away his jacket to grab his hip. "And are we to hang our livelihood on the integrity of a man we all know to be a recreational consumer of his favored *tonic powder*?"

Dorian hurls himself to his feet. "I beg your *pardon*?"

"You shall not have it, good sir. If you'd invested as much time in the lumber business as you do cans of hop, you might have made more friends and fewer enemies around this table."

"What do you care?" Dorian spits the words out like a little boy taunting his mate on the playground. "I hear you've been shut out of the lumber business—the coward prancy who couldn't save his own brother!"

The silence hits hard, the room taking in an inaudible gasp. Hiram's burning eyes leak with disdain and guilt as his jaw tightens.

Heck stands, his palms up to calm the commotion. "Regardless of his misfortune, Mr. Wilmington is right. Furthermore, *I* sent Rose to speak with you. She's a part of this as much as I am."

"Did you send her to kiss me as well?"

Dorian's indictment recharges the room, some barons pulling at their suit lapels while others grab their papers to leave.

Heck hunches his back, slamming his palms on the table. "You will stop these accusations at once before I pin you to the goddamn wall!"

"You can't afford to!"

Okay, fates . . .

It's time.

I LOWER MY HEAD WITH ONE LAST SILENT PRAYER. THE shouting in the room has become a blessing as I begin to sing one of my own.

> *Abre los corazones de toda violencia*
> *Dulce amor, consume nuestra indignación*
> *Aguarda hasta que nos juntemos*
> *Y da a conocer la verdad*

They don't see the sky opening up nor feel the tiny roots of the ferns reaching into their soil. The stars, embedded in magenta and indigo sky, invite me to join them one day. And I will. One day. Because we are simbiótica. The witches of the North might want to claim I'm otherwise—the stars, even my own mother thought I might be a bruja de maldiciones, but I know in my heart I never wanted this power to hurt. I want to be part of something, be *with* something. I need the fates, and they need me. For what is earth magic without the earth's blessing?

As the ceiling closes off the sky, the stars wave farewell, and the warmth of calm blankets my skin. The tightness in my joints dissipates, and I clamp my mouth shut as the barons all stop their fussing to stare at me. I must have still been singing. I flash them an embarrassed smile, shrugging my shoulders. "It's just that I can't whistle like Hiram."

The leader of the lake faction gives me a slow blink with a shocked smile below the handlebar of his mustache. "A noble effort, Mrs. Kessler, even if a tad pitchy." My cheeks warm as he encourages them all to take their seats. "Now, let's iron out these contracts like gentlemen before someone breaks out a harmonica."

Hiram's ease has the entire room chuckling, save for Dorian, who pouts in the corner with his arms crossed. The spell can't force anyone to be kind, but it definitely calms them enough to see reason. After several minutes of discussing various clauses, barons from all around the table pull pens from their jacket pockets and seal the next year of Heck's development ventures—and mine.

The spell worked, thank the fates. *Finally.*

Heck reaches over and squeezes my hand, his tight smile

echoing the relief he shares with me. We've got the contracts. Even the barons from the Bootheel are signing . . . except for one.

"Dorian," a man next to the grummy baron's empty chair says, "let's move on with it, huh?"

"I'm not signing a damn thing. This is all hooey."

The men in his crew roll their eyes, one of them exhaling loudly as he holds a paper toward the corner of the room where Dorian sulks. "Stop being such a debutante."

"My own cousin betrays me, then? You say this after you heard what that gambler tried to do."

"What we know," the man says, "is that Javi probably abandoned your offer after the way he was treated." He pushes on as Dorian tries to argue. "And Giuseppe likely attacked you for the same reason."

"I've had enough of this!" The Bootheel prince straightens his jacket.

"And I've had enough of *you*. We want this contract— that's why we came to Kansas City in the first place, if you'll remember. Now, if you do not stop making trouble for us, I will go to your father and tell him everything," his cousin says, lowering his chin for emphasis. "*Everything*."

As the silence in the room swallows the tittering, Dorian shifts on his feet before snatching the contract from his cousin's hand, jerking a pen from his lapel. Griping and swearing, he scratches the ink into the signature line, then rushes from the room. The paper floats to the floor.

Despite himself, Heck's hand hits his mouth, but he recovers quickly, standing to shake each man's hand as they head on their way. The last to leave is Hiram, his sandy eyes wet as he hands us a contract without a signature. Heck grips the deflated baron's shoulders, his eyes watering as well.

"You've done more for us than any contract could promise to provide."

Hiram nods in thanks, tapping a hand to Heck's cheek as he turns away. "You two have fun celebrating. I have to go see a man about a dog."

I wish he wouldn't hang his head so low, the door creaking closed behind him. I worry he may be drinking too much. The last time he had a few rounds in him, he was saying some crazy things. I'm sure he doesn't mean he wants to die. Hell, I've heard drunk men say all kinds of things. But don't we all? I surely can't blame him for feeling miserable and hopeless.

We'll have to find a way to cheer him up later. We owe him that much.

"We did it, kitten," Heck says, lifting me from the floor and spinning around. I wouldn't mind if he carried me out of here. I'm ready for a three-year nap. I don't have that long, though. Still, I need to recharge if I'm going to heal my brother.

Burying my nose in Heck's neck, I pretend to snore. "I'm beat, Mr. Kessler."

"Let's get you something to eat, at least, Mrs. Kessler," he says. "Maybe a little hotel restaurant where no one will recognize us."

Bother us, he means. And that sounds amazing to me.

"JUST WHERE DID YOU LEARN TO SMOKE?"

Heck dabs the corners of his coy smile with a napkin. "I've been practicing since the barons came to town. It's absolutely *vulgar*. Don't count on me continuing."

"Well, you did look a little green toward the end."

"I vomited in the men's room after."

My eyes roll upward to the high beamed ceilings, then survey the rest of the hotel restaurant Heck describes as "little," the walls made up of dark wood and murals depicting pioneers along the Santa Fe Trail. The oak bar, which would normally be serving up an array of cocktails, is now covered by hanging curtains to curtail suspicion from law-abiding patrons in the daylight. The drapes are a weak cover-up for a felony. I suppose the Savoy Hotel and Grill doesn't try too hard because it doesn't have to.

Kansas City won't ask. Kansas City doesn't care.

The menu is renowned, however—so delicious, I can't take another bite. I don't know why we never frequent this joint, other than my personal boycott against establishments with separate dining rooms for men and women until only a few years ago. Without Heck's loose pockets, I'd never drop this much green on steak and seafood either.

"You know, darling, I've been meaning to ask," Heck says, reaching across the tablecloth to take my hand. His hesitation meets my skin as he stares at the emerald on my ring finger. He's conflicted about something, but I back out of his mind to give him time to say it. "Would it be so bad to have a bad reputation for divorce now that Pendergast is sending the trustee away?"

I certainly wasn't expecting that. Sure, I've thought about it a hundred times. Heck is no longer forced to marry now that he's inherited his fortune. But I would never betray our agreement as long as he needed me. *Is that what he's saying?*

My best friend in the entire world tilts his head, his small smile filled with affection. "I know you're unhappy."

"But I'm not. I just—"

"You are," he says. "And I can't continue denying you something just because I can't have it."

My heart splinters. He means Javier—an open relationship without hiding. Slipping into Heck's thoughts, I find a stack of reasons why we needed to stay together—and all of them have been satisfied. We got the clubs. We got the contracts. We won the barons' favor. Heck has no intention of ending our financial partnership—our friendship remains the same; yet something about him saying it carves a hole inside me. I don't want to lose what we have. But he worries a breakdown is coming if we keep going like this. He wonders if our ruse is worth the fight anymore. Maybe it's time to stop climbing and start building where we're at.

Heck squeezes my hand and sends me a message that fills the hole—at least a little bit. *We'll always be there for each other.*

"Are you sure you don't want dessert?" our waiter asks, glancing at the plate I've cleaned up. "We have an award-winning blackberry cobbler."

I look at Heck like I can't believe he's even considering it, given the way he scans the menu. A smirk follows his shaking head as he pulls out his money clip to pay the bill. "We appreciate it, but I need to get my wife home. It's been quite a day."

Quite a day. And month. And year.

But this is a new year. I'm ready to heal my family and return to boring ledgers and moonshine inventory.

"Oh, thank you, Mr. Kessler!" The waiter's eyes grow large at the stack in his hand. "Truly."

So much for no one recognizing us.

Still, no one bothered us, so it worked out. Where that's left the two of us, though, I'm not sure, and I wonder when we'll be able to pick this conversation back up. As Heck scoots my chair back, I tug at the belt in my trousers, thankful it doesn't pinch so badly when I stand. I'd tear the damn thing off if I weren't in the middle of a restaurant. I might not eat for another week.

Taking my gallant husband's arm, we stroll into the hotel lobby and my heart sinks a little at the title. It was nice having a husband who didn't want to strip me of my identity and choices. I'm sure Gio wouldn't either, but with Heck, there's no risk of heartbreak—or actual babies. No risk of it not working out because it wasn't real in the first place. Our sham, admittedly, was becoming my safe place . . . a safe place that has kept me from giving an open commitment to Gio.

I let out a sigh as the coat-check man takes his sweet time, as though he's never coming back at all.

Heck checks his wristwatch, tapping his loafer against the tile. He cranes his neck around, looking for any staff member at this point. The valet hasn't even come to take our vehicle ticket.

Where is everyone? I'm so damn tired.

"Well, this is some poor service, honestly," Heck says, dinging the bell on the counter. An entire age passes before a room services maid runs by, ignoring his greeting. "Excuse me, miss. Just what in the world is . . ."

She picks up the telephone from the counter, the candlestick holder quivering in her grip as she spins the dial. Heck and I look at each other as someone on the other end of the earpiece finally picks up. "Yes, ma'am," she says. "We need police at Ninth and Central. There's a man, he's . . . he's been found dead in his room."

Heck pulls at my arm. "Um, darling, let's get our own coats. Then I'll locate the car."

"S . . . sure," I stammer, a wave of nervousness threatening to expel the first meal I've been able to enjoy in days. Nearing the coatroom, I run into a wall of air, my heels freezing over the threshold.

Heck's narrowed eyes turn back to me. "Rose . . . are you all right?"

The buoyant atmosphere is unmistakable—a fluidity he can't sense.

My breath becomes shallower, my heart quickening as I push my hand through an invisible wave, lifting it in front of my face. "I don't know, it . . . it feels like water."

I'm sure he thinks I've gone delirious from exhaustion as I wiggle my fingers in the air; I half suspect I'm losing it too. Hell, I wish I was. Then I wouldn't have to admit what's really haunting this hotel at the moment.

"Magia," I breathe, dropping my arm when the unearthly feeling stops.

Heck meets my wide eyes, studying them for a moment. "You're certain?"

"Unfortunately."

"Then we definitely need to get you out of here."

"Wait." I pinch the cuff links on his sleeve, thumbing the imprinted ivy. Commotion gathers in the lobby behind us. "We have to go up there."

"Rose. *No.*"

"We have to, Heck."

His hand covers mine, steadying my fidgeting as he silently tells me how afraid he is—how he vows to protect me. And that he also trusts me.

Wonderful. At least one of us does. I was kind of hoping he'd tell me I'm crazy.

Following the buzz of waiters and maids, we find our way to the second floor, gathering at the rear of a small crowd outside an open doorway. We slip through the various huddles toward the front, then lean around the doorframe with the subtlety of two kids sneaking out after bedtime. The scene we witness makes me wish I'd stayed in bed and never left the boxcar.

No, por favor. Not again.

Gawking at the lifeless tangle of lanky knees and elbows, I brace myself against Heck's arms just as he's holding onto mine. A rancid smell assaults the back of my throat, but I realize it's the climbing bile and not the body lying on the hooked rug. The woven pattern of fruit baskets and floral sprigs is free of blood or any other indicator as to how he ended up here.

I told Pendergast not to do this. I wanted the investigator out of the city, not out of this world. I don't realize I'm entering the room until Heck tugs on my wrist, sending me a signal to look to my left. To anyone else, the miniature evergreen on the windowsill appears to be a symbol of the recent holiday, a traveling trustee's way of celebrating in a lonely hotel room. To me, however, it's an ominous promise from a person disturbed enough, powerful enough, to take a man's life for no foreseeable reason.

Leveling my gaze at the sharp edges of the evergreen, I press my magic into the soil, its roots reverberating back to me. A spell has just been used. And not just any spell—a curse of perpetual sleep. Thankfully for the rest of us on the edge of the room, it would take another incantation to awaken the plant, much like the sleeping fern. The dirt's power is already waning.

But even reaching for the roots has drained what strength I had, my legs buckling. The floor pitches beneath me, and Heck folds me into his arms.

"Excuse me," he says, pushing through the crowd and into the hallway.

"Heck, I'm okay."

"Bushwa." He struggles down the stairwell, his own apprehension flowing through his arms. Once we reach the Chrysler, he lays me in the passenger's seat, tucking his jacket between my head and the seat. He says it's for comfort, but his hands tattle his concern about the leather if I become sick on the ride home, and weirdly, that makes me feel like I'm just a little safer, knowing Heck is still so . . . Heck. The scent of patchouli oil is comforting too.

With my arms cradling my head, the car rumbles over the boulevards, the gyration shaking my insides. A hot tear pushes its way down my temple. "That wasn't my plant, you know."

"The thought never crossed my mind, kitten." Heck brushes a few wet strands behind my ear, leaving his thumb to run across my cheekbone. Reading him only makes me cry harder. If I could see myself the way he sees me, I would never doubt my magic again. Nor his love for me and my brother. He's never lied to me. And I promise to cherish his heart forever.

"Such an odd happenstance," he says, the streetlamps

glowing out the windows, "the trustee at that very hotel. Certainly, we didn't know the man was staying there. It has me worried, Rose."

"I know . . ."

We *didn't* know where the investigator was hiding out. But someone did.

Idoya.

The thought comes to Heck the same time it comes to me. It has to be her—and her vile sister. Perhaps they know I read Archibald's memories. Are they after me because the willows by the river gave them up? Maybe it's fallout from the fates for killing Gus. It was an accident, but I don't know how the stars measure deeds and misdeeds. This feels like a game of dominoes, and we're just waiting around for the next one to fall. How many more people are going to die?

My tears soak into the wool under my chin. "Heck, we have to . . . I have to figure out why those witches . . ."

"Shhh." His thumb continues soothing the skin beneath my ear as the cabin fills with his whispering song.

> *Like to feel your cheek so rosy*
> *Like to make you comfy, cozy*
> *'Cause I love from head to toesie, lovey mine*

Like a spell all its own, Heck's silky voice slows my tears enough to let my eyes close. His determined thoughts and the exhaustion weigh me down as a soothing blanket, and I feel myself drifting to the hum of the engine. I will never wonder how my brother became so entranced by such a man. I don't have to hope that we will always be there for one another as he says. I know we will.

17

I'M FAR FROM REFRESHED AS I TRUDGE DOWN THE NARROW
steps into the basement of the Kessler mansion. The earthy
smell carries in the stairwell. Our crew and I have decided
there's no better place for a private meeting than a stone
room with a dirt floor. Especially where there's bruja magic
involved.

I hadn't bothered to change into something more appropriate, such as the slacks and blouse Heck laid out for me,
instead donning my warmest clothes. Tonight's business
requires comfort over silk. He hasn't arrived yet to critique
my pairing of an oversized shirt with my cotton sleep pants.
He's probably tucking Javier in after I tried to no avail to heal
my brother. There's only so much dirt, and clearly, I don't
have enough. I'm on the verge of exhaustion and tears, and
it's not helped by the knowledge that if I can't heal Javier, I
won't be able to help Mamá Sunday.

Hopelessness swallows me like my ensemble. At least my crew is in decent spirits.

Penny wraps her arms around me, the curls of her wig tickling my neck. Mauve is a good color on her, although she can wear just about anything and make it spectacular. Her warm thoughts and embrace have me wanting to lay my head on her shoulder all night. I fight the lump in my throat.

Doris and Nickels throw their arms around me as well, my boyfriend joining the huddle, holding his smoke away so as not to burn anyone. My family of misfits has me welling up, and we haven't even said anything. I can hear their thoughts, and much like Heck's, they believe in me.

How can they? I've failed. I've failed my brother.

"You're going to make it, Miss Rose," Penny says as the group pulls away. Her hands cradle my twisting face. "And we're all gonna be here when you do."

Doris tosses the blond mass on her head, holding a cigarette out to Nickels for him to light. Even under the single bulb, the rouge on her cheeks glows. She takes a quick drag before she hands the smoke to me with a determined nod. "You saved a lotta more lives than you took. Hell, I'd turn a few guys' brains inta' spaghetti squash if I had your powa'."

"Pos-i-lutely," Nickels says, his arms bulging as they cross. "You done good things, boss. We all know it. We think those otha' witches are responsible for Gus—responsible for everything. And we ain't gonna let 'em keep comin' afta' you."

Everyone agrees, echoing Nickels's sentiments as my boyfriend pulls me close to his side.

"I know you're not doin' all right," he says. "But are you doin' all right?"

All I can do is nod, pressing my back to his chest as we fill the room with smoke.

"Is that really necessary?" a cosmopolitan voice calls out. "There are no *windows* in here."

Betraying my despair, I trade a smile with Gio, and we let our dinchers fall to the floor, stomping them out with our shoes as Heck reaches the landing.

With his arms tucked behind him, he points his nose at my oversized wool garment. "Is that my sweater?"

"I'll answer that once you've returned my hand cream and bath powder."

He scowls, but before he can say anything, Gio leans around me and asks, "Whatcha got there, Heck? Please tell me it ain't cordial."

My elbow pokes his ribs. "I happen to like cordial."

"Don't we all know it."

Batting at my boyfriend's fingers as he tickles my ear, I swivel away, my grin suspended by the large tome in Heck's hands. *¡Imposible!* Where did he . . . how did he?

"My dearest flower, I think it's time to start healing again."

Like the treasured artifact that it is, he lays the book in my outstretched arms, as Gio's happy kiss wets my cheek. He knew. I think they *all* knew. No wonder they were all so giddy.

The hole in my chest closes further. We really are there for one another.

My fingers stroke the twisting tree on the cover, the limbs of all three branches of magic represented. Not one limb is greater than the other—they're all a part of the same tree. This is where I come from. This is who I am.

"Heck Kessler, how did you *get* this?"

"I think I really am Gloria's favorite."

In a flurry, the crew begins pulling out the boxes we have hidden in the shadows, and I sink to the floor, laying the spell book on the bare earth. I might as well see what our ancient text has to share. There must be something I haven't thought of—maybe I'm missing a word during the incantation, or maybe I need to add a rare herb to my abuela's mixture. I have to try. It's not like Javier can get any worse.

Diving into the cream pages, I pass the first section on charm magic, using my thumb to flip to the second. The sapphire stone etched into the pages' corners wraps around a variety of healing spells, but as I scan the notes about mending a broken mind, my hope deflates. I've already tried these spells.

"Aww," Doris says above me, "they look like little recipes."

"Maldita sea," I growl, flipping through the rest of the book like it's a shuffling deck of cards. The emerald pages catch my eye. The lessons on soul-splitting and divination seem anything but a good hand. I should fold now and think of something else. But my eyes are steered toward the rudimentary drawings at the bottom of the pages.

Whoa.

A rodent lies opposite a man, a beam of light exiting the man's body and entering the rat. My finger points to each line as I silently read the Spanish text.

Life force, also known as "light," is extracted from a living soul and may be kept in another host. Dead or alive, it does not matter as long as the host is not human and is kept within one hundred feet . . ."

Dios mío. It's talking about criados. This is how Idoya and her sister are able to bring dead animals to life to do their bidding. Dread peppers the inside of my cheeks. Where did they get the life force to do that? Images of the dead investigator send a warning to my guts.

My eyes race across the page.

Extracted light may also be kept in a place where there is no life at all, such as an enchanted jar or the tusk of a hog, for safekeeping. These will last as long as they are sealed and unused . . .

So, a person's life force can be collected—collected like dead rats floating in bottles of moonshine. Idoya had the nerve to call them "gifts." I swallow my disgust. These are some bad little brujas.

"What did you find?" Heck squats with his arms on his knees. "I think she's found something."

My thumbnail tucks between my teeth, my eyes glued to the spell book. "The witches are stealing life force from people and storing it in animals—and possibly jars. I don't know why, but that's what they're doing."

"Aw, shit," Gio says near my shoulder. "I knew this was gonna get creepier."

Penny lets out a loud gasp. "They're stealing people's *souls*?"

"No, just their life force. It's the light that keeps our bodies alive."

"So, they're tearin' this light from our bodies and keepin' it in jars?" Nickels asks. "Where does the soul go?"

"I . . . I don't know." I shake my head, skipping a few more pages. We don't have time to study the whole book. These witches are gunning for me. For *us*.

The words on the following page halt my frantic turning. *Curses defeat curses.* Hope returns as a small spark of victory.

The diagram of a spotted egg is all but unrecognizable, the notes unlocking the secrets of where I've been getting this wrong.

"'Curses defeat curses,'" I say aloud, as though everyone else understands the text in front of me. "I'm sure this is it, you guys!"

Gio squeezes my shoulders. "That's wonderful, Rose. We're one hundred percent behind you."

His thumbs on the back of my neck tell me he has no idea what I'm talking about—and he might be more than a little freaked out—but he's got some serious faith in me. Which in turn means I have more faith in me.

With renewed confidence surging past my doubts, I glance around the dim room, pressing my palm to the floor. "I'm going to make another egg."

"Oh, uh . . . sure, if that's, uh . . . what you gotta do."

"And I need cursed dirt."

"I think that's where this comes in," Heck says with a grin in his voice.

Hovering in front of my face is a sealed mason jar filled with soil—my cursed soil. I never thought I'd be so glad to see it. This will definitely save me some time. And energy. I sit up on my knees, clasping the jar in my hands. "Heck Kessler, you shouldn't be carrying this! I'm glad you were, but you shouldn't have."

He shrugs, flicking his eyebrows with nonchalance. "Your mother said it was safe."

Oh, Gloria. I can't help my smile. It's nice to know she believes in me too.

After sending Nickels for a bucket of water and two eggs

from the crisper, I have my crew keep their distance for their own protection. Soon, my lips begin uttering a spell I've never uttered before. The recitation is ghostly, like the melody that drizzles from the open ceiling as a chilled rain no one else can feel. The songs from the heavens are somber, the stars tucked away behind a wall of gray clouds.

The realization hits me. The earth isn't hiding because it's ashamed of me. It's hiding because it's sad. The stars know there's a time and a place for curses—a time and place to fight, and never for one's own gain. Knowing the difference is what's important.

I think I'm finally learning.

MY BROTHER LOOKS LIKE THE SLEEPING BOY WHO ONCE shared a bed with me and our abuela, save for the raven scruff over his lip and around his chin. Between meals, the morphine has kept him in a restless sleep, full of unending nightmares. But it's also kept him safe in the fortress of our guest suite. He would hate all of the fuss and the large room we've given him. The sizable bed he rests on is one he's used to, but not for just one person.

Perhaps without me pouting around the house, he and Heck can finally have some time for themselves here. They've both evaded society's eye for this long, both separately and together. Love always finds a way.

As Javier's eyelids begin to stir, I lie beside him, slipping my hands beneath my cheek. We ordered the nursing staff to wake him a while ago, slowing the drip in his arm. The golden lighting from the bedside lamp is the most they can provide to keep him calm while he's awake, however.

His groan, which typically unnerves me, now fuels my determination. *Not long now, Javi. The earth is coming to fight for you.*

He grips the soaked sheets, his bloodshot eyes shooting open. "Please, Luna. Don't make me go back. I won't hurt anyone else. Don't make me go back."

"Hey, hey, hey," I say, keeping my tone light. "Trust me for once, okay?"

He glances at the tiny pot on the bedside table. "Is that for protection? Is it cut from one of Abuela's?"

"It is," I say with a cozy smile.

"It won't let her take me, right?"

"I won't let anything happen to you, hermano."

My brother side-eyes the sprouted fern, his wild ovals turning to a slow blink as I hum a childhood tune our mother used to sing to us at nightfall. The chirping of crickets and cicadas joins with it until his face relaxes, his body going still. His steady breathing tells me he's ready.

Signaling to the peeking head around the doorframe, I encourage Heck to act quickly, reminding him to shove the bowl completely under the bed after cracking the egg. He follows my instructions with the precision of a guy who's hell-bent on saving the man he loves. As Heck slides onto the pillows on the other side of Javier, I wrap my arms across my brother's bare chest, which is sticky with a fresh layer of dew. The torment from Sol has already begun.

My teeth clench in retribution. Dreams are where healing happens. And dreams are where the monsters live. *Not for long.* This is the last time those witches touch my brother.

Vengeance leads me past his eyelids and onto the arid field where the crimson sun has already begun setting. My brother stands on the cracked ground, dressed in his favorite slacks and suspenders. The back of his head trembles as he watches the woman on the horizon take shape, his feet shifting in preparation to run.

I cup my hands around my mouth, charging forward. "Javi!"

He pivots, chest heaving and eyes wide, swiveling his head at the sound of my voice. "Luna?" He runs to meet me, gripping my elbows as his desperation blows through the empty field like an impending storm. His fears are on the wind, flying and spinning up dust in swirling madness.

"You can't *be* here," he cries, his eyebrows cinched together. "I don't want her to find you!"

Heat builds from the glowing figure on the horizon as she draws closer. His panic has the wind in a frenzy, the dust stinging my cheeks. I grip his shirtsleeves, begging him to look at me. "I'm gonna end it, Javi! I'm ending this right now!"

"Por favor, Luna. Don't make her angry." He turns his face to me, peering down with the same defeat that echoes across the field. "She said she'll let me keep my soul."

My brother's fears confirm what I've suspected since reading the spell book. They want my brother's life force. Nickels's question hangs on the edge of my thoughts. *But where does the soul go?*

I shiver despite the heat. I don't want to know. I just want my brother back.

A burning gust whips my hair back and forth, the strands slapping my eyes, but I keep my gaze steady on the hag who advances on all fours with her claws in the ground. *Just try and come for my brother.*

Sol isn't the only bruja de maldiciones. I *am* a curse—a curse to my enemies.

As her hunched gait towers over us, her fiery dress fades into scarlet rags. I want to shrink away from the drool pooling around her cracked teeth, but I hold my ground without daring to flinch. The shadows grow longer beneath her gnarled limbs that contort where her arms should be. Javier ducks, his fingers laced around the back of his head at the sound of her stretching. The crackling is fiercer than the howling air.

Five fingers of bone and bark reach high against the gale, which flays her skin, splintering the wood. My brother's emotions are fighting back. This is his mind, after all. But the witch just smiles before a cruel song swirls around her teeth. The melody is too low, yet too high. It jingles like a child's song harmonizing with the notes of a monster under their bed.

What spell is this?

I want to strike—to tear her limbs from her body with a song of my own.

But these songs *aren't* my own. They belong to the earth. They belong to us both. And they always seem to know when it's time to start singing.

The witch's teeth clamp together until tiny cracks run through them, splitting until they shatter, her pulsating tongue retracting. Dust and wind shift direction. Sol's toes root themselves into the ground. The spin-ups racing into her gaping mouth sound like agony as her mouth drags the air across the field around us.

I chance a look at my brother now that the witch's eyes have disappeared from their sockets. Still covering his head,

Javier pitches forward, fighting the suction with his eyes squeezed shut. *Javi?* I don't know why I can feel it, yet it's not pulling me too.

She said she'll let me keep my soul.

A twist in my brother's direction answers the questions beating in my chest. As the hag consumes the atmosphere, Javier's eyes unfasten, the whites trembling at his captor. Pinned against an invisible wall, his back arches, sending his chest forward as it begins to radiate with a glow so intense I have to shield my eyes. My eyelids struggle to open. *It's so bright!* I can't see anything.

I don't need to.

If agony can be described as a scream filled with guttural terror, if wailing is a gale tearing at all love, all kindness, all mercy, it wouldn't compare to the chaos my ears must endure. No one should ever have to listen to such torment. And it's coming from my brother.

The ground vibrates the heels of my shoes like the ferns when my abuela would sing to them. A strange memory at a time like this. *Sing. Time.* I don't need it drawn out for me. Tearing my T-straps and stockings from my feet, I plant my bare feet on the hard earth and plunge them into the ground.

My roots shoot forward, meeting Sol's as they twist around each other in a struggle that shocks her, and I begin to read.

Get out of my head, you stupid bruja!

Get out of my brother's!

Not until you give me what's mine. I've got you, silly girl.

Her mind pushes against me, repeatedly, until I'm not sure I have the strength to keep going. But I have to. I can't lose this time. I have to figure out exactly what she . . .

What did she just say?

I've got you, silly girl.

I've heard something like that before—in the thoughts of a man just as devious as these brujas.

I dive in further, immediately picking up on the putrid scent of rotten fruit. The witch tries to pull back, but I'd recognize that smell anywhere. *Dorian.* I was right. These awful excuses for brujas used another scoundrel to use my brother to get to me. It was subtler than their deal with Archibald, offering Dorian what he thought was a deal to buy tonic powder. He didn't know he was snorting a spell to have him fixate on Javier. It was easy then to get my brother to ingest a pinch of the cursed opium in their first drink together. Another plan foiled by me . . .

And Sol isn't happy.

Her intentions are a wicked admission, confessing her and her sister's plan to drive my brother mad so I would seek them out for help. Abuela's ferns, the protective ivy around his club, and the Kessler mansion have kept them from being able to cross over to us. Sol needs to be near my brother in person. And she needs me as well.

With a frustrated growl, Sol's roots wind tightly around mine and rip away from our connection. The air tugs harder at my brother, the air blinding me, but my sight is not necessary for earth magic. I dig my roots deep into the soil and let the melody take over.

> *Malditas son las raíces que no dan fruta*
> *Muertas son las almas sin luz*
> *Perdidas son las vides sin agua*
> *Y desaparecidas son las estrellas sin canción*

Claps of thunder—or perhaps the ground is splitting, it's hard to tell with my eyes covered—rattle the arid terrain as my feet return to me. My nose lifts to the earthy smell of the air after a storm as the vibration becomes a distant rumble. The blinding light no longer seizes my eyelids, and I blink away the blur.

In place of the field is the workshop behind our abuela's house, a place where my brother used to practice his carpentry before misery took him. He seems anything but miserable now as he scrapes a block of sandpaper over a tabletop, looking up at me with an excited smile.

"What do you think, Luna?"

The thoughts in his dream tell me he's working on a piece for his and Heck's dining room—something he's been designing for a while. The grand humidor with curved legs is a birthday present. And he can't wait to see his lover's face when he gives it to him.

Javier goes back to sanding, forgetting my presence as he whistles a tune about riverbeds.

"He's gonna love it," I whisper, floating back away from the shed. His subconscious is none of my business. I'd cry from joy, but there are no tears to be had here.

My eyes flutter open in the golden light of the guest room, and I smile. Heck's nose rests against my brother's cheek, the fern sending him to sleep as well. *Good.* They both need the rest.

Nickels's bulky hand knocks on the doorframe. "Safe to come in now, boss?"

"Definitely," I say, swinging my feet to the floor.

"So, uh, find anything in there I should know about?"

Nickels's eyebrows pinch together; he's as concerned

as ever. It's sweet that he wants to protect me, and he has been a big help to my entire crew. I should remember to take him out soon or buy him a new car. God knows I can't just tell him; I'm terrible at expressing gratitude. But I hope he knows what he means to us.

"Dorian," I say, standing to face my bouncer's chest. "The sisters used him to get to Javi."

My bouncer's body tenses. "You think he . . . he knows? I mean, about you and your, uh . . ."

"No, not like Archie. He shouldn't be a problem now."

Crouching on our bellies, we pull the bowl from beneath the bed with a light gasp. The water is thick with sinewy threads, as though it were filled with slimy ash. I say we leave it until morning. My brother's nightmares began before the wicked sisters came along. But he will have good dreams tonight. Healing dreams—which gives me an idea.

"Hey," I say, propping my elbows on the rug. "Where's Hiram?"

Nickels tilts his head in a shrug. "He's been drinkin' away his sorrows at the River Rose, but I can get 'im for ya afta' droppin' off that egg for your grandmotha'. I got a shift tonight to hold the place down for Javi, anyway."

"Great." Groaning like an old spinster, I hoist myself from the floor. "And listen, we all need to stay together. Keep a fern on you at all times. No plants or dirt unless I give it to you myself."

"Yes, ma'am."

The brujas north of the river are exposed, sure. But that doesn't make them any less dangerous. For now, I just want to lie in my bed and pass out. As if my body will give me another choice. I just fought hell tonight.

* * *

WAKING TO THE SOUND OF THE PHONE RINGING, I FALL OUT of bed and slink through the darkness to the phone in the hallway. *Who the hell is calling at this hour?*

A frantic Nickels is on the other line.

"Whoa, slow down," I say, stretching my back from its rigidity. "Did you find him?"

"Yes, boss, I did." His sniffles scratch my ear through the earpiece. "In the storage room. He musta' been there all night. He was already gone by the time I found him! God help me . . . I didn't know till I was lockin' up."

My body stiffens once more. "What do you mean, gone? As in, not breathing?"

"Boss . . . he was hangin' from the raftas." Nickels breaks down, his wailing making my bottom lip tremble. "Who knows how long he been there—all alone. I cut him down soon as I saw 'im."

A flood of anger and devastation burns in my chest, rising to my nose and threatening my eyes. Are those brujas just picking my crew off one by one? My teeth grind at the sound of Nickels's crying and the quiet of my home. They're never going to stop until they get to my brother. *Why him?*

"Those bitches," I hiss.

I have to stop them. I have to stop all of this.

"I don't think it was them, Miss Rose," Nickels says.

"How so?"

"He, um . . . there was a note—a letta' inside a gin bottle. He . . . I guess he just didn't wanna be here no more."

My eyes widen, blinking hard. I'm stunned. The staff said he was laughing at the paper over breakfast yesterday, making fun of the article announcing his absence from negotiations.

He was also half-seas over. I should have instructed them to serve his cranberry juice without the vodka.

Once again, everything feels like my fault. We should have kept him with us. But he's a grown man.

Or was.

"There was no plants, no nothin'," Nickels's crying gasps say into my ear. "Can't you do somethin'? Magic him up? I lost my sista' a few years ago and . . . Hiram—he unda'stood that. And we . . . he's like a brotha' to me now."

The pain from the people I love is a thick marinade in my stomach. I won't let this happen. Not again.

"Nicky," I say, "did anybody see him? Anyone at all?"

"No, I don't think so, Miss Rose. Wasn't nobody in the cella'. It was a slow night."

Good.

"Take him to Penny's willow—and dress warm. I'll find you there."

18

THE FEW PLANTS LEFT IN MY ABUELA'S GREENHOUSE GREET me under flickering light as I turn up the lantern on a hook in the corner. Their shadows are long, but darkness doesn't scare me. Facing down two powerful brujas when I've only just learned to use my power—that sets my hands to trembling.

Using the adrenaline, I rage like the blizzard on the other side of the windows as I set the spell book on the bench. My eyes squint at the pages, doing their best to decipher the instructions under the lantern.

Curses make desires stronger. According to the book, whatever a person's inclinations are, they hit a boiling point. How people react to that, however, is different for every person.

Something about these pages rings true. *But how?*

How did the sisters' magic get ahold of Hiram?

The man wanted to die, but we all face that moment. Most of us never follow through, hope finding us again—which is why we set him up in a room with a vine that should have kept him from sinking. Even the River Rose would have had the same effect on him.

Something must have pushed him over the edge. But how did evil follow him into our sanctuary?

"Mija?"

I lift my face from the book, my mother's silhouette rushing to my side with a quilted blanket. "It's freezing out here—and after midnight! What are you doing, silly girl?"

She stays her lecture as she gets a good look at me. I'm sure my swollen eyes and spotted face can still be seen even in this lighting.

"Oh, Luna . . . how can I help?"

My mother's wisdom leaks through her palms as she cups my face, wiping the tears from my cheeks. She's been around brujería her entire life. She knows Mamá Sunday's spells better than her tamale recipes. And, like my abuela, she's a bruja without her magic. If anyone knows how to defeat evil in this world, it's Gloria Alvarado.

I lift my chin, straightening my back like she always reminds me to do.

"Mamá," I say with the pride she instilled within me. "Teach me how to kill a bruja."

TWISTING THE TOP OF A LARGE POTATO BAG, I TIE IT OFF with a piece of thick twine.

There. We had to knock on about twenty doors to locate

enough ingredients for this spell, but at least my neighbors were willing to help. Or perhaps they're just scared of me, knowing what I'm capable of. But my neighbors are not the ones who should be nervous. I narrow my eyes toward the north. The end of all of the sisters' chaos lies at my feet, and I can't wait to throw it at theirs.

A silent recital of spells plays in my head. I've never done these spells before, which has me more than a little nervous. I've got to keep Hiram's soul from venturing too far, to give me time to crush those witches before I heal him. I strap another potato bag full of blessed dirt over my shoulder, patting the side with an earnest prayer. If bringing Hiram back takes my powers, so be it.

The world needs loving hearts more than it needs magic.

Bending my knees to lift the potato bag, I sigh at the shuffle near the door. "Don't worry, Mamá. It's not heavy."

"Luna."

I jerk my body up at the familiar male voice, my head shaking. "Javi. Where's Mamá?"

"Praying in her bedroom," he says, charging across the greenhouse. "Luna, you're not going there alone. I forbid it."

"H . . . how did you know?"

"Doris kept calling. She couldn't find Nickels. Woke me up."

My eyes search the darkness of the house behind him. "Is Heck with you?"

"No," my brother says. "He fell asleep after I did, I imagine."

The fern. The spell has a time release, and my brother's must have ended.

Dammit. He can't be here. And he's definitely not going to face those witches now that we know what they want from him.

"You're not going, Javi."

"Then neither are you." His loafers step closer. "I will not let you do this. We'll find another way."

I know he's worried—probably terrified. But he can't go with me. And I will make him stay if I have to. *I'm sorry, Javi.*

The menagerie around me reaches for me as my magic reaches for it, searching the pots for the original fern I used to cut smaller rootings from. It's weakened—needs time to grow.

I can certainly relate.

Backing away at my humming song, my brother tears through the greenhouse, shoving pots aside to find the offending plant. But his eyes haven't had time to adjust to the darkness. And the spell is already working. His knees lower to the concrete, his breath slowing as he looks up at me with sadness and betrayal in his eyes.

"Luna . . . what did you do?"

I swallow the lump in my throat, and I rush to help him as he falls back. As I lower him to the ground, he grabs my hands, but his grip can't hold me.

"I'm saving you, Javi," I whisper, unwinding his fingers from mine. "But please believe me . . . I'm so sorry."

I know he's probably still nervous his dreams will turn on him. I know the last six months have been a waking nightmare, even without bruja curses. But if I can end his pain and all of this chaos, even at the cost of his trust, I will. It's an honor to give myself for love.

My brother thumbs the leaves of the long ivy around him, his breath becoming steady. Snatching the tied ends of the bags, I tug my hat down over my ears and run with the fates leading the way.

• • •

THE SNOW COVERING MY WINDSHIELD MAKES IT HARD TO SEE the willow grove. The fog from my racing breath doesn't make it any easier. The figure ahead lifts a massive arm, shielding his face from the headlamps. Silence replaces the rumbling of my car as I shut off the engine, my door squeaking open.

"Darlin'," he says, "is that you?"

Darlin'? I know Nickels spent a lot of time with his new friend, but I've never heard my bouncer speak like him.

I shove both bags onto the floorboards and shut the door. As the flying snow stings my face, I pull my fists into my coat sleeves. "Um, Nicky, where's the body?"

His bulky coat turns, and my eyes follow the footprints to the spot beneath Penny's willow, its limbs weighed down by the snow. A lifeless baron lies near the trunk.

"I was a handsome thing, wasn't I?" Nickels drawls, shaking his head. "We never do get what we ask for."

My mouth drops open, cold flakes salting my tongue. I almost couldn't sense the magic with the frigid wind blasting my face, but it's here. It's all over my club's bouncer.

My chattering teeth manage to stammer, "H . . . Hiram?"

Nickels gives me a slight bow, his expression as dark as the night around us. *Oh God.* I sent them both into another trap. Maybe I *don't* know what I'm doing. Javier was right. I shouldn't have come here.

"But . . . the fern. It was supposed to protect him."

"Nicky's a good boy, but he's not exactly known for his attention to detail."

No, no, no, no, no. This is wrong. It's all so wrong.

My bones tremble despite the layers I'm wearing. "Hiram, I was going to bring you back!"

"Now, why would you *do* that?" The sternness in his voice makes me take a step back, but he follows me, his fingers pinching my chin as Nickels's frame towers over me. "Do you know the peace I felt?" His thumb presses my dimple, leading me backward toward the river. "My God, it's worse this time. The pain is worse!"

"Hiram, I'm sorry, I . . . we'll figure this out."

His stale sob spills through clenched teeth, water filling his wild eyes. "Send me back!"

"I don't know if I can," I say, glancing behind me. We're getting awfully close to the water. *This is Hiram.* He won't hurt me. But he's not exactly himself. "Listen, I know Nicky was special to you, and you meant a lot to him. He gave his *life* for you."

Hiram's grip rips away from my chin as he grabs at his sandy hair. "Nicky? Is that who's in my head? Get out of my head!"

What did he just say? This can't get any crazier. Why the hell didn't I brush up on soul-throwing? A spell like this shouldn't even exist.

The conflicted man lifts his squirming face. "It's gonna be okay, Miss Rose. I ain't gonna let nothin' happen to ya. Or you, Hiram."

Nickels?

"I said get out of my head!"

Echoing laughter spins us both around to the river, where a lone figure in a tattered dress stands on the ice, which stretches across the water like a bridge to the other side. She's small enough to keep from falling through the frozen layers. But it's clear what a danger she truly is, regardless of her innocent stature.

A hundred feet from the shoreline, Idoya's hair whips around her playful smile. Curled through her tiny fingers, the netting of bones lies against her boots.

I lock my teeth together with my jaw. This is the witch who sent Archibald and Dorian after my family. This is the witch who murdered Giuseppe—*and* the investigator. She and her sister tormented my brother and ripped Hiram from his body. My clenched fists shoot out from my coat sleeves. I'm anything but afraid. I'm pissed.

Nickels grabs the fur of my jacket as I start forward. "You'll go right unda' if that ice ain't thick enough, Miss Rose."

"Return Hiram at once!" I shout, twisting my arm. "And stay away from my brother!"

Idoya bounces with glee, clapping her hands together. "Cats and mice never play kindly!"

My eyes drop to the frozen sheet over the water. The edge looks a couple of inches thick, maybe more. She wouldn't be jumping like that if it weren't safe. But she's also insane.

"Is that all you can do?" I taunt back. "Haunt Javi's dreams and send rats to chase at my heels? I'll crush your criados and whatever game you're playing."

I want to slap the giggle that emanates from Idoya's mouth at my words. "Crush them? They're already dead. We like playing with dead things, and so do you . . . why else would you steal the light from my criado to heal that saxophone player?"

Huh? I didn't mean to use the rat's life force—not that it belonged to it in the first place. My mind flips back to the pages I skimmed in the greenhouse. Well, that explains why healing Clip didn't drain my energy. *Holy hell.* It also explains why I was able to heal him without consequences in the first place.

So witches like us *can* heal—if we take life from something else.

"I was going to give you Hiram's," Idoya muses, lifting her leg to balance on the other like a girl playing hopscotch. "But you're not being nice. Now he and Nicky have to share."

I pull away from the mountain behind me, but Nickels's grip is like iron. I take to growling at the river instead.

Idoya lets down her foot, her shoulders drooping in a feigned pout. "Oh, stop acting so sour, Luna. You're a full bruja. We saw you bring a dead man to life. Heal Hiram when we're done with Javi if it's so important to you."

What? "But, I'm not . . ."

I let my words dissipate into the snowfall. She doesn't know I'm not a healer like my abuela. She and her sister obviously want my power for something. I'd rather not leave time to figure out what that is.

"Nicky," I whisper, hanging on to his wrist. "I need you to get something out of the car for me. Can you do that?"

"Miss Rose, I"—his eyebrows wrinkle over his baby blues as he stares at the witch, then back at me—"I can't."

"Sure you can," I say, glancing down at the fist gripping my fur collar. "What are you talking about?"

Idoya's laugh accompanies the scraping of my boots as they slide from the riverbank and over the water.

"Nicky, what are you doing? You said the ice wasn't thick enough."

"It's not!" he gasps, pushing me forward. "She's makin' me do it, dammit. I can't stop."

I press my heels to the ice, but they keep sliding. I won't say this isn't possible. I'll never say that again.

"Stop this, Idoya! He's not one of your criados!"

The little witch's delight fades from her face, her chin lowering to level her gaze. "*He's* not. But the other one is."

Hiram. Fates help him. His life force belongs to her now. At least I don't have to go looking for it in a jar when this is all over. For now, it's creating a serious problem.

"It's just like me and my sister when we had the accident," Idoya says. Her palm faces the sky, drawing Nickels closer. "We had just learned—didn't know what we were doing . . . it's a terrible thing to lose a sister. It was a terrible thing to be a witch who couldn't bring her back—not the way you brought Javi back."

Is that *what this is?* She wants me to give life to her dead sister's bones?

My feet spin like a bicycle pedaling backward. "What you're wanting isn't possible. Her soul's been gone too long."

Hopefully, wailing in the pits of hell.

"I kept her bones and her soul!" Idoya shrieks, stomping her foot down. "You can't keep a life force if you don't have somewhere to throw the soul, stupid bruja."

But . . . where did the soul go?

"Spent too much time kissing the boys and not enough in the books, I see." The little girl sneers, ready to answer my dumbfounded face. "I threw my sister into my own body. In fact . . . you can meet her if you want."

"Um, no, I don't think I want to."

One last laugh crosses the girl's lips before her face smooths into a wicked smile.

Great. Her again.

The worse of the two sisters curls her fingers, tugging at the air between us, Nickels shoving harder.

"I'm sorry, Miss Rose," he gasps. "I'm trying to fight it."

"Quiet!" Sol snaps, her sister's tiny features full of fury.

"Oh, uhh, I—"

Sol tilts her neck, her eyes searching her periphery. "I wasn't talking to you."

Her jerking head and mumbling lips remind me of the homeless man outside Gio's rooming house. I wonder how many other souls have been stolen and tossed away by these witches who have determined their lives to be disposable.

I also wonder what the sisters are arguing about.

"We would never risk our magic for a stranger." Sol's hold on Nickels pauses. I guess they have some things to work out. "Even she hesitated with Clip's life. Idoya—idiota, there *is* no good in this world."

As she continues lecturing her sister about the evil deeds of men, I slide my fingers along the fur of my coat, pushing the first few buttons loose from the holes. I peer over my shoulder. We're farther out than I thought. But I can still make it to the car if I can get Nickels on the trolley.

"Hey," I whisper, his body frozen behind me. "See if you can let go, huh?"

"Miss Rose, I been tryin' this whole time—sorry, darlin', those ladies are crazier than you are."

"Enough!" Sol screams, pulling at us once more. "You will give me your brother. You will give me your power, or I will take it from you."

Sliding forward, I tuck my elbows down through my overcoat, never more thankful for a silk lining. "Nothing can bring dead bones to life, Sol. Even Javi was almost too far gone to save him that day, and the spell took my abuela's powers. We're not God!"

Sol thrashes about in a tantrum fit for a toddler. "Your brother has been to the stars and back! He's not just another soul!" Her fingers reach for my collar, the few feet between us closing. "It will work! You know the spell! We can help you!"

"Do what?" I ask her fingertips. "Murder someone else so I can keep my magic?"

Her hand stops just inches from my chest, a mournful expression shadowing her face. "If you don't help us, I will kill you and store your life force with all the others."

"You're not putting me in a jar—or anyone else."

"Dios mío, Luna, jars? You know almost nothing." She lifts the netting, showing me her bone collection. "I keep them in a sacred place."

Her laughter is as foul as ever.

They *are* insane. Obsession with power is a hungry beast with no satisfaction. My arms shimmy down to my sides. I have to make my move.

I tilt my head to catch the witch's fuming eyes. "You already have my power."

"So you agree, then?"

"No," I say. "You're not listening."

"What are you talking about?"

"You have my power because I have the same powers. I'm not a healer. I can only perform curses . . . just like you."

The distraction shocks her just enough to allow me the half a second it takes to slip through my overcoat, my knees hitting the ice. Scrambling between legs the size of tree trunks, I take off for the shoreline, Sol's screeches tarrying on the wind.

Keep moving, Luna. The air blasts through my sweater, but my beating heart carries me over the thick snow and up to my vehicle. As I jerk open the door, I glance behind me, Nickels charging like a bull in a parade. *Dios.* He's faster than he looks. Snatching the potato bag from the floorboard, I duck as a lumbering hand reaches for my neck. Giving Nickels the slip for the second time, I sprint for the river, untying the bag when I reach the ice.

"So, so, so, so sorry, Miss Rose!"

My sweater cuts at my neck as my feet leave the ground, Nickels's eyes welling with tears. His hand closes around my neck, and I slap my palm down hard onto his head. The tiny crack opens the egg beneath my hand, the yolk running down his wrinkled forehead. The gooey membrane darkens to gray.

My feet hit the ground.

"Don't let her go, you idiot!" Sol screams, holding her hand out to a wind that is no longer listening to her. The earth always answers back—unless you're a psychotic bruja with a control problem.

Unsteady and gasping for breath, I twist the bag closed, then lift it with both hands over my head before slamming it onto the ice. Sol shakes her head, tearing at her cheekbones. "What are you doing!"

On his knees, Nicky brings down his bulky fists, crushing the remaining contents, the tiny crunches sending her pitching as though the earth were moving. Another crackling sound, not so tiny, has us all frozen in place. With our eyes on the limp potato sack, we follow a blue line as it makes its way from Nickels's fist to Sol's boots. Like an invisible hand drawing on the surface, it rushes between her legs before splitting and spreading in all directions.

"Hey, Nicky, I think we oughtta—"

"Right behind you, Miss Rose."

He and I break for the shoreline as the shrieking witches swear at each other, cursing me in two different languages, but their screams are quickly cut off by the frigid water below the ice.

Idoya was right. The dead can do everything we can do. Even die.

I turn to hug my favorite bouncer, but stillness and the rush of water meet me instead. With the ice broken, the river shoves the broken sheets down the shoreline, carrying the crushed eggs into the night.

"Nickels?" I spin around, searching the darkness. He was just here—right behind me. Turning my eyes to the river, I scan the shore, my trembling steps halting at the two giant handprints in the muddy snow. Claw marks lead all the way to the water, sending a freeze inside my chest more than does the cold air on my skin. *No.*

My heart races up to my aching neck.

He must have slipped when we were running. The river took him and didn't even tell me. I could have fixed this— him and Hiram. I didn't even get the chance.

One more—no, *two* more—bodies in my ledger.

I didn't even get the chance.

19

MY MOTHER'S HOME IS WARM AND QUIET BENEATH THE twinkling lights of her tree. We waited to celebrate the holidays together. But instead of laughter and buñuelos, my family lets me sit in silence, my untouched food still in the kitchen from breakfast. My only comfort is the tinkling from my abuela's knitting needles as she works a piece of wool from her seat on the sofa.

My legs fold against my chest as I stare out the window. I'm in a conservative dress, but I don't care. At least it's a pretty day. In just a week, Missouri weather has turned from fierce to frolicking, the sun smiling as though nothing awful has happened. It still thinks Nickels is at the bar throwing a few back with Hiram, jabbering on about their fathers and how many times they got punched in grade school.

Our bouncer was the only one of us brave enough to carry the boxes of floating mice to the cellar—the only one strong enough to carry four crates at once. I don't even know what to do with such foul creatures, but my abuela said I should keep them. They could be useful one day. I can't possibly think how.

I honestly don't want to think about magic for a while.

"Mija," my mother says, "your brother will be here any minute. Can't you eat something before the funeral?"

"I'm sorry, Mamá. I'll have him stop at the deli after my meeting."

I wish she'd give me a break. Three funerals are a lot to put on a girl. We held Nickels's memorial under the weeping willow since there was no body to bury. We didn't even report it. He had no family, and we all agreed that having the cops scraping the bottom of the river could unearth more questions than we could answer—all Doris's idea. She's been holding up pretty well, given the circumstances. Sadly, she's grown accustomed to violence and loss, which is what made her into such a scrapper in some ways. But I know she's hurting. I can't even imagine losing Gio. I was a mess when I *nearly* lost him back in the summer. I'm glad she'll be staying with Penny for a while. The last thing I want is to lose our lovely, caustic Bearcat.

Hiram was sent back to southern Missouri, where his friends and family believe he passed from getting drunk in a blizzard. We raised a toast to him last night, most of us heading home early. And Giuseppe . . .

I don't know why we saved him for last. The only family he has is in town, and none of them wanted to come.

I tuck my chin back onto my knees, wrapping my arms around my legs. Everything joyful tastes like sorrow. Even cordial sounds like seawater to me.

"Ah, my Luna girl," my abuela sings, pinching her mouth between her gums. I hope her eyes always twinkle like that when she looks at me. "No weep when I go."

"Abuela," I say, the shock throwing my mouth open. "You're not going anywhere."

"We all go. And you no cry."

I push down my legs. What a morbid thing to say. "I will be destroyed if you leave me."

"Why?" Her rounded shoulders lift as she gives me a knowing smile. "You know where they are?"

"Not exactly . . ."

"Sí," she says, wagging a wrinkled finger. "If you know, you not ask them to come back."

My legs warm in the rays from the window, and as I did when I was a girl, I poke at the light with my fingers, letting them heat up before pulling them into the shade again. I think back to Hiram's desperate face when he pleaded with me to send him back—back to his death. I suppose it would be something awful to be yanked out of heaven only to wake up by a frozen river, a lunatic witch his only company. Well, her and Nickels, if sharing a body counts as company.

Geez. I'd beg to be put out of my misery too.

Outside the window, a Chrysler pulls up to the curb, and my brother shuts off the engine. He's another one who's been to heaven and back—apparently legendary among bruja circles. I never asked him how he felt about it.

I open the door before he can knock, throwing my arms around him. He lets out a surprised laugh, teasing me for wrinkling his suit. When I let him go, the smile fades from his face, his hand holding mine. "What is it, hermanita? You got a secret crush on Gus?"

"No," I say, shaking my head to shake away the grin that threatens my lips. "I, uh . . . just wanted to know . . ."

"¿Síí?"

"What was heaven like?"

A soft smile returns to Javier's lips as he drops his gaze, looking into a world I have not seen. "Well, it's . . . better."

"Better than what?"

"Everything else."

It crushes me, and I wrap my arms around him once more, crying.

"Oh . . . I'm so sorry, Javi."

"Why?"

"For snatching you from it."

"Don't be."

"But—"

"Don't be, hermana. Heaven's not going anywhere. And in the meantime, there are wonderful, beautiful things here. I wasn't ready for all that . . . I mean, I'm not even sure I deserved it. But knowing it's waiting for me . . ." He creates a little separation so he can look into my eyes.

"Thank you."

And it's the best thing I've heard in a long time.

AS BEFITTING AS A VISIT TO PENDERGAST'S OFFICE IS ON THE day of a bootlegger's funeral, the last place I want to stop on the way to Gus's memorial is the brick building on Main, where a mobster spends more time imprinting his rear in a chair than actually out mobstering.

Entering the tiny office, I see I was right.

He glances up from his papers, pushing his spectacles to the end of his nose.

"I'm not some dog on its leash, Mr. Pendergast," I say with my hand on my hips. I'm done with bribes and threats. My actions have had unintended consequences, and that isn't okay with me."

"Hold on there—"

"No!" Circling around his desk to the window, I dump a handful of blessed dirt into the aloe plant on the sill. I don't care. He's looked at me like I'm crazy before. "My businesses and my crews are to be left alone. And I'll sleep with whomever I please."

He pulls on his spectacles, letting them fall to his chest as they're held by a chain. Studying me for a quick moment, he shrugs a shoulder. "Fine. But that better be the good stuff you put in there."

"I . . . I'm sorry. The what?"

Pendergast's chair squeaks as he leans back, his hands folding over his belly. "At least you know what part of the life you like and which parts you don't. Even brujas gotta have boundaries."

He did not just say that word. Is he having me followed? I know what comes after this—more threats, more bribery. But why call me out today? He could have taken my whole family hostage by now, demanded money . . . or more.

"Hang on," I say, sweeping the air with my hand. "How long have you known?"

"I think the question you really wanna ask me is what do I want from you."

I really don't want to ask that.

"Look," he says, "someone like you, if they didn't have no heart, could make *me* their puppet—like that creepy girl up north. You ain't done that. You've shown who you are and who you're not. Moretti's first mistake was tryin' to control that." He nods to the aloe. "I ain't no fool. But I also ain't afraid. You and me—we gotta work togetha' in this city, pure and simple."

Damn. Was not expecting that. I need to stop expecting things.

I lean my hip against the windowsill, dusting my hands off. "So . . . what do you want, then?"

"I want Kansas City to be the greatest city in the world."

I find myself nodding because a lot of me wants the same thing. Just maybe in a different way. Still . . .

The side of his mouth presses into a flat smile. "Just keep it prosperous for me, will ya?"

"That's it?"

"No," he says, "one more thing. Shut the door on your way out. And don't eva' fuckin' touch me, eh?"

THE WORLD IS RID OF HORRIBLE EVIL. BUT IT'S RID OF SOME damn good souls too.

As much as I love seeing my crew at the River Rose, I hate how somber we all are. Heck tried a few cheerful subjects like how well Margaret's circular is doing, at the forefront of women's rights. Even the ladies at the Guadalupe Center are playing less Parcheesi and spending more time in the soup kitchens. But the National Woman's Party's plans to revive their campaign to put women in Congress just wasn't the boost to our crew he hoped it would be.

It should be a happier day than it is. Instead, we're standing around my club with drinks in our hands, remembering a slimeball we never knew we'd miss.

I step to the center of the dance floor, raising my glass of gin in the air. "I just want to say . . . Giuseppe, although he had his struggles, was a great . . . gambler. And . . ." A few clear their throats as I kick myself for not writing this down. ". . . and he always took me wherever I wanted to go. And he never asked any questions. So, I'd like us all to have a toast for a man who was—"

"A no-good, dark-skin-hatin', gross Barney!"

I do a double take at the purse-lipped lounge singer downing her glass. "Doris Fenton, now is not—"

"Oh, Nicky couldn't stand 'im and neitha' could I. He smelled like onions, and his breath wasn't any betta'—"

My crew's lips twitch around the room, as they ignore my warning glare. I'm not really mad. It's the kind of send-off a creep like Gus probably deserves, but it's not like there's any stopping Doris once she gets going.

"Hell, he even tried to get in my knickas a time or two. Offa'd to pay me. But like my mama always told me, 'Don't eva' let a man pay you for no nookie.'" Her head jerks in a sharp nod. "I give that shit away for free."

"Hold on right there, Bearcat," my brother says, trotting to the dance floor. "I think Gus has shown that a man can change. I mean, we've all changed, haven't we?"

Guilt mixes with Doris's irritated frown as she weighs Javier's words for a moment before raising her glass, to which the room responds with, "To Gus."

"Yeah," she says, "I guess life ain't easy for a guy who's gotta stand on a chair to look down my dress."

Javier nods in understanding, using his glass to gesture. "Sí, it was just a couple of weeks ago, I was carrying boxes out to the alleyway, and he saw me and said the nicest thing that ever passed his lips at me:

"'Hey.'"

Gio's gin sprays from his mouth; Doris buries her head in Penny's shoulder. I shake my head at this room full of ill-mannered criminals, mostly to hide the smile I'm fighting.

"Oh my God, Javi," I say. My brother hasn't stopped laughing.

Gio tilts his hat low over his brow like Giuseppe used to do, his cigarette dangling from his lower lip. "'Ey, all I wanted in this life was to schmooze da' boss in that flivver she calls a car."

My brother's eyes spring with tears, his laugh so big it's nearly silent as he clings to Gio's shirtsleeve.

"You goddamn bindle punks," Javier says, his voice squeaking as he barely keeps it together, "always stinkin' up da' joint!"

Doris snaps her fingers before pointing in the air. "Yeah! And Nicky'd say, 'Hey, boss, ain't that smell the dog shit you dragged in on your own shoe?'"

My brother's feverish nod has my eyes rolling. "Yes! And then Gus—he'd lift up his foot to take a sniff, and look back at him and say—"

The rest of the gang lifts their glasses in the air, all shouting together, "'Shut the hell up, Nick!'"

I turn to the only gentleman in the room, my mouth dropping open. "Heck."

"All right, all right," he says, sidling to the center of the floor. "Rose is right. Giuseppe had his demons, but surely he deserves a respectful send-off out of this cruel world."

Everyone sobers quickly as Heck bows his head, the men removing their hats. I knew the man was poetic, but the prayer he offers up is one for the spell books. Some even dash away a few tears from their eyes.

He lifts his face upward as though he's staring into heaven itself. "And God, if . . . if you're actually a woman, for Gus's sake . . ." I turn a slow, flat stare to his twinkling eyes, which roam the ceiling as he lets out a somber sigh with a wide grin. "Hike up dat skirt and show us them gams, will ya?"

Including me, the room erupts into a display of laughter and merriment that I can no longer get control of.

And I don't want to control it. I want laughter and love to have me—to fill me with faith again. And I hope it never lets go. The joy on Javier's face renews my will to believe again—bigger dreams involving less money, this time.

In the cheerful room, I realize I'm rooted in something deeper than earth magic. And if there's one thing I know about flowering trees in a storm—they withstand. And I will too. All of us will. Until we go someplace better.

20

"WHOA, MARGARET REALLY DID A NUMBA' WITH THIS FLUFF piece on you and Heck."

I haven't laid in Gio's bed in so long, I almost miss the screaming neighbors and wailing children on the other side of the walls. Our smoking dinchers lie in an ashtray, their smoke trailing in a lazy dance toward the ceiling. Margaret's circular has been the talk of the town for sure, her forward views on conservative rhetoric challenging the status quo. I'm really proud of her for choosing to stay in Kansas City after all to raise her baby while fighting injustice on her home front. Plus, buying a plot of land away from curious eyes will afford her and Penny a safe haven to support each other. More shocking, even Doris has agreed to leave the city life to join what the public will view as a few spinsters living their lives in unmarried loneliness in the country.

Peace is more like it.

Gio's lips trail down my neck as he reaches for the news-paper we incidentally threw on the floor during our first twenty minutes in the door.

"I missed this," he says, giving my neck a final kiss before settling back with the newspaper. "Feels bad but good—like barnymuggin' a married woman."

"Mr. Cattaneo, you should be ashamed of yourself."

His hand pinches my nipple as he goes back to reading.

I'm definitely going to be talking to his employer about this.

I cozy myself against the pillows as he points to the ink. "Do you know what they're writin' about you, babe?"

"Yes, I've read it."

"They're alleging," he continues with an ornery grin, "that Mrs. Kessler has been accused of having a heated love affair with a certain Hiram Wilmington—*the Third*."

"I said I *read it*."

"Adding to the list of nefarious rumors, it says, the in-famous heiress has been seen with an array of eligible bach-elors, including Dorian Luxberg of Ozark, Missouri, and Stuart Kensington—oof, that's a name I haven't heard in a while."

"You're really loving this, aren't you?"

"Ooh!" My boyfriend slaps the corner of the newspaper, a snort coming out with his laughter. "There's even a rumor you had a tryst with your old bartender."

Ew.

I snatch the paper from his hands, tossing it to his feet. Reaching for my sides, he tickles my ribs, and I fall to the bed, squealing for mercy.

What he didn't read was that the list of scandals and

antics makes me a popular figure in the papers. I'm the flapper "It Girl," taking the city by sass and storm. I almost can't believe the shift in the city's views on an improper woman. The blessed dirt in Margaret's circular definitely turned the public eye in my favor. More people are apparently reading it than are letting on.

"Somebody must have tipped off the presses," I say, taking a few deep breaths from my fit of giggles. "I guess Heck will have to divorce me out of shame, now." Gio raises up onto his elbow, and I grin at the shock on his face. "Don't worry. It was his idea."

I'm as relieved as Gio looks as he celebrates with another cigarette, offering me one, but I wave it away. I've had my fill of buzzing for one hour.

My boyfriend nods to the fallen circular in his lap. "So, is that gonna be the, uh, official announcement later?"

"Margaret is ready to print it next week," I say with a grin.

My boyfriend's face is stupefied with shocked gladness, but he quickly recovers with a short sniff, clearing his throat. "In a week. I'm sure the press is gonna have a ton of questions. I'm ready to lay low if you and Heck need to—"

Grabbing Gio's hand, I give it a reassuring squeeze. "Heck is going to be spending a lot more time with Javi on a 'yearslong development' for new businesses, and the only thing I need is to be right here." I shake my boyfriend's hand to turn his misting eyes to me. "Sitting in the back seat together when we go to a party and, I don't know, picking out a house . . . maybe?"

Gio shakes his head, leaning over me to smash the dincher into the ashtray. His nose brushes my cheek as he locks his arm onto the mattress beside my hip. "You askin' me to marry you, Miss Lane?"

My mouth drops open, forcing him to chuckle. *Marry?* Of course not. Or maybe I am. I'm not used to being excited about such a concept. Yet I am, and it must be showing because his orneriness is back with an expectant smirk.

"Well, me asking you would be extremely improper, Mr. Cattaneo."

"You're wantin' to buy a house with your boyfriend, and you're worried about bein' proper?" Gio lies on his back, tucking his hands behind his head. "I mean, I guess we'll have to get hitched if we're gonna explain that baby."

"I'm not having that baby. It says so on page three."

"That's okay. We can have more."

It's my turn to pinch *his* nipple and he cries out with hoarse laughter that gives me more joy than a big night of winnings at the clubs. Pulling me down to lie on his chest, Gio's fingers comb through my hair. He leaks feelings of both gladness and uncertainty—just like I have. He doesn't want me to break his heart and he wants to take good care of mine. *Well, that's good.* At least we're both panicking together. And I suppose that's the point of such a partnership.

My eyes travel across the room to the lonely jacket still perched on a chair. I meant to give it back to Hiram after he let me borrow it the night we met. My heart sinks for his family. I'll have to send his wife a comforting fern as my condolences. It won't heal her heart. Only time can do that. But it's something.

I didn't know the man long. But I know the pain he carried. I know the kindness and love he carried too. I didn't think he'd do anything to hurt his family, even if they might grieve for a while.

And I can respect that. I have blood on my hands and soul to save the ones I love. Hiram does too, even if it's just his own. It's a simple yet powerful commonality we share—*la familia es todo*. My brother, Heck, Gio, Penny, Margaret, even Doris, have all filled my heart with such a fierce sense of protection, it almost overwhelms me. I'm growing more accustomed to letting a tear fall as it hits Gio's chest.

"Hey," he says, lifting my chin to look at me. "We're gonna be all right."

"I know," I reply with a sniffling smile that shakes the worry from his face. "I think I'm just . . . happy for us all. Heck is taking a big step, and it's all for my brother."

"The most romantic divorce eva'."

"You're off your nut. You know that?"

Gio and I laugh and tease each other in the warmth of the bedroom, a freedom afforded by the bravery of folks like Heck, whom I adore as though we were raised together. Because of his strength, Margaret's child may never know the cruelty he and Hiram faced as children. I hold out hope that the world she grows up in will, in time, embrace love in all facets. One day, perhaps in the farther future, men will hold hands. Women will share a bedroom in peace. And their daughters will hold office in Congress.

As I snuggle close to Gio, I imagine Margaret's child as a little girl bouncing up the steps of the Capitol, readying her notes to fight for justice and truth. Perhaps she too will fall in love with a humble young man, much like Javier. Or perhaps he will be a jazz musician with skin as dark as the evening.

It's cruel, the way we associate darkness with evil. I've seen evil. And it's full of hatred and blindness.

Gio pulls his face back, pinching my chin. "Whatcha thinkin' about?"

I give him a long look before laying my hand over his. "You're a good guy, you know."

A flush creeps up his neck and he looks away with a sheepish smile. "Yeah, I don't know."

"Well, I do. And the stars do too."

"Look, I already said I'll marry you."

"I'm serious, Gio."

Shaking his head, he buries half of his face into the pillow to hide his welling eyes as they close. "I know you are. And it means a lot . . . *you* mean a lot."

The way he pulls me close to him is exactly why I do want to marry him. His heartbeat makes me think of peace after the sun sets, when the stars begin their twinkling, their patterns pointing this way and that. It makes me think of rest as I send a silent song to the heavens in thanks that I'm surrounded by love, and I will be for a long, long time.

ACKNOWLEDGMENTS

TO GOD, MY AMAZING CHILDREN, MY FAMILY, LOVED ONES (BOW!), and solid friends—I could not have done this without your constant support and encouragement. I'd like to send a special thanks to the book lovers in Kansas City, including the Kansas City Public Library, KCUR NPR, podcasts, the Kansas City Historical Museum, the *Kansas City Star*, the Thorpe Menn Reading and Event Committee, Rainy Day Books, and so many more. Thank you for giving the Bindle Punk series a place to shine.

Also, much love to Gilly Suit, my go-to interpreter and support friend. You're a star.

Ace Money, as always, you're a true life-saver. Thanks for kicking my butt every single day.

To all who love to hope in the pursuit of peace. To laughter and silliness.

To pirates and poetry.

ABOUT THE AUTHOR

DESIDERIA MESA IS THE AUTHOR OF THE HISTORICAL fantasy debut *Bindle Punk Bruja*. Her craft often focuses on celebrating the successes and exposing the struggles of Latinx culture through Mexican folktales in historical settings. Aside from churning out novels, she enjoys writing songs, poetry, and short stories.

More by
DESIDERIA MESA

Boardwalk Empire meets *The Vanishing Half* with a touch of earth magic in this sexy and action-packed historical fantasy set in the luminous Golden Twenties from debut author Desideria Mesa, where a part-time reporter and club owner takes on crooked city councilmen, mysterious and deadly mobsters, and society's deeply rooted sexism and racism, all while keeping her true identity and magical abilities hidden—inspired by an ancient Mexican folktale.